MY FATHER'S GHOST

GWAMBI TETRALOGY
BOOK TWO

A. C. WILSON

My Father's Ghost, volume 2 in the *Gwambi Tetralogy* by A. C. Wilson

Interior illustrations by Shelby Elizabeth

Cover by Kirk DouPonce

ISBNs:

978-1-959666-04-2 (paperback)

978-1-959666-14-1 (ebook)

Published by:

Wise Path Books

a division of To A Finish LLC

12407 N MoPac Expy #250

Austin, TX 78758

www.wisepathbooks.com

To my wife Magali:
I could not have written this book
without you, my Love.

CONTENTS

GWAMBI TETRALOGY

GWAMBI TETRALOGY

BOOK TWO

The Year 1026 KA
Entwerp Coastal, Llaedhwyth

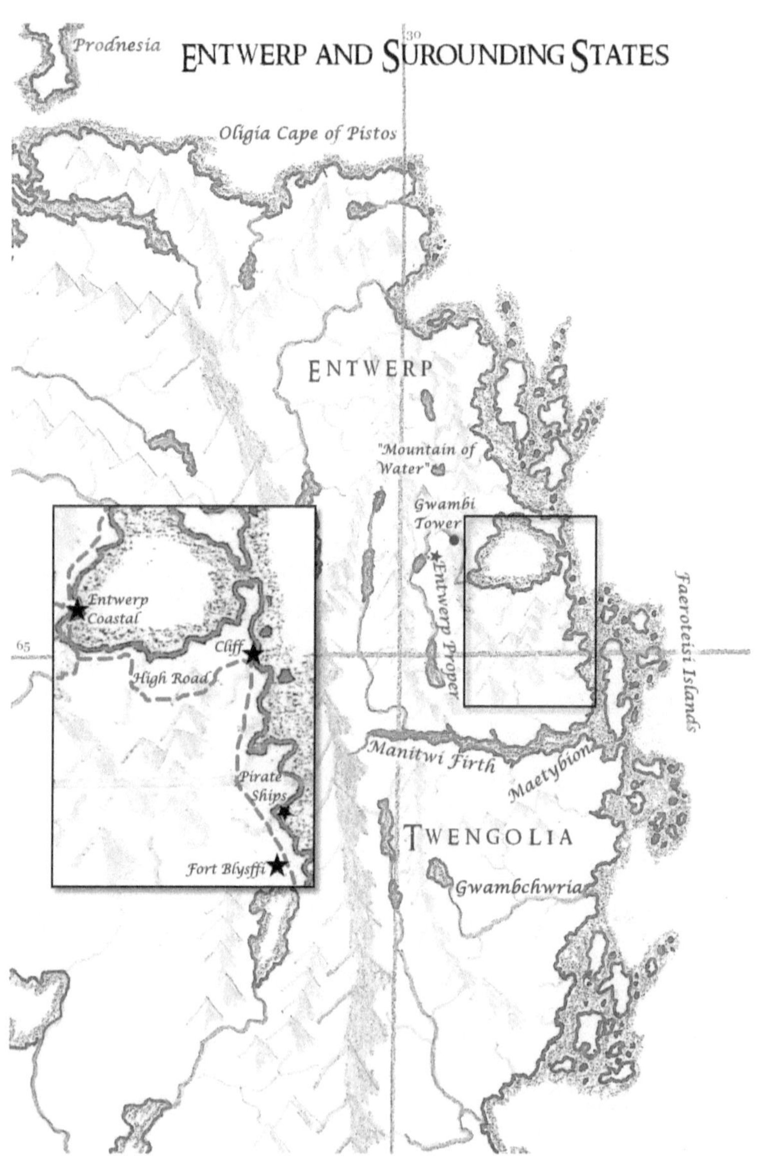

Prodnesia
ENTWERP AND SUROUNDING STATES
30
Oligia Cape of Pistos
ENTWERP
"Mountain of Water"
Gwambi Tower
Entwerp Proper
Faeroteisi Islands
Entwerp Coastal
Cliff
High Road
65
Pirate Ships
Fort Blysffi
Manitwi Firth
Maetybion
TWENGOLIA
Gwambchwria

MEIGALIAS OCEAN C. 1020 KA
BORIA
KELMAR
EMPIRE OF KELMAR
SLYZWIR
Hulacos River
Blisa
Laccitan Sea
EMPIRE OF KERYNA
REPUBLIC OF DORPT
NORTHERN LOCNISH ISLES
SOUTHERN LOCNISH ISLES
Cape of Pistos
Entwerp
LLAEDHWYTH
MELWYN
SOPHEZ
LYDHWI
NEW SLYZWIR
DHAERRYQ
HINTERCHORA

1

CONSCRIPT

*E*rnest's hand trembled as he set it on the door's handle. He could hear low laughter from inside the pub — was it his father's? Ernest swallowed and tried to stay steady.

He was thirteen today — he was a man now.

Ernest slowly pushed the door open and entered the dim barroom, the stench of vomit and alcohol assailing his nostrils. Only four hazy lanterns lit the small room, hanging from the ceiling. A few dozen men sat inside. Some played cards, some laughed and hooted, and some simply lay in a stupor. All were drunk. Ernest trembled as he looked at these men. They were huge workmen — humans, dwarves, gnomes, faeriefolk — almost all sailors or stevedores from the docks. They were heavyset and strong from their manual labor, but sour and bitter from their meager pay.

Ernest scanned the room slowly, and his eyes fell on a man leaning up against the bar. He was taller than any other gnome in the bar, wicked, and dead drunk. Ernest swallowed. That was his father.

Two other men stood by his father, laughing uproariously and drinking hard *usquebaugh* liquor. The landlord stood in front of these three men; Ernest couldn't tell if he was drunk or not. The landlord was prying open another bottle of *usquebaugh* for his customers with a long knife.

Slowly, Ernest walked across the room towards the bar, the rough, wood floor scratching his bare feet. At every step, his heart sank nearer to his toes. The closer he got to his father, the taller his father looked, the larger his fists appeared, and the more Ernest could smell the rank alcohol in his laugh.

Finally, Ernest stood beside his father. His heart pounded in his chest, and his mouth was completely dry. His father didn't seem to notice him yet.

For a moment, Ernest considered turning around and running all the way home. His mother didn't expect his father to come back anyway, so why was he trying? Ernest tried to calm himself.

He was thirteen today — he was a man now.

He couldn't run.

"Papa?"

Still, his father didn't seem to notice him.

Ernest reached out his hand and touched his father's greasy trousers. His father turned and looked down at him, foam still dripping from his oily beard. Ernest shrunk back at his father's hollow stare.

"What'tre'ya want?" His father slurred. "Get'tya back home, brat."

Ernest stumbled back a step and tried to speak. "Eh...Mama...eh...Mama sent me..."

"Did'ya hear me?" His father growled, pausing momentarily to drink down the last of his glass.

Ernest swallowed. "Mama sent me...eh...to bring you home."

His father leered down at him. "I amn't going home. Now you get, 'fore I beat you out'tta here, scrawny boy."

His father turned back to the bar and motioned for the landlord to fill his glass again.

A feeling of hatred welled up inside of Ernest — a hatred that surpassed even his fear of his father. His fists curled up tight, and he stood straighter. His father had called him 'scrawny boy' enough times. He was thirteen today — he was a man now.

"You will not."

His father turned and stared at him blankly.

Ernest stared his father full in the face. "You willn't beat me ever again. And you willn't beat Mama, either. I willn't let you. I'm thirteen today — I'm a man now. I willn't let you hit us ever again."

Ernest saw his father's fist double too late. Stars exploded in his head, and he felt his body hit the floor. Ernest tried to get back to his feet, but another punch threw him to the ground again. He curled up in a ball, whimpering in terror as his father rained down blow after blow.

"I will never hit you again, will I?" his father yelled, "I will never hit you again?"

Suddenly, Ernest felt his father's hands close around his throat. Ernest squirmed to get free, but his father lifted him from the floor, holding him in a stranglehold with his feet dangling in mid-air. Ernest could hear the other men in the pub laughing, but his vision swam. His father's leering and hollow face danced before his eyes.

"I will do whatever I want with you, boy," his father said.

Ernest kicked frantically and clawed at the air with his arms, trying to find something to hold on to. He couldn't breathe. He was desperate. He had to find something to brace himself against to get the pressure off his neck. Suddenly, his hands hit the bar. He grabbed at the edge of it when his fingers closed on the handle of the landlord's knife.

Without thinking, Ernest snatched the knife from the counter and swung at his father with it. The blade hit his father in the belly, and it sank to the hilt.

His father roared in pain and surprise. Stumbling backward, he let go of Ernest.

Ernest collapsed in a heap by the base of the bar, but he wasted no time in scrambling to his feet and running like a hunted rabbit toward the door. In a moment, he was out in the moonlit alleys, careening over the black cobblestone.

Had he just killed his father? If not, then his father would kill him. Ernest slipped in a wide puddle and crashed into the street. The cobblestone tore at his hands, face, and clothing like the claws of an angry alley cat.

Hurriedly, Ernest got onto his hands and knees, crawling against a dark wall. His whole body ached with pain, and his mind raced with terror and guilt.

What was he to do now? He couldn't go home; his father would kill him. But where else would he go? He couldn't go to the cathedral. The bishop would have nothing to do with a boy who had killed his own father. That was a mortal sin, wasn't it?

Ernest curled up in a ball and wept. He was on his own now. That was all there was to it. He was a poor gnome boy of thirteen, thrust out into the cruel world to starve and die.

No, he couldn't just die, but if he stayed in that town, his father would find him and kill him. He would go to the docks. Maybe there was a ship that would take him? He could swab decks or clean bunks easily enough. Maybe the ship would drop him off in another port, hundreds of miles away from his father...

Ernest woke with a start. Who had shaken him? It could hardly be midnight yet. Ernest sat up, winking his eyes like an owl as he tried to make out anything in the pirate ship's dim cabin light. Yes, there was Bill, the long-armed gnome, leaning over him.

"What's this for, Bill? What's the time?"

"It can't be more than an hour past sunset," Bill replied with a grin.

Ernest stretched. "Then why are you waking me up? You should be asleep, too."

"Captain Holgard's orders," Bill replied with a grin. "We're going on a raid."

Ernest dropped from his hammock and looked at the gnome levelly. "Raiding for what?"

Bill sneered and walked off.

Ernest sighed and quickly pulled on his clothes. Then, looking both ways to see that no one was watching, Ernest pulled out his prized pepperbox pistol from his locker and slipped it into the breast pocket of his coat.

With that, he hurried off after Bill.

He met up with the gnome in the galley, where a few dozen other pirates also waited. Not a lantern was lit; Ernest could only make out their faces by the oven fire's light. There was the lumbering form of Tell, Bill's messmate, and many other faces that Ernest recognized. Boatswain Killjelly, the leprechaun, seemed to lead the group. Ernest looked closely for the Albino but couldn't see him. He sighed in relief; just thinking about the Albino made him shudder.

Ernest's messmate, Lewis, was busy in the galley, stuffing provisions into satchels and then passing them out to the pirates. The smell of freshly baked bread wafted through the dim air. Lewis finished packing one satchel and handed it to Ernest.

"Here you are, boyo. Hope that's enough for you." And Lewis winked.

"What's this for?" Ernest asked.

"Not so loudly, sure," Killjelly hissed.

"What's this for?" Ernest asked in a whisper.

"Weren't you telled?" Killjelly asked. "We're going raiding."

Ernest shrugged. "What for? Don't we have enough provisions?"

Killjelly eyed Ernest carefully for a moment, then he spoke so softly that only Ernest could hear. "Do you remember the door?"

Ernest stumbled back involuntarily at the mention of the door. Memories flooded back over him, memories that he had tried to erase. He could almost see that door, iron bolted and secure, and feel the air pulsing with power as the Albino cast spell after spell to free the locks. He could almost hear the desperate screams of the leprechaun maid with the rabbit-lip.

It was the Albino's dreadful voice that sounded in his ears. *"Where is the key? Where is the key to that door?"*

Ernest shook visibly, and Killjelly smiled.

"We're going on a raid so that we can find the key."

Ernest nodded. "Who has it?"

Killjelly stared at Ernest for a long moment, and his reply echoed the rabbit-lipped housekeeper's desperate and wild death-shrieks.

"Stifyn Blysffi, the gardener."

2

HOMELY

*H*aeli's heart rushed as the wind washed through her raven hair. Beneath her, the horse rose and fell in a steady lope. With no saddle under her, she could feel every ripple of the horse's body, and she matched it movement for movement, her whole body following in the horse's steady, rolling motion.

She touched the horse's neck with her reins, and the horse turned, wheeling back towards the other side of the paddock. With the evening sun now falling against her face, Haeli closed her eyes and breathed deeply. This was the life—just her and Hope, with the world before them.

After a moment, she opened her eyes and reined Hope in. For a moment, she sat still, panting, and soaking up the beauty of her home valley. The mountains sloped gently to either side of her, climbing steeply to the great coastal peaks. Her pasture lay in a dale between these mountains, and if she looked out to the east, she could see the dale running down to the ocean. The sun touched the peaks behind her, bathing creation in a golden glow and casting long shadows behind every bush and outbuilding. The air tasted of autumn, with a hint of damp leaves mingled with yellow clover, and there was an invigorating chill in the breeze. All the aspen trees on the mountain were changing colors, trading their green for a dozen shades of fiery gold. The first frost would come soon enough; then this dale would be a riot of colors. The fort lay before her, beyond the barn and the corral. Like a gentle invitation, smoke rose from the chimneys.

Haeli took in a deep breath and let it out slowly. She could never look out on the dale the same way since her Da had taken her up here two years ago and waved his big, hard-working hands over the landscape.

"This, Haeli," her Da had said. "This is our home, but it is not ours. Take a good look and enjoy it while we live here."

"What do you mean, Da?"

Da shook his head and smiled ruefully, running his fingers through his coiled hair. "The Company owns this fort, Haeli, and the Company will do with it as they want. We can put our heart and soul into this ground, child — and God knows that is what I mean to do — but all it takes is one owner changing his mind, and they can kick us out at a moment's notice."

"But that is not fair."

"No, child, it is not fair." Her Da sighed and looked her in the face. "I have brought you to the fairest world I could find, but there is Empire even here. Now there's no point worrying about the future. All you can do is live the moment that you are living right now."

Haeli sighed again, taking in another breath of that crisp, mountain air. That was one of those memories she would hold for the rest of her life. And this was one of those moments she wanted to live as long as she could. This was exactly where she wanted to be. She could never live anywhere else after living here.

After several long minutes, Hope shifted her weight under Haeli, snorting.

The Blysffi Trading Fort

"You ready to go, girl?"

Hope cocked her ears back, and her withers trembled like she was shaking off a fly.

Haeli laughed. "Merri well."

With a touch of her heels, she pointed Hope back towards the corral, trotting back over the pasture. They passed through the gate, coming right up to the corral fence. About five other horses were tied up here, and Haeli's Ma stood in the middle of the corral, lunging the stud, Vengeance. Of all the horses, Hope was Haeli's favorite. She wasn't the fastest by any means, but she wasn't as jumpy as the other horses.

The stud was another matter entirely. He was fast, but he was also reckless. Haeli could hardly get that horse to obey her — in fact, the stud was the only horse that had ever thrown her. But her Ma knew how to handle him. Ma was the only person Vengeance seemed to respect. Haeli shook her head as she watched the stud circling her Ma.

Just as she reached the gate to the corral, her three-year-old brother Dafid came toddling up to her, under the close eye of her nymph foster brother, Yohni.

"Dafid wants to ride with Yali," Dafid said, grinning up at Haeli. His big brown eyes twinkled up at her, and his coils of black hair seemed to have lost a fight with the wind.

Haeli slid from Hope's back and walked her up to the fence. "How do you quire?"

"*Please*, can Dafid ride with Yali?"

Haeli took off Hope's reins and then put a halter on her, tying her to the fence with the other horses as she replied, "Dafid can only ride with Yali if the horse has a saddle."

Dafid frowned. "Sad. Crying."

Haeli couldn't help but smile at her little brother's antics. "I know it is sad. How about you quire Yohni to fetch a saddle for Yali and Dafid?"

Dafid grinned widely and turned to Yohni. It was funny to

see the two interact. Yohni, being a nymph, wasn't more than a foot taller than Dafid. He stood somber and quiet most of the time, while Dafid could hardly stand still for a moment and chattered incessantly.

Dafid jumped up and down as he asked Yohni, "Can I fetch a saddle for Yali and Dafid?"

Haeli grinned, "Say, 'can *you*' Dafid, 'can *you* fetch a saddle.'"

Yohni nodded and padded off on his webbed feet.

Haeli took her brother by the hand and led him up to the fence where he could watch Ma lunging the stud.

"What is that?" Dafid asked, pointing at the stud as it circled around and around in the corral.

"What *is* that, Dafid?" Haeli replied.

"The stud." Dafid replied, grinning from ear to ear.

Haeli nodded. "Yes, that *is* the stud. And what is the stud's name?"

Dafid furrowed his brow as if in deep thought. "Vengeance."

"You are right," Haeli squeezed Dafid's hand. "Does Dafid want to ride on the stud?"

Dafid shook his head emphatically.

"What horse does Dafid want to ride on?"

"Dafid wants to ride on Chastity." Dafid pointed enthusiastically to an old bay mare, opening his mouth wide, trembling all over, and jumping from one foot to the other in his excitement.

"Does Dafid like Chastity?"

Dafid nodded.

In a few moments, Yohni came back with a saddle. He looked at Haeli inquiringly.

"Chastity," Haeli replied to his unasked question.

Yohni walked over to Chastity, and with the dexterity that only a nymph can muster, he swung the saddle up over her high back and then strapped it on. Haeli always enjoyed watching the nymph putting on saddles. He could put any human stable-hand to shame. Sure, he was almost half Haeli's height, but then again, that meant he didn't have to walk around the horse but could simply duck under Chastity's belly.

As Yohni strapped the saddle to Chastity, he frowned deeply as if he were apprehensive.

"What is the matter, Yohni? Why are you frowning?" Haeli asked.

Yohni looked up at Haeli soberly. "It is a bad day."

Haeli couldn't help but smile a little at this statement. "What makes you say that it is a bad day? We have a bright sun, a fresh breeze, and all the grass is green. How is that bad?"

"The rain-crows are restless," Yohni answered, returning to his work, "and the fog clings about the tower." Yohni motioned toward the mountains, where an ancient tower stood out against the sky. It seemed to be made of rocks from the mountain, blended in so perfectly with the surrounding granite cliff faces that it hardly appeared to be a tower at all, but simply the mountain's highest pinnacle that some freak of nature had carved with ramparts.

Haeli looked back at Yohni and shook her head. "That is a little superstitious. Do not you think?"

Yohni only stared back at her darkly. "We will wait and see."

Just then, Ma came up, leading Vengeance behind her. Sweat covered the stud's body, and he panted. Ma, however, grinned from ear to ear as she looked at Haeli and Dafid. She was panting herself, though she hadn't exerted herself nearly as much as the stud had.

"Ma!" cried Dafid, shouting excitedly and jumping up and down. "Can Dafid ride with Ma? Can Dafid ride with Ma?"

Ma winked. "Dafid wants to ride on Vengeance?"

Dafid shook his head adamantly. "On Chastity."

Ma laughed. "Not Vengeance? What about Lamentation?"

"Lamentation?" Haeli asked. "Who's that?"

Ma tilted her head to one side, trying to get a stray lock of hair out of her face without releasing her hold on the stud's lead rope. Ma was not as dark-skinned as the rest of them, and her hair was oddly straight. Apparently, Ma owed her hair texture and high cheekbones to her indigenous tribe to the south.

"That's what I have named the new filly," Ma said. "Lamentation. Sounds good to me."

Haeli shook her head. "Ma, you name our horses the weirdest things."

"It is an object lesson," Ma replied with a wink.

Haeli nodded.

Dafid continued hopping up and down, drawing attention back to himself. "On Chastity. Dafid wants to ride on Chastity with Ma!"

"Ma will ride with Dafid," Ma said finally, "If Yali can take Vengeance back to the stable?"

Haeli nodded, though not without a little nervousness. "Of course I can take Vengeance."

Ma handed her the lead rope, and Haeli led Vengeance out of the corral. She looked back to see Ma mounting Chastity before taking Dafid in her lap.

"You see, Dafid," Ma said, "our emotions are like these horses, Hope, Joy, Vengeance, Regret, Lamentation... God gave them to us as tools, to help us do what we need to do."

"Dafid likes Chastity," Dafid interrupted.

Ma urged Chastity forward, riding in circles around the corral while Dafid chortled with delight.

"Some people will tell you," Ma went on, "that you shouldn't listen to your emotions, that you should only listen to your reason. But that doesn't work."

As Haeli walked away, Ma's voice faded away slowly, but Haeli knew exactly what she was saying. She had said it many times before, and the words were etched into Haeli's memory.

"Like a horse, you must break in your emotions, but then — once there is trust between the two of you — you can ride them to accomplish great things."

Haeli smiled, looking up at the sun. They still had an hour before the sun set completely behind the mountains.

Soon, Haeli came to the stable and led Vengeance down to his stall. She was careful to act confidently and authoritatively as she led the stud. He was tired, sure, so he wasn't likely to pull anything on her, but she could never be too careful around him — he was a stud, after all.

Opening the gate to his stall, she led him in. She left the gate partially open, but stood in the opening as she reached out to untie Vengeance's halter. Seeing his chance, Vengeance started forward as if about to dash Haeli aside and fly from the stall.

Haeli caught him by the halter and yanked back forcefully a few times. Vengeance halted at the first yank and backed up quickly. His eyes rolled back, and his nostrils flared. Haeli still clung to the halter, waiting several minutes for Vengeance to calm down.

"What is all this about?" Haeli said soothingly. "There is nothing to be alarmed at. Calm down. I will not hurt you."

Vengeance's muscles relaxed, and he began licking his lips.

"There we go," Haeli said. "See? There was not anything to be alarmed at."

She gently untied Vengeance's halter and slid it off.

"There we go." Haeli backed up to the gate, exiting the stall and bolting the gate behind her. When this was done, Haeli sighed deeply. The stud looked at her innocently as he ate some straw that still lay in his manger.

"Do not think you can fool me," Haeli said. "I know what devious thoughts go through your mind."

Vengeance looked up at her and snorted.

"That is right," Haeli continued, grinning despite herself. "You have been planning this all day, have not you?"

Vengeance went back to eating his straw.

Haeli wagged her finger at the stud. "I still won." And with that, she walked from the stable.

She first faced the direction of the corral to see Yohni gathering up all the horses to bring them back into the stables. Ma was now holding Dafid, as she untied Hope's lead rope from the fence. Haeli turned back to the house — Da might want some help preparing supper.

She found Da kneeling in the garden, cutting sprigs of kale with a long, serrated knife. He looked up as Haeli approached, wiping beads of sweat from his brow with the back of his hand. Soil caked his trousers and apron up to his knees, and it lay smeared on his face. Haeli couldn't help but smile at her dear Da.

"Do you need any help, Da?"

Da smiled, and his eyes twinkled. There was a sort of gleeful childishness in his face anytime he got his hands in the dirt. "Thank you for asking, love. Can you ceive this basket of kale into the house? I will be right after you once I check on the raspberries."

Haeli took the basket from Da and marched up to the house.

'House' was a loose term in these beacon-tending forts. What she referred to as 'the house' was more of the fort's main lodge The fort itself consisted of two wooden palisades covering the fort's south and east sides. The fort's west side came directly up to the mountain's cliff face. Standing in the north, the stable, the corral, and all the various fenced paddocks closed the gap between the eastern wall and the mountain. Inside the fences was a wide courtyard with fruit trees and bushes, the garden, and several outbuildings — a few sheds, an auxiliary storehouse, a bunkhouse, an outhouse, and a smokehouse. Exactly in the middle of the courtyard was the 'house,' or main lodge.

The lodge was built of thick spruce logs, fitted so tightly together that it might have withstood a battalion's worth of rifle-fire. The lodge served as the main storehouse, the trading center, the tavern, and the home for the fort manager and his family.

As Haeli approached the house from the back, she saw two swarthy figures appear at the open gateway. They were indigie huntsmen; both short and stocky, with webbed feet and oily skin. Their eyes were dark, narrow, and squinted, giving them an air of sobriety and stoicism. Long, raven-black hair fell in unwashed tangles down their shoulders, and the setting sun glistened off their bare upper bodies. Strapped onto their thick frames, they bore bags of skins in various stages of tanning.

"Da!" Haeli called out to the garden, "Da, we have some hunters here. Looks like trade!"

"Right," Da called out from behind the raspberry bushes. "I will be there in a minute. Can you ceive them while I clean up?"

"Absolutely!"

Haeli hurried in through the back door to intercept these two indigies at the trading counter. Ducking through the pantry, she left the basket of kale on the kitchen counter and then slipped out to the bar. Here, she stood behind the counter, having just enough time to wipe off the bar top with her apron before the huntsmen entered the main door. They entered slowly through the main hall, past the many dining tables, and up to the bar. They nodded in greeting to Haeli and then laid out their skins carefully on the counter.

Haeli smiled and addressed them in Tylweni, the indigies' language. "Good greetings do I give unto you, and welcome into my fort."

The larger huntsman nodded again, "May the Great Aeparon repay your good hospitality unto us. We come with the wish and free intent of trading of our wares to you."

"My father, the fort-chief for the Mighty Tribe, will be here presently and at a time close at hand, while my mother is currently training the mighty-four-legged-creatures. Shall I entertain you until he or she returns to oversee your transaction?" Haeli couldn't help but smile at the vocabulary she was forced to use to communicate with the indigies — there were no words in Tylweni for 'Beacon Company' or 'horse.'

The larger huntsman shook his head. "Our wares must be able to please the young women of your people, the east-folk. Therefore let them be evaluated by a young woman, even by yourself."

Haeli nodded. "It shall be even as ye have said. Have ye traded amongst us before?"

The two huntsmen nodded.

"Please dictate unto me your names." Haeli reached into a file underneath the counter.

"Aerlyn-Withlygwyr of the Twengoli tribe," the larger huntsman said.

Haeli thumbed through the papers until she found the one marked with that name. She pulled it out and then looked at the second huntsmen inquiringly.

"Felhedh-Llasaryni of the Twengoli tribe."

Haeli found the paper with this name and placed it next to the first. On each paper was written all the transactions these huntsmen had made with the trading house — lists of the types and numbers of hides they had traded, along with the amount of trading credit each had with the fort and the dates these huntsmen had frequented the fort. Haeli noticed these huntsmen had been here only three times before, their first visit being a year ago. They must be young hunters, then.

"Shall I give drinks unto you, while I calculate and ascertain your credit?" Haeli asked.

The two huntsmen nodded.

"We will both accept *kombucha*."

Haeli smiled, grabbing two tankards from their pegs on the wall. She filled each from one of the tapped kegs on the back counter and then handed each huntsman a tankard.

As they sipped slowly on their beverage, Haeli inspected the hides they had brought. Most were light-tanned, with the hair still on, but there were a few dark-tanned hides and a few scraped to raw leather. She looked them over carefully, one after another, deducting the price for bald spots, holes, or stiffness in the hides. With some satisfaction, she noted that nearly all the hides were supple; these huntsmen knew how to tan their hides. Haeli wrote everything down on the transaction sheets for each huntsman, calculating the price as she went.

After several minutes, she finished with the first huntsman's pile of hides, writing down her final calculation. "Aerlyn-Withlygwyr, these will give unto you a hundred and seventy-five cubits of credit with this fort — and ye appear to have twenty-three cubits and two han'readths of credit still left unto your name from your last transactions among us."

The larger huntsman nodded soberly. "Even this is a fair calculation."

Haeli turned to the second pile of hides when her Da walked in from the back. He grinned broadly at Haeli and the two huntsmen as he wiped the last smudges of dirt from his hands with his handkerchief.

"Well now, Haeli, I could practically retire and leave you to man the fort. It would be in better hands then, I am sure." And he laughed loudly at his own joke. Haeli laughed too — she couldn't help but laugh when Da laughed. His deep belly laugh was too contagious.

"What have you got now?"

Haeli showed her Da the calculations she had made. "I was about to start on the second man's trade."

"Merri good, merri good, you do that." Da turned to the huntsmen. "Do you understand the common tongue?"

The larger huntsman looked at him soberly, searching for the right words. "They understanding of a leettle."

Da nodded and spoke in Tylweni. "I will make address unto you in Tylweni then."

"That is most preferable unto us," the larger huntsman replied.

"Follow me, therefore, to the storeroom in which we may in all ways conduct our trades among us." Da motioned to the larger huntsman, and they walked back into a room that opened off of the main hall.

3

AN ANCIENT WOE

aeli finished tallying the second huntsman's credit and gave him the paper, motioning him to follow his comrade.

Soon, the first reemerged from the storeroom loaded down with sugar, new *karambit* skinning knives, fishhooks, coffee, tobacco, and other goods. He sat down at the bar again and pulled out a large leather bag. He placed each of his new acquisitions into his bag with great care, leaving only his massive *kukri* knife, a walrus-tusk pipe, and pouch of tobacco on the bar. When this was done, he calmly and seriously picked his nose clean and then lit his pipe.

Haeli watched with great interest. The indigies intrigued her a good deal. They were a fascinating people. She had heard people call the indigies 'wild' and 'savages,' but she knew better than to call them that; just because they were heathens did not mean they were savages. The indigies had elaborate manners of their own — though they seemed peculiar to the "civilized" world — they were civilized by their own standards. She counted herself lucky to live in indigie territory and see them as they really were, instead of having to base her knowledge of them off the biased travelogue writings of others.

"Ye are of the Twengoli?" Haeli asked.

The huntsman looked at her soberly and nodded. The fort was built on Twengoli tribal land, so naturally, most of the huntsmen that came here to trade were Twengoli — though it wasn't uncommon for a Skratsi tribesman to come up from the south, and they had even had a few Uquibiwi tribesmen come in from the Megalytia Cape, seeking better prices for their hides. Her foster brother Yohni was himself born a Skratsi tribesman.

"Do ye bear with you any stories?" Haeli asked.

The huntsman looked up again. "I bear no news as of the current happenings which are happening, yet I have many tales of the ancient days which are of old."

Haeli smiled. She had hoped as much. She found the ancient Twengoli tales particularly fascinating and was always glad to hear a new one — or an old one if that was all that was to be had.

The huntsman gave a long draw on his pipe and leaned back. After a moment, he began.

"In the ancient days, the Twengoli ruled these lands — but they were not called the Twengoli then in those times of the ancient past. And then came unto the shore a new and weird people, and none have seen them before, and none have seen the like of this people since. They were *Kwawpi*."

"Kwawpi?" Haeli interrupted. She had heard this word a few times before — usually as a curse or a derogatory term.

"The *Kwawpi*," The huntsman replied, pausing for a moment. "They were mighty and fell, for they were led in battle even by one of the gods. And they fought a great war all round about the land and joined battle over and against it, and wasted it, and enslaved all the tribes round about within it." The huntsman took another long draw at his pipe. Haeli grabbed a stool and sat down on the other side of the counter from the indigie.

"And this *Kwawpi* people took the Twengoli and embondaged them with the fetters of slavery and serfdom, and required them to work even amidst the Mountain of Water."

Haeli raised an eyebrow. She had heard the Twengoli reference this place before. "The Mountain of Water?"

The huntsman nodded. "It is here even to this day, and a holy place it remains."

"But what is it?" Haeli asked. She had never received a straight answer from any Twengoli huntsman she asked, though she had met several who claimed they had seen it.

The huntsman looked at her seriously. "It is a mountain made even of water. And it stands alone in the midst of the Closed Valley, and none but the wise and cunning and holy may enter or escape from that valley."

"Have you seen it before?" Haeli asked.

The huntsman shook his head vigorously. "No Twengoli alive today has seen the Mountain of Water, save only the shamans, nor would any Twengoli dare to risk entering that valley, lest he never return, for it is holy and haunted by the spirit of the god of the *Kwawpi*, and to enter the valley is death."

Haeli nodded knowingly. None of this made much sense to her. It was hard to tell how much indigie belief was pure superstition and how much was based in reality. But she wanted the huntsman to continue.

After another draw of his pipe, the huntsman went on, sweet-smelling tobacco smoke curling around his square frame.

"The Twengoli were thus imprisoned within the valley, and there was found no way of escape, but they must continue to work for the *Kwawpi* in all things. But a man of the Twengoli, preeminent among them, Iasaqi-Kanwyr was even his name by which he was called. And this man was in the far reaches of the valleys when a spirit appeared to him even in the shape of a bird, and the spirit led him through the Valley of Mushrooms even to the exit of the valley and bid him take his tribe from the midst of the Mountain of Water, and bring them out of their embondagement to the *Kwawpi*. And there the spirit gave him a mushroom as the sign of his deliverance, and thus are the Twengoli called the Twengoli or the People of the Mushroom."

The huntsman took another draw at his pipe and then opened his mouth to continue, but a loud crash interrupted at that moment.

The huntsman turned suddenly to look at the door, setting his pipe down forcefully on the counter and then remaining stock still as if he had turned to stone.

Haeli stood up with some alarm when suddenly she heard gunshots — dozens of shots discharged almost from within the fort itself. This was now joined with sounds of shouting and whooping. Before she had much time to think, the front door burst wide open, and in walked almost a dozen men, each armed with dirks, cutlass, sabers, rapiers, muskets, pistols, and nearly every other weapon known to man. They were sailors, if Haeli could judge by their clothing, probably pirates — all leering, dirty, and loathsome. They stank even worse than the indigies.

The leader — an olive-skinned leprechaun with two brass hooks where his left hand should have been — leaped forward into the hall, overturning a table as he did so.

"All stand and deliver this fort!"

Haeli stood stock still, her heart pounding in her chest, her mind all a blur, hardly able to process what was happening.

Suddenly, Da burst out of the storeroom with the small huntsman close behind him. "What is the meaning of this?"

"Stand where you are!" The leprechaun produced a pistol and fired it in Da's general direction. Haeli cried out in fear. Da stood where he was, but the huntsman crumpled into a heap at his feet.

Haeli looked on in growing horror. She had just conducted trade with that huntsman; he had come here in peace, probably securing provisions for his family and tribe members. How could someone so callously kill him? Haeli breathed deeply and deliberately. She had to get control of herself. Panic was overtaking her. Da had taught her how to defend herself, but she couldn't do that unless she had control over herself. She couldn't let herself get tunnel vision. She had to calm down. In her mind, she imagined her panic as a horse galloping off without her permission. As she took a deep breath, she reined panic in, slowing her to a trot. Her heart still raced, but she was in charge. She could use the energy of panic's trotting pace to do whatever she needed to do to get out of this situation.

The leprechaun with the hooks produced a second pistol and pointed it straight at Da. "Stand where you are! I mean business, and I willn't be trifled with, sure. Put your hands where I can see them."

Da raised his hands slowly. Haeli could see his jaw muscles working in and out slowly. A fresh wave of panic swept over Haeli as she realized even Da was afraid. Again she visualized pulling back on the reins as she inhaled.

"What do you want?" Da finally said.

The leprechaun sneered. "We want what you have, sure."

"The storeroom is behind me, then." Da wasn't looking at the invaders now; he stared over their heads. Haeli followed his gaze toward the rifle which hung above the door. Haeli's heart pounded in her chest. How would he reach it? These pirates stood between Da and that gun.

"I don't want your provisions," the leprechaun replied. "I comed for what *you* have; what you taked. You were the gardener for Saemwel Pickering once?"

Da's face seemed to pale for a moment, but he quickly recovered. "I do not understand you."

The leprechaun laughed, motioning toward his men. "Secure the fort. Find anyone else living here and bring them into this room, sure."

The pirates whooped, and half of them dashed from the room in all different directions. One pirate, a swarthy human, leaped over the bar and brandished a knife at Haeli.

Haeli backed away, holding up her hands to show that she had no weapons. The man sneered at her and inspected under the bar, probably looking to see if she had a musket back there. Seeing nothing, he shoved a stool towards her.

"Sit and keep your hands on the counter where I can see them."

Haeli looked at the pirate for a moment. She could feel the energy of panic like a steady trotting gait through her whole body. She could use that energy now. Her Da had shown her frequently how to disarm someone of a knife, pistol, or musket, and was confident that she could take the knife from this pirate now. With the added energy of her panic, she was certain she could disarm and dispatch this pirate in a matter of seconds. Would it be wise? She looked at her Da. He shook his head.

Obeying the pirate, Haeli sat down. The pirate now pulled out his musket and held it ready, eyeing her menacingly.

"You don't move, understand?"

Haeli swallowed. Panic was trying to pull out of her trot. Breathing steadily to calm her heartbeat, Haeli stole a glance at the pirate guarding her. She could envision catching his wrist and then breaking his elbow over her knee. After that, she could snatch up his musket and crush his skull with the heavy butt. When her Da gave the signal, she would know what to do.

In her mind, she could hear her father's voice from one of their many training sessions. "Act without hesitation. God knows it's best not to have to kill at all, but when you need to, do it quickly. The last thing you want is an injured and angry opponent. Besides, it is more merciful to make it quick."

Haeli remained where she was, as still as she could be. She hardly dared to move her head to either side but looked straight forward at Da.

Out of the corner of her eye, she saw the larger huntsman — still sitting at the counter — move ever so slightly. She looked closer. His hand closed over the handle of something underneath his leather bag. Could it be his *kukri*?

Just then, another pirate burst through the front door, hauling in Yohni by the collar. There was blood running down Yohni's forehead, and he looked to be only barely conscious.

The pirate threw Yohni down between two tables and addressed the leprechaun with the hooks. "This one nearly taked my thumb off. Can I kill him?"

The leprechaun shook his head. "He's a stable hand, not one on the savages. We could use him as bargaining power," he looked at Da menacingly, "to make him talk."

Da didn't even flinch. He seemed to have completely regained his composure now.

Suddenly, the huntsman leaped from his seat at the bar. Haeli heard a metallic ring as he drew his *kukri* from the counter. The indigie wailed an almost unearthly battle cry and a pirate turned towards him in alarm. The huntsman caught this first pirate in the throat with his *kukri*, throwing him in a bloody heap to the floor.

The indigie struck out with his *kukri* again, planting it in another pirate's belly, but before he could get any further, at least half a dozen muskets fired, filling the entire room with gunpowder smoke. Haeli recoiled, as much in shock over what she was witnessing as at the putrid smell of gunpowder. The indigie stumbled back, but he was still on his feet. With one accord, the pirates rushed him.

Haeli closed her eyes, shaking all over. She could hear the pirates yelling and cursing, their feet pounding against the floor, almost drowning out the soft sound of the indigie moaning,

Haeli finally opened her eyes to see four pirates standing over the huntsman's body with bloody bayonets. The pirate who had received the stomach injury sat slumped against the wall. His face was ashen, but he was still breathing.

Haeli shuddered all over. Her stomach churned, and she could feel bile rising in her throat. She swallowed it back forcefully, trying to control her breathing, trying to keep from sobbing. Panic was fighting the reins now, and Haeli wasn't sure if she could keep her from galloping off.

The leprechaun discharged a last shot into the indigie's body and then turned on Da. "No sudden moves, do you understand?"

Da flashed a smile, though Haeli could tell it was forced, "I understand that if I *do* decide to move, I had better kill you quicker than you can kill me."

The leprechaun stepped forward and lashed out at Da with his fist doubled. Da took the blow calmly and smiled back at the leprechaun. "I am sorry if I have done anything to offend you."

The leprechaun looked as if he were about to strike Da again, but at that moment, four more pirates returned from the kitchen door, ushering in Ma between them. Ma's face was pale as she clutched Dafid desperately to her chest. Dafid whimpered, and Ma rocked him slowly side to side, as her eyes darted between the pirates and Da.

Da smiled broadly as she entered and winked reassuringly. Seeing this, Haeli grew a little more confident and sat a little straighter. Da had a plan.

"What do you gentlemen want?" Da said as he walked towards the bar.

A dozen muskets lowered on him as he moved, but Da hardly seemed to blink. The leprechaun put a hand to his own musket, obviously debating if he should kill Da for moving. The entire room stood in tense silence, the only noise being the sound of Da's footsteps. Off in the distance, Haeli thought she could hear a distressed whinny from the horses.

Da walked behind the counter and turned back towards the pirates, raising his eyebrows inquiringly.

"We have a door to open," the leprechaun finally replied. "You will give us the key, or we will peel and kill everyone on your family members in front on your eyes before skinning you alive." A sinister smile played at the corner of the leprechaun's mouth. "I'm a trained surgeon, too, sure. I'd keep you all alive for days while you feel all on the agony."

Da smiled again. "No, I mean, what do you want to drink?"

The pirates looked at him blankly.

Da slapped his hand on a keg on the back counter. "Beer? Whiskey? Rum? Or you could have goat's milk, or we have *kombucha*, too, if you have a taste for that. I have dozens of barrels in the back as well."

The pirates looked at the leprechaun, like curs watching their master's hand for permission to gorge themselves. The leprechaun looked at his men, then back at Da. A wide smile spread across his face. "Drink what you want, sure."

The pirates rushed towards the bar. Da pulled tankards quickly from the wall, offering them to Haeli so that she could fill them for the pirates.

The leprechaun with the hooks sat down on a table, facing the bar and eyeing Da with a kind of perverted humor in his eye.

"It will do you no good. My men obey orders better when they're drunk, sure."

Da smiled again as he poured tankards of ale for the pirates. He began whistling a popular song, stopping at the refrain to sing the words: *"And they'll will be happier, too, until the hangover."*

4

———

STABLE

*H*aeli filled tankards as fast as she could amidst the pirate's clamor.

"Give me a pint of beer, now."

"Hey missy, some whiskey."

"More here, and fast!"

Haeli had served them three rounds each and was rapidly filling up fourth rounds when the barrel went dry.

"What are you stopping for?" a pirate hissed.

"We are out of whiskey," Haeli said, turning to her Da.

Da shrugged. "We will get another barrel then. Here, help me fetch one from the back."

Da walked towards the door to the kitchen, and Haeli made as if to follow, when the pirate who had been guarding Haeli held up his knife in her face.

"You two aren't leaving so easy."

Da shrugged. "Vene with us then. We could use a third hand."

As they left the room, Haeli chanced a look back over at the leprechaun with the hooks. He had finished loading his pistols and eyed them carefully as they left the room.

They passed through the kitchen and into the pantry. Da moved a crate aside in order to get to the whiskey barrels better.

"Here is the whiskey, all three of us can grab one?" Da looked back at Haeli and the pirate guarding them.

The pirate stood behind them with his pistol trained on them, but his eyes went wide at the sight of the whiskey barrels, and he lowered his pistol slightly.

Da bent down to lift a barrel and grunted heavily. "Here, can you give me a hand?"

The pirate motioned with his pistol for Haeli to help. Haeli looked over at her Da. He was up to something. What was he trying to do? Da looked up at her meaningfully.

Haeli turned towards the pirate, smiling weakly as she held out her hands. "I cannot lift those barrels."

The pirate gave a low growl, and then, shoving his pistol into his belt, he bent down to help Da.

No sooner had the pirate reached his hands under the barrel than Da dropped it on his fingers. The pirate inhaled sharply, but Da slapped his hand over the pirate's mouth before the pirate could yell. With the ferocity of a puma, Da seized the back of the pirate's head with his other hand and twisted violently.

There was a sickening snap, and Haeli winced. The pirate crumpled to the ground. Da stood up, burning anger in his eye. Haeli doubled back a few steps at his ferocity.

Da breathed heavily, calming himself. He was reining in his own horse.

"Haeli," Da finally said between deep gulps of air, "you have to get out of here. Get help as quickly as you can. Martyn should be on the mountain, trive him, or Aarushi, or anyone. Tell them what is happening and get them here as fast as you can."

"How, Da, how?" Haeli's heart raced now as she glanced between the pirate's corpse and her Da.

Da put his hands on her shoulder and looked her directly in the eye reassuringly. "It is all right, Haeli. You can do this. I am fully confident that you can do this."

Haeli breathed deeply, trying to slow her heartbeat.

"Climb out the window," Da said in a low voice, "and get to the stables. I will buy you as much time as I can. You can take a horse. You should be able to get help within an hour."

"But will you *tain* an hour?" Haeli asked.

Da smiled weakly and hugged her affectionately. "I love you, Haeli. Now cede along."

Haeli turned towards the window when Da stopped her again.

"Wait, ceive these."

Haeli turned to see Da offering her the dead pirate's loaded pistol and two iron keys tied onto a leather strand. Haeli took the pistol and eyed the keys curiously, feeling almost a sense of doom as she looked at them.

"This is what they are garding for," Da said in a low tone. "They can not ceive them, no matter what. You can not let them get these. Get them as far away from here as you can, and never let them out of your sight. You cannot tell *anyone*, understand? *No one* can know about these keys."

Haeli tucked the keys into her bodice, then stuck the pistol into her apron pocket. She looked at her Da desperately. What was going on?

Da looked back at her with a tired and helpless look in his eyes. "You can give them back to me when I trive you after this is over."

"Where will I trive you?" Haeli asked.

Da forced a weary smile; then he set his jaw tightly in determination. "I love you," Da replied. "Be strong, tain courage, and wait on the Lord. Now cede along."

With that, he yelled loud enough for anyone in the house to hear. "Get your hands off her, villain!" Da growled, imitating the dead pirate's voice. "Now, you take one more step, and I'll blow your brains out."

Haeli didn't wait to see anything else. She shoved the window open and slipped out, dropping to the ground outside the house.

As she stood to her feet, about to run towards the stable, a gunshot rang out in the twilight, followed by a horse screaming. Haeli backed up to the house wall, trying to stay in the shadows while she looked around. The sun had set by now, leaving only a shimmer of gold and carmine above the western mountains. Yet a full moon was out, casting ample light to see by. The day-star, too, shown out of the sky. Haeli took a deep breath. While this meant that she could easily see her surroundings that night, it also meant that the pirates could easily see her.

Haeli could make out figures moving about in the corral beside the barn. She strained her eyes to look closer. There appeared to be about six pirates in the corral. They had brought several horses out; some were trying to ride while others were herding them back and forth, purposefully frightening the horses with their guns. Haeli bit her lip in anger and frustration. Hopefully, they didn't have all the horses in the corral.

She crept along the house's shadows. There was a window on the barn's west side, which was in shadow from the moon-light; that would be her target destination. But how was she to get there? She scanned the area between her and the stable for hiding places. There was the raspberry patch about halfway between her and the window on the barn's west side, but other-wise, there was no other cover.

Haeli shook her head and bit her lip. She would have to make a dash for it.

Looking in all directions to make sure no one was watching, she sprinted across the yard, throwing herself flat on her belly in the raspberry patch's shade. After satisfying herself that no one had seen her, she rushed the rest of the way to the window.

Though she was in shadow from the moon, she still felt exposed. Hurriedly, Haeli pulled the window open and scrambled through.

She landed on a pile of straw inside. Ducking behind the walls of a stall, she remained still for a moment, crouching low and looking all around to assure herself that no one was in the stable. She tried to calm her breathing and remember what her Da had taught her. She had to keep panic at a trot.

It seemed like he had rehearsed over and over emergency situations with her — how to respond if the lodge caught fire, how to respond if the indigies attacked, how to defend herself from a single attacker — but she still felt completely unprepared for this. This was real; her Da had only simulated the situations. Still, she had to think. She had to concentrate. She could make it through this. In her head, she knew she was prepared, even if she couldn't feel it in her heart. But she would use that emotion of uncertainty, ike her mother had taught her. It was her horse, and she would use the energy of her emotions to get her through.

She could almost hear her father from those many training exercises. "You will never think clearly enough in the moment. Make a plan beforehand."

Breathing deeply, she felt her pulse. She was too nervous. She needed to calm down. After another minute, she looked back at the stables. Her heart sank as she saw stall after stall, completely empty. Tack was strewn carelessly across the floor, and several doors to the stalls lay broken on the ground.

Just then, Haeli heard a low whinny. Looking over at Vengeance's stall, she saw the stud still standing there, calmly eating straw. Haeli breathed a sigh of relief. There was a horse for her. She would have preferred Hope, but Vengeance was the fastest horse in the stable, anyway. So long as he didn't act up, he would be the perfect horse to make her escape on.

She studied the stable for a moment. Both the north and

south doors were open. Since the north one led into the corral, Haeli knew she would have to take the south door. Assuming the gate to the fort was still open, she could mount Vengeance and be out of the fort in less than a minute.

Silently, she crept toward Vengeance's stall, picking up a pair of reins from the ground as she went. There was a saddle hanging inside the stall. Would she have time to put it on the stud? A better question would be, would Vengeance let her put the saddle on him without making a scene?

Haeli slowly opened the stall door and slid inside, leaving the door cracked. Vengeance raised his head when she entered and snorted.

"It is all right, Vengeance. We have a ride ahead of us tonight." Haeli dropped her right arm over the stud's neck and began putting on the reins. He took the bit with no trouble. Haeli sighed with relief; he wasn't in a fighting mood.

She gently slipped the reins over his ears and fastened the chin strap. Just as she turned to take the saddle from the wall, she heard a voice entering the stables, only catching the tail end of what he said.

"...a good deal on excitement!"

Haeli ducked below the stall wall and peered out through a crack in the slats. Sure enough, a pirate had entered through the north door and was walking towards her, looking in each stall as he passed. The pirate stumbled badly as if he were drunk. Haeli's heart began racing again. She tried to calm herself. The pirate may not see her. He might walk out of the stable. But what if he looked in Vengeance's stall? What if he was coming *for* Vengeance?

"Make a plan beforehand."

Her father's words repeated themselves in her mind. She set her jaw firmly and tried to control her breathing. Very well, she would stay where she was, but if the pirate entered Vengeance's stall, she would not hesitate; she would shoot him dead.

There. She had made her plan. She couldn't hesitate now.

As she watched the pirate come closer, she reached into her apron pocket and pulled out her pistol, cocking it back to full position. Panic was trying to pull into a gallop again, but she reined her in with several deep, steady breaths.

Sure enough, the pirate walked right up to Vengeance's stall. He stumbled forward, pausing momentarily with one hand on the gate as he messed with the lock — apparently too drunk to tell that the gate was already open.

At that moment, a wave of doubt washed over Haeli. Could she kill this man? Haeli pushed her hesitation back. She had already decided; she was not about to rethink this. An image of the two dead and mutilated indigie huntsmen flashed before her mind. She gripped the pistol tighter, every muscle in her body poised and ready to spring. The pirate had brought this on himself; he shouldn't have attacked her fort.

The pirate swung open the gate, looking up at Vengeance, when his eyes fell on Haeli. His eyes went wide, and his mouth curled in a leering smile, but that was as far as he got. Haeli gave panic a little rein, and a wave of energy passed through her. She stood, pointed her pistol straight at the pirate's head, and fired. She was too close and too well-practiced to miss.

The shot echoed through the stables, and the pirate crumpled into a heap in the gateway. Vengeance leaped back at the pistol's report and screamed. From outside the stable, Haeli could hear shouts from the pirates as they hallooed their dead comrade within. Haeli's mind reeled with a mixture of panic over the fact that she had just killed another person and anger at her own stupidity for firing a gun in such circumstances. Now she had startled Vengeance – and there was no telling how long it would take to control him again – she had alerted the pirates that she was in the stable and had killed someone in the process. Part of her wanted nothing else but to curl into a ball and give up, but she knew she had to continue. For the sake of

Da, for the sake of Ma, Yohni, and little Dafid, she had to get out of the fort and tell Martyn what was happening.

Haeli stuck her pistol back into her apron pocket and snatched Vengeance's reins. "Easy, Vengeance, calm down."

Vengeance reared again. Haeli yanked on the reins to bring the horse back down to his feet, terror and anger getting the better of her. She knew she had no time to fight with Vengeance and no time to worry about saddling him. She needed to get out of the fort before the pirates found her again.

"Baptize it, Vengeance, get down!" She yanked on the reins again, too overwhelmed to care that she had cursed.

From the corner of her eye, Haeli saw a pirate entering the stable. At that moment, Vengeance stood still for just an instant. Haeli wasted no time but flung herself onto the stud's back, drove her heels into his sides, and clung to him for all she was worth. Vengeance leaped out of the stall, bucking and snorting, trampling on the dead pirate, and throwing hay and tack in all directions.

The pirate whom Haeli had seen entering the stable shouted. "There's another one in here! Get her boys – she's taked a horse!"

Haeli tugged on the reins hard and kicked her heels into Vengeance's side, trying to get him to leave the stables. The stud, however, paid no attention to her but only bucked harder.

Suddenly, another gunshot rang out through the stables. Haeli winced, expecting Vengeance to crumple dead beneath her, but instead, the shot seemed to alert Vengeance to the imminent danger he was in. Vengeance took one last leap into the air before darting off like a lightning bolt through the south doors.

Haeli looked up, relaxing her grip ever so slightly now that Vengeance was galloping and not bucking. She guided the stud gently, trying not to frighten him. There was the fort gate, and yes, the pirates had left it open. Haeli leaned a little to guide the horse, but Vengeance had already seen this path of escape.

Continuing his mad-dash pace, Vengeance flew through the gate and down the Ocean Road outside. Haeli breathed a deep sigh, trying to calm her heart. She was out of the fort now. The worst was behind her.

Now, how would she find help?

5

CHIVALRIC

*H*aeli let herself breathe easier. The worst of her fears were behind her. She was out on the open road now and riding fast. She could easily reach Martyn's station in twenty minutes — ten if Vengeance could keep up this pace.

Vengeance showed no signs of slacking, but continued at top speed, almost flying down the road. The stud had obviously still not recovered from his terror. A hint of concern crept over Haeli. What would Vengeance do once he reached the intersection with the High Road? She needed to head south to Martyn's station, but would Vengeance obey the reins?

Just then, Haeli glimpsed the High Road ahead of them. Vengeance still showed no signs of slowing. Haeli leaned back and pulled hard on the reins, but Vengeance plowed on heedlessly. Haeli's heart raced. She had to get control of Vengeance, but how?

Vengeance mounted a small incline, and the High Road was in front of them. The Ocean Road ended abruptly at this intersection, but that didn't appear to stop Vengeance. Haeli hauled hard on the reins to the right, but Vengeance paid no attention.

In an instant, he had crossed the road, jumped over the ditch on the other side, and hurtled on, continuing with no road before him. The land here was fairly open, a few copses and clumps of bushes peppering the open land, looking like nebulous dark masses in the moonlight.

While the full moon provided enough light for Haeli to see the way ahead, Vengeance either couldn't see where he was headed, or else he didn't care. He continued at the same incredible pace, crashing through bushes and tearing through a copse. Haeli winced as thorns and branches slashed across her legs and face, but she still sat upright, hauling hard on the reins.

"Whoa, Vengeance. Whoa!"

Vengeance continued on until, while hurtling through another clump of bushes, he tripped. He stumbled heavily, and for a moment, Haeli thought he would throw her. She held on tightly with her knees, and Vengeance caught himself just in time. Finally, he slowed his pace, wheezing.

Haeli patted the side of his neck — it was covered in sweat.

"Easy, Vengeance."

Vengeance snorted and came to a stop.

Haeli looked back at the High Road. She was panting too, but feeling a lot calmer. At least she now had control of her horse. Hopefully, she could get back to the road quickly and recover the time they had lost. Haeli was about to turn Vengeance back towards the High Road when she felt something hot and sticky on her right leg. Was she bleeding?

Looking down, she did indeed find blood all over her leg. But wait, that was blood on Vengeance's side. Haeli leaned over. Sure enough, Vengeance was bleeding steadily. How did that happen? She hadn't been driving him that hard. Besides, she didn't even have her spurs on. Haeli recalled the gunshot in the stable just before Vengeance bolted. Had he been shot?

At that moment, Haeli heard a nasal whistle from overhead.

Looking up, she saw Aarushi, the harrier, hovering above her, the moonlight gleaming on her plumage.

"Aarushi! Oh, thank God I trived you."

Aarushi whistled inquiringly, looking at Haeli with some perplexity.

"I need to trive Martyn. They attacked the fort. Pirates, I mean. I need to... we have to..."

Aarushi nodded and fluttered upwards a little way.

Haeli breathed deeply. She had to get going and find Martyn quickly. She could only pray that Vengeance's injuries were not fatal. Haeli clicked with her tongue and turned Vengeance around to face the High Road.

Haeli looked up at the ridge the High Road ran across and then sat stock still. There were five pirates on the High Road. They were all on horseback, but they weren't riding. They simply stood where they were, scattered across the length of the road, scanning the entire area. Haeli tried not to move; she tried not even to breathe. They were still a long way away. Could they even see her from where they were? She could see them.

One pirate pointed in her direction and shouted. Haeli's heart sank. The pirates yelled enthusiastically and spurred the horses off the road toward her.

Haeli bit her lip. She had to get back on the road and head south as soon as possible. However, the pirates were now between her and the road. Any way she rode, they would cut her off.

"Make a plan beforehand." Her father's words came back to mind.

She forced herself to breathe deeply and slowly. There was a lot of ground between herself and the pirates; she could hazard taking a minute to think and orient herself to her situation.

She scanned the open land before her. About half a mile to the south, the ground rose steeply into a hill crest. To the north, the ground lay open for several miles before it too sloped upward into the foothills of the mountains. In front of her and to her right was a thick copse, and to her left was a small stream — about six feet across — with steep banks on either side. Before her, the ground rose steadily up towards the road, which sat on the ridge of this slight incline.

Haeli took another deep breath. Vengeance was fast, and he was a good jumper. Only a few other horses in the stable could surpass Vengeance in either of those skills. Haeli breathed out slowly. She could only pray that the pirates hadn't grabbed any of those horses.

Haeli tapped her heels against Vengeance's side and drove him forward, toward the pirates.

The pirates yelled again, and a few fired their muskets. Haeli wasn't very concerned about being hit — they were only muskets, after all, and were not likely to hit her at this distance. However, it looked like one of the pirates had a rifle. She would have to keep away from him. He was the only one likely to pose a risk to her, so long as she kept her distance.

Haeli turned Vengeance abruptly, riding hard north to the copse on her right and hiding herself from the pirate's view. No sooner was she out of sight, than she turned around abruptly and reined Vengeance to a halt. Her heart pounded in her chest.

"Lord, please guide me," she breathed.

The pirates should pass on the north side of the copse, thinking to cut her off. However, she would ride south. That would be her chance to get back between them and the road.

She waited for about a minute as the sounds of the pirates' horses grew louder and louder, steadily moving to the north.

Suddenly, a pirate burst through the copse on the north side. Haeli dug her heels into Vengeance and urged him forward.

Vengeance leaped like a thunderbolt, flying straight for the stream. Haeli could hear the pirates yelling and turning their horses to follow her. At least they were now behind her instead of in front of her.

Vengeance reached the stream and, without hesitating, leaped to the other side. Haeli continued to urge him on, chancing a glance behind her. The first pirate reached the stream, but his horse balked, throwing him headfirst into the opposite stream bank. The other four pirates, however, made it successfully over, though three of the horses stumbled on, landing on the other side, slowing them down. Still, one pirate kept hot on Haeli's tail.

Haeli looked ahead again to see Vengeance charging directly into a thick copse. There was no time to turn aside. She ducked down and clung tightly to Vengeance's neck.

The stud hurtled through, branches and thorns tearing across Haeli's arms and face. Bursting out the other side, Vengeance stumbled. Haeli urged him forward. She couldn't lose time.

A horse burst through the copse behind them, but its saddle was empty.

"Come on, Vengeance, get-ye-up!"

Vengeance wheeled and pointed towards the road. At that moment, the pirates rounded the copse to her left. The one with the rifle was the foremost of the group. He leveled his gun and sighted down the barrel.

Haeli dug her heels into Vengeance's side, urging him forward again. Her heart beat hard in her chest. If that pirate was even a half-decent marksman, she would be dead in a moment.

Suddenly, a shrill cry broke through the air, and a blur of feathers and talons fell like lightning on the pirate with the rifle. It was Aarushi.

The harrier caught the rifle in her claws and threw it aside as the pirate fired. Then, with another shriek of indignation, she darted into the pirate's face, slashing mercilessly and pecking at his eyes. The pirate yelled in pain, trying to shield his face. The pirate's horse started in alarm and reared, throwing the hapless pirate hard to the ground.

Haeli did not stay to see how this ended, urging Vengeance on toward the road. In a moment, the stud mounted the bank, leaped the ditch, and landed in the road. Haeli could hear Vengeance breathing heavily. She bit her lip, praying he could keep running. Glancing down at his side, Haeli could see his wound still running with blood, though now the blood was thick and dark.

Another eighth of a mile, Haeli guessed, and they would be at the foot of the trail that led to Martyn's station—just one more eighth of a mile.

"Come on, Vengeance," Haeli whispered. "Come on! You can do this."

Behind her, Haeli could hear the last two pirates mounting the bank of the High Road. She glanced back in time to see Aarushi swoop in front of one horse's feet. The horse screamed, rearing up on its back legs and throwing the rider from his saddle. The last pirate leaped the ditch, swerving to avoid his comrade as he entered the road.

Haeli drove her heels into Vengeance's side; she could feel his pace slowing. The pirate behind her was gaining ground on her. Glancing behind her, Haeli could see that her pursuer was a gnome. He was fairly young yet and looked like he had never ridden a horse before from the way he bounced around in the saddle.

Haeli looked forward again to see the trail to Martyn's station branching off the High Road to her right. Before she had time to congratulate herself for coming this far, Vengeance collapsed beneath her. Haeli caught herself on her shoulder as she hit the ground and rolled a few times to reduce the impact, ending halfway between lying on her back and sitting up.

The gnome pirate behind her reined to a stop in front of Vengeance, leaping to the ground and reaching for his rapier.

Haeli pulled the pistol from her apron pocket and pointed it directly at the pirate. She forced herself to breathe deeply and steadily. The pistol, of course, wasn't loaded, but the pirate didn't know that.

Haeli cocked the pistol back to full position. "Do not vene any closer."

The gnome froze, and his eyes went wide.

Something about the startled look on the pirate's face gave Haeli more confidence. She stood boldly to her feet, keeping the pistol trained on the gnome the whole time. Her heart pounded like the ocean surf inside her chest, but she forced herself to stand straight and steady.

"Drop your guns and your sword," Haeli commanded. "Do not try any fast-handed stunts, or I will shoot you dead."

The gnome trembled all over. "Please don't shoot me."

"Then drop your guns and sword." Haeli spoke as harshly as she could. At that moment, Aarushi fluttered down behind her. The harrier alighted on the ground to her right.

The gnome took a step back, staring in terror at Aarushi. He hurriedly let his musket down from his shoulder and then unbuckled his belt, letting it fall to the road with his rapier and pistol.

"I wouldn't have tried to hurt you... if'n... I knew you haved a gun..." the gnome stammered.

A rush of anger flooded over Haeli. She marched forward, and the pirate backed away from his weapons.

"If you had known that I tained a gun?" Haeli fumed. "You would have willingly attacked a helpless girl, but once you know she is armed, you lose all your fight? You sick and disgusting coward! I should kill you right now. The world would be a better place without you."

Haeli picked up the gnome's pistol from the ground and trained it on him. Now she had a loaded gun. She clenched her jaws tightly, pure rage running through her veins. Why not pull the trigger and kill this contemptible pirate? Look what they had done to her house and her family, and those two poor indigie huntsmen.

The pirate stood still, the wide-eyed look of fear still on his face. She had already killed a pirate today. The very thought of it made her sick, and much of her anger gave way to disgust. She couldn't do it again. Then again, how could she let this man live? Who knows who he might harm next? Under Llaedhwythi law, he could be shot on sight.

Haeli looked again at the terrified pirate. He had no fight left in him. All her anger left her as she realized the absurdity of this situation. Here was a full-grown pirate, who had probably fought in many a raid, and boarded many a ship in battle on the high seas. He had probably killed men before. Yet here he was, cowering before a girl who had not even seen her seventeenth summer. This gnome was no dread evil to be exterminated; he was only a coward.

"There is nothing honorable about you," Haeli finally said, still keeping both pistols trained on the pirate, "but I would rather fight a cowardly evil than a fearless one. Get out of here as fast as you can, and remember that you should have died tonight. Your life is a gift from me. Do not abuse it."

The pirate turned around and sprinted off down the road. In a few moments, he had disappeared from Haeli's sight.

6

THE COWARD

*E*rnest's heart pounded in his chest as he ran down the road. His lungs burned, and his legs ached, but sheer terror drove him on. All he could see was that grim, dark-skinned girl standing behind him like the angel of death.

"You should have died tonight."

The words echoed in his mind again and again.

"You should have died tonight."

He hurtled forward, the darkness a blur around him. His mind was void of any thought, like the primal emotion of a beast. Fright completely overwhelmed him. Strange and wild images danced around in his mind, memories of a painful and buried past. Fear beyond reason gripped him, like the fear of a child, like the fear that he had once felt years ago...

That dark-skinned girl — he had seen her before. The anger in her eye, the moonlight like a fire in her hair, the raptor bird as it hovered above her. But she wasn't holding pistols; she held a sickle.

"Death has found you! No one can escape death!"

He could almost hear the words of his old parish priest in his ear. In his mind's eye, he could see the scene again, the monastery, the courtyard, the torches, the monks in somber black — and the mystery play.

A dozen weird and wild images flooded his mind. He had been so young at the time that he didn't know that they were only performers. To him, it was real, all too real, as if it happened to *him*. Death, the judgment, the sentencing, the eternal torment, the damnation — all these scenes and many others acted out before his little eyes, with demons and vices scurrying about on stage as if they were actual creatures, all intent on stealing his soul and dragging him into the sulfur pits of Hell.

But above all, the confused memory of those plays stood the ominous figure of Lady Death. She stood taller than any other performer, her coiled black hair falling in a torrent of disarray, cascading well below her waist. Her eyes burned like coals, her hands snatching at any little boy in their reach. She held a large sickle in her left hand, and on her shoulder perched a mighty raptor bird.

"Death comes swiftly! Who can escape her? All men are equal before her: young, old, rich, poor, weak, powerful — all will fall beneath her. And falling, all will be cast into judgment!"

Again, that black and primal terror flooded his soul. He ran harder, stumbling slightly in the darkness. From even that young age, he had felt the deepest of all fears. A fear beyond the fear of death. The fear that perhaps we will be held responsible for all the dark deeds we do on this earth. The fear that perhaps there is a God.

Ernest tripped, and he landed face-first in the road. The physical pain broke through his unbridled emotions. For a moment, he could think again.

That play was only a play, nothing more. It was a show put on by the monks. They just meant to frighten little boys like him into being good.

Lady Death

The terror still nagged at him. He still felt like Lady Death was behind him. Her sickle was even now prepared to level him.

"You should have died tonight."

Ernest fought the impulse to leap back to his feet and keep running. In his mind, he knew there was nothing behind him. Death was not imminent. It was only a traumatic memory — a permanent childhood scare. His heart, however, would not listen to his head.

For a while, he lay there in the road, curled up tight, as the terror continued to wash over him. Yet slowly, it ebbed. Bit by bit he regained control of himself again.

It wasn't real. That play wasn't real. Lady Death wasn't real. None of that was real. It *felt* real, but it couldn't be real. At least if it was real, it was too terrifying to be admitted to.

There was no Lady Death. She was not coming for him. That girl with the pistol had reminded him of her, that was all.

Ernest's pulse was still rushing, but at least he could control himself now. The key was not thinking about death. After all, with no fear of death, there could be no fear of whatever followed — or worse still, the fear that Someone willed it all.

Ernest lay still for several more minutes until the unearthly terror had completely subsided. Only then did he stir. Slowly and carefully, he stood to his feet. He felt rather small and vulnerable, standing there in the road under the moonlight without his sword or his musket. Then again, he still had his pepper-box pistol. It lay hidden inside his coat.

Just then, Ernest heard the sounds of hooves on the road to the south. He slipped off the road and ducked behind a large clump of sagebrush. As he looked out from his hiding spot, he could make out three figures in the full moon's light. Two were on horseback, and one ran alongside them, somehow keeping pace with the galloping horses.

Ernest stayed still until they passed him and only rose back to his feet once they had disappeared down the road to the north.

As he stood up, Ernest sighed deeply. Those three men looked as if they had guns. What were they up to?

The question was now, what was he to do? Killjelly and the others were still at the fort, so perhaps he should return to them. Then again, Killjelly would not be thrilled to hear that the dark-skinned girl had escaped. Besides that, returning to the fort would mean following those three men who rode by. Ernest did not like that idea.

His only other option would be to return to the galleon without Killjelly and the rest of the raiding party. That would look suspiciously like deserting. He wasn't deserting, though. After all, that girl had attacked him, and he barely made it out alive. He wouldn't be deserting — maybe he would be abandoning his comrades — but he wouldn't be deserting.

It had already been a long day, and if he were to head back for the galleon now, it would take him several hours to hike back through the wilderness and find the ship. He'd be lucky if he could get back in time for morning chores. Ernest groaned inwardly at the thought of starting another full day of work with no rest after a long night of raiding.

There was his solution. He would simply walk off the road a little ways and find a place to sleep. Come morning, he would head back to the galleon. With any luck, Killjelly and the rest would already be back by then, and his straggling in would give extra credibility to his story.

This decided, Ernest turned off the road and soon found an old deer hollow. He curled up here and closed his eyes.

He wasn't sure if he got any sleep or not, for what seemed like only a moment later, a gunshot roused him. Come to think of it, he had heard several gunshots previous to this one. However, this one was closer and more startling.

Ernest was now fully awake, and the thought of armed men nearby made him nervous about lying back down again.

Slowly, he stood up, still bent low to avoid being seen in the brush. He reached into his vest and pulled out his pepper-box pistol. Yes, it was still loaded. Ernest cocked it into half-cock position but didn't put his finger to the trigger.

He chanced to stand a little higher so that he could see what was happening. At that moment, another gunshot rang out, and Ernest could hear the bullet whiz through the air not too far from him.

Ernest ducked again, his heart pounding. Had someone found him? Was Lady Death coming for him again? He cocked his big ears, listening intently.

Now he could hear the sounds of people rushing through the long grass towards him. In a moment, they would be in the deer hollow with him. Ernest cocked his pepper-box pistol fully and trained it in the noise's direction. He didn't know how many people were likely to emerge, but if they were in close formation, the eight-barreled gun would silence a few of them.

Just then, the grass burst aside, and six forms entered the hollow.

"Stand!" Ernest hissed in as intimidating a voice as he could muster under the circumstances.

The six threw themselves to the ground, and the leader produced a pistol, aiming it in Ernest's general direction. In a moment, the two recognized each other.

"Killjelly!" Ernest gasped as he lowered his pistol.

"Ernest," Killjelly replied as he stood back to his feet.

Ernest looked at the five pirates following Killjelly. "Where's the others?"

"Where's the girl?" Killjelly asked almost at the same moment.

Just then, another gunshot sounded in the air. Ernest could

hear the bullet embed in the ground not two inches from his foot. Suddenly, Ernest heard hoofbeats coming towards them.

"Move!" Killjelly hissed as he threw himself back into the long grass. Ernest fell in line with the others, hunched over as low as possible but rushing forward as fast as they could.

Ernest recognized the pirate running in front of him as Tell, the thickset human messmate of Bill.

"What's going on? Where's everyone else?" Ernest asked.

Tell only panted in reply. "They're... Gotta..."

Just then, they burst out of the long grass into the road. Killjelly continued forward in a dead sprint across the road and down into the shrubland on the other side.

As Ernest followed, another gunshot sounded, and the pirate to his right fell dead in the road. Ernest ran faster now, leaping over the bank on the far side of the road and careening after Killjelly and the others.

Killjelly headed straight for a copse of small trees about a hundred yards from the roadside. No sooner had he reached the edge than he threw himself flat on his belly beneath the small trees — out of the moon's direct light. Ernest and the others followed suit, though Ernest landed right in a briar patch as he flung himself to the ground.

The briars stuck in him from all over, but he lay perfectly still, hardly daring to breathe. His heart pounded in his head from the run. What was going on?

Ernest glanced back up at the road in time to see a figure appear in the moonlight. He was very tall — probably close to eight feet in height. Even from this distance, Ernest could make out two horns curving back from the figure's head.

They were being tracked by a giant — or a satyr, as they were commonly called. Ernest had seen many satyrs when he was a young boy in Keryna. All those he remembered were fearsome habiru warriors, or bounty hunters — all huge and powerful. Never in all of his sea voyages, and never outside of Keryna, had he seen another satyr. The thought of being hunted by one did not sit well with Ernest. Weren't they the most renowned hunters in the world? Couldn't every hair on their body hear noises? Couldn't they smell your trail more keenly than a bloodhound?

The moonlight glinted off the satyr's rifle as he looked down its barrel and scanned the valley below him. Ernest almost gasped at the gun's size — it was probably a good foot taller than he was! That satyr could probably hit his mark from a quarter mile with that rifle. Ernest's heart raced at the thought. How would they ever escape with a beast like that tracking them?

Killjelly lay perfectly still in the copse, setting an example for the other pirates. Ernest hardly dared to breathe as he stared up at the great satyr on the road.

The satyr continued to scan the shrublands below him meticulously. Ernest looked on with dread in his heart. The gun passed slowly over the copse where they lay.

"If'n we runned," Bill, the long-armed gnome, said to Killjelly in a low whisper, "If'n we runned, he couldn't take more than a few on us before we got outta range…"

Killjelly gave a low hiss. "Stay where you are, and motionless, sure."

So they lay still for several more minutes — several more terrible, death-defying minutes. The satyr's gun passed over the copse again. Still, he did not seem to see them.

Ernest tried to breathe normally now. They had passed detection twice. That was a good sign, wasn't it?

Then, like an angel of death, that raptor bird fluttered down from the heavens above the satyr. Ernest looked at it in fear and apprehension. He could hear Lady Death's voice plain in his ear.

"Death has found you! No one can escape Death!"

Ernest could feel the primal panic coming over him again.

With an effort, he stuck his hand into his mouth and bit down hard. The pain seemed to bring him back to reality.

The bird settled down on the satyr's shoulder and looked this way and that. It seemed to motion to him with her head and then fluttered away. The satyr raised his rifle and turned away, too, disappearing in an instant down the road.

The pirates lay as they were for nearly twenty minutes after the satyr had left. Only then did they dare to stir.

Killjelly stood to his feet and turned on Ernest darkly. "You do'edn't get that girl, sure?"

Ernest shook his head. "She nearly killed me! I was the..."

Killjelly waved his hooks for silence. The pirates stood there for another moment, looking at one another.

Ernest was almost afraid to speak as he looked at the five comrades that were left of the original raiding party. "The keys?"

"They were with the girl," Killjelly replied, finally moving from the circle and stepping out of the copse. "Holgard willn't be happy, sure."

The other pirates followed gloomily as Killjelly struck out towards the coast. It would be a long, long journey ahead of them, back to the ship. Yet, as Ernest stepped out of the copse, he heard the flutter of wings above his head. Could that be the raptor bird? No, surely it was a pigeon or some other bird. Still, the sound of the wings made him jump. Again, Lady Death's words rang through his head.

"Remember, you should have died tonight. Your life is a gift from me. Do not abuse it."

7

COUP DE GRÂCE

Several minutes after the gnome had disappeared down the road, Haeli lowered the pistols and let them drop to the ground. Now that the excitement was over, her stomach tied itself inside her like a knot. She felt sick and weak. All she wanted to do was curl up in a ball and weep. Panic had run her course. Haeli could not use her to ride any farther tonight. She would have to find some other emotion — or else sheer willpower — to drive her on. Haeli set her jaw firmly. She had to keep going. She had to get to Martyn.

She turned back to Vengeance. He lay on the road almost without moving. Haeli's heart sank as she looked at the wound in the horse's side. The blood had almost ceased to flow, encrusting the stud's side, and even covering one of his legs.

Haeli walked slowly up to Vengeance and put her hand on his neck. His eyes fluttered ever so slightly, and his nostrils flared.

"Goodbye, Vengeance," Haeli whispered. "You have been a magnificent horse."

She could feel a tear coming to her eye, and thought it ironic. This stud had irritated her more than any other horse in the stable, but she couldn't help but feel deeply grieved that he was dying. After all, she owed her escape — probably her life — to him.

Haeli rubbed his neck affectionately. "You deserve your rest."

She stood up and sighed. Now she would have to walk up the trail to Martyn's station.

Just then, her eyes fell upon the horse which the gnome had ridden as he pursued her. The horse still stood in the road, looking at her quizzically.

"Hope!" Haeli exclaimed. "Well, at least they did not harm you."

Haeli took the horse's reins as quickly as she dared without frightening the horse, and then she sprang onto her back, urging her towards the trail that would lead to Martyn's station. Aarushi flew low behind her like a guardian angel watching to see that she would be safe.

Sweat covered Hope's body from the long chase, but she trudged forward doggedly at Haeli's prodding, plunging at a full trot up the narrow mountain path. Haeli looked at the moon to guess the time. Perhaps thirty minutes had passed since she left her Da in the storage room. Was he safe? What would become of Ma, Yohni, and Dafid?

Haeli urged Hope on. They still had several miles to go before they reached Martyn's camp.

They had not gone up the path more than half a mile when Haeli heard the sounds of hoofbeats coming down the path toward her. She reined in her horse. In the moonlight, three shapes materialized in front of her, two on horseback and one — over eight feet tall — beside them. Haeli knew them in a moment to be Martyn and Laendon Blaeith, with their trusted friend Meriwedhr Daerl. Aarushi fluttered up beside Martyn's horse. Even in the moonlight, Haeli could see the prodigious number of rifles and blades that hung about their steeds and persons.

"Haeli!" Martyn cried when he saw her in the road. "What is the meanin' o' all o' this?"

"They attacked the fort, Martyn," Haeli replied, now only barely containing the emotions that flooded over her. "They have Da, Ma, Dafid, and Yohni. They killed the huntsmen and would have killed me — I killed one of them..." Haeli began sobbing.

Martyn nodded seriously. "Vene to the camp, Haeli. We'll will be back in a little while. Make sure the camp is ready fer the rest o' yer family. We will bring them safe, Haeli." With that, Martyn spurred on his horse, and Laendon and Meriwedhr followed close behind, rushing past her. Aarushi gave a single shriek as she swooped after Martyn.

Haeli urged Hope forward at a much slower pace. Both she and her horse were desperately exhausted, yet they plodded on up the mountainside. It was a long and worrisome trek that night, without hardly a sound to break the darkness but the trudging *thud, thud, thud* of Hope's hooves upon the trail. Twice, Haeli fancied she heard gunshots, and she reined Hope in to listen. But she knew it was little more than pitiable fancy. There was very little chance of hearing gunfire from this distance.

Finally, she reached Martyn's beacon-tending station. This camp stood in an open area amidst the lower mountain crags. Martyn and the others had abandoned it in haste, without a single weapon left in the place. There were the two spare horses, shut into their shed for the night, and several stacks of firewood leaning up against the shed's side. Three small tents lay at sundry angles, wedged into the rock crevasses and under various granite ledges, and in the widest of these crevasses sat the beginnings of a rustic shack.

In the camp's center was a fire ring, still glowing with embers, some supper still roasting above it where the three beacon-tenders had left it in their haste. Above the camp and up a craggy path some ways, Haeli could make out the dim lights of another dying fire — the beacon, surely, perched at the topmost point of some cliff-faced outcropping whose nose pointed directly to the sea.

Haeli slowly slid from Hope's back and tied her to the horse-shed gate. She was near total exhaustion by this point, but knew that she must tend to her horse. She slowly and deliberately loosened the saddle straps from Hope's back. The saddle slid off and tumbled to the ground at the horse's feet. Hope was too tired to even jump at the noise.

Haeli grabbed a bucket of water and placed it before her horse. Hope drank from it gratefully as Haeli stumbled off to the fire ring. Collapsing on an uncomfortable wooden chair that sat before the fire, Haeli gazed absentmindedly into the embers. She hurt all over, both the sharp pain from a million cuts, and the dull ache of the bruises which now covered her body.

But for all her misery, she could hardly dwell on it for very long. What would become of Da? What would become of Ma, Yohni, and Dafid? Would Martyn be able to help them? Had she gotten to Martyn too late? Had she simply sent him to his death in a suicidal attempt to save her already-dead family?

Haeli shuddered at the thought. She hugged her knees tightly to herself and rocked back and forth. "O Lord, help them," she breathed, "O Lord, help them."

To a certain extent, it was a silly prayer. Deep down, she knew that was not how God worked anymore. Martyn was going to help — he was the help God had sent.

As she rocked, her hands strayed to the two keys which still lay concealed in her bodice — those two heavy, iron keys — had she not felt that they were doomed when her father first gave them to her? What was their purpose? Did they bring doom to the bearer, or was that just her imagination?

But there was another horror in them. Da had said that she could tell no one about the keys. She, and she alone, bore them. Was there anything more horrifying? She was all by herself in this, with no help from her community — with no help from anyone but her Da. At least Da was one shoulder she could lean on.

Haeli shuddered again as a wind blew across the camp. With the wind came an odd sound, almost like a chanting or the pounding of some primal drums. Haeli listened closely but could not decide whether she heard it or whether the pounding was simply the echo of her own heartbeat in her ears.

Haeli held tighter to her knees and rocked more violently. She was thoroughly exhausted and would have liked to fall asleep where she sat, but she knew she had to wait for her family. Martyn would bring them back; he said he would. If he came back at all, he would have them.

"Oh Lord, help them."

She sat thus for only a few more minutes before she heard a flurry of wings beside her. She looked up to see Aarushi. The faithful harrier rubbed her head against Haeli's arm. Haeli stroked the bird's beautiful feathers. "It will be all right, will not it, Aarushi?"

The harrier looked at her and whistled dolefully. Haeli looked at her closely. "You are rather ominous tonight. What is your meaning?"

As if in answer, Haeli heard hooves coming up the path to the camp. They moved slowly this time. Haeli's mind raced. Was slow a good sign?

Martyn came into view, leading his horse with Ma and Dafid in the saddle. Ma looked about with a blank numbness as she held Dafid's sleeping form to her bosom.

Yohni padded stoically behind them — bruised, but without further injury — with Meriwedhr towering above him.

Laendon entered the camp last. He led his horse, too. Haeli looked closely, expecting to see her Da mounted on the horse, but there was only an obscure bundle slumped over the horse's back.

Haeli rushed forward as her Ma dismounted. "Ma! Are you all right?"

Ma embraced her tightly. Haeli looked at her closely. She was pale. "Ma, are you all right?"

"Not harmed," her Ma mumbled weakly.

"What has happened? Where is Da?"

Dafid woke up at this moment and howled miserably. Ma held him tightly, trying to soothe him, but she collapsed on the ground. Haeli looked to Yohni, who only looked back at her darkly.

Haeli turned from Laendon, to Meriwedhr, to Martyn in desperation. There was a hint of panic now rising in her voice.

"What has happened? Where is Da?"

Laendon slowly took the obscure bundle down from his horse's back and laid it gently on a rock ledge. Haeli looked at it with wild desperation on her face.

Meriwedhr inclined his horned head pathetically. "I am sorry, Miss Haeli. We did our best."

Haeli only looked at them and at the indistinct bundle. She refused to believe what she saw. It wasn't real. It couldn't be real. If it was real, why wouldn't they answer her?

Dafid wailed again. "Da, Da! Where is Da?"

Haeli looked back at Ma, now beginning to tremble all over. "What has happened? Where is Da?"

Ma took Haeli's hands in hers. She was barely middle-aged, but now deep lines of pain ran over her brow, and the bags under her eyes wrinkled with care. Her features were hard and seemed impossible to bend when under her determination, yet now they were malleable to her sorrow.

Even at the look in her eyes, Haeli could feel her heart sink. Gone was her desperation, and in its place was sheer grief — and grief was speeding up to a full gallop.

"Your Da," Ma said, slowly licking her lips, "is safer than he could ever have been on this earth."

Haeli collapsed against Ma, weeping uncontrollably. Ma wrapped her arms around her and stroked her hair sympathetically, but she said nothing. Haeli could hardly think for the pain.

"He said to leave him," she finally blurted out through the sobs, "I did right to do what he said?"

"You did right, Haeli, you did right, indeed."

Haeli only buried her head deeper into Ma's chest and wept more bitterly. Ma let out a deep keening wail, her whole body convulsing as she hugged Haeli and Dafid tighter. Grief was at a full gallop, and neither Ma nor Haeli was going to pull on the reins now.

8

MANNERISM

The fire shone cheerily on the dining room hearth of the Pickering Manor the following morning. Oak logs crackled and spat as the flames danced around them, the light smoke curling up the chimney, and the fragrant smell of burning oak filling the dining room. The morning sunbeams streamed through the tall windows and sprawled across the floor as if they were sentient beings curling up for a nap.

Ella Donne Pickering stood in attendance by the very large, yet cheery, cedar table, her jaw set in determination. Every morning since they took Sir Saemwel to the doctor's house had been a total disaster. Either Ella herself would burn breakfast, or else the young Elsi Sara Pickering would fall to weeping after the first bite. Ella wasn't upset, though. She knew that Elsi and herself had plenty of things to weep about, between Sir Saemwel's illness, and the brutal torture and murder of their friend and housekeeper, Olyfia. No, Ella didn't blame Elsi one bit, yet for all of that, she was determined to have one — just one — good morning. Miss Nansi, Elsi's aunt, puttered around the table, pouring the tea and placing it at each person's place, muttering to herself as she went.

"Now there is fer ye, deary, an' I am certain the sheriff would ceive some warm beer with this."

Sheriff Laei entered the room as if on cue, with Clerans Blaeith behind him. These two venerable souls had spent the night in the manor's lower rooms to guard it in case of another attack by pirates. Several other militia members had served as the manor's guards — Pastor Daerl, Mr. Fflemins, Miss Flalowen, Mr. Hydmenton, Lexi, and many others who slipped Ella's memory at present. Today, however, the sheriff and Clerans were their personal guards.

All took their seats for breakfast except Ella. She served each a bowl of oat porridge and some smoked ham, but she looked anxiously for Elsi to arrive. It was on her and her alone that the morning's cheeriness depended.

The poor young girl was still distraught over her father's sickness but still refused to see him. If she were to come out now and fall to weeping — as was not at all unlikely — then the entire morning would be ruined. Ella bit her lip. She had just as good a reason to cry as Elsi did this morning, as she was separated from her family too, and she didn't even have a father anymore — well, she had a step-father, but he didn't count. The point was that she held it in this morning to make a clean start of it. Couldn't Elsi do the same?

Ella did not have to wait long for Elsi to arrive. The young Miss Pickering entered from the hallway, perfectly groomed and looking as determined to have a good day as Ella was determined to make it one. The two met eyes, and Elsi smiled wearily. Ella smiled back.

"Thank ye, merri much, Ella, fer another fine breakfast."

"It is my pleasu'e," Ella replied through her lisp.

Clerans cleared his throat, "Now, Elsi, it would be a merri more o' an pleasure if ye'll would sit down an' eat! These two starvin' souls here cen no bear much merri waitin'."

Elsi smiled good-naturedly. "Ay, I'm sure."

Ella served Elsi, and after Miss Nansi said a blessing over the food, the 'starvin' souls' began to eat.

Elsi looked at Clerans quizzically.

"An' may I quire, Mr. Clerans, what makes ye such a starvin' soul this fine morning?"

Clerans shrugged carelessly. "I dreamed o' fightin' pirates all night. Jist a lot o' physical labor. That is all."

"Away with yer stories," Sheriff Laei said between bites of smoked ham, as if he could tell that Clerans bordered onto a subject that might now distress Elsi. "This is merri good ham, wos it ye, Miss Nansi. Who cooked it?"

Ella bit her lip, glancing at Elsi to see that she was not about to cry before looking at Miss Nansi. Hopefully, she could steer the conversation away from pirates. Smoked ham was a much more innocuous subject.

Miss Nansi, however, turned on Clerans with a twinkle in her eye. "Ye say that sleepin' is physical labor?"

Clerans looked defensive. "No, it wos no the sleepin' that was the labor but the dreamin' that wos the labor."

"Curious," Miss Nansi replied. "I ha' never trived imaginin' things to be a laborious past-time."

Elsi giggled at this. Ella breathed a tentative sigh of relief. So far, so good.

Clerans raised his finger in the air as if he were about to deliver a speech. "No, that is no the half o' it. It wos no the imaginin' which tired me out an' ceived me an appetite. It wos the pirates themselves."

Sheriff Laei cleared his throat. "Who should I compliment fer the ham, then?"

Miss Nansi glanced between the sheriff and Elsi. Elsi's face turned long and somber as she looked at Clerans.

"Are ye givin' me to believe," Miss Nansi said, "that these imaginary pirates somehow wore ye out?"

"Ay!" Clerans replied triumphantly. "That would be it."

"Did they pirate the food from yer bowels?" Miss Nansi asked.

Elsi giggled lightly at this.

Clerans shook his head. "It wos no the pirates themselves that ceived me my appetite."

"Ye *jist* said otherwise," Miss Nansi broke in.

"Do no interrupt," Clerans replied with a high-minded wave of his hand. "I wos sayin', it wos the *longing* fer the pirates that ha' filled my bowels with hunger."

The sheriff frowned. "It is reckless for anyone to wish the pirates to be here." And the sheriff gestured to Elsi.

"Oh no," Clerans replied hastily, glancing at Elsi himself. He flushed red as if suddenly realizing that what he had said might be inappropriate. "Oh no, I do no long fer the pirates to be here. What I ha' been meanin' to say is that I am longin' to fight the pirates — real pirates."

"Ye could ha' said that from the beginning," the sheriff said stiffly.

Miss Nansi chuckled. "Ye cen never get Clerans to say something from the beginning. It always comes out at the end after he ha' tained the chance fer acting out some drama."

"Fightin' pirates," Clerans went on, putting his hand over his heart, "is in my blood. It wos what I wos born to do. I will be a ship's captain, or perhaps an admiral."

Sheriff Laei shook his head. "An admiral would need to learn more polite conversations."

Clerans waved his hand. "That is true. I never did like the politics an' policies, anyway. I will be a free-fighter then, a privateer fer good, like a second Jock Blowhoarder."

At the name Jock Blowhoarder, Ella sat up straighter. She vaguely remembered the pirates calling Jock 'the Blowhoarder'. How would Clerans know about Jock?

The sheriff sat back and chuckled. "So that is what this is about?"

Clerans looked confused. "What do ye mean?"

"Jock Blowhoarder? This is because o' that poem ye read about him."

Clerans made a face of mock perplexity. "I do no know what ye are talkin' about."

"I fer one," Elsi broke in, "think ye would make an excellent second Jock Blowhoarder."

Clerans doffed his imaginary hat. "Thank ye, thank ye."

Ella licked her lips. "I feel silly fo'h asking, but who is Jock Blowhoa'de'h? You all seem to know, but I don't have any idea who he is."

Clerans spread his arms wide. "I am astonished! Ye do no know o' the feats o' Captain Jock Blowhoarder?"

Sheriff Laei chuckled and shrugged. "He wos a privateer."

Clerans raised his hand in objection, warming to his subject. "No jist a privateer, by any means. An' does no the entire nation o' Llaedhwyth owe him a debt o' gratitude?"

Miss Nansi laughed. "Here ye cede again, dear. Ye an' yer dramatizin' an' yer exaggeratin'."

Clerans shook his head vigorously. "An' I *challenge* ye to point out *any* exaggeration in what I jist said."

Elsi nodded at this. "He is merri right, Aunt Nansi. We owe a debt to Captain Blowhoarder."

"I'm so'y to say so," Ella broke in again, "but I still do not know who this man was."

"Ah!" Clerans interjected. "An' that must be rectified." Clerans leaned against the table intently, as if he were a renowned lecturer about to teach a dozen pupils.

"Ye see, durin' the war, we did no tain a navy. The Hrufangi tained few ships themselves, but mostly they jist hired pirates to be privateers fer them and ruin our trade and shippin'. Now the worst o' these Hrufangi hired privateers wos that pirate Longfinch. He attacked the capitol o' Chiryapolis itself, an' destroyed all the merchant ships that tried to land there. He stayed there fer three months straight an' would no let anyone bring food or trade into Chiryapolis. Well, this would no do fer Caedmon Wilkins. So he talks to Parliament, and Parliament issues a decree an' gives out letters o' marque to hire privateers o' our own — see, that was the only navy we tained."

Clerans paused his oration and looked at Ella. "Are ye followin' so far?"

Ella nodded. "I believe so. This Longfinch that the H'ufangi hi'ed, he's the same one that attacked Entwe'p?"

Clerans nodded. "Ay, the merri same one. But as I wos sayin', Parliament hired our privateers, an' one o' the first ones to answer the call wos Captain Jock Blowhoarder. Now Blowhoarder venes up to New Serron, and he starts attackin' the Hrufangi privateers, an' sinkin' them, an' makin' a name fer himself. An' it wos no long a'fore he ha' vened to Chiryapolis an' there he met with Longfinch."

Clerans paused for dramatic effect, but Miss Nansi took advantage of this and cut in herself. "Well, to make a merri long story short, Blowhoarder defeated Longfinch an' raised the siege o' Chiryapolis."

Clerans raised his hands in protest. "No jist that! He broke the Hrufangi navy there, an' from then on, *we* had control o' the high seas. An' if no fer that, it is doubtful that Caedmon Wilkins would ha' been so successful on land."

"There is truth to that," the sheriff nodded. "The Hrufangi might ha' starved us out, but that Blowhoarder an' his other privateers kept the Hrufangi on the run."

"An'" Clerans continued, "Blowhoarder is the only person, *to date*, who ha' ever defeated that pirate Longfinch in open battle. He made up an entirely new strategy fer sea warfare and outsmarted the un-outsmart-able Longfinch. See, since the ships could only load one side at a time, Blowhoarder pretended to load one side o' his ship, an' Longfinch vened at him to attack him broadside from that side, yet at the last minute,

Blowhoarder *switched* to the other side, which wos the side he tained loaded this whole time."

Clerans waved his finger in the air with a military flourish. "Well then, so Blowhoarder had a whole round o' broadside to give Longfinch, an' that dastardly Hrufangi privateer did no tain a single cannon shot to exchange. But as Providence would tain it, one o' Blowhoarder's cannon balls struck Longfinch's ship and rolled into the powder magazine, and the entire ship went up in flames."

Clerans paused and regarded his audience with an intense look on his face as if trying to impress on them the gravity of what he said. "An' so, ye understand why Blowhoarder is a national hero, but that is no the end o' it. See, after his victory, Jock Blowhoarder gave up his life as a pirate. He gave his crew the slip an' left the high seas, an' he ha' never been heard o' since. An' how is that?"

Elsi started clapping. "Well done, Clerans, as always."

"Thank ye, thank ye," Clerans replied with a bow.

Ella couldn't help shaking her head at Clerans' antics. Still, this story intrigued her. Was this Jock Blowhoarder, Hero of Llaedhwyth, the same as the Jock whom the pirates now held as their prisoner? It would make sense of the antagonism between Jock and Longfinch. But how had this famous privateer ended up as a beggar in her home village of Blisa?

Sheriff Laei stood. "I regret I must be on my way. I tain my business to attend to in the city. Clerans, will ye be vening with me today? I expect I'll will be able to run ye through a few drills this mornin', if ye'll like."

"Ay, sir," Clerans said with a wink. "I do tain my fetcher work to get to."

Clerans and the sheriff kissed Ella, Elsi, and Miss Nansi before they trudged out the door.

"Thank you fer the delicious breakfast," Clerans called out as he left.

"Thanks ye fer the entertainment," Elsi replied.

"Anytime!"

The sheriff closed the front door behind them, and their boots trudged down the front steps. Ella sighed contentedly. This was the good beginning to the day she needed. Maybe Clerans was all they needed to make a fresh start.

9

WHALING

*E*rnest, and the other five surviving pirates, stood before Captain Holgard in his cabin at the aft of the galleon. They were all rather disheveled from the raid the previous evening and all very weary from the long trek back to the galleon through the night. These raiders were themselves not a terrible picture of the galleon that they now stood inside, for it too, was still disheveled and badly damaged from its most recent attempt on the Entwerp Battery. Ernest had noted, with some disappointment, that the carpenters didn't seem to have made much progress in repairing the ship. Still, it was in better condition than Longfinch's battered man-o-war, whose main mast still hung in a shattered mess.

Killjelly looked even wilder than usual, with his raven-black hair now a tangled mess hanging to his shoulders, and his leprechauni skin showing a hint of green from his hunger and lack of sleep. He stood foremost among the pirates gathered in the cabin, directly before the captain's desk. The potent smell of alcohol filled the cabin like a mist, making the entire room feel uncomfortable and tense. This conversation would not go well if Holgard had drunk even half the grog that it smelled as if he had.

Captain Holgard sat behind his desk, eyeing them all suspiciously, but most particularly Killjelly. He took a draught of ale from the tankard before him. "This is all you bringed back to me?"

Killjelly squinted his eyes. "Do you think that you could have done better?"

Holgard shrugged and took another sip of his ale before glaring at Killjelly again. "Weel, a fine mess I will have explaining this to Longfinch."

"It was a raid gone wrong, sure," Killjelly replied, carving idly with his hooks upon the desk.

"A raid what he never condoned," Holgard reminded. "And why did we raid without him telling us? How will we answer that question, eh? What're we supposed to do now that you've let the keys slip from you?"

Holgard stood, displaying his massive form. He was a dwarf, true, but he was a giant of his race, just shy of six feet in height. Though he was only taller than a few of those present, he still seemed to tower over them all simply with his massive frame and muscular bulk.

Killjelly did not seem intimidated. "We will tell him that the raid was a rash decision, sure. That we only meaned to scout it out, but getted carried away. He may reprimand us for our stupidity, but he willn't ask further, sure."

Holgard still surveyed Killjelly angrily. "We're both in this together, you know. One on us failing will drag the other one down with him."

Killjelly nodded. "Very true, sure."

Holgard snorted and sat down again, taking another sip at his ale. After a moment, he spoke again. "And what on the girl? You're quite certain that she haves the keys?"

Killjelly nodded.

Holgard slammed his open hand down on his desk emphatically. Everything on the desk — tankards, knives, compasses — jumped at the blow's force. "Then baptize me! How the sacrament do we get those anointed keys?"

Killjelly licked his lips slowly. "We will find the girl. Surely she will return to Entwerp with her family…"

Holgard banged on the desk again. "We can't let her reach Entwerp. We are certain to lose her then. How are we to locate her, eh?"

Killjelly smiled as he continued carving with his hooks on the table aimlessly. "That might require *darker arts* than I possess, sure."

Holgard looked at him abruptly. "Darker arts?"

Killjelly nodded but looked pointedly at the crew standing behind him.

Holgard seemed to get the gist, for he snorted. "Weel, I will send him to shore."

Ernest shuddered all over. He guessed at who Holgard referred to. He had seen the Archeomancer, that mysterious albino human, use some of these 'darker arts,' and he did not much relish the thought.

"Very weel, now," Holgard said, standing up again, when at that moment, there came a scratching sound at the door.

All the pirates turned as the door swung open and in bounded Cweel, the Eagle Griffin. "*I* bring news from Longfinch," he hissed. He looked around at the pirates gathered suspiciously. "What is *this*?"

"A discussion," Holgard replied curtly. "Now, what have you comed to say?"

Cweel took one more suspicious look around, then stared at the captain warily. "There has been a *whaling* ship sighted, following the coast north towards *us*," Cweel replied.

"A whaling ship?" Holgard replied. "At this time on year?"

"That *is* the case," Cweel returned with a hostile growl.

Holgard snorted. "That's all one to me. It will pass us in the Faeroteisi, and even if'n it do'ed see us, it wouldn't dream on attacking two pirate ships even if'n we are a little battered and bruised."

Cweel's eyes flashed. "Where is *your* sense of plunder?"

Holgard laughed slightly. "You said a whaling ship, ay? There isn't plunder in a whaling ship, even if'n our ships were fit enough to fight."

"That *is* to be seen," Cweel replied. "But the *whaling* ship has good masts to replace *our* broken ones, and solid boards to shore up *our* broken ones." Cweel looked at Holgard meaningfully. "*You* will sail in front of the *whaling* ship when it passes by the mouth of *this* bay. Longfinch's pirates will then circle the *whaling* ship from behind in the shore boats. *Together,* you will board and take the ship."

Holgard snorted. "Very weel, I will see to it."

With that, he motioned with his hands to Ernest and the other crew members in his cabin. "Out then, get outta here! Get to your posts, prepare for action!"

Ernest and the others tumbled out of the cabin hurriedly. In a matter of moments, the deck burst to life as the pirates dropped their carpentry tools and took up muskets and sabers in their stead. Others brought in the anchor and released the sails. The beaten ship groaned a little as she moved forward again, and the foremast bowed with the wind's strain. Yet enough rigging lines remained intact that the galleon began moving forward slowly. Ernest looked at the galleon with some satisfaction. They could count on her yet. At least she was in better shape than the man-o-war.

Ernest armed himself with a musket and a rapier from the armory. Ducking into a dark corner where no one would notice him, he checked to see that his pepperbox pistol was loaded.

Coming back out onto the deck, he could see Longfinch's pirates climbing down from their man-o-war into skiffs, all armed to the teeth. Leaping nimbly into the shrouds — and avoiding the damaged ropes as he ascended — Ernest climbed high enough to see out of the bay where the ships were hiding. Sure enough, Ernest could make out another sail among the rocky islands, moving steadily north. A few more minutes would bring it up to the bay's mouth.

Ernest dropped again lightly to the deck and looked about him for something to do in this upcoming attack. He, being cook's-mate, did not have a defined role in combat — either as a sailor, boarder, or gunner — but was simply supposed to do whatever was necessary at the moment. There seemed plenty of sailors coaxing the wounded galleon forward, and there were enough boarders, too — though they could always use another hand. He was about to join the boarders in their group, when he heard the words of Lady Death again in his head:

"You should have died today!"

Ernest shuddered. There wasn't much to worry about, really. He was long past that now. Still, he had tested his luck so much yesterday that maybe he shouldn't test it again today. On the other hand, what risk was there in boarding a whaling ship? There probably wasn't a fighting man on board. Still, perhaps he had best find a gun crew who was short-handed. That would probably be the safest thing for him.

Just then, Killjelly strode past. "Follow me, Cook's-mate."

Ernest obeyed, following Killjelly as he picked several more pirates before climbing over the gunwale and into a shore boat that waited for him in the water. The pirates who Killjelly had selected quickly descended the galleon's side and dropped into the boat with the leprechaun boatswain. In a moment, they pulled away at the oars, with Killjelly at the tiller. The shore boat skimmed lightly towards the bay entrance, passing ahead of the battered and struggling galleon.

Ernest could see four more shore boats — all full of Longfinch's pirates — speeding through the water in the same direction. There were many islands around, most of which were tiny, rocky, and often very tall, rising like granite pillars from the heaving sea. It was to the lee of one of these small islets that Killjelly now directed his shore boat. Here they halted.

Ernest looked out to see the galleon looming over them as it passed out into the open sea. What a sight it must have looked to the whalers as she hove into their view; a broken ship, hardly fit for the ocean, and yet bristling on all sides with cannons. Ernest could hear whistles and shouting, and he guessed the whalers had spotted their leviathan.

"Now!" hissed Killjelly, and the pirates rowed for all they were worth.

The shore boats leaped forward, nimbly passing from the bay.

Ernest looked all around as the boat skimmed into the open water, heaving hard against his oar. Yes, there was the whaler ship not far off, in a flurry of commotion. All the whalers rushed every way at once, as if uncertain whether to engage this phantom ship which bore the appearance of a patchwork dragon, or else to flee before its decrepit onslaught.

Even as the shore boats passed in front of it, the galleon let loose a volley of cannon shots. To Ernest, the volley sounded pitiful compared to the mighty cannonades he was familiar with. The cannons sounded more like the wheezing of an old man smoking a bad batch of tobacco than the mighty blasts of war. It was then that Ernest realized that there was no real help from the galleon. It could never chase down the whaling ship. All their hope in taking this ship was in the shore boats success-fully boarding.

Ernest pulled harder on his oar, and the shore boat skimmed even faster towards its target. The fresh smell of saltwater pene-trated Ernest's nostrils, and the spray of seawater peppered his face as the boat careened on.

"Grapnels!" Killjelly ordered, though they were still a rifle shot away from the whaling ship. "Hold in ready!"

Ernest pulled harder, looking over his shoulder at the whaling ship in front of the shore boat. The whaling ship was turning now, as if it meant to flee. It couldn't head straight south, directly into the wind; thus, Ernest supposed it would flee east into the Faeroteisi Islands, not far away. Killjelly must have expected this move as well, for he had steered his shore boat very wide to catch the whaling ship almost from the west.

Ernest looked back to see Longfinch's four shore boats spreading out in all directions. No matter the whaling ship's route, one would catch it.

Ernest heard a gunshot from the whaling ship and looked up. Apparently, they had no cannons, though there appeared to be a musket or two among the whalers. Most held harpoons, though some held hatchets or merlon spikes.

"Pull, now!" Killjelly yelled. "We can't let her slip away, sure. Pull, if'n you're sailors, sure, pull!"

Ernest heaved harder on the oars, and the shore boat veritably flew through the foamy brine. The whaling ship was now turned completely westward, and the wind filled the sails nicely. With a good wind, it would easily outrun the shore boats, and the galleon was not fit for pursuit.

Where was Cweel in all of this? Ernest thought to himself. Hadn't that Eagle Griffin disabled ships before? Where was he now?

Killjelly turned the boat hard, sending it directly at the whaling ship. "Grapnels! On my command!"

Ernest bent hard over the oar, straining every muscle in his body as he heaved against the salt water — he could feel each oar stroke from his fingers down to his toes.

Suddenly, he heard another gunshot. Ernest looked around at the other shore boats. They, too, bore down on the whaling ship. Time was in the balance. If the wind could accelerate the ship fast enough, it would soon outpace the shore boats — or else bring the rowers to exhaustion. The shore boats were gaining on the whaling ship, yet the whaling ship was slowly picking up speed. Ernest looked over at the other shore boats. Was it just his imagination, or did they seem to slow down? Where was Cweel in all of this? The whaling ship was certain to get away from them.

With resolution printed across his brow, Killjelly locked the tiller in place and stood to his feet. They were yet a hundred feet from the fleeing whaling ship. Killjelly snatched a grapnel from the bottom of the shore boat and, swinging it above his head for a moment, heaved it with all his might towards the whaling ship. There was a moment of breathless anticipation as the missile flew through the air, arching high over the waters and bending low toward the ship.

The pirates stopped rowing for a moment as they watched the grapnel with bated breath.

"It isn't going to make it!"

"No, he haves the distance."

"It will fall two inches short."

"I'm betting on it..."

And with a resounding clang, the grapnel caught the gunwales' edge. The pirates raised a terrific cheer as they started hauling away at the rope. Ernest tugged for all he was worth, despite the blisters he was already feeling on his hands.

"Pull hard!" Killjelly laughed as he grabbed another grapnel. "Pull hard for a new mast, sure!"

The whalers fell on the grapnel, trying to work it loose. Finally, one of them reached out with his knife and began hacking at the thick chord. Longfinch's pirates let loose a volley of musket shots and curses from the other shore boats, but both proved harmless to the brave whaler who cut at the rope.

Killjelly now threw his second grapnel, which landed as true as the first. "Pull away! Pull hard for a new mast!"

The shore boat closed in fast. Almost as soon as the whalers had cut the first grapnel free, Killjelly landed a third. The whalers seemed to realize it was a lost cause to stop the pirates from coming. They now rushed to the gunwales with one accord, brandishing harpoons, hatchets, skinning knives, or anything else they could get their hands on.

Killjelly took Ernest by the shoulder and looked him earnestly in the face. "You have it on you, sure?"

Ernest touched the pepperbox pistol hidden in his breast pocket and nodded.

Killjelly flashed a wild smile. "Fire on my command." Then, turning to the other pirates, he said, "Prepare to board! This will be a ripe party for Holgard's honor, sure!"

The pirates raised a cheer.

The shore boat now pulled alongside the whaling ship. The whalers greeted it with a barrage of harpoons. Two pirates fell back, writhing in the boat's bottom, impaled by these missiles. Ernest pulled out his pepperbox pistol and cocked it into full position, looking to Killjelly.

"Throw your grapnels, boys! Climb for death and glory!"

"Death and glory!" the pirates cried in response.

The whalers leaned over the gunwales again, another line of harpoons in their hands, preparing to throw them down on the pirates now scaling the ship's side.

"Now, Ernest! Baptize them with fire! Send them to hell!"

Ernest pointed his pistol toward the whalers and fired. The eight barrels fired as one, sending eight separate charges into the mass of men above. The whalers fell back with shouts and swearing, some wounded, some dead, and most others terrified.

With one accord, the pirates scaled the ship's sides, taking full advantage of this hole in the whalers' defenses.

Killjelly was the first to mount the deck with his saber in one hand. Catching a hatchet from the hand of a whaler with his hooks, he sliced the unfortunate man to the deck.

"Here's for the glory of Holgard!"

Ernest climbed up after all the others, first reloading his pistol properly. Upon reaching the deck, Ernest looked around for an attacker. The whalers seemed all in one mass in the middle of the ship — their comrades' bloody and desecrated bodies strewn all around them.

Suddenly, Ernest's eye caught on a middle-aged man cowering up against the gunwales, looking on wide-eyed as the pirates fell to their slaughter.

Ernest raised his musket, leveling it at this hapless man. Suddenly, above his head, he heard the clap of wings. Ernest looked up in surprise to see a raptor bird streaking through the gunpowder smoke. Fear gripped Ernest.

"You should have died. Your life is a gift from me. Do not abuse it."

Ernest tried to push his fears aside, raising his gun to his shoulder again. Just as he did so, the middle-aged man toppled over the gunwales. The raptor bird dove after him and was gone.

Ernest now turned to look towards his comrades, seeing Vania Bloodrummer and a host of Longfinch's pirates pouring over the opposite side of the ship. Vania had his sword drawn and now looked around in his customary manner.

"Who's the captain on this ship?"

"Silence, Bloodrummer!" It was Killjelly who called.

With one accord, the pirates halted in their slaughter and turned to look upon their captains.

Vania stood with his sword drawn and a look of perplexity on his face. Killjelly also stood with sword drawn, blood and gore on his blade and hooks. His eyes gleamed with fire and determination.

"Which is! What's this, whatever?" Vania asked.

Killjelly spat. "We have no need on your challenges to single-handed combat, sure. The ship is taken — and that by the might on Captain Holgard and his crew."

Holgard's pirates raised a cheer as they fell anew on their victims. Vania raised an eyebrow.

"The ship is ours, whatever. We may now *both* repair our ships."

Killjelly nodded, raising his saber high in the air. "For death and glory! For the honor on Captain Holgard!"

A MIRROR

*E*lla began clearing the breakfast dishes. Elsi stacked her dishes neatly and handed them to Ella.

"Thank ye, kindly."

"It's a pleasu'e," Ella replied. And she took the dishes into the kitchen, where she placed them in the washbasin. Returning to the dining room to wipe the table, she saw Elsi retreating to the parlor with her tea. Miss Nansi slipped past Ella into the kitchen, and when Ella returned, she found Miss Nansi busily scrubbing away at the dishes.

Miss Nansi looked up at Ella as she entered, waggling her eyebrows mischievously. "Now, what are ye venin' back in here fer?"

Ella smiled pleasantly. "I am the maid now. I believe it is my job to wash the dishes."

Miss Nansi clicked her tongue reprovingly. "Ye may as well give it up now, fer *I* am washin' the dishes, an' *ye* cen no stop me. Now set down an' read a book or something' useful like that."

Ella opened her mouth to object, but Miss Nansi held up her hand. "I do no want to hear any objections, now get ye cedin'. *I* will take care o' the kitchen fer now."

"But I'm the maid," Ella objected. "It's my job to wo'k."

"It is no yer job anymore," Miss Nansi replied with a good-natured smile.

"But the Picke'ings a'e paying me to wo'k. I can't just sit down and be idle."

"Ye most certainly cen," Miss Nansi replied. "I ha' cognized more than enough girls yer age who would jump at a chance to read. Do no ye like to read?"

"I love weading, ma'am," Ella replied. "That's what I always did at home, in Slywi'h..."

Miss Nansi nodded. "Then cede an' read now. I will take care o' the chores this mornin'."

"But I'm the maid," Ella repeated weakly.

Miss Nansi raised her hands in despair. "If ye'll must feel useful, then dust something or other. Dust the bookshelves, fer instance."

Ella smiled. "Ve'y well. If you insist."

Grabbing a duster from the broom closet, she left the room. She entered the parlor and began dusting the bookshelves. Elsi sat in her chair in the corner with the piano, reading a large tome. Ella stole glances at her as she worked. She felt certain, particularly with Miss Nansi's injunctions, that she was justified in cracking open a book and reading to her heart's content, but she couldn't bring herself to do it while Elsi sat there.

Finally, when Ella had dusted her way into the corner where the piano hid Ella from Elsi's sight, she pulled a book free and cracked it open. To her disappointment, she found it not written in the common script, but entirely in the strange Pistosian script. Opening several other books, she found them all to be in this script. Not a little disappointed, she slipped the books back into place and resumed her dusting.

After dusting as much of the shelves and ornaments as she could, Ella moved from the parlor into the hallway, recollecting that there was a great deal to dust in Sir Saemwel's bedroom.

Hastily, she headed to that side of the house as if afraid that someone would find her. All she was going to do was dust. There was no harm in dusting, was there?

Ella found the door to Sir Saemwel's bedroom and entered. She took little time to look around but set about dusting this room as well, the hearth, the wardrobe, the bookshelves — whose books (alas!) were also all in the Pistosian script — and finally, she came to the portraits on the wall. Yes, those three portraits, one of Sir Saemwel Pickering, one of Mrs. Pickering, and one of Silas Pickering.

Ella felt a tingle run through her even as she looked at the portrait of Silas. Looking at this portrait, she was more convinced than she had been at first that this Silas Pickering was the same as the Silas Pickering who had brought her into the world; the same Silas Pickering who left her before her fifth birthday in the mountain village of Blisa, Slyzwir; the same Silas Pickering who had died before her fifth birthday — so she had been told. Yet now here his portrait hung, proof that he had out-lived her fifth birthday, only to be killed again at about her seventeenth. So he was dead — again — and she had no more hope of knowing him now than she had before.

As Ella stared into those painted eyes, she could almost see through them into her own heart, realizing with some astonishment what she found written there. This Silas Pickering — or the lack of him, rather — had molded her more than she had ever realized until this point. Why did she befriend that beggar Jock in the first place, if not to learn what trials her father might have gone through in his brief stint at sea? Why had she gone out late that night to bring Jock bread, if not because she would have wished another girl to do the same for her father were he in a distant land?

Ella could see now with startling clarity that this passion for Silas Pickering — the father she would never know — was indeed her master passion and driving force for everything she did. On the rare occasion she had disobeyed her stepfather, it was always because she did what her father would have done.

Her very hatred of her schooling and yet love of learning anything and everything was, in its own way, an imitation of her father. Even now, her attempts to find the Gwambi Treasure were not so much driven by a desire to save the city, or even to ransom Jock from the pirate's hands; no, she was driven to find the Gwambi Treasure because it was that treasure which her father had died seeking. Deep within her, she hoped that in finding that treasure, somehow she would find something of her father too.

She stared long and hard into the portrait's eyes, and for a moment, she couldn't tell whose face she was looking into — that of Silas Pickering, or her own, as if reflected in a mirror of canvas. Ella started at this thought. Were they so similar, then? Yes, very similar indeed. Both walking the same path, seeking the same treasure, probably making the same mistakes along the way.

Ella furrowed her brow. Her father's mistakes — whatever they were — had proved fatal to him twice, if that were possible! Had she walked so much in his way that, even now, she would fall into his same fate?

Ella shook herself all over at this idea. What a silly thought it was, anyway. The painting was simply a portrait of Silas Pickering, her dead father, and that was all there was to it.

Ella lifted her duster to the portrait, when a thought came to her. Sir Saemwel had left them a clue behind the portrait of his wife. Might Silas have left a clue behind on his portrait as well?

Ella took a chair over to the wall and, mounting it, took the portrait from the wall. She scrutinized it, turning it over several times, until, on the third pass, she saw a piece of paper cleverly concealed against the inside frame.

A Mirror

Her heart leaped into her throat. With bated breath, Ella pulled the paper free, then carefully hung the portrait back on the wall and moved the chair back to its proper place.

A rondel of blue wax sealed the paper she now held in her hand, and it was this wax which had held the paper to the picture frame. Ella's hand shook as she slipped in her thumb to break the seal. Yet now she hesitated. Suddenly, there was a vague heaviness in the air, and Ella thought she could hear a dull drumming — or else chanting — but perhaps that was just her heartbeat. Why had a sense of doom fallen on her so suddenly?

Just then, she heard the voice of Miss Nansi calling from the kitchen.

"Ella dear, I cen no tell fer the life o' me where the brooms are kept! Ella dear, where are you?"

Ella slipped the mysterious piece of paper into her apron pocket and stepped silently out of the room. She would have to look at the paper when she had a moment to herself later.

11

PATERNAL LOSS

The sun had not yet risen as Haeli sat up from where she lay before the fire ring. Dafid, Ma, and Yohni slept not far away while Meriwedhr and Laendon snored soundly in their nearby tents. Martyn was not in his tent — he must be tending to the beacon.

Haeli slowly stood to her feet. There was a dismal mist over the entire camp, its moisture congealing on every surface. The oppressive dampness seemed to cloud Haeli's nose. She shivered. She was cold. Taking the blanket she had slept on, she wrapped it tightly around herself. After a moment's thought, she walked up to the little path leading up to the beacon, which still glowed faintly above her in the mist.

It was not, however, her intention to climb up to the beacon. She only wished to be alone. She hadn't climbed the path more than a few feet when she came to a small rock ledge a little away from the path. It was situated above the campsite, holding a view to the east. Haeli slipped out onto this ledge and sat there motionless and in complete silence. The damp settled on the granite rocks, making beads of dew all across the stone. As Haeli sat, the wet slowly seeped into the blanket where she sat, and she knew if she sat there too long, it would seep into her dress and leave her wet and chilled. She shivered, trying to ignore the damp, looking out into the fog.

She knew that if the mist were clear, she could have seen for miles out into the world. She would have been looking out over the morning ocean, with the Faeroteisi Islands to the south and the Gwambi mountain range standing like a menacing guard over the inland behind her. If she could have looked to the north, she probably would have seen Entwerp Bay and perhaps even wisps of smoke rising from the textile factories along the river.

Haeli gave a deep sigh. It was appropriate, she supposed, that her physical view was so clouded, even as her mind was so clouded that she could hardly think. When she let herself think, her mind would always drift back to that shapeless bundle tenderly laid before the fire — as if he might still need warming from the cold.

Haeli felt a sob coming to her throat, but even as it came, her hands felt the keys in her bodice. She had almost forgotten about those doomed keys. Oh! That she could throw them from her even now and watch them sink into the ocean! Still, her Da had said not to let them out of her sight, and throwing them from the cliff would certainly have done *that*.

Haeli pulled the keys from their hiding spot. She looked at them closely, comparing the two. They were of similar size — both were a little longer than her smallest finger — though slightly different weight and shape. They were of a curious design and seemed rather heavy for their size. Why could no one know of these keys? What secrets did they hold? What would happen if they fell into the pirates' hands? Could they work their will with only one of these keys? What if they had both?

Perhaps she had best take some precautions. Haeli took one

of the keys from their common ring and fixed it carefully inside her headscarf. She then replaced the other key in her bodice.

As she did so, there again fell on her the feeling of doom that she had felt the night before when her Da handed her the keys the first time. Was she hearing drumming somewhere far off in the distance? Perhaps there were indigies about playing on their drums — surely not at this hour. Could she even be certain that she was hearing a drum? Perhaps it was only her own heart that she heard pounding in her chest.

As quickly as this wave of doom washed over her, it passed. Haeli simply sat where she was for several more minutes, watching as the dim mist far out to the east slowly changed from steel gray to rose gold. Down below her, she could hear sparrows chirping, proclaiming the coming dawn. Now and then, the call of a wren or a thrush cut through the damp morning. Haeli felt a lump forming in her throat. To think, this was now the first sunrise that Da would never see.

Just then, Haeli heard a movement nearby. She looked up to see Martyn climbing out onto the ledge. He smiled at her sympathetically as he sat next to her, putting his arm around her comfortingly. The two sat motionless for several minutes. The rose gold seemed to bloom brighter now, growing from a single bud of a star into a line of fire across the eastern horizon.

Martyn sighed. "Haeli, are ye all right?"

Haeli took a deep breath and let it out slowly. "Of course not. That is a merri silly question."

Martin pursed his lips, looking out into the mist. "I am sorry, Haeli. I wish I had something to say."

"You do not need to say anything," Haeli replied, her voice soft and passionless. "Maybe don't talk about it at all right now."

And so they sat together on the ledge for several more minutes. Neither looked at the other, but simply stared out into the mist, watching as the golden glow of the sunrise spread all around them, the fiery carmine hue defused in the water droplets around them.

"Like blushin' ice," Martyn breathed.

Haeli looked up. "What was that?"

Martyn shrugged. "It is beautiful, is no it?"

Haeli nodded. "Ay, that it is."

"God is merri good to us," Martyn said in a voice barely above a whisper. "He gives us rain, an' cloud, an' sun, an' yet through it all he blends its transitions together into sich a marvelous patchwork o' praise, that it will keep artist busy forever tryin' to reduplicate what He duplicates every mornin' an' evenin' on the thinnest parchment ever made."

Haeli looked up at Martyn, eyeing him critically. It was good to get her mind off of yesterday. She didn't want to ride that horse again for a while. Contemplating the physical world — the present moment — seemed like the right thing to do. "I believe you have turned poet from your long stints on this mountain, Martyn."

Martyn cracked a wry smile. "Llifsa! I am no a poet. Though this reminds me o' one o' Clerans' poems, now that ye bring it to mind."

Haeli furrowed her brow, her surprise tempered by her emotional exhaustion. "Clerans? A poet?"

"Ay, he is no a merri *good* poet, though. He does no let on. I am sure one o' these days he'll *will* be a good poet, as he'll writes a good poem every now an' then."

"I did not know," Haeli finally said as she looked back at the sunrise.

"Now this poem," Martyn went on, still in a low voice, "I do no remember it merri well — some o' the rhymes were poor — but it wos a good poem fer all that. There was something' in there about the clouds blushin' with embarrassment when the sun vened from her bed, catchin' them at dancin' all night." Martyn smiled, "An' the sea, as if in jealousy fer the sun's choice o' husband in the sky, would reflect the same blue surface as if to woo the sun into returnin' into his aquatic embraces."

Haeli looked back at Martyn again.

Martyn shrugged. "It wos merri good imagery, at any rate."

"You are *quite* certain that Clerans wrote those lines?" Haeli asked.

"Well, it wos no those lines, but something' o' the same effect," Martyn replied.

Haeli still studied Martyn closely, and then finally looked away. "I do not cognize Clerans as well as I thought I did, then."

Martyn laughed shortly. "I do no think that *Clerans* cognizes Clerans as well as he thinks he does."

Again, they faded into silence. After several more minutes, Martyn sighed and stood to his feet. "I believe I ha' better start on some breakfast fer you. Will ye vene down with me?"

Haeli nodded and let Martyn help her to her feet. She took one last look at the blooming sunrise through the misty morning and sighed.

After descending the little path into the camp, Martyn coaxed the fire back to life while Haeli sat down on a wooden stool and watched him. It was impossible to keep her eyes from straying to the shapeless bundle not far away. She could feel another lump in her throat, her eyes beginning to water again. That bundle of cloth couldn't be Da. Da couldn't be gone. Haeli started sobbing.

Martyn looked down and blew on the hot coals a couple more times. Once he had brought the fire to life, he sat on a stool beside Haeli.

"It is a merri good thing to weep."

Haeli didn't reply.

Martyn pursed his lips. "It is written in the scriptures, 'I am the resurrection an' the life.' Do ye believe that?"

Haeli nodded, but she still made no audible reply.

Martyn put his arm around her again. "Well, at least we tain hope, even if there is a merri o' sorrow with it."

It was a silent breakfast that morning in the gloomy mist of that camp. All they had to eat was an insipid oat porridge that had no taste or smell and clung like glue to the back of Haeli's throat. She tried to wash it down with a little beer Martyn had warmed up, but Haeli gave up before she had eaten half the porridge.

Laendon forced his food down in a few bites and then headed up to the beacon while Martyn and Meriwedhr sat behind with Haeli, Ma, Dafid, and Yohni. Dafid was still asleep, lying curled up in a mound of blankets by Ma's side. Ma stroked Dafid's curly black hair and stared blankly into her untouched porridge bowl.

Looking into her Ma's blank eyes seemed to stir up new resolve inside Haeli. Her dear, poor Ma! Haeli knew she needed to be strong for Ma. She could put on a brave face. She could do whatever was needed, for Ma's sake.

Then again, what were they going to do now? Would they go back to the fort and begin working as usual? Just at that thought, a sob caught in Haeli's throat. How could she go back to work without Da? There was too much to do — between taking care of the horses, trading with the indigies, and giving out provisions to the beacon-tenders — none of them could do Da's work for him.

Just then, Martyn cleared his throat. "Mrs. Blysffi, I am curious to know if ye'll tain any thoughts as to how to proceed from here?"

Ma looked up at him blankly.

Martyn licked his lips. "While we are more than happy to let ye stay here at the camp, we are only supplied fer three workers, an' I am sure these accommodations are no merri comfortable fer ye."

Ma nodded and gave a weak smile. "That is true."

Martyn nodded. "Meriwedhr an' Laendon ha' volunteered to hold down the beacon fer me so that I cen bring you wherever ye'll wish. I could bring ye back to the fort; if that is what ye'll want?"

Ma took a deep breath at this suggestion, glancing at the shapeless bundle not far away. Haeli could tell that she fought away tears.

"Or," Martyn added hastily, "if ye'll would prefer, I could duce ye back to Entwerp. I do no know if the Pickerings will be up to hostin' ye, with Sir Saemwel absent an' all, but I am certain that Ma would ceive ye in."

Ma sighed deeply. "Martyn, I know what I need to do. I just have to do it."

Martyn sat silent, looking at Ma until she spoke again.

"We can not just return to the fort. Now that Stifyn is dead, we are not under the Company's charter. The fort is no longer ours."

Haeli's stomach lurched in anxiety. She couldn't lose her Da and the fort at the same time. The fort was her home. "No!" Haeli cried. "That can not be true!"

Martyn took a deep breath. "Did Stifyn not put yer name on the charter, too? The Company would surely want ye to stay on as fort-tender, if fer no other reason than that it makes good business sense to keep on the family who knows what they are doin'."

Ma swallowed. "I will tell you about the Company's business sense." She looked Martyn in the eyes. "Stifyn tried to put me on the charter back when the Company signed us on. But they would not accept me as a fort-tender."

Martyn raised an eyebrow. "Why ever no? They tain many female fort-tenders."

"Because I am indigie," Ma replied, a bitter edge to her voice. "And while the Company will hire indigie beacon-tenders, they will not hire an indigie fort-tender."

Martyn scratched his head pensively. "Well, that's juvenile."

"Bigoted Kelmarian aristocrats run the Company," Ma replied. "So, ay, of course they behave like spoiled juveniles."

Martyn sighed. "I cen see why ye would say that."

Ma held up her hands. "So there it is. Stifyn's name alone was on the charter. He is dead, so now we tain no right to the fort. It is at the Company's discretion to give it — horses, stock, and all — to anyone they choose."

"So long as they are not an indigie," Haeli added bitterly. Her stomach hurt, and she could feel a lump rising in her throat. She again remembered her Da's words to her, but now she understood what he had tried to tell her.

"The Company owns this fort, Haeli, and the Company will do with it as they want. We can put our heart and soul into this ground — and God knows that is what I mean to do — but all it takes is one owner changing his mind, and they can kick us out at a moment's notice."

Martyn sighed again and shook his head. "I cen no conceive that they'll would be sich idiots. We will write a petition. We will get the whole kirk to sign it. My Da works at the Company offices in Entwerp, anyway. We'll see that they listen. The Company will ha' to listen."

Ma shook her head. "The Company is no listening to the thousands of strikers currently protesting all across the capes. You think they would listen to *us*?"

Martyn shrugged. "We would never know until we tried."

"Martyn," Ma said with a sigh. "We have tried. Stifyn tried repeatedly. He already got your Da to petition for us. Every time he went to Entwerp for provisions, he tried to add me to the charter."

Haeli could feel anger rising in her throat. Her first

instinct was to swallow it back. But Ma said that her emotions were like a horse and that it was good to ride them. She had good reason to be angry. She may as well mount up. Clenching her fists, she groaned in frustration. "How can they do this to people? This is not idiotic or juvenile; it is immoral!"

Neither Ma nor Martyn said anything to this, so Haeli went on, shaking her fists. She let her anger go at a trot. "They can not do this to people, to people made in God's image. How can they do this? What do they tain against indigies? Have the owners even met an indigie before? How could they make such an immoral rule?"

Martyn shrugged. "They probably have no met an indigie a'fore. It is jist ignorance on their part."

"Ignorance?" Haeli replied. She was nearly yelling now. She waved a hand around the camp. "And what about this? Are they ignorant, too, of the conditions they make you work under? A week up here in the harsh weather, and they will not even give you the funds for a hut, but you must make one yourself in your spare time. And what are the owners doing? Attending fancy dinners and balls, and cruising in luxury in the Acspian aisle while they eat cockatrice eggs and veal?"

Martyn sighed.

"The money they spend so freely on their luxury," Haeli went on, "isn't their money. It should be yours by right. You are the one who worked to earn it, yet they are the ones spending it."

Martyn stared Haeli in the face, and a tear slipped from his eye. "Haeli, yer father lives on with ye. As long as ye are here, yer Da has never really left us."

The horse of anger came to an abrupt stop, and a wave of grief washed over Haeli. She sobbed, burying her face against Ma's shoulder.

Martyn took a deep breath and wiped his eyes. "I'll will miss hearin' his politics, even if I'll could never agree with him."

More tears came to Martyn's eyes, and he wiped these away, too, taking another deep breath.

Tears streamed down Ma's cheeks, and she hugged Haeli tightly.

Martyn took one last breath and let it out slowly. "If there is anything we'll cen do, we would be happy to help. If you'll need it, one o' us will accompany you back to Entwerp."

"And leave the beacon short-handed?" Ma replied.

Martyn shrugged. "It is the least I cen do fer you."

Ma wiped the tears from her cheeks and glanced at the shapeless bundle by the fire. "For now, I would accept your help in burying my husband."

Martyn nodded. "Where shall I do it?"

"Back at the fort," Ma replied. "Next to Tomas. That is where he would have liked it. We'll go back there one more time."

And so it was decided.

TO RECOVERY

Meriwedhr ascended to the beacon to tell Laendon the plan while Martyn saddled the horses. When this was done, Ma roused Dafid, and they headed down the road to the fort.

Meriwedhr accompanied them to assist Martyn in digging a grave. Upon arriving at the fort, Ma directed them to the other grave in the courtyard with the small gravestone that said 'Tomas Blysffi.' Next to this grave, Martyn and Meriwedhr dug a new one for Da. Once they had a sufficient hole, Martyn and Meriwedhr lowered the shapeless bundle into the grave.

"'I am the resurrection an' the life,'" Martyn quoted. "'He who believes in Me shall live, though he die.'"

As Martyn and Meriwedhr shoveled the dirt back over Da, Ma turned abruptly and walked towards the stables.

"Ma!" Haeli called out, and would have gone after her, but Yohni grabbed her by the arm and shook his head.

"Ma!" Haeli called out again.

"I have to ride a horse," Ma called back, not even turning to look at Haeli as she spoke.

Ma disappeared into the stables and a moment later came

out, leading a horse by the halter. A lump formed in Haeli's throat. Even from this distance, she could see Ma had the new filly, Lamentation. Switching halter for reins, Ma mounted Lamentation and galloped off into the pasture.

For several minutes, Haeli stood there, watching as Martyn and Meriwedhr filled in the grave shovel-full by shovel-full. Yohni stood beside her in stoic silence while Dafid stood next to her, holding her hand.

"What are they doing?" Dafid finally asked.

Haeli tried to swallow the lump from her throat. "They are burying Da."

Dafid furrowed up his brow. "But why? Why can't Da be with us?"

"Because—" A lump caught in Haeli's throat, and she could say no more.

Martyn put his shovel down and held out his arms to Dafid. "Here, little man, how about ye vene with me? We will see if there are any more raspberries."

"All right!" Dafid cried enthusiastically, toddling after Martyn. Haeli wrapped her arm around Yohni's shoulder. He was the only person close enough to hug at the moment, and she needed the comfort of physical touch. She felt like she was a very little girl again, when her pet sparrow had died. Her brother, Tomas, had held her and rocked her repeatedly, telling her it would be all right. She could still hear Tomas' voice in her mind.

"It will be all right, Haeli. It will be all right."

Haeli sobbed. Now all she had left of Tomas and Da were her memories of them. Yet those memories were indeed tangible things.

After several minutes, Ma returned from the pasture, riding Lamentation at a brisk trot up to Haeli and Yohni. She was flushed with exertion, her hair a tangled mess, and streaks of tears lined both cheeks from uncontrolled weeping. Yet there was now a look of resolution in her eyes.

Ma dismounted, offering the reins to Haeli.

Haeli swallowed. "I am all right, thank you."

"It helps," Ma replied, still holding out the reins. "When you ride your emotions until the end, you can finally move on. Let them out, and they will be your friend."

Haeli took a deep breath, but still didn't take the reins from Ma.

"I will," Yohni suddenly said, taking the reins and leaping onto Lamentation's back.

Ma and Haeli stood back as Yohni dug in his heels, urging Lamentation into a gallop. As the horse lurched forward, Yohni threw his head back and vented an unearthly wail of grief. Haeli shivered all over. She had never seen Yohni show such emotions, and the sight of him letting loose now disturbed her.

Ma put her arm around Haeli's shoulder and sighed. "Come on then, let us find some dinner."

Haeli glanced up at her Ma. "What now?"

"From the storehouse," Ma replied, "Let us find something to feed everyone."

"But did not you say that the Company now owns this place, and we tain no right to it?"

"Technically," Ma replied, "But they can not grudge us a meal before we leave."

Ma led her towards the door to the main house. Haeli couldn't help but gasp with astonishment and grief as they entered. The entire bar area was a wreck of tables and chairs. Blood stained the floor, and various weapons lay strewn about where the pirates had dropped them in their haste to escape. Martyn must have cleared the bodies out already, but simply seeing the room's upheaval was almost more chilling without the dead bodies present.

She could see the splotches on the wall where the wounded

pirate had sat slumped over after the huntsmen stabbed him. There were the bloodstains in front of the counter where the pirates had bayoneted the larger huntsman to death. Hook marks marred the table where the leprechaun leader had sat. She could see that they had been there, yet they were all gone — the huntsmen, the pirates, and Da — all gone. This was the last room many of them had ever seen. Simply this knowledge made Haeli feel as if ghosts haunted the room. In her mind, she could still see every one of those dying souls, gasping out their last breaths on the floor amidst the puddles of their own lifeblood.

Haeli shuddered again. She felt like crying, but she couldn't.

Ma lifted a chair and set it back on its feet before walking through the kitchen and into the storage room. Haeli followed, but stopped stock still as she entered the room. This was the last room where she had seen Da. She could still see him snapping the pirate's neck. She could almost smell the drunken fumes of the air that night.

Haeli shrank back, but she knew she must enter that room. She took one step forward when she saw a dark blood stain on the storage room floor. She paused again, and she felt light-headed. That pirate had not bled when Da snapped his neck. A mixture of horror and grief washed over Haeli as she realized this dark blood stain was Da's blood. So this was the room where he died.

Haeli would have fallen into a ball weeping in a moment, but her Ma caught her by the shoulder and looked into her eyes earnestly.

"Da gave you something?"

Haeli was speechless, her emotions still far too present to let her make a coherent reply.

"Last night, when he let you out, he gave you something?"

Haeli recovered herself enough to talk, but she hesitated. Da had said not to tell a single person about the keys. Surely that didn't include Ma?

Ma seemed to understand her hesitation and sighed contentedly. "Good. It is better that way. But do not tell a single soul — no one. You were good not even to answer me. That doom has passed on to you, love. I pray you may guard it safely."

And with that, Ma turned away abruptly.

Haeli sobbed, leaning up against the doorpost.

Ma was on her hands and knees, looking through the crates and casks on the bottom shelf of a storage rack, but she spoke in comforting tones to Haeli.

"That's it, love, let it out. Ride it."

Haeli's voice trembled. "If I ride it, how do I know it will stop?"

"It will." Ma replied, still digging through the bottom shelf. "If you trust your grief, then it will end eventually. It is only if you do not trust it that it will ride on forever."

Ma dug to the back of the shelf so that only her legs remained visible. After some grunting and clanking, Ma backed out of the shelf, a small chest in her hands. Ma's face was grim, and her eyes narrowed.

Haeli wiped the tears from her eyes, looking critically at her Ma. "What is that?"

"This?" Ma held up the chest. "This is a revolution."

After collecting enough cheese, dried berries, nuts, and jerky to last them a week, Ma and Haeli left the storeroom. Haeli cast one last look over the wrecked bar area before hurrying after Ma, leaving the main house — maybe forever.

Ma still carried the chest under her arm as she walked up to Da's new grave. Martyn and Meriwedhr sat by the grave, tossing crabapples, while Dafid giggled and tried to catch them. Even as Haeli and Ma came close, Yohni trotted back towards them. His face was once more its normal stoic self.

"I have food," Ma said simply, sitting on the grass by the two beacon-tenders.

Dafid cheered. "Dafid is hungry for food!"

Setting the chest next to her, Ma handed out the provisions. No one spoke much as they ate. Only after Martyn finished his wedge of cheese did he finally clear his throat.

"Well now, shall I escort you to Entwerp, then?"

Ma didn't answer right away, so Martyn looked up at the sun. "It is too late in the day to make it all the way tonight, but we'll could make a good start."

Ma picked up the chest and set it before her. "Martyn and Meriwedhr, I want to give you an opportunity to leave now, so you don't have to be involved in this. I realize you are the Company's employees, and it could go badly for you if they found out you were involved in this."

Martyn raised an eyebrow. "I am intrigued."

Meriwedhr smiled broadly. "If I'll could get in trouble fer it, then I want to join."

Ma looked at them grimly before opening her chest.

Haeli peered inside, a little disappointed to see nothing more than stacks of papers, legal documents, and lots of silk bills — Haeli had rarely seen so much money in one place.

Ma sighed deeply. "Stifyn worked on this. It was his life's mission. He had all the evidence and affidavits he needed years ago. He was just looking for the right time to start."

Martyn was also looking at the box's contents, and he frowned. "What exactly is this?"

Ma's eyes were as cold as stone as she looked Martyn in the face. "This is emancipation. Freedom of all fort-tenders from the Company."

Martyn nodded slowly. "I am still in the dark as to what exactly this is."

Ma took a deep breath. "I am going to the Twengoli. They have a permanent settlement nearby. There, I will assist them in prosecuting the Company."

"Prosecuting them fer what?" Meriwedhr asked.

Again Ma's eyes turned cold. "Stealing the indigies' land."

Martyn folded his arms over his chest. "How so?"

"This fort," Ma waved her arms around her, "was built on Twengoli land. The tribe was not compensated. Company officials simply found this place and built on it. There was no treaty, no conversation with the Twengoli. They just did it. They stole this land, plain and simple."

"And ye cen prove this?" Martyn replied.

"Ay," Ma pointed to the legal documents in the chest. "That is what most of this is. Proof."

Martyn pursed his lips and nodded. "So ye mean to sue the Company so that they'll return this fort to the Twengoli?"

"Not just this fort," Ma replied. "Every parcel of land the Company occupies which is within tribal territories."

Martyn raised his eyebrows. "Every parcel o' land? That would include beacons?"

"Ay," Ma replied. "It would."

Martyn nodded. "I admire yer idealism, Mrs. Blysffi, ye are jist as radical as Stifyn." And with that, he stood. "I wish ye the best."

Meriwedhr looked between Martyn and Mrs. Blysffi and frowned. "Ye know if ye'll are threatenin' the ownership o' the beacons themselves, the Company will fight this vice an' vail, do ye no? This would take years in the federal courts. Will ye live with the indigies all that time?"

A light came into Ma's eyes. "Who said I would take this to the federal courts?"

Martyn and Meriwedhr looked at Ma suspiciously.

"Ay," Meriwedhr finally said, "an' how else would ye do it?"

"Tribal law," Ma replied. "The federal courts have no jurisdiction here since the constitutional convention passed the Indigie Law."

Martyn's eyes grew large, and Meriwedhr sat back.

"Llifsa!" was all Martyn said.

Haeli looked between Ma and Martyn, pursing her lips. She was missing something.

"I am sorry if this is silly of me to ask," Haeli broke in, "but what is the significance of the Indigie Law?"

Martyn shook his head. "It recognized fully autonomous tribal law within tribal lands."

"To all people within tribal lands," Ma added, "not just the tribes."

Haeli nodded slowly. "And the significance of that is?"

"If anyone," Ma replied, "indigie, Kelmarian, beacon-tender, fort-tender, huntsman, or owner of an international company, commits a crime within tribal territory, then they must be tried by traditional tribal means of justice, and the Llaedhwythi government is bound to uphold the tribal ruling. There can be no appeals to the federal courts."

"It was a way to get the tribes into the constitutional convention," Martyn added. "We had to grant them absolute autonomy. We cen no coerce them into joining the government, but the hope is that if we'll show them we mean to respect them an' treat them as equals within the government, that they will help us create a unified law code that can apply to all."

"But until then," Ma added, "the government has sworn to uphold the tribes' absolute autonomy."

"In other words," Meriwedhr broke in, "jist to make sure I understand what is going on, you mean to sue the Company and demand that they give their land back to the tribes, but ye mean to sue them in tribal courts so that the judges o' the case are the traditional judges o' the tribes themselves — the very people who will benefit from the land the Company gives back?"

Haeli could not help but laugh at this. "Ma, you are brilliant!"

Martyn shook his head. "It is no altogether fair."

Ma nodded grimly. "And do you think the Company played fair when they stole this land? Or shall I read you the names of the forty-seven indigies whom Company agents killed while 'taming' this area?"

"Llifsa," Martyn replied, rubbing his forehead. "This will change the Company as we know it. First the free-riders, then the strikers, now this? The Company will go bankrupt fer sure. They may no ha' been the most just in their dealings all the time, but they ha' done a lot fer these capes."

"Ay," Meriwedhr broke in, "before the Beacon Company, these were jist out o' the way fishing villages. Look at all the profit they ha' brought to us."

Ma's gaze was as keen as flint. "Then tell me: would you rather have justice, or profits?"

Martyn and Meriwedhr both exchanged glances but said nothing.

Ma took another deep breath. "I mean to go to the Twengoli and bring this before the court of the Iasaqi-Woni. I will take Dafid and Yohni with me." She turned to Haeli. "I mean for you to go to Entwerp."

"Alone?" Haeli gasped.

Ma gave a sideways glance to Martyn and Meriwedhr. "I had hoped you would have company."

Haeli took a deep breath. "What do you want me to do?"

Ma pulled out a small packet of papers. "I need you to bring this to the Company office in Entwerp Proper. This outlines our conditions for a negotiated settlement."

Martyn raised an eyebrow. "What sort o' a settlement?"

"We will pay the Company," Ma replied, "the price of the infrastructure on this land — the fort, the outbuildings, though not, of course, the price of the land itself, because we do not recognize that they own the land."

"Fair enough," Martyn nodded.

"In return," Ma went on, "and assuming the Iasaqi-Woni grants our family permission to stay on this land, we will reopen business with the Company, providing the same services as before, though this time as private individuals, outside of the Company's hierarchy."

"In other words," Meriwedhr replied, a bitter edge to his voice, "this all comes back to yer Rectificationist ideals o' abolishing hierarchies?"

"Is not that what justice is?" Ma replied hotly.

"Come now," Martyn held up his hands. "Let's not turn this into a war between our two kirks."

Meriwedhr folded his arms over his chest. "I'm beginnin' to think that is what this always was."

"That is enough o' that," Martyn replied. "Meriwedhr, ye clearly want no part o' this—"

"Ay," Meriwedhr replied.

"Merri good," Martyn went on. "Then ye need no take part in this. Ye cen always return to the beacon an' help Laendon."

"An' ye?" Meriwedhr asked, looking up at Martyn.

Martyn pursed his lips. "I will accompany Haeli to Entwerp."

Meriwedhr snorted.

A flash of anger crossed Martyn's eyes. "Meriwedhr, Stifyn was a good friend to us. Ye, an' I, may object to his politics. But I must honor the man. It is the least I cen do fer him." Martyn then looked at Ma and Haeli. "An' the two o' you. Your whole family has been good to us. This is the least I cen do fer you."

Ma now turned to Haeli. "Will you go to Entwerp for me? I know we are stronger together, and I hate to leave you to do this without me. But I know you are strong."

Haeli took a deep breath. This was her Da's life mission. She could do this for her Da. Besides, she had her memories of her Da and her brother and their teachings inside her. They were stronger together, and they would always be together, if only inside her heart.

"Ay Ma," Haeli said, but she choked on the words, a lump forming in her throat and an unexpected wave of emotion washing over her. "Ay, Ma, I can go to Entwerp for you."

Suddenly, Dafid looked up from the dried fruit he was eating.

"Ma, where is Da? Should not he eat with us?"

Ma swallowed. "He is dead, love. We buried him there, remember?"

Dafid's face fell. "Can I see him?"

Haeli burst into tears.

"One day, love," Ma replied, sobbing herself, "one day you will."

13

PATRONYMIC

Ella thought herself perhaps too happy to finish her chores and retreat to her bedroom for the night. Pastor Daerl had arrived to guard the house for the night, and Clerans, too, had returned to his post. These details hardly seemed to be important, however. Ella's chief concern was to find a quiet moment so that she could read the piece of paper she had found on her father's portrait in Sir Saemwel's bedroom.

Ella closed the door to her room behind her and sat on the small chair next to her dresser. She now pulled the paper out and looked at it closely. On a whim, she stood up again and locked her door. It seemed appropriate. At least, the heroes in all the books would have locked their doors before a moment like this.

But what was this moment?

Ella looked back at the paper carefully. It was folded neatly — almost like a letter — and sealed shut. *Was* it a letter, perhaps? But a letter *to* whom? A letter *from* whom?

Ella breathed softly. Could it be another part of the puzzle in uncovering the Gwambi treasure? Or else was it totally unre-

125

lated? But why had it been stuck to the back of that portrait frame? Who was it meant for?

Slipping her thumb inside, she broke the seal. She couldn't help but feel excited about this find. There was so much mystery here, so much to discover.

Ella slowly unfolded the letter, and her heart sank as she saw the first lines:

tw maei direst tshaeild, shud shi efr traeif thys vωt,

Ella put the note down on her dresser and put her head in her hands. Why did it have to be in Pistosian script? Why was everything in this house in Pistosian script? Wasn't there any decent person who used the common script?

Ella drummed her fingers in frustration. Well, this was a fine fix. She would, of course, have to ask someone how to read Pistosian script, but she would need a good excuse for why she asked. No one else should know that she had found the note.

But why couldn't they?

Ella looked back at the note. Why did she feel she had to keep it a secret? Well, she wouldn't keep it a *complete* secret. She would show it to Haeli whenever she came back. Would she have to wait that long?

She could ask someone how to read Pistosian script in the morning and read the letter later in the day. Ella ground her teeth together in frustration. That was the best plan, she supposed. What a dreadful disappointment.

Folding the note back, she dropped it in the top drawer of her dresser, and then, taking off her over-clothes and blowing out her lantern, she crawled into her bed.

Ella closed her eyes. The sooner she fell asleep, the sooner she could wake up to ask someone about the Pistosian script. She lay like this for several minutes before she suddenly threw the covers from her and stood up. It was no use. She would never sleep until she could read that letter. The suspense was simply too much for her. She would have to ask someone, but whom?

She could ask Elsi, but that might not be wise. This letter might contain more information on Sir Saemwel and his trips into the Gwambi catacombs. Elsi was already far too worried about her father. She did not need something else to make her anxious.

There was also Pastor Daerl or Miss Nansi. They both seemed to be good people, yet Ella didn't feel she knew them very well. She didn't feel like she could share such delicate information with them.

Ella bit her lip. Wasn't Lexi supposed to arrive tomorrow afternoon to replace Clerans for her militia duty? She could trust Lexi with the contents of that note. Could she wait until then?

Ella opened the dresser drawer and pulled the note out. Again she unfolded it and looked inside.

No, she simply couldn't wait. She couldn't sleep. She would be a nervous wreck by the time Lexi arrived, if she hadn't read the note by then.

Very well, there was only one other person in the house whom she could ask: Clerans. Ella felt confident she could trust him, though she wasn't sure how he would receive her confidence. Anyway, he was the only person in this house at the moment to whom Ella felt like she could show the letter. It was worth a try.

Ella hastily lit her lamp again, and, unlocking her door, she slipped quietly out into the hall. She padded softly downstairs. There was still a light on in the kitchen. Pastor Daerl and Miss Nansi were apparently still talking. The big satyrian pastor leaned back in a chair by the kitchen table, and Ella could hear the indistinct murmur of conversation mixed with the sweet scent of tea and Miss Nansi's maté.

Ella passed down the hallway and came to the room where

Clerans stayed. There was light coming from underneath his door, so he must still be awake as well. Ella knocked lightly on the door.

"Ay, ye may vene in," Clerans called from inside.

Ella pushed the door open and stepped in, closing the door behind her.

Clerans looked up from a book he was reading, marked "ffn-foryt pωams" on the cover. "Good evenin', Miss Ella. May I help ye?" And he looked concerned when she closed the door behind her.

Clerans put his book down and peered at her closely. "I say, Miss Ella, are ye all right? Ye gard as if ye'll ha' seen a ghost!"

Ella shook her head, suddenly feeling embarrassed that she had come down in her nightgown. "No, I'm fine. I've come to ask fo' you'h help."

Clerans raised an eyebrow, glancing past her at the closed door again. "All right, in what way do ye need my help?"

Ella slowly handed him the note. "You can wead Pistosian script, I assume?"

Clerans unfolded the note and looked at it. "'To my dearest child, should she ever trive this note.' Ay, I cen read it. What is it?"

"I found it behind the po't'ait of Silas Pickering in Si'h Saemwel's woom," Ella explained.

Clerans looked at her blankly. "Behind the portrait o' Silas Pickering? Why ever were ye gardin' there?"

Ella sat down on the corner of the bed. "It's a long sto'y. See, I came he'e because... actually, I was kidnapped because..."

Clerans gazed at her intently.

Ella let out her breath slowly. Where was she to start? "Silas Picke'ing was my fathe'h," she finally said bluntly.

Clerans jumped. "Tar and needles! Silas Pickering — your father?"

Ella nodded.

Clerans raised an eyebrow. "An' what does all o' this ha' to do with this note?" He waved the note above his head emphatically.

"Well, I think it's a clue."

"A clue to what?" Clerans pressed, still obviously very confused.

Ella breathed deeply. She didn't want to go over her entire life story again. "I think it will be in the lette'h. Can you wead it to me? I'm su'e that I will not be able to sleep fo'h suspense until I've wead that note."

Clerans looked down at the note, glancing over it briefly. "Ay, it is signed by Silas Pickering."

Ella's heart nearly skipped a beat. It was a note from her father? To his 'dearest child'? Her father had left this note for *her*?

"Oh, please, Cle'ans, wead it."

Clerans flashed a roguish wink. "Better than that, I'll will teach ye how to read Pistosian."

Ella sighed with relief. "Thank you, Cle'ans."

"Do no thank me yet," Clerans replied, grinning now. He held the letter over to her. "See, the trick to this is ye jist ha' to read it phonetically. Our script is no like yer continental script — with all its extra letters and silent letters, an' letters that make different sounds in different circumstances. None o' that. Sound everythin' out with its proper sound."

"But 'Tw' is not a wo'd," Ella protested, "and it doesn't sound out phonetically into anything."

"Ay, it does," Clerans replied indignantly. "The 'w' says 'oo,' like in loose."

Ella shook her head. "Well then, it says 'to,' I suppose, but 'maei' doesn't sound out phonetically to 'my,' unless you have a ve'y vivid imagination."

Clerans only smiled halfheartedly at this. "Well, I suppose if ye gard at it like that, ye are right. However, that vowel combination, '*a*,' '*e*,' and '*i*,' says the sound of 'y' in 'my.'"

"Fine then," Ella said, "it says 'to my.'"

And Ella struggled on in this manner, Clerans pointing out how to read it as she went along. No, 'i' by itself always says 'e,' as in 'eat.' No, that 'v' says 'n' as in 'night.' Ay, and that 'n' was a vowel, and it says 'ay,' as in 'hay.'

And so she pieced together the whole note:

"To my dearest child, should she ever trive this note:

"It is with great pains that I now write you. You can not imagine what pains I have ceiven to conceal this from you, nor can you imagine the pain that has duced me to keep this from you. Even now, I can not trive it within me to deliver to you the whole truth. It is yet too much for me to bear.

"Half the truth, or a penumbra of it, must, for the present, suffice. I know not whether I will ever disclose the truth or whether I will even now take it with me to the grave. No, it is for another person to share. It is not for me. He surely is vening, this dear friend of mine. His vening is long overdue already.

"I have indeed trived out the Gwambi Treasure. It has taken me merri more years than I had wished to trive it, and I have even been counted dead to my family these sixteen years on account of it. I should have returned long ago. I can not right that wrong. No, that is for another man to do.

"However, I have trived out the Gwambi Treasure and entered their cities — if they can be called 'cities.' By my reckoning, I have entered those catacombs eight times, and once with a friend. I have explored them to a merri extent and left anything of value that I could trive up in the alcove. Perhaps there is more to trive in those catacombs, but nothing could induce me to enter again.

"My dear child, I have seen *it* — or perhaps I should say '*him*,' as it seems nearly to be a person in its own way. *He* is in those catacombs. His presence haunts my dreams. I am sure that his curse will vene on all those who enter those halls. Since I can not forbid you to enter the door — I'm sure the temptation will be too great — but I beg you, in the name of God Almighty, not to enter past the alcove. He is there.

"I have gone by many names in my pursuit of this treasure. I am afraid that at this present hour these names have vened back to harm me. Many who cognized me by another name now seek me by that name. I am grieved that the innocent will be punished for the crimes of myself — the guilty one. This grief is almost more than I can bear.

"My dearest child, I can hardly bring myself now to say what I must. Let it, for now, be sufficient. I sign my name for the first time to you, my dear child.

"Signed, Silas Pickering."

When Ella finished reading the note, Clerans looked up at her inquisitively. "I am no sure that note ha' enlightened me a smudgeon."

Ella could hardly breathe. She scanned the note over several more times. "Papa found the t'easu'e! Oh, I knew he must have — o'h, I hoped he had, at least."

Clerans raised an eyebrow. "Why's that?"

Paying no notice of him, Ella continued, "He left the t'easu'e fo'h me and told me whe'e to find it, too. He w'ote me this note so that I could find it fo'h him."

Clerans cleared his throat. "With no disrespect intended, Miss Ella, cen ye please explain this whole thing to me? What is so significant?"

Ella took a deep breath. "We thought Papa died sixteen yea'hs ago. I neve'h thought he had lived long enough to find the t'easu'e."

Clerans nodded. "Well, he is certainly dead now." He suddenly looked at Ella awkwardly. "I am sorry. I did no mean to be that blunt."

Ella almost laughed. She was too exhilarated after reading the note to be particularly upset about her father's death at the moment — besides, she had lived with that fact her whole life. "Don't wo'y."

"Well," Clerans continued. "He left Entwerp somewhere around three years ago. We never heard from him, but finally, a privateer trived up the wreck o' the ship near Prodnesia. They must ha' been caught in a storm an' lost their water, or something' o' that nature, fer most o' the crew wos dead from thirst, an' the rest garded as if they'll ha' been killed by pirates. We think it was the elfin pirate captain Longfinch since he wos in the area at the time — it wos either him or his subordinate, Captain Pennywraith."

Ella nodded. "I had hea'd about that. And I'm su'e it was Longfinch because he is back."

Clerans raised an eyebrow at this statement. "What makes ye say that?"

"The pi'ates who attacked the city," Ella said. "Longfinch is their leade'h. I hea'd them talking about him."

Clerans leaned back and squinted his eyes in thought.

"The pi'ates we'e looking fo'h the Gwambi T'easu'e," Ella continued. "I hea'd them talking about that too."

Clerans licked his lips. "So ye mean to say that Longfinch knew that Sir Silas ha' trived the Gwambi Treasure, an' so he killed him, an' now he ha' vened back to seize the treasure himself?"

Ella nodded.

"Why did he wait three years?" Clerans asked, tapping his finger to his chin.

Ella shrugged. "I don't know."

Clerans leaned forward again and looked over the note. "What I want to know is who is 'he?' — the thing in the catacombs, I mean. Who or what was Mr. Silas talkin' about? What does he mean that 'he' is there? It does no make merri o' sense to me."

Ella took the note back and looked it over herself. "I don't know."

She looked back at Clerans, who shrugged.

Ella folded up the note with a sigh of satisfaction. "Well, thank you, Cle'ans. That was weally helpful. I'll be su'e to let you know how things p'og'ess from he'e, but fo'h now, I'll let you get you'h sleep."

Ella hurried back upstairs and entered her room. She still trembled with excitement. She put the note back in her dresser drawer and flopped into bed.

Her father had found the Gwambi Treasure! Her father had written a note to her!

14

MALCONTENT

After guiding the whaling ship into their bay, the pirates had stripped it down, taking its rigging, shrouds, and sails to replace their own tattered and ripped equipment. The quartermasters of both crews marched up and down the decks, blowing out orders on their whistles, the shantymen sang as loudly as they could for the workers, and the carpenters on board the pirate ships beat in time with their hammers, while their comrades on the whaling vessel worked busily with their saws and crowbars to bring back all the good lumber they could find.

Then there was the great excitement when the carpenters, under the direction of Killjelly, brought down the whaling ship's masts. The pirates swarmed onto the magnificent pieces of lumber like muskrats onto a log, wielding long poles and oars to float the masts over to their ships. Longfinch's pirates took the mainmast and the mizzen to the man-o-war, leaving the fore-mast for the galleon.

The commotion began all over again as the pirates hoisted the masts out of the water and replaced the splintered masts with these new ones. As the sun sank beneath the mountains, the carpenters put in their last rivets to the ships' hulls and the last bolts to secure the new masts.

Ernest turned from his work to go below deck. Every muscle in his body was sore from the work, but he felt content with what they had accomplished. The ship was now watertight again and ready to take on battle in the open sea — well, so they still had the new sails to hang up, and the new rigging to run, and the forecourse yard hadn't been touched yet, but that would be tomorrow's work. They had done well as it was.

He looked over his shoulder at the whaling ship's remains floating in the hidden bay. The poor vessel lay stripped of all of its masts, its ribbing open in a few places. The bright crimson sunset reflected off the surface of the bay around the whaling ship, making the vessel look almost like a slain sea monster, languishing in its own lifeblood, its ribs open to the sky.

Ernest smiled to himself. Yes, that was a job well done.

As he stepped below with the other pirates, a soothing smell wafted up to them from the galley. Ernest's belly rumbled at the smell. Oh, the pure joy of finishing a hard day's work only to feast on Lewis' prime cooking.

Lewis met Ernest at the entrance to the galley with a twinkle in his eye.

"Oh ho ho, boyo! How's some warm soup sound to you, eh?"

Ernest nodded. "And a pint on whiskey or two."

Lewis handed Ernest a bowl and a chunk of dark bread. "Well then, boyo, scarf this down real quick, 'cause I need you to pass out the grog for me."

Ernest downed the soup in two mouthfuls and then stood by the barrel of grog, rationing out each pirate a portion as they shuffled through.

"We do'ed good today, do'edn't we?" one said with a wink.

"Oh, ay. The ship will be ready to fight in no time at all."

"No one could keep Holgard and his mighty galleon down for long."

"Ay, no, they can't!"

Several pirates gave a hearty cheer at this, and a stocky gnome in the corner pulled out a fiddle, playing '*Fighting Past Death*' at a quick tempo. The pirates may have been tired, but the food, drink, and music livened them up. Many started clapping their hands to the rowdy music while some nymphs banged with their webbed hands on the tables as if they were drums. One or two pirates stomped about in a manner that resembled dancing.

Ernest now retired from his post by the ale barrel and drew himself another bowl of soup from the pot Lewis had on the stove.

"Now then, boyo," Lewis said, perching on the edge of a stool and looking at Ernest intently, "I hear you haved quite the adventure?"

Ernest nodded and grinned. "Ay, I was one on the first to climb onto that whaling ship, and me the cook's-mate and all, too! They should write a song about me for that."

"That they should," Lewis nodded with an air of mock solemnity. "Dread Ernest Redfoam, pirate extraordinaire, terror on the whaling crews."

Ernest grinned. "Ah, maybe I should be a captain then. I'd make you boatswain."

"Helen Maria! No, thank you," Lewis objected, pouring himself a pint of whiskey. "I'd bargain away my tongue for pigs' food before I became a boatswain. Blind prelates, no! Then, I'd have to engage in the fighting. If'n I must be anything more than your cook, Captain Ernest the Terrible, make me your poet."

Ernest raised an eyebrow. "My poet?"

Lewis raised one finger in the air emphatically, as if delivering some great oration.

> "Look here or there
> In sea or air
> No other man you'll find
> To match or to out-fight
> Our cap'n Ernest's might!"

Ernest smiled. "Ay, only 'find' and 'fight' don't rhyme."

"Not rhyme, no, it's called 'affluence,' or something on that sort."

"'Assonance,'" Ernest corrected. "You forget that I do'ed have myself some learning when I was younger."

"Eh," Lewis winked broadly. "So I see, so I see. You're a talented gnome, you are."

At this moment, a commotion among the eating pirates interrupted their conversation.

Ernest looked up to see Boatswain Killjelly walking down the steps into the galley. The fiddle player stopped his tune abruptly, and the pirates settled down in the presence of their officer.

Killjelly slammed his hooks into a table and grinned, looking over the group of pirates.

"You have all done a fair day's work, sure."

"Ay, sir!" a couple of pirates answered back.

"And I trust you will do just as well tomorrow, sure?"

No enthusiastic cheers greeted this comment.

Killjelly smiled again. "Well then, Captain Holgard sends me with this command." Killjelly now fixed his eyes on Ernest. Ernest looked back uncomfortably.

"Cook's-mate," Killjelly said, "double rations on grog for all hands."

"Ay, sir!" Ernest saluted enthusiastically. This brought a cheer from the men, and the fiddler sawed out the first few chords of another reel. Killjelly held up his hands, and everyone went quiet again.

"Now, you all deserve it, sure. I seed you myself today. We taked that whaling ship with no help from Longfinch, and we've fixed up our ship smartly, sure." And then he added under his breath, but loud enough that everyone could hear it, "despite Longfinch and his scum."

This brought nods of approval.

"Long live Captain Holgard!" Killjelly finally said. "I hope you drink our good captain's health because I know we will drink the health on the crew in the captain's quarters. We couldn't wish for finer men, sure. Long live Captain Holgard!"

"Long live Captain Holgard!" The crew echoed, and with one accord, they lined back up for another pint of grog. The fiddler started playing again, this time *'Jolly Old Captain Mulligan.'* Ernest stood up and speedily rationed out the grog, tapping his toes to the lively music. And when the tune ended, the fiddler struck off again, first *'I Drank a Gun of Whiskey,'* then *'Never You Fear the Sea, Boys',* and on and on the music went.

Ernest dished out the last of the grog to Bill, the long-armed gnome, and his hulking mess-mate Tell.

"Oh, ay," Bill said after sipping his grog. "Do'ed you see Longfinch's pirates working? They were lazier than a pack on sea elephants lounging in the sun."

"That's true," another pirate joined in. "We must've done half the work on their ship besides fixing up our own."

"And their boatswain," Bill remarked. "What's his name? Vania? Vania Bloodrummer?"

"Ay, that's him," Tell said with a meek smile.

"Vania Bloodrummer," Bill continued. "Strutting about and ordering us to do our work while he never lifted a finger."

"And it was him, too," Quartermaster Harold said from where he sat at the head of one of the tables, "what was walking past when we were lowering the mainmast, and it looked well nigh like it would fall, and I says to him, says I 'grab a hold on that rope and help us get the mast down gentle!' and he turns to me and says, 'I'm an officer. You can manage.'"

"No!" another pirate protested, standing on the table dramatically. "That's not *quite* what he sayed. He was like this:" and the pirate strutted about on the table, then stopping, looked at Quartermaster Harold and said in his thickest imitation of Vania's accent, "*Which is!* I am an officerrr." And he trilled out the 'r' obnoxiously while the other pirates hooted in laughter. "'You can manage, *whateverrrrrr.*'"

"And all that time," Bill added, yelling over the guffawing and drunken laughter, "all that time, there was our Killjelly with his shirt off, an officer no less than Vania, sweating up a storm with the best on us."

The fiddler now, apparently thinking that there had been too much talk already, sawed away at a few chords and then launched off into '*Give me a Cheer for a Wife.*' The pirates clapped their hands and pounded on the tables to the lively beat.

The pirate who had been impersonating Vania clicked his heels neatly as he jumped down from the table. "I wish that Vania Bloodrummer were here now; I'd give him a thing or two to think on! I wouldn't mind even to give Old Longfinch a good rap on the pate!"

"I wouldn't give a conversion!" another pirate roared. "Here's a toast for you, then! To Longfinch and his crew: baptize the lot on them!"

The pirates hooted at this new jest, the beginnings of a string of curses and profanities directed at Vania Bloodrummer, Longfinch, or various other pirates in the other crew.

Ernest couldn't help but find this rather amusing. He did like Longfinch — he at least seemed to be a good captain — but the rest of his crew *was* snobbish. Maybe it would serve them right to be mocked.

Killjelly now climbed up the steps and back onto the deck. Ernest almost thought he saw Killjelly look at Lewis meaningfully as he left. For the briefest instant, Ernest thought he saw Lewis returning the glance. But then Lewis leaned toward Ernest with a wide smile.

"Now, a moment ago, when I sayed you haved been on a grand adventure, I wasn't talking about the whaling ship. I meaned your raiding expedition. Helen Maria! You should've heared Longfinch yelling about it."

"Longfinch?" Ernest asked, confused. Was Longfinch supposed to know?

"Oh ho ho, boyo," Lewis replied. "Yes, Longfinch. He comed aboard while you were cutting down the mast and gived Holgard a regular dressing down about engaging in a raid without his permission. It was quite a show."

"The raid?"

"No," Lewis laughed, "I meaned that Longfinch's yelling was quite a show, but I'm sure the raid was a show, too."

Ernest settled into a stool solemnly. He did not like to be reminded of that raid. The very thought of that girl with the raptor bird behind her made Ernest uneasy.

"It must've been quite the adventure, eh? You didn't get into too much fun now, do'ed you?" Lewis looked at him meaningfully.

Ernest shifted positions nervously. "'Fun' wouldn't be the word I would use to describe it."

Lewis looked at Ernest closely, his carefree look giving way to sincere empathy. "It *was* a disaster, then? What happened?"

"I almost died," Ernest whispered. "She almost killed me..."

"Blind prelates, Ernest, you look like you've seen a ghost! Are you all right?"

Ernest shrugged. "It wasn't that bad; I shouldn't have been so scared. It just reminded me on..."

Lewis still looked at him closely. Ernest could hardly bring himself to look Lewis in the eye. Remembering how terrified he had been that night — even construing a young girl to be

Lady Death incarnate — he felt ashamed. Why had he been so afraid?

"Reminded you on what?" Lewis prodded.

Ernest sighed. "Do'ed you ever see mystery plays?"

"Like in the monasteries?" Lewis asked, raising an eyebrow.

"Ay," Ernest nodded, "where they would act out the mystical stories on holy days, stories like the 'Day on Death,' 'The Day on Damnation,' 'Mortification on the Flesh,' 'Vices and the Consequences.' Do'edn't you see any on those?"

Lewis shook his head. "We never went near the Orthodox monasteries. We were strictly Weldronists, so we never messed with prelates or monks."

"Well then, you mightn't understand," Ernest sighed. "They were frightening. And when I was a boy, I was convinced that Lady Death and Dame Hell were real, living people who might come up at any moment to drag me down to the fiery tortures on damnation."

"Ah," Lewis nodded knowingly. "The prelates would do all sorts on things to convince you to be a good little boy who always obeys the rules. The fear on death — now that would be a fear that would make a boy behave."

"That's it," Ernest said, nodding. "That's it exactly."

Lewis pursed his lips pensively. "Death is much to fear. But we aren't really afraid on death, are we, boyo? No, we're afraid on what *follows*."

15

———

BENIGHTED

*H*aeli stood atop a craggy pinnacle with fog and wind whirling around her. The fog was thick and moist, drenching her from head to toe, almost as if she were being beaten by the ocean waves. Was it raining? Was that the boom of thunder she heard in the distance? Now there was a low, rhythmic sound, like some tribal drumbeat, or perhaps the chanting of some mystic cult. The pungent smell of sulfur assailed her nostrils.

There was just room on that rock to stand, and she held out her hands for balance. Another gust of wind raked across her body. Haeli crouched, gripping the rock with her hands now. Still, the mist drove at her. Water dripped from her nose and fell down, down, down from the rock. She could see through the heaving fog below her for a moment, and there was the angry ocean bashing itself against the giant rock.

As the drop rushed down to meet the ocean, the ocean rushed up to meet it. The waves now splashed against Haeli's feet and hands, slicing them as if with briar branches. Still, the rhythmic chant continued; was it coming from inside her head?

Above the chant, there was the sound of wings — great reptilian, or perhaps mammalian, wings.

A dark shape loomed above her in the mist. Its great wings beat back the mist for a moment, and Haeli could see the shape of an Eagle Griffin. Then the mist obscured it again, and it assumed the shape of a pteranodon, its great wings folded back as if it was preparing to dive at her. At that moment, the sea rose with a sudden fury and swallowed her into its great mouth. With a clap like thunder, it swept her from the rock.

For a moment, she whirled in the furious waves. She gasped for breath and flailed about wildly. Her hand caught on a post of some sort, and she clung to it for all she was worth. The raging sea subsided all at once, and she could see that she held onto the posts of one a food shelf in the storage room back home.

Haeli looked around to see that she was indeed standing in the storage room. An obscure, bloody mass lay on the floor before her. Towering over this body stood the leprechaun with the hooks. He fired his pistol into the obscure mass.

"Where are the keys, fool? Where are the keys?"

Suddenly, all went dark. She was no longer holding the post. All around her, the air was cold and musty, with a strong odor of mildew. Beneath her bare feet, she could feel something like cold stone. In her ears, the rhythmic chanting continued and seemed to grow louder and louder.

Haeli clamped her hands over her ears to block out the noise, and in a moment, all was silent.

She removed her hands. All was quiet as death. Then out of the darkness, like the low breaking of a rotten egg, a voice spoke:

> "Ys ffayewsy ene eytacwsy ene,
> Ys agwraswsy ene athebwsy ene,
> Ys chreyswsy ene aeydhwffwyeyswsy ene."

Haeli shuddered at the sound of the voice. She hardly dared to breathe, lest whoever had spoken should find her in the darkness. The voice spoke again:

> *"Those who make me do not need me,*
> *Those who buy me do not want me,*
> *Those who use me do not know me."*

A bloodied knife flashed in her vision as a scream sounded in her ears.

Haeli sat bolt upright. Perspiration was clear on her brow, though it was still freezing out. Martyn stirred and sat up, rubbing his eyes and looking at her from across the campsite.

"Are ye all right?"

Haeli breathed heavily, looking all around. All was as it should be. The fire had died down to embers, and Martyn lay on the other side from her, his tomahawk and rifle close at hand. The sweet smell of the pine forest mingled with the last wisps of smoke from the waning fire. They were still in the little hollow off the High Road, where they had bedded down for the night on their journey to Entwerp. Haeli checked to see that her letter for the Company was still safe under her bedroll. She listened hard for the rhythmic chanting but could hear nothing.

It had just been a dream.

Martyn turned to her with more concern. "Haeli, are ye all right?"

"I am fine," she mumbled.

It had to be more than a dream. There had been that leprechaun with the hooks, and he had shot Da. That *had* happened. It couldn't just be a dream. It had to mean something.

At the thought of Da's death, Haeli trembled and sobbed. Just then, she felt Martyn's hand on her shoulder. She looked up to see him looking her in the eye; his brow furrowed with sympathy.

"Ye are no all right, Haeli. I cen tell that much."

Haeli tried to smile, but tears came to her eyes. "I am sorry. It was just a bad dream."

Martyn nodded understandingly. "I am merri sorry, Haeli. I really am. I wish I'll could help ye."

Haeli forced another smile, swallowing hard and wiping back her tears. "Do not be silly, Martyn. You are helping us." Another sob caught in Haeli's throat, and she stopped.

Martyn took her hand and squeezed it encouragingly. "Ay, but I wish I'll could be a merri o' *more* help."

Haeli laughed cynically but then stared soberly into the dying embers. "Ma always said that it was more important to be with someone than to help them. Listening is better than doing things, sometimes."

Martyn gave a wry smile. "That's ironic, coming from a Rectificationist. Are no ye all about helpin' people? *Doin'* things?"

Haeli pursed her lips. "Do you remember what people say to you? I mean, can you hear people's voices — your Ma's or your Da's or your pastors — telling you what you need to hear in the moment?"

Martyn looked at her critically. "Cen ye?"

Haeli nodded. "I have always wondered if other people are like that."

Martyn shrugged. "I cen no speak fer other people, only for me."

Haeli took a deep breath. "It is like…" she searched for the right words. "When I climb a tree, I can hear Tomas coaching me like he did when he taught me to climb. Or, when I go to the ocean, I can hear Da telling me about how treacherous the ocean is. Or, if I am feeling overwhelmed by emotions, I can hear Ma teaching me horse riding…" Haeli trailed off and glanced over at Martyn. "You do not do that?"

Martyn pursed his lips. "Sometimes, I cen hear my sister gigglin', the way she did a'fore she got sick. That is about it, though."

Haeli looked away, and Martyn sighed deeply. "I am merri sorry, Haeli. I miss yer Da, too."

Haeli tried to swallow back the lump in her throat. "I think thoughts — memories — are real things. They are physical things, like our emotions."

Martyn raised an eyebrow. "Emotions are no physical things, are they?"

Haeli shook her head. "You are hopeless."

Martyn laughed softly. "I mean, I realize that ye are a Rectificationist, an' fer ye, everything is physical. So I will accept yer argument at present."

"How merri patronizing of you," Haeli replied.

Martyn shook his head. "All right, then. 'Memories are physical things,' ye were sayin'? Go on."

Haeli looked back at the fire, the lump returning to her throat. "If memories are physical things, then Da is not really gone, is he?" Haeli tapped the side of her head. "He will always be here."

Martyn's face softened, and he touched Haeli's shoulder. "Is that enough fer ye?"

Haeli looked away, fighting back a sob. "No."

Martyn took a deep breath and let it out slowly. "When my sister died. I trived it easier no to remember." he bowed his head. "It feels heartless now that I am sayin' it out loud, but *there* it is. Sometimes it is easier no to remember."

Just then, a loud thud sounded over their heads, almost like canvas snapping open in a squall. Haeli looked up to see a dark shape circling the trees above them.

Martyn furrowed his brow as he looked at it. "That is no a pteranodon, is it?"

As if to answer this question, the shape fell like lightning from the sky, opening its wings and beating them to slow itself before it touched the ground.

It was an Eagle Griffin, nearly the size of a full-grown tiger. Its back legs were sleek, muscular, and feline-like, splotched with dark brown and black spots in its fur. Slim and scaly forelegs, with four wicked talons on each foot, raked the earth in front, and a long and lizard-like tail, with broad feathers at its end, swished back and forth behind. Its head was wicked, with a hooked upper beak and a lion-fanged lower jaw, slitted eyes, and wolf-like ears laid back dangerously. Its golden wings were nearly twenty feet as it folded them back over its wiry body.

Overall, the beast bore the appearance of a fierce, avian, reptile cat, with its sleek fur, feathers, and scales. It crouched about five feet away from them. Haeli regarded it with some apprehension. The images of her dream flashed through her mind. Hadn't she seen an Eagle Griffin, or was it a pteranodon?

The beast eyed them for a moment with its narrow golden eyes. It seemed most keen on Haeli as it looked her up and down closely.

Haeli noticed Martyn's hand slowly moving towards the rifle hanging from his shoulder. The beast must have seen this too, for it gave a low hiss.

"Do *not* touch your gun. You can not resist *me.*"

Martyn's eyes narrowed. "What do ye want?"

The beast looked at Haeli again. "I *am* looking for a blonde girl. *She* is about the same size as this one *you* have with you. *You* have not seen her?"

"If I'll ha'," Martyn replied, "I would no tell ye."

The griffin hissed viciously. "*Her* name is Ella Donne Pickering."

Haeli gasped. How did this beast know about Ella?

Martyn suddenly unslung his rifle, but before he could level it and fire, the griffin sprang at him and swatted it from his hands. As the beast turned to slash at Martyn with its fangs, Martyn lept nimbly aside, pulled a long horse pistol from his belt, and discharged it into the griffin's side.

The griffin screamed and launched himself from the ground, flapping his wings furiously and rising rapidly out of the hollow. Blood dripped from his side as he flapped frantically.

Martyn snatched up his rifle from the ground and leveled it at the retreating griffin. The beast veered sharply to the right as Martyn fired, then flew off into the night sky, still beating its wings heavily. Haeli could hear the beast screaming back at them and guessed he must be spewing a string of curses at them.

She glanced over at Martyn in shock as he frantically reloaded his two guns.

"I half wish that it'll would vene back. I'll would be sure to finish him, then."

"What was that?" Haeli finally gasped.

"Do ye want a gun, too?" Martyn replied.

"But how did he cognize Ella?" Haeli asked, looking back after the griffin in apprehension.

Martyn sighed. "He must be the griffin that works with the pirates."

"They are still looking for Ella?"

"Llifsa!" Martyn replied. "I am afraid they still tain some unfinished business at the Pickering Manor."

Haeli nodded, her head spinning. She knew what the pirates were after. But why had she dreamed of that griffin even before seeing him? Had it been a vision?

Martyn finished loading his guns and let the flint hammers down to a closed position. "You ha' best be gettin' back to sleep. I will keep watch fer now. We'd best be off at first light."

Haeli tried to settle down. "How far from here to Entwerp?"

"Eight, ten miles," Martyn replied.

Haeli pursed her lips. "Shall we just go? Walk through the night?"

Martyn shook his head. "Ye need yer rest. Try to sleep."

"I am not sure that is possible anymore," Haeli replied.

16

COMMISSIONS

*E*rnest slept very well that night, with the grog inside him and his body already exhausted from the day's work and the previous night's raid. Still, a light in the kitchen awakened him before daybreak. He opened one of his eyes to see Lewis sitting down before the just-started fire with his scriptures in his hand. Killjelly stood nearby.

Ernest knew better than to get up, as he had done the last time he saw these two conspiring together. But he could hardly hear them from his hammock. He strained all of his hearing power, tilting his big ears towards them as best he could, but he could not make out a single word from either Lewis or Killjelly.

What were those two up to? Ernest wondered. And what was that meaningful look they had exchanged last night? Just then, Ernest heard someone coming up towards his hammock. He lay perfectly still and snored loudly so that whoever it was would think he was fast asleep.

He felt a hand on his shoulder and opened up his eyes. It was Lewis.

"Sorry to wake you," Lewis said. "Killjelly needs you."

Ernest tumbled out of his hammock, stretching and yawning outrageously.

"You waked me out on a *sound* sleep." And Ernst yawned again.

Lewis smiled dryly but moved on to rouse Bill and Tell as well.

Ernest entered the kitchen and looked at Killjelly. The dark leprechaun stood menacingly in the shadows cast by the fire, playing with his hook absentmindedly.

"What's going on, chief?" Ernest asked.

Killjelly scowled. "Wait for the others."

Ernest sat down on a tall stool and nodded. "If'n you insist."

Bill and Tell now stumbled into the kitchen, with Lewis right behind. Tell still rubbed sleep from his eyes, and Bill fought back a yawn.

Killjelly now stepped out into the light.

Tell looked over at Killjelly groggily. "Hey, what are you doing down in the kitchen?"

Bill jabbed Tell in the ribs with his elbow. "Shut up, you idiot. Listen to the officer, now."

Ernest stood at attention. "We're all listening to the officer now; if'n he would only speak, though, that's the issue."

Killjelly frowned darkly in annoyance. "I need you three again," he said flatly.

"Ay, and isn't that the truth? And who doesn't need the three on us now?" Ernest added cheekily.

Killjelly ground his teeth together and walked up to Ernest, staring him straight in the eye and stepping so close that Ernest could feel his hot breath on his face.

"You waked up feeling confident, do'edn't you?"

Ernest swallowed. "I thinked I was always supposed to be confident."

Killjelly smiled slightly. "I like you, Ernest, and it's a baptized good thing for you, or I might have killed you years ago." Killjelly touched his hooks suggestively.

Ernest nodded, now regretting his devil-may-care attitude of a few moments ago. "Very good, sir."

Killjelly stepped away and looked grimly at the three pirates assembled before him in the kitchen. "You all may as well laugh and smile now because I doubt you will have time for that soon."

Bill, Tell, and Ernest stood expectantly, waiting for their commissions. Ernest could feel his gut tying itself in a knot inside of him. This did not sound like it was going to be enjoyable.

Killjelly stared them levelly in the face. "The Albino..."

Ernest felt his whole body go cold at the sound of that name, and he heard Bill and Tell gasp involuntarily.

"The Albino," Killjelly repeated, "requests aid. He haves finded the keys, sure."

"Keys to what?" Tell asked blankly.

Killjelly glared at Tell.

Ernest cut in. "You shouldn't have selled your brain for a block of cheese."

Tell looked confused. "I don't remember doing that, but I do like cheese–"

Bill elbowed Tell, and Tell closed his mouth.

Killjelly's eyes narrowed, and he looked the three pirates up and down with a hint of disgust. "What is this to you?"

"Sir?" Tell looked up.

"Is this just some merry cruise on the ocean? Is this only a romantic treasure hunt to you? Don't you realize we are on the verge on uncovering the Gwambi civilization? Does that have any significance to you?"

Ernest spoke before Tell could say anything else stupid. "Ay, it means we will all be richer than kings!"

Killjelly looked Ernest over disdainfully. "Is that what you think? Rich, eh? Perhaps we will be rich, sure, but more importantly, we will be powerful."

"Powerful?" Tell asked.

Killjelly nodded and replied elusively, "What do you think kept that treasure hidden for so long?"

Tell wrinkled his brow pensively, nodding sagely. "Ah, I see."

Killjelly curled his lip in disgust, spitting on the floor. "That power is not the sort on thing that we will want to share, now is it?" Killjelly looked at Ernest, Bill, and Tell, who nodded dutifully. "We must work hard to gain that power, and we must do so before Longfinch, sure?"

Ernest nodded. "We will take the treasure for ourselves, then?"

"If'n we can," Killjelly shrugged. "Why should more than one pirate crew take that power?"

Bill grinned hideously. "That's something to look forward to."

"And that," Killjelly said, "is what I need you to do. If'n the Albino can retrieve the keys, then we have no need on staying with Longfinch. We could find the treasure ourselves."

"And the Albino needs our help?" Ernest asked.

"With the girl," Killjelly added.

Ernest felt another chill run down his spine. As if it wasn't enough to be forced to work with the Albino, he had to track down that girl again. The one who had almost killed him?

"The Albino has come to me in a dream," Killjelly continued. "He haves finded the girl and needs you to help him capture her so that we can retrieve the keys. Is that clear?"

"Where will we meet him?" Ernest asked.

"On the high road to Entwerp," Killjelly replied. "That's the way the girl taked. He's been following her ever since he leaved."

Ernest nodded. "And how do we get to shore?"

Killjelly smiled. "Well now, Longfinch would miss a boat if'n you taked one, so I'm afraid you will have to swim to shore."

"That will be cold," Tell whimpered.

Bill elbowed him in the gut again. "Don't whine, you baptized wimp. We will have time to dry off when we get to shore." But Ernest could tell that Bill did not relish the thought of swimming through that cold bay any more than Tell.

"Any more questions?" Killjelly asked.

The three pirates looked at each other, but none had anything else to add.

"Very good," Killjelly said. "I would like you to be gone in ten minutes, sure. The quartermaster is waiting to give you some arms, and then you should be off."

Ernest nodded and stepped outside the kitchen to his hammock. It only took him a moment to grab what he needed for the journey — namely his pepperbox pistol — and then tie his boots and shimmy into his overcoat. That done, Ernest turned to climb up on deck but found Lewis behind him.

Lewis smiled broadly and handed Ernest a leather bag. "Some food for the way."

Ernest took it. "Thanks."

"I'm sure it will come in handy," Lewis winked. "It's in a watertight container, too."

Ernest nodded. "What were you and Killjelly talking about?"

"What?" Lewis looked startled.

"Just now," Ernest asked, "you two were talking about something before you waked me."

Lewis grinned roguishly. "Ah, yes, politics, just discussing politics."

Ernest grunted and then climbed up to the deck, where he found Quartermaster Harold waiting for him at the door to the armory.

"It's about time you showed up," he growled as he unlocked the door and led Ernest inside. He handed Ernest a musket and a pistol. "That's what the boatswain said to give you. Now get going."

"What about a rapier?" Ernest asked. "Can I have a rapier?"

Harold sighed. "You *would* want a sword, wouldn't you?"

Ernest shrugged. "You know I'm better with it than a musket."

"Fine." Harold took the musket back and handed Ernest a rapier instead.

Ernest ducked back outside and made his way to the gunwales. He looked back to see Bill and Tell coming up on deck and heading into the armory, receiving a similarly grouchy treatment from Harold.

Ernest took a deep breath. This was it, another long day starting — and it would probably be a very unpleasant day if it involved the Albino and that girl. Ernest shook his head as he looked out into the cool and still morning. It was so dark that he couldn't see the shore, and the stars glimmered above him like tiny pin-points of amber light, winking and blinking as if they, too, were waking up. The daystar alone shone brightly in the darkness. Ernest sighed. Why couldn't he live like those stars? Surely they didn't have to worry about wars, or raids, or archeomancers, or Lady Death. When this was all over, he deserved a little peace and tranquility.

Just then, he thought he heard voices in the air. They came from Holgard's cabin. Someone had left the window open by accident. Ernest cocked his big ear to listen, walking closer. He only made out the end of Holgard's statement.

"...the summoning."

Then everything was quiet again. But after a moment, Holgard spoke again. "And the crew?"

"Ripe for the picking, sure," came Killjelly's voice in reply.

"Ernest!"

Ernest looked up to see Bill and Tell coming up to him.

"We're ready, are you?" Bill asked.

Ernest nodded.

"Over we go then," Bill said glumly.

Ernest tied a spare piece of rigging to the gunwale and threw it over the ship's side. He then vaulted over the gunwale and began lowering himself into the frigid water.

"And it begins again," Ernest mumbled.

Bill laughed sarcastically.

17

SECRETS

*E*lla lay in her bed, not fully awake, but neither was she fully asleep. As if in a dream, vivid images from her memory flashed before her. The pirates storming the Pickerings' porch; the door flying open at a word from that white-haired beggar. She could almost still hear Olyfia's footsteps as she fled up the stairs. Ella shuddered. Would she ever be rid of that horrid memory of that horrid day?

Suddenly, Ella's eyes snapped open. Olyfia had been running upstairs. Why had she been running upstairs? She could have run out the back door by the kitchen and made it safely out of the house. Maybe there was a pirate guarding that door? But why run upstairs?

Ella sat up and looked out her window. She guessed it to be maybe half an hour before sunrise. She had time to investigate before her breakfast duties.

Quietly, she slipped out of bed, wrapped a shawl over her nightgown, lit her lantern, and crept from the room. There was no noise in the house, and as she was the sole occupant of the upper story, she needn't be very concerned about disturbing anyone — so long as she didn't make too much noise.

But where would she look? There were dozens of rooms up here; Olyfia could have been running to any one of them — assuming she had run anywhere in particular. Ella screwed her lips to one side. The best she could do was start looking in rooms, starting from the kitchen staircase and moving on from there.

She came to the first door and tried it. Locked. She grabbed the knob of the next door. Locked again. Finally, on the fifth door she tried, the door opened. Ella pushed it open slowly and couldn't help but gasp at what she found inside.

It was a small room, with only a single window in the far wall, which let in the murky light of predawn. The room smelt heavily of mothballs. In one corner was a bed with a white cloth draped over it, but the cloth was disheveled, and there was blood on it. An armchair lay on its side with one leg broken off, and a dresser was pulled out into the middle of the room.

Ella entered the room slowly. She had thought they had cleaned up the house after the pirates' raid, but they must have missed this room. She looked at each piece of furniture and shuddered. This must have been where the pirates captured Olyfia before they dragged her down to the basement. But why had Olyfia run into this room of all rooms?

Ella looked carefully around the room. There was nothing peculiar as far as she could see. She walked over to the single window on the far side from the door, stepping around the dresser as she did so.

In front of the window, she noticed a line of dust. Looking closer, she saw that dust covered the entire floor, but in front of the window, there was a rectangular shape with no dust on it. Of course, that must have been where the dresser stood before the pirates moved it.

Ella paused. Why had the pirates moved the dresser? She understood they might knock over chairs that were in their way, or even tear down pictures from the wall, and slice open mattresses for the sheer joy of mayhem, but why would they move a heavy dresser from the wall? Perhaps if they had done such things downstairs, it wouldn't seem strange, but come to think of it, this was the only dresser that the pirates had disturbed.

Or had the pirates moved it at all? Perhaps Olyfia moved it?

Ella got down on her knees and looked at the floorboards in front of the window. It was all solid wood flooring, but she noticed a crack between one board and the wall, just big enough for her to fit her fingers into. She slipped her hand in and felt a leather strap on the other side. Ella's heart raced. It was the handle of a trapdoor. Hastily, she swung the door open. The rich smell of soil and old wood wafted up towards her, and several cobwebs blew into her face. Holding the lantern down to see what it would reveal, Ella peered down the dark shaft she had uncovered.

A wooden ladder led down from where she knelt, reaching about sixteen feet down before it ended on a dirt floor. Ella took a deep breath and descended the ladder, brushing cobwebs out of her way as best she could as she went. Reaching the bottom, she turned around and held her lantern up. She could see that she was inside a small, wooden tool shed, with several hoes, shovels, scythes, and an old wheelbarrow leaned in disarray against the walls. There was a small door on the far side, and peering through a crack in it, Ella could see outside into the early morning.

Ella looked around the shed one last time. This was rather curious. Sir Saemwel had a secret passageway in and out of his house. Had he foreseen a raid like this?

Ella stood there in the toolshed for a moment. What did all of this mean? This house seemed as if it bred questions but never gave answers. Ella kicked absentmindedly at the dirt floor, breathing deeply of the earthy-smelling air as she sighed.

Answers, yes, she needed answers. The pirates might return any time, and she had to find that treasure before them.

But how?

Did she have to wait until Stifyn Blysffi came back to Entwerp before she could get more answers?

Just then, the light of her lantern flashed against something on the wall. Looking closer, she could see it was writing — four names carved into the wall. They were in the Pistosian script, but Ella could now read them easily enough. The first three names on the list were crossed out, and someone had underlined the last name. "Saemwel Pickering, Sam Pickerwright, Sym Carterwright, Syd Cartwright."

It almost seemed like someone was playing with a name, starting with Saemwel Pickering and mutating it until they came up with a new name. Syd Cartwright. What did this mean? Who was Syd Cartwright?

As helpless as Ella felt she was at answering any of these questions, she knew there was yet one man who might answer them for her: Sir Saemwel. It was his name at the top of this list, after all. If only he weren't so sick! Perhaps if he got well enough to talk again, she would ask him some questions.

Ella turned and ascended the ladder to the room. Miss Nansi would wake soon, and Ella would need to make breakfast. Besides, she hadn't even got dressed yet. She would have to investigate this passage more later.

After breakfast, Pastor Daerl excused himself to the parlor to study for his sermon, and Ella and Miss Nansi cleared the table. Elsi sat in her seat pensively, and Clerans stood, looking first at Elsi and then at Miss Nansi and Ella, as if trying to decide who to join.

"Is there anything' I'll cen do to help ye?" Clerans finally asked Miss Nansi.

"Oh, ay," Miss Nansi replied. "I tain a merri o' dishes to wash. Ye cen do that, I am sure?"

Clerans nodded. "I most certainly cen."

Ella brought her platter full of dishes to the kitchen and returned to the dining room to clear the rest, passing Clerans on the way as he whistled vociferously, rolling up his sleeves and heading towards the pile of dirty dishes. Ella reentered the dining room as Elsi addressed Miss Nansi.

"Aunt Nansi, do ye tain any news from Papa?"

Miss Nansi shook her head. "I do no believe I ha' heard anything' about him recently. I am sure he is jist fine, though."

Elsi sighed. "I am sure he is, but all the same, it would make me feel better if I'll knew fer certain."

Miss Nansi nodded.

"Ye do no think," Elsi began, then she stopped. "Ye do no think that ye, or Ella, or someone could cede over to Doctor Heyl's house and check on Papa fer me?"

Miss Nansi shrugged. "Why do no ye go yerself?"

Elsi smiled softly. "I am afraid that I would no leave him. I will cede and visit him, I am sure, but I am no ready now. Please, would ye check him fer me?"

"I will," Ella said on impulse. "I would love to visit him fo'h you." She felt it might do her good to get out of the house and get some fresh air. All of this mystery in the house — the note, the passageway, the list of names — was getting to her. Perhaps she could think more clearly if she got away from it all. Besides, if Sir Saemwel was doing better, then she could ask him some questions.

Elsi smiled, "Thank ye, Ella. I merri greatly appreciate that. Ye remember where Dr. Heyl's place is, do no ye?"

Ella nodded, but shuddered at the same time. The last time she had been to Dr. Heyl's place, the strikers in Nychweni

Square had nearly attacked her. "Would you mind," Ella started. "I mean, if Cle'ans has nothing else he needs to do, do you mind if he comes with me?"

"No, he would no mind!" Clerans yelled from the kitchen. "An' as much as I *love* washin' dishes," he added sarcastically, "I much prefer escortin' beautiful women."

Ella blushed a deep crimson.

"Llifsa!" Miss Nansi called back to Clerans. "The real question is, do these said 'beautiful women' appreciate bein' escorted by a rascal like yerself?"

Clerans marched out of the kitchen, waving a dish towel as if it were a military baton. "A rascal indeed?" He gave an affected cough. "Yer own private opinions aside, madam, I do trive that beautiful women prefer to be in the company o' handsome young men." He gave a mock bow and an affected look of arrogance.

Miss Nansi looked back at him mischievously. "Ay, that may be the case, so it remains to be proven that they enjoy *yer* company."

18

OVER-HEARING

*E*rnest, Bill, and Tell had hardly swum ten yards from the galleon before they heard the heavy beating of wings over their heads. Ernest looked up in alarm to see the dark shape of Cweel passing over them. The Eagle Griffin beat his wings frantically, almost as if he was having a hard time staying in the air. Was he wounded? Ernest strained his eyes upwards but could make out little in the predawn darkness, though he heard Cweel muttering a string of curses as he passed.

Ernest stopped swimming and started treading water where he was as he watched Cweel. The mighty Eagle Griffin was losing altitude rapidly, despite his best efforts to stay aloft. In a moment, he had reached Longfinch's man-o'-war. He extended his front claws to catch the gunwales, but must have barely missed them. Ernest could hear his frantic scratching as he slid down the ship's tumblehome side and splashed heavily in the water.

"What's up with him?" Tell asked loudly.

"Shh!" Bill hissed. "Not so loud. It looks like he's been injured."

Tell must have heard the first part of what Bill said but not the second, as he dropped his voice to a stage whisper and asked again, "What's up with him?"

Bill growled and made a swipe at Tell's head. Tell, however, ducked nimbly underwater and resurfaced a few feet away — out of reach of Bill's long arms.

As Ernest continued to watch, Cweel burst out of the water, flapping his wings frantically and growling loud enough to wake a bear from hibernation ten miles away. Cweel mounted the gunwales and flopped over the side in exhaustion.

"Baptize *it!*" Cweel screamed over the waters. "Anoint *it!* I am going to kill *him! I* will!"

Ernest could see several people moving towards Cweel on deck, and they seemed to quiet him down. What was going on over there? What had happened? Ernest knew he was on a mission, and shouldn't take any time to dillydally, but his curiosity got the better of him. Besides, he wasn't looking forward to meeting the Archeomancer again, so why *should* he hurry?

"You don't have to follow me," Ernest said to his comrades, then Ernest changed course and thrust himself towards the man-o-war. He was an excellent swimmer — he'd been swimming most of his life — but his gnome body was also particularly well-suited for swimming, with long arms, a lithe frame, long feet, and large hands to thrust himself forward. Within moments, he had reached the man-o-war.

Ernest could hear confused voices from the aft of the man-o-war and recognized one as Cweel's. Again, he plunged himself underwater and swam swiftly and silently over to the aft end of the ship. Emerging again, he positioned himself directly under the captain's cabin window. The window was closed. Ernest could hear the voices of several people inside — arguing together, if he were to judge by the tone of their voices. Ernest, however, could not make out what they said. Looking around to see if there was a way to get closer to the window, Ernest noticed a rope-and-board scaffolding hanging off the ship's side where a carpenter must have been working the day before.

Ernest seized onto this scaffold and pulled himself out of the water, climbing until he came to a board of scaffolding which hung below the window. Crouching here, he could hear the conversation clearly through the glass.

"I will, I will, I will!" Cweel screamed.

Ernest risked peeking through the window for an instant, and he could see the griffin storming about the cabin like a cornered honey badger. His wings were partially unfurled, and one hung almost limply from his body, dragging on the floor as he paced back and forth. Ernest recognized Vania Bloodrummer in the cabin as well, chasing Cweel in circles across the floor. Longfinch sat comfortably in an armchair with his back to Ernest. Now and then, he flicked out his long, elfin tongue to taste the air, but otherwise, he remained motionless.

Ernest now ducked back down below the window, hardly daring to breathe as he hung there, clinging tightly to the scaffolding.

"Which is! Stand still, whatever!" Bloodrummer said.

Ernest could hear more sounds of a scuffle. He imagined Cweel was still evading Bloodrummer as he raged around and around the room.

"*You* can not stop me. *I* will kill him! I will, I will, I will. Baptize *it*!" There was a loud crash, and Cweel hissed and snarled as if in intense pain.

"There!" Bloodrummer said again. "Look what you've done, whatever. Now stand still, anoint it, if you ever want to use that wing again, whatever!"

"Stand still, Cweel," Longfinch said. "Calm yourself."

The scuffling stopped, and for a moment, there was only the sound of Cweel hissing and growling.

"Look at what you've done." Vania said in a low voice. "How'd this happen, whatever?"

Cweel's voice rose to its former pitch of fury. "That is what *I* said! *He* did it! Baptize him! I will kill *him*. I will, I will, I will!"

"Which is, it's a gun wound," Bloodrummer said.

"Get the bullet out," Longfinch said. "And mend his muscles. I need him whole."

"*I* flew on it all the way here. Baptize *it*! It hurts like the sacrament! Anoint *it*!"

"Stay still, whatever," Bloodrummer growled. "Stay still, you beast."

Cweel snarled angrily.

"Calm yourself, my pet," Longfinch said.

Again Cweel seemed to settle down.

"It's badly swollen," Bloodrummer said. "Which is, it's terrible, whatever."

"I've seen you mend worse," Longfinch replied. "You have the power. Quickly now."

"*I* will kill him. I will, I will, I will!" Cweel said again, but this time more quietly, almost as if he were talking to himself.

Ernest thought he could hear Bloodrummer muttering something to himself in another language. It sounded strange and made Ernest shudder all over. It reminded him of the Albino.

"There!" Bloodrummer said after several minutes. "There's the bullet. Soon now, whatever, you will fly again."

Cweel hissed in delight. "Let me kill *him*. I must kill *him*."

"We have another task at hand, Cweel," Longfinch replied.

"For *me*, only this once," Cweel whined. "Let me kill *him*. It will not take any time."

Longfinch let out his breath slowly. "We have others on the ground. I do not know what they are planning. Unless I miss my guess, they may be very close to this man who shot you. You risk compromising *his* operation."

Cweel leapt from the window

Cweel whimpered like a spoiled child who couldn't get his way. "I can settle it with anyone, any time *you* like. Let me do this for *me*, this once! Let me kill *him*!"

"We have other plans at stake," Longfinch replied firmly. "Holgard is very close to getting the key for himself, and then there will be no time for anything else but finishing this operation. Your revenge could impede that."

Cweel whined again. "But he hasn't found the key yet!"

"There," Bloodrummer said, "as good as new."

There were more scratching noises as if Cweel had resumed his fuming circles around the room.

"Who is he?" Longfinch asked.

"That fighter," Cweel replied. "The beacon-tender. *He* was among those who defeated us at the dike. He was with the *girl*, too, and among those who took *her* in and protect her now."

"The girl?" Longfinch asked. "Do you mean Ella Pickering or this other one?"

Cweel hissed. "Both. *He* is now protecting the fugitive from Holgard's raid."

There was a moment when none of the three spoke a word. The only sound Ernest could hear was the rasping of Cweel's claws against the floor as he paced in circles.

"Very well," Longfinch said at last. "Kill him if you wish."

Cweel squealed in ecstasy. Suddenly the window above Ernest burst open, and Cweel exploded from it like a living, breathing, fuming cannonball. Ernest watched the Eagle Griffin as he tore across the bay. He didn't have the slightest evidence of the wounds he had borne only moments before.

Ernest stayed perfectly motionless, hardly daring to breathe. He could hear Longfinch and Bloodrummer walking up to the window. They must be standing right there at the open window. They could have reached out and touched him. Ernest trembled in terror. He had to stay still. He couldn't be found eavesdropping.

"Who is he killing?" Bloodrummer asked. "I never understood that, whatever."

Longfinch gave a short laugh. "He was rather excited, wasn't he? It must be one on the Llaedhwythi locals. Though he seems to be involved with both Ella and Stifyn Blysffi's daughter."

"Which is! One on those who ran off Killjelly?" Bloodrummer asked.

"Presumably," Longfinch answered. "If'n he's foiled our plans once already, we may as well risk foiling Holgard's plans — whatever they are — to take this man out and prevent him from stopping us again."

Bloodrummer grunted in acknowledgment, and then one of them closed the window.

Ernest breathed again. Had he been holding his breath? He didn't feel like risking anything else. That was enough eavesdropping for one morning.

Slowly and shakily, Ernest lowered himself into the water again and swam off towards the beach, all the time trying to make sense of what he had heard. Cweel was going to kill someone — someone related to Ella and a man called Stifyn Blysffi. Wasn't Stifyn the name of that fort-tender they had killed the other night?

Ernest rolled that question around in his mind. Was Cweel about to kill one of those men who chased them out of the fort? The satyr, perhaps? Or else one of the two men who had galloped past him on the road?

But how did Cweel and Longfinch know about the raid? How did they know Holgard was planning anything, and how did they know that Stifyn Blysffi had a daughter? And how had Cweel healed so quickly? Surely he wasn't exaggerating his wounds when he flew up to the ship.

Ernest could now feel the ground beneath his feet, and he stood up in the water, walking the rest of the way to land as a thought occurred to him. Longfinch knew that Holgard had planned to do something *that morning*. Killjelly had commissioned him, Bill, and Tell *that morning*. Longfinch was also fine risking the failure of Holgard's mission for Cweel to get his revenge on this anonymous man. However, this mission that Cweel put at stake was *his own*.

Ernest shivered. That meant that Cweel would probably run into them today. Ernest's heart sank. What kind of mission was this that he had to face the Albino again, and Lady Death, and Cweel? What had he done to deserve this?

19

STRIKE

*E*lla and Clerans left the Pickering manor a few hours later, heading down the road to Entwerp Proper. Clerans walked briskly by Ella's side with his hands thrust into his pockets, whistling merrily as he went along.

Ella took a deep breath of the clear mountain air and sighed. Maybe it wasn't as mountainy as the air around her little village of Blisa in Slyzwir, but it still held that same distinctively romantic scent. She looked out across the dale at the broad city of Entwerp, hemmed in so picturesquely by the green mountains, with the little whiffs of smoke rising from the factories on the city's west side along the river, and the neat houses all in their rows, blooming with flowers and greenery. Yes, it was a distinctly beautiful city.

In some ways, she was glad that the pirates had kidnapped her and dragged her all the way across the ocean. She had always wanted to visit these far-away, exotic cities, but never had the means as the daughter of a logger in Blisa. Thanks to those bothersome pirates, here she was! So there was something to be thankful for in all of her wild adventures with those pirates. Still, she would be elated if they all drowned in a ship-wreck. It would simplify things for her.

Suddenly, she realized that Clerans wasn't whistling anymore. She looked over at him. He seemed almost pale. "Cle'ans a'e you all wight?"

"What?" Clerans forced himself to smile. "Oh, ay, I am perfectly fine. Perfectly fine."

Ella looked at him closely. "You'he pale, Cle'ans. You look like you saw you'h double."

Clerans laughed. "No, no, nothin' o' that sort." He frowned and kicked at a rock in the road. Then he looked up again with a roguish wink — Ella didn't think it looked entirely genuine. "How good are ye at riddles, Miss Ella?"

"Well," Ella began.

Clerans cut her off. "Never mind, I am about to tell ye it anyway: Those who make me do no need me, those who buy me do no want me, and those who use me do no know me. What am I?"

Ella stopped dead in her tracks and looked Clerans straight in the eye. She could almost hear a pounding — or maybe a rhythmic chanting — in her head. "Whe'e did you hea'h that widdle?"

Clerans looked down at the ground and breathed deeply. "It wos in my dream."

Ella felt a chill run down her spine. "So, you have had the d'eam too?"

Clerans raised an eyebrow. "What is that?"

"I have had the same d'eam seve'al times," Ella said, "The one with that widdle."

"An' the chantin'?" Clerans asked.

Ella nodded. "And the chanting."

"An' Sir Saemwel?"

Ella looked at Clerans closely. "I have not d'eamed about Si'h Saemwel."

Clerans swallowed. "I dreamed that the whole village wos on fire. I wos gardin' fer Sir Saemwel in the Fflemins' house, though why he wos there, I do no know. When I trived him, he looked dead. I tried to drag him out o' the flames, but it only bruised my arms. But then, it was no Sir Saemwel," Clerans looked at Ella closely. "It wos Mr. Silas Pickering."

Ella stared at Clerans for a long time. "And the widdle?"

Clerans shrugged. "Why would we both ha' dreamed that same riddle? Answer me that."

Ella shrugged, but she felt the hair on the back of her neck rising. "It's the Gwambi T'easu'e. I shouldn't have given you that note. Now it will haunt you, too."

Clerans laughed at this and winked again. "Well, if that is all it is, I'll will make sure to help ye trive it quickly so we cen sleep in peace again." He laughed and started whistling again as he marched off, though it sounded halfhearted to Ella.

Ella followed Clerans somberly. She had a vague feeling that something was very wrong. Clerans should not have dreamed the same riddle that she had. Should she be concerned? She didn't see that it would help anything.

By this time, they had entered the city's outskirts and now passed through the busy crowds. Clerans took Ella by the hand — a courtesy she was still getting used to. The shoppers and city folk of Entwerp were as bright and cheery as ever, tipping their hats to her as she passed and stepping aside to keep from jostling her.

"Ay," Clerans whispered, "I'll should be sure to bring ye with me every time I'll walk the streets. It is easier walkin' with a lady along."

"I don't know," Ella replied. "Most times you walk the street, Lexi says you a'e vaulting ove'h fences and walking ove'h wooftops. Would you take a lady along for that?"

Clerans flashed a roguish smile at her. "Are ye sayin' that ye do no want to walk across a roof with me?"

"Not pa'ticula'ly." Ella replied.

Just then, Ella heard a distant shout coming from further down the street. Ella glanced at Clerans, but he looked off in the noise's direction.

The shout came again, but this time it was louder. It sounded like the voices of maybe a hundred people.

Clerans caught a passerby by the sleeve. "Halloo, sir, God bless ye. Do ye know what that sound is?"

The man shook his head. "I cen no say."

Clerans arrested another man similarly.

"God bless ye. Do ye know what is goin' on?"

The man frowned. "Ay, younker, it is the strikers."

"The strikers?" Clerans asked.

"Ay," the man replied. "They are leavin' Nychweni Square."

Clerans raised an eyebrow. "An' where are they venin' to?"

The man shrugged. "Yer guess is as good as mine," and he walked on.

Ella looked at Clerans closely. She was stiff with the recollection of those strikers. She did not like them at all. Why were they leaving Nychweni Square? This didn't seem to bode well.

Clerans stood on his tiptoes, trying to see what was going on over the crowd.

"If I'll could only get a gard at 'em," Clerans breathed aloud. "I wonder which direction they're venin' in..."

Just then, there was another shout — very close this time. The crowd cleared away in an instant, leaving the street wide open. Clerans took one look before he pulled Ella into an alleyway off the street. Marching down the middle of the road in a shoddy, military style, came the strikers. It was the same motley group Ella had seen before — mostly humans but with a few gnomes, leprechauns, and faeries. They made a conspicuous appearance with their long, unkempt beards, rough clothing, and scowling faces. Many also bore weapons — an axe, a pistol, a knife, a tomahawk, a rough-worn rifle.

They marched past slowly and deliberately. Now and then, on some unseen signal, they would all let out a single shout in unison.

The memory of Ella's previous experience in the strikers' camp came to her again, and Ella shivered. She did not like these men. They were gross, filthy, and terrifying.

Yet the strikers took no notice of anyone as they marched by, keeping their course in the middle of the road, hardly even looking to either side as they plowed ahead. They set their jaws in determination — almost a cruel determination, Ella imagined.

Clerans tapped his finger to his chin as he watched the strikers pass. "What do ye think they'll could be up to?"

Ella didn't reply.

"They are headed due west," Clerans mused. "They could no be after the National Bank, then. Ye do no think they would vene to the factories, do ye?"

At that moment, Ella heard a low *click* from behind her. She wouldn't have thought anything of it except that Clerans sprung to the side like a startled wildcat, throwing her flat on the ground.

There was the sound of a knife coming clear of its sheath, and something metallic hit the pavement. Ella looked up to see Sheriff Laei standing behind them. His hand was out as if he had been holding something, but Clerans gripped the sheriff's wrist tightly, holding his skinning knife poised in his other hand.

The sheriff smiled. "Well done, Clerans. Ye are merri intuitive."

Clerans smiled, letting go of the sheriff's wrist and sheathing his knife. "Thank ye, sir."

Clerans bent down and picked up a pistol that lay in the alleyway nearby. He handed it back to Sheriff Laei.

Sheriff Laei nodded in thanks again and turned to Ella as he stuck the pistol back in his belt. "Ye are in good hands, miss, one o' the best bodyguards this town tains to offer."

Clerans smiled and shrugged his shoulders. "Aw, now..."

The sheriff raised his hand. "But I did no simply vene to test yer reflexes, Clerans, though I am sure ye could learn something' if ye'll stuck around to watch."

"The strikers," Clerans said, motioning with his thumb over his shoulder. "Are they cedin' to the factories?"

The sheriff nodded grimly. "Ay, there are about fifty o' them there already."

Clerans frowned. "What do they mean on doin'?"

The sheriff furrowed his brow in response. "I do no know. But I mean to trive out. Do ye wish to follow?"

Clerans nodded eagerly. "Ye'll need another hand, sure, if it'll venes to a fight!"

The sheriff turned and marched down the street after the strikers. "Let us hope it does no vene to that."

As Clerans dashed out of the alleyway to follow the sheriff, Ella stepped in line behind him, her heart sinking down into her shoes. Yes, she thought, let us hope it does not come to that.

20

DAY BREAK

aeli woke with the slowness of ice melting from an alpine lake. She first felt a cold sensation at the tip of her nose, which slowly seemed to spread to her entire face. Her first instinct was to huddle back down into her blankets, but she opened her eyes for an instant. She lay with her eyes shut again for a moment until her brain registered what she had seen. She snapped her eyes back open and looked around. Sure enough, all over the campsite sat a pale frost.

The sun had just poked its head above the eastern horizon, and the first golden sunbeams now filtered through the trees, reflecting off a million minuscule rows of crystal on every leaf and blade of grass. But it was only a light frost, and as Haeli watched, it melted into vapor, which floated like misty ghosts in the air. Martyn sat hunched over the fire, his hands stretched out, the frost steaming off his over-jacket, earmuffs, and tricorn hat. The smoke from the fire seemed to mingle inseparably with the mist from the melting frost so that Haeli could almost imagine that the fire itself was nothing more than frosted logs welcoming the frosted morning.

Haeli sat up, wrapping the blankets tightly around herself

and shivering. She sighed deeply and watched as her cloudy breath danced above the frost's lingering steam. She smiled broadly and shivered again.

Martyn looked up at her and grinned. "First frost," and his eyes danced.

"It is so beautiful," Haeli gasped in wonder, still watching her breath as it steamed from her mouth like vapor escaping a boiling cup of tea.

Martyn nodded, "Ay, one o' the most beautiful things ye'll will ever see." He paused and looked around again with a dreamy light in his eyes. "First frost," and he said the words almost as if they were sacred. "What a merri sight it is. An' to think that it only lasts fer a small portion o' an hour, before it all vanishes into the mist, an' then the mist itself clears."

Martyn sighed. "Ay, God is a queer artist to paint a sight o' sheer beauty an' only leave it there fer sich a small time. Ye would almost miss it if ye'll were no gardin' fer it. An' yet, ye cen no gard fer it, since ye do no know when it'll will happen. Ye'll will jist wake up one day, an' there it is. Or ye'll will sleep in too long, and it is gone, an' ye ha' missed it."

Already Haeli could tell that the frost on the trees was gone, and frost on the grass was also quickly melting. "I wonder if this is what Heaven will look like."

Martyn grinned widely. "Only that it will last forever?"

"But is it the *same* forever?" Haeli asked. "Or maybe it will be moments like this, moments of sheer ecstasy and beauty all one after another."

Martyn squinted up his eyes and looked out at the sunrise. "Ay, perhaps. With God there in the middle o' it all, directin' each moment like a conductor o' an eternal symphony. Oh ay, perhaps."

They sat silently for a moment. Suddenly, Haeli thought she could hear some kind of tribal drumming, then realized that it was the sound of slow footsteps on the road, accompanied by the *tap, tap, tap* of a cane.

In a moment, they could see the shape of a man through the trees as he made his way slowly down the road. Haeli looked at him closely but couldn't see much through the foliage. She could only tell that he was a rather large man with a cloak wrapped tightly around him, and he walked along using a cane. Just then, the smoke from the fire blew into Haeli's eyes, and she turned away with a loud cough.

The blind man paused in the road. "Hello? Is someone there?"

Haeli looked over at Martyn. He seemed uncertain.

"Hello?" the man on the road called again.

"Do no be alarmed," Martyn replied. "We are jist fellow travelers, like yerself."

"But you are off the road," the man replied.

"Ay," Martyn replied. "We ha' been spendin' the night on our way to Entwerp."

"Does that mean you have a fire?"

Martyn looked over at Haeli quizzically, and she looked back at him. He had better have something to say, because she would not get involved.

"Ay," Martyn finally said.

"Ah!" The man on the road sighed. "What a relief. I have been looking for somewhere I could cook my breakfast."

With that, the man turned off the road and began making his way toward the camp. He picked his way slowly through the underbrush, feeling forward with his cane, until he came to the little clearing. Haeli looked the man over carefully. He seemed to have a large frame but was bent slightly with age. He wore a very large coat to stave off the cold and a white rag tied loosely across his eyes, mingling with the bleach white of his hair. Feeling his way with his cane, he came to the fire.

"Ah," he sighed again. "You do not know how hard it is to get a fire going when you are like me." And the man laughed at his own joke.

Haeli smiled but still studied the man. His voice was deep, and Haeli couldn't decide if she found it soothing or intimidating.

The man sat cross-legged before the fire and pulled out a small parcel from the folds of his cloak. Carefully, he unwrapped it, revealing some raw meat and spices. Haeli thought that the parcel's wrapping was itself odd. It almost looked like an old piece of parchment, and she could see odd shapes and symbols, like an ancient script, scrawled all over the inside. The man sprinkled the spices onto the meat.

Martyn also watched the man closely, glancing back and forth between him and Haeli. Finally, Martyn cleared his throat. "Ay, well, ye are free to enjoy the fire, but we oughtta-should be cedin'."

"So soon?" the man asked. "I would be much obliged if you would stay and chat for a little. Few people have the decency to do that anymore, you know."

"Ay," Martyn said, "We do no want to be late..." He looked over at Haeli as if looking for her support.

Haeli nodded. "We do not mean to be rude, sir, but we were about to cede on our way, anyway. We must–"

The man suddenly threw the rest of his spices into the fire. Haeli stopped in mid-sentence.

"You do not need to leave," the man said.

At the words, Haeli felt herself weighed down with the distinct sense that she didn't want to leave just then. She wanted to sit by the fire and relax. What was the hurry? She *should* want to leave; she *should* want to get on her way so that they could make it to Entwerp in good time, but she didn't. For some reason, though she felt like she ought to be concerned and suspicious, but she wasn't.

Haeli looked over at Martyn to see him blinking and shaking

his head as if trying to shake off drowsiness during a long night watch.

"Let me introduce myself," the man continued, placing his meat on a stick and holding it out over the fire. "My name is Syd Cartwright." He paused and studied Haeli and Martyn closely. "Does that name mean anything to you?"

Martyn shook his head, still as if fighting sleep. "I do no know; what wos that?"

"No?" the stranger said. "What about Jock Blowhoarder? Does that name mean anything to you?"

Haeli felt as if she had heard the name before but didn't feel like she could say so.

The stranger smiled disarmingly as he stirred the fire with his stick. Haeli felt as if it was mildly odd for him to do so, considering he had meat on the end of the stick.

"I believe I ha' heard the name," Martyn said, blinking owlishly.

"What about Silas Pickering or Saemwel Pickering? Have you heard those names before?" The man asked, still smiling.

Haeli nodded. "Ay, we know both of them." The words seemed to come unbidden to her mouth.

"Ah," the man said, "that is the *key*, isn't it?" He looked at Haeli pointedly.

Haeli again felt that she should be alarmed, but she wasn't. She felt almost comfortable sitting there with the stranger. She found she was laughing, as if the stranger had cracked a joke.

A light breeze played in the trees, and the smoke from the fire shifted. For a moment, Haeli felt as if a wind had blown away a thick fog from her brain, and she felt a complete panic flood through every fiber of her being. Then, the mist settled again, and she slumped forward, feeling like weights held down every part of her body.

Martyn, however, leaped to his feet. "Here now," he cried. "What's the meanin' o' all o' this?"

The stranger looked surprised. "I do not understand. What are you so alarmed at?"

Martyn's eyes narrowed. "Who are ye, an' what are ye?"

"Just a poor, blind mendicant; who else would I be?"

"A sorcerer, mayhaps!" And Martyn's hand strayed towards his tomahawk.

The stranger raised his hand, and Martyn's knees seemed to buckle in exhaustion. He fell to the ground.

"There is no reason for alarm," the stranger said. "This is all very easy." He turned to look Haeli in the eye.

Haeli felt as if she would fall asleep in a moment, but she strained to keep her eyes open as the stranger peered at her.

"I have a door — a very particular door — that needs to be opened, and I believe that you, my dear, have the key."

Haeli felt words forming, unbidden, on her tongue. "Ay–" she caught herself and, with an effort of great willpower, forced herself to close her mouth. As she did so, a fresh wave of exhaustion flooded over her, almost as if some dark and nebulous force were swallowing the air around her, leaving nothing to breathe. She felt very dizzy.

"Do not be afraid," the stranger said soothingly. "You look very sick. Let me give you something for your head." He reached back into his pouch.

Just then, Martyn leaped back to his feet as if throwing off a great chain. He drew out his pistol and leveled it at the stranger. "Do no move, or ye are a dead man!"

The stranger turned towards Martyn with that same disarming smile and raised his hand again.

At that instant, there was a loud *crack* like some great canvas snapping against itself in a high wind. Haeli looked up as the Eagle Griffin from last night dropped like lightning into the camp, his claws extended as he streaked towards Martyn.

Martyn collapsed to the ground before the stranger's outstretched hand, and the griffin missed his mark, landing instead directly in the fire. The griffin cursed loudly as he danced about, scattering coals in every direction and fanning them back to life as he beat the air with his mighty wings to raise himself off the ground.

Again, Haeli felt as if a fog had lifted while the rushes of air from the griffin's wing-strokes wafted over her. She felt as if she were breathing air for the first time in a very long time, and she breathed deeply and greedily of it.

Martyn was on his feet in an instant, firing his pistol at the griffin.

The griffin screeched and thrust down with his wings again as he wheeled at Martyn. Smoke wafted into the air from all across the hollow now as each coal from the fire warmed under the steady rushes of air from the griffin's wing-strokes.

The stranger leaped to his feet, his hands extended towards the griffin. "Not him, you fool, the girl. What are you doing?"

Martyn struck out with his empty pistol and caught the stranger across the face with the still-smoking barrel. The stranger pitched backward with a tremendous yell, and Martyn snatched up his rifle to face the griffin.

Haeli struggled to her feet, staring all the time at Martyn, where he stood with the smoke from a dozen different embers curling around him.

"What is happening? What do I do?"

At that moment, a cedar tree on the hollow's edge burst into flames. As the griffin wheeled now and struck out at Martyn. Martyn beat the griffin back with his rifle butt.

"Run, Haeli, run!"

Haeli turned and took a few steps toward the road. There, in front of her, stood the blind stranger. He smiled benignly and held out his hand. Haeli didn't even wait for him to speak but took off at a dead sprint in the opposite direction. She hardly thought as she leaped the small ditch on the other side of the road. Her body simply moved with no input from her brain. She was on Panic, riding it like a horse at a mad gallop. She did not have time for thoughts. By the time thoughts registered in her mind again, she was careening downhill too fast to stop herself.

In front of her, the earth dropped off in a wide cliff, and the boom of surf echoed up from afar. She screamed, waving frantically with her arms for anything to stop herself. Her hands caught a thorn bush almost on the cliff's edge. The thorns gouged into her flesh and tore at her dress, slowing her greatly. Her foot landed with her heel on solid ground and her toes hanging in thin air. Her heart pounded in her chest as all time seemed to slow. She could see the swelling ocean far below her, the stinging smell of salt assaulting her nose. But she was still moving forward. She was in the balance now, only a hair's breadth from tipping over the cliff. Then, the thorn branch she was holding snapped, and she toppled forward over the cliff's edge, nothing but the wind's mercy between her and certain death at the ocean's hands below.

21

HARANGUE

*E*lla and Clerans followed the Sheriff as closely as they could through the crowd. Gone were the merry faces of a moment before, and the whole town seemed to have turned at once pensive and melancholy. As she passed, Ella could hear many of the townspeople whispering to each other.

"Where do ye think they are venin'?"

"What are they about?"

"Wos no that the sheriff, jist now passin'?"

And from some, Ella heard the phrase, "Baptize those strikers," muttered emphatically.

After following Clerans for what must have been half a mile, the shops and houses stopped abruptly to make room for a wide square. Unlike the other squares Ella had seen, this was not entirely made of cobblestone, but had several circles of grass and flowers planted regularly among the cobblestones. A tall aspen tree stood in a few of these circles of greenery, standing out like an island amidst a sea of red brick. The plaza was about a hundred yards square. The neatly laid-out greenery gave the square a cheery look, and the air was fresh, tinged with the sweet scent of the blooming flowers. At the far end from where

Ella had entered, a wrought-iron fence ran about eight feet high with an arched gate directly in the middle. All about the fence were more trees and flowers, and it looked like there was even more greenery on the fence's other side. Behind the fence rose the huge sides of the factories. They couldn't have been any older than Ella, and they appeared to be well kept — no peeling paint on their white gables and no cracked mortar between the rows upon rows of neatly laid brick. Ella glimpsed the river behind the factories as it rushed by, turning the waterwheels with tremendous flow. That was undoubtedly how the factories powered all of their machinery.

The strikers rapidly filled the square outside the factories — now, maybe a hundred of them — standing before the fence. An even larger crowd of curious onlookers ranged on the square's perimeter, keeping their distance from the strikers. On the other side of the fence, another crowd gathered, too.

Ella guessed that these must be the factory workers. They all appeared to be rough and hardworking men and women, not nearly as wild or ferocious as the strikers. As with the rest of the population, they were mostly human, though Ella identified several dwarves, nymphs, gnomes, and faeriefolk among them. Several of these workers — Ella guessed they were supervisors by their cleaner clothing — ranged directly in front of the fence, scowling at the strikers through the wrought-iron bars. Among these supervisors, Ella noticed a familiar face. Mrs. Blaeith stood near the front, watching the strikers assembling and frowning. Ella felt her heart leap. Hopefully, nothing would come of this. She would not want any harm to come to Mrs. Blaeith.

Just then, Ella saw a lanky man come striding out of the crowd of onlookers. He walked briskly and confidently right along the fence between the strikers and the factory workers. Reaching the gate, he turned to face the strikers. Ella could get a good look at him now. He appeared to be middle-aged, though with more wrinkles and care than he should have had for that period of life. Every part of his body seemed to be rather too long, with little girth, from his lanky arms and legs, to his narrow torso and face. His shoulders were broad, and Ella guessed he must have been a sturdy man in his younger years.

As this tall man looked over the strikers sternly, the right side of his face twitched involuntarily, almost as if he were a clock, alerting the crowd to the passing of each second. There seemed to be some kind of pus oozing from this same right eye, but he wiped it away with the cuff of his sleeve as if out of habit.

Clerans leaned over and whispered in Ella's ear, "That is Governor Braedhwyc. He wos a cannoneer fer Caedmon Wilkins durin' the war."

"What is it you want?" the governor asked in a harsh and wheezy voice.

There was an indistinct murmur from the strikers, and one of them stepped forward. Ella couldn't help but think that of all the rough and vile individuals in that group, this spokesman was the roughest and vilest. His clothing was filthy, wrinkled, and stained, with no regular buttons to hold it together. His greasy black hair fell back to his shoulders, and his matted and unkempt beard reached down to his cockeyed collar, where a bear-claw amulet hung out from behind it. He stood cocked back on one leg, his head tilted askew, and his eyes squinted — like a sailor straining to see the first signs of land.

"What do ye think we're after, eh?"

Governor Braedhwyc's face twitched, but otherwise, his grim expression didn't change.

Seeing no answer, this spokesman sneered and went on. "Ye know why we are all here: the Company ha' fired us. All o' us what worked so hard to keep them beacons runnin' fer so long."

The other strikers grumbled in approval.

"I still wait to hear an explanation o' why you are standin' in front o' this factory," Governor Braedhwyc said levelly.

"Oh, ay, is that no enough o' an explanation fer ye?" the spokesman taunted.

"No," Governor Braedhwyc replied, wiping his eye absent-mindedly. "Typically, men who lose their jobs trive up some other useful job so that they tain food to give their wives and children."

A low snicker rose from the factory workers on the other side of the wrought-iron fence.

The spokesman smiled cheekily. "Well, mayhaps that's why we're here, then, eh?"

At this, a man on the factory side of the fence pushed his way up to the gate. He wore cleaner clothes than even the supervisors, with a well-pressed suit, a starched collar, and an impeccable cravat.

"Not a single one o' you is about to ceive a single job at my factory if that is what ye'll are venin' fer!"

This set the entire crowd of strikers into a loud murmur. The spokesman simply smiled and winked. "Sure, no, cap'n, I do no think anyone o' us would want to work fer *ye* neither."

"What is it you want?" Governor Braedhwyc asked again, his face ticking as if disdainful of the joke.

"We want work!" a striker yelled, apparently tired of the spokesman talking for him.

"Ay, ay!" the strikers returned.

"You will tain none from me!" the factory owner shrieked back.

The strikers murmured loudly in reply, and many pulled out their weapons. One striker unslung his rifle and fired it into the air viciously. The factory owner stepped back from the gate, and Ella winced at the sharp report.

"Hold!"

All eyes turned to Sheriff Laei as he stepped from the crowd behind the strikers with two horse pistols drawn. "The next man to fire any gun — be it a threat or even an accident — I will shoot him dead."

Before any striker responded to this, Governor Braedhwyc spoke again. "All o' you know why you ha' been released from the Company's services: The Company cen no afford to keep you employed. Ye would no ha' any better luck here even if ye'll could convince Mr. Eosterling to hire ye. In a month, he could no afford to pay ye either, an' back ye would vene to the street."

"We want work!" the same striker yelled again.

"And what the conversion do you want me to do about it?" Governor Braedhwyc roared, totally losing all composure.

"We are workmen. We must tain work," the spokesman sneered.

"You are no workmen," Governor Braedhwyc replied, still yelling at the top of his lungs. "You are baptized, lay-about, hibernatin' sloths is what you are! You do no work, an' you are no *men*. You are toddlers in a pout, stampin' your foot since someone told you 'no.' I do no care if the Company does fire a thousand more cabbages like you, and I do no care if every single one o' ye starves. Baptize the lot o' you!"

The strikers yelled back in reply, but their cries were so loud and confused that Ella could understand nothing they said. Finally, the spokesman raised his hands, and the strikers grew silent again.

The spokesman flashed a cheeky smile. "Now see here, Gov'nor, ye know as well as any that without work, we'd be forced to *desperate* measures an' may no strictly keep in legal bounds, eh?"

The governor's face ticked, and he scowled darkly. "Ay, you are criminals too, then."

The spokesman held his palms out defensively. "Ah, now, Gov'nor. Now, o' course we would no *willingly* stoop to crime, but without a job... who knows what we may do? Ye see, it is in yer best interest to make us well-situated. Ye would no want a hundred more privers to clean off o' yer streets?"

"Stop blatherin', ye fool," Governor Braedhwyc growled, "and tell me what ye are here fer?"

The spokesman smiled. "Ay, oh, what are we here fer?" The spokesman gave a low chuckle. "Ye know — and we know — why the Company fired us. Oh, ay, we know! The Company cen no survive. It is about to die — an' probably soon. We are jist the very first o' the layoffs, and we are about to see a merri o' more. We could all scatter across Megalytia an' Oligia an' trive up work in the factories, but what about the next beacon-tenders what lose their jobs? Where will they trive up work? An' where will the next batch after that trive up work? And then, who will hire the last batch when the whole Beacon Company falls apart? An' too, who will make sure the beacons stay lit so that the merchants keep venin' around our coast? An' when the merchants stop venin', and the money runs out — then what?"

The spokesman paused for dramatic effect.

Governor Braedhwyc wiped his eye. "Yer point?"

"Oh, ay," the spokesman replied, "the point, ye ask? Were the Beacon Company to fail, it would cause a national crisis fer everyone. Whether ye will believe it or no, the Company *is* failing, an' we are only the harbingers o' that failure."

"Do ye propose, then, that we *all* quit our work an' lay about in the town square to prepare fer the fall o' the Company?" Governor Braedhwyc asked. "Mayhaps we should bang on gongs and keen about this approachin' doomsday?"

"Oh, no, Gov'nor, we all need work," the spokesman replied with another cheeky smile. "The fact is, without the Beacon Company, we could no all tain work. What we need is someone to *ceive over* the Company and keep it afloat. An' that, Gov'nor, is where ye arrive on the scene."

The governor's face ticked, but he made no reply.

"There's only one institution what even *begins* to compare to the Company in size. Ye know o' what I speak, Gov'nor: the government itself. That's the only thing what cen ceive over the Company, eh?"

Governor Braedhwyc snorted incredulously. "The government would never ceive over the Company. It is no their goal, wish, or purpose to employ brutes like ye to protect a few merchant ships. Sich measures would be totally outside constitutional bounds."

"A few merchant ships?" the spokesman replied. "Oh, no, Gov'nor, the whole economic backbone o' the country, that's what the Company is protectin'. An' it is the government's solemn responsibility to protect them fer the sake o' the citizens. Why put that much responsibility in the hands of greedy, corrupt businessmen?"

Governor Braedhwyc wiped puss from his eye, visibly irritated with the strikers' spokesman. "If the Company fails, it fails. Whether the merchants are the backbone o' our country or no, is beside the point. Those *useful* workers will simply trive out new work to create a new backbone o' our country. It is no up to the government to decide which businesses need protectin' and which ones do no, and as the governor o' this city, I reject yer plan!"

"Well," the spokesman said, grinning from ear to ear, "I s'pose we're reduced to hagglin'."

The governor's face ticked a few times before he answered. "I do no haggle with rabble."

"Ay, but I do," the spokesman replied cheekily. "An' here's what I say: ye will recommend our plan to the Government — to the Lord Protector Caedmon Wilkins himself if ye'll ha' to — an' we will stay here until they enact our plan. An' until then–" the spokesman paused for dramatic effect, a leering smile playing about his lips, "–until then, no one leaves or enters the factories."

2 2

OVER-PASSING

*E*rnest pulled himself out of the water, his mind still reeling with the implications of the conversation he had overheard. He could hardly make sense of everything. He found Bill and Tell waiting for him on the beach. Tell lay spread out obnoxiously, displaying his massive body as if sunbathing, while Bill huddled up tightly, his spindly frame wrapped around his bony knees like a dead spider.

Ernest felt something warm on his face. Looking to the east, he could see the smallest etchings of red on the horizon above the mountains, heralding the dawning of another day. Ernest sighed.

"There you are," Bill hissed as he saw Ernest emerging from the water. "What do'ed you leave us for?"

"Yes," Tell said, sitting up and rubbing his jaw. "Where were you?"

Ernest swallowed. His throat was dry — surely that was only because of the salt water. "Ah, nothing much. I was just curious."

Bill raised an eyebrow. "'Curiosity is the antelope's doom.'"

Ernest shrugged.

Tell looked over at Bill in confusion. "How's that?"

"What?" Bill asked.

"'Curiosity is the antelope's doom?'"

"True; that it is."

Tell scratched his head. "How's that?"

"Eh?" Bill looked at him with irritation.

"But how *is* it?" Tell asked again, just as irritated.

Ernest knew he had best intervene. "How's some breakfast sound?"

Bill and Tell both looked over at him.

"You have breakfast?" Bill asked skeptically.

Ernest nodded as he pulled out the sack that Lewis had given him. Opening it, he found it still dry inside — much to his satisfaction. "Ay, Lewis gave it to me before we left."

"Good old Lewis," Tell breathed with a contented smile on his face.

They ate their breakfast rather hurriedly and then set off inland with the rising sun in their faces. It was rather rough going at first, as they had to force their way through the woodlands. This close to the bay, the forest was dense and full of thorn bushes and vines, making their hike rather tedious. Added to this, they were all cold and wet. Ernest plowed forward doggedly, trusting that the physical exercise would eventually warm him up.

As they climbed up the mountainside, the underbrush thinned, and the trees started growing farther apart. Soon they passed into open aspen groves and through the denser pine groves. Still, the going was rough and slow as they continually ran into cliffs and boulders — both large and small. They diverted their path accordingly as they continued their steady, if tortuous, ascent. Finally, the woods petered out all together, and before them stretched a narrow space of open ground. Ernest could see the high road ahead, almost at the end of the plain.

Once they reached the road, they took a brief rest. Ernest guessed by the sun's position that they had been walking for about three hours. As he looked out over the way they had climbed, he could barely see the bay far below, but he couldn't make out either pirate ship. The morning fog still clung to the low places and hollows along the mountains' lower slopes, and Ernest was pretty sure he could see a light frost in the shadowed recess which had not yet seen the sun.

Within moments they resumed their journey, now heading due north down the High Road. They couldn't be far from Entwerp, Ernest guessed. They were over halfway between the fort they had raided the other night and the town of Entwerp itself.

Now they made rapid progress, all three of them walking briskly with no impediment. With the sun warming them more directly, and with the energy of their exercise, they took off their overcoats and held them slung over their arms. They were finally beginning to dry off fully from their icy swim that morning.

Soon enough, Ernest noticed some trampled underbrush branching off to the left.

"Look," Ernest said, pointing to the makeshift trail. "What do you make of that?"

Tell squinted at where he pointed. "Eh..." he said with his mouth hanging open. "It looks like grass, maybe?"

Bill made as if to punch Tell in the ribs, but Tell stepped out of the way before the blow fell.

"On course it's grass, idiot!" Bill turned on Ernest. "What on it?"

"It's a trail," Ernest replied.

"Hardly that," Bill said with a sniff.

Ernest shrugged. "It looks like maybe a path that a group on people would have taken to set up camp just off the highway, is what it looks like to me."

Tell gasped in awe. "Why do'edn't I think on that? That makes a lot on sense."

"Maybe you should start thinking in the first place," Bill muttered.

Ernest left the two messmates to continue their argument while he stepped off the highway and followed the footpath down into a little hollow. Much to his own satisfaction, he found this hollow was indeed the site of a camp. Yet this camping ground was in a total state of chaos. The coals that were left from the fire lay strewn about all over the hollow, many of these embers still glowing hot. A cedar tree at the far end of the hollow was smoldering and burnt down to the trunk. A couple of blankets still lay on the ground, wadded up as if kicked about in a great commotion. As Ernest examined the ground more closely, he could see blood sprinkled in a few places.

Ernest raised his eyebrows and shook his head. This was a mess. Just then, he heard Bill and Tell coming into the hollow behind him.

"Baptism," Bill cursed. "What happened here?"

Tell shook his head. "*Something* happened here."

Ernest noticed some strange marks on the ground right around where the fire must have been. Bending down and examining them, he could tell it was a footprint of an enormous cat, or maybe a wolf. He glanced around the campsite again, noticing another track that looked like the talons of a massive bird of prey. Only one animal could have made both tracks.

Ernest stood up again and dusted himself off. "It's Cweel's doing, whatever it was."

Tell looked astonished. "How do you know?"

Ernest shrugged nonchalantly. "I can see into the past."

Tell's eyes bulged in further astonishment. "Why do'edn't you say so?"

Bill punched him neatly in the ribs. "He's making a fool on you!"

Ernest turned out of the hollow, meandering back to the

High Road. Tell followed behind after a moment, and Bill pursued him.

"I amn't a fool," Tell said, crossing his arms over his chest. "I might be slow, but you willn't make me a fool."

"You're doing it to yourself," Bill replied.

No sooner had Ernest reached the road again than he saw a solitary figure trudging up the High Road to the south. He hissed back at Bill and Tell, and instantly Bill was silent.

"What is it?" Tell whispered loudly.

Ernest peered at the figure. He was still a good way off, but Ernest could tell he was wrapped in a dark cloak. Could it be the Albino? No, surely not. This man was limping and slumped over. He walked like a defeated man. The Albino didn't walk like that.

Ernest, Bill, and Tell remained motionless as the figure continued to approach. Ernest kept his gaze fixed on that solitary figure.

"Should we hide?" Bill whispered, "If'n he looks up, he could see us."

As if on cue, the figure stopped and looked up, staring the three pirates in the face. It was indeed the Albino.

"Finally, you are here," he said, and even from that distance, Ernest could sense the frustration in his voice.

The Albino again bowed his head and trudged forward. The pirates remained where they were, not sure what to do. Ernest watched the Archeomancer intently. He was *limping*.

The Albino didn't look up again until he had walked right up to the pirates. Then he again stopped, regarding them closely.

Ernest was surprised to see a welt all along the left side of the Albino's face and what might be the beginnings of a black eye. He slouched over, keeping weight off of his left leg. Ernest had seen the Albino fell trees and demolish oak doors with a few muttered words, and he couldn't help but wonder what kind of power could have done this to the Archeomancer.

The Albino's pink eyes burned with vengeful anger. "Well?"

Ernest saluted smartly. He wasn't sure what else to do under the circumstances.

"You are rather late."

Ernest swallowed. He didn't enjoy talking to this man. "I do'edn't realize we haved a time–"

The Albino raised his hand to cut Ernest off in mid-sentence. "I do not want to hear a single excuse from you. You *are* late, and that is that."

"What happened to you?" Tell asked.

Ernest felt like crawling into a hole for mortification at Tell's question.

The Albino's eyes flashed with a sudden dreadful fire of anger, and all three pirates stepped back. "What happened, you ask?" The Albino seemed to calm himself. He breathed deeply and stood more squarely on his two feet, resuming more of his wonted composure. "I was rebuffed, we shall say."

Ernest still held his breath. 'Rebuffed' sounded like an awfully short word to describe an incident that would bring the Albino down to such a level. Even as Ernest thought this, the Albino straightened himself up, resuming his former intimidating size.

"You did not appear to be coming here soon, so I made an attempt on the girl myself, and nearly succeeded. I should have waited for you before making such a bold move. As it is, that baptized griffin spoiled the entire operation, and I was physically assaulted by one of those anointed beacon-tenders who has spent the last two hours hunting me all over this mountainside. He would probably be hunting me still if I had not evaded him with a cloak of darkness."

The Albino paused. Ernest tried to picture this scene in his mind but failed. He had particular trouble imagining a Pistosian beacon-tender attacking the Albino without being struck dead on the spot by a lightning bolt. Then again, if this bacon-tender was anything like that satyr who routed Killjelly and his men, this scene might be a little more believable.

The Albino's eyes flashed with anger again. "I could not cast a spell on him! Nothing would–" He cut himself short, again regaining his composure. "It was rather humiliating, as you can see, to be routed by a common man — though I suppose I should take it as a lesson. It was my overconfidence that had me attempt to get the keys in the first place, and I should not give way to it again."

The Albino now turned back to the pirates, eyeing them all over. "But now, what am I to do with you?"

Ernest swallowed. "They sent us to get the key from that girl?"

Just then, the Albino bristled. He whipped his head around. "Is it him? Again?" After only a brief look behind him, the Albino hissed in warning. "Down! Get down, all of you. In the brush — hide!"

Ernest, Bill, and Tell did as they were told, throwing themselves flat on the ground and scuttling for cover behind the nearest tree or into the nearest bush.

23

DISSOLUTION

"You cen no keep us in!" a factory workers yelled from behind the wrought-iron fence.

"Cen no we, eh?" the spokesmen said. "We tain weapons to keep you there. But I reckon you do no tain weapons to help you get out."

There was a low murmur from the factory workers.

The spokesman turned back to the governor. "If ye'll will still refuse to grant our wish, then after the factories die, we will cede to the bank, an' ye know merri well that if the bank is to fail, all o' Llaedhwyth would feel that! What do ye say, Gov'nor?"

Sheriff Laei answered in a low voice. "This is what I say, slug: You will all — everyone o' ye — leave this square, or I will hold you as public criminals."

"To what end, eh?" the spokesman replied with a sneer.

"A bloody one," he replied from behind the strikers.

The strikers turned to face the sheriff now, murmuring among themselves.

"To put it briefly," Sheriff Laei said, "I will give you the space o' twenty minutes to leave this square. At the end o' twenty minutes, I will shoot anyone who remains."

Several strikers — and the onlookers, too — took a step back from the sheriff, but the spokesman stood his ground, laughing cynically. "Ye cen no fight us all at once."

"Who says I am alone?" Sheriff Laei asked.

As if in answer to this, a couple of men in the crowd of onlookers held up rifles for all to see.

"Besides," the sheriff said, "how would you'll stop me? Would you'll mob me? Attack me? Would you'll shoot me or lynch me? An' what would any o' that be but an obstruction o' justice an' open violence against a minister o' the law — an' that deed done, too, before the eyes o' an hundred witnesses. No, my misguided fellow, be sure that this deed would send all o' you to your deaths."

The strikers shifted positions nervously. Some fingered their weapons as if ready to strike the sheriff dead where he stood, while others looked this way and that, like frightened animals looking for a way of escape.

The sheriff eyed the mob, fixing the spokesman with a special gaze. "I know no why you'll ha' chosen Entwerp o' all places fer your strike. Fer though it will make your strike the more public, it will also make your straits the merri o' more desperate. Therefore, I think it fair to warn you further: Lord Protector Caedmon Wilkins himself ha' been summoned."

This brought an audible gasp from the onlookers, strikers, and factory workers alike. Ella looked around to see the look of shock in every face present, though she could see in Clerans' eye a look more akin to eager anticipation.

Sheriff Laei continued, "Be advised then, that what deeds you do here will be merri well brought back upon your heads with justice ten times over." He looked at the strikers steadily, contempt and determination in his eye. "There, two minutes ha' passed already, each o' ye tains eighteen left to save his life."

The strikers looked at each other, many visibly nervous. The spokesman only smiled, "Yer threatenin's do no sway us, cap'n!"

Now Governor Braedhwyc spoke, his face still ticking out the time, "Your choice is simple: stay, an' you are condemned, fight, an' you are condemned. If you'll would hope fer any mercy fer your miserable plight, then you must return to Nych-weni Square."

The strikers looked from the governor to the sheriff and then to each other, but no one spoke a word. Sheriff Laei cocked his pistols back to full position but kept them pointed at the ground. The spokesman's face clouded with what might have been uncertainty, and he looked as if he were about to speak, but Sheriff Laei spoke first.

"Ay, that is your choice. Now I will count fer the seventeen minutes you tain to decide."

He stood there silently while the three groups stood facing each other: the factory workers, peering through the iron fence bitterly, the onlookers watching and hardly daring to breathe while they positioned themselves to either run or join in should a fight ensue and the strikers between the two of these groups, standing between resolution and dissolution.

Ella could feel the tension in the air. The sheriff stood nearly motionless, with his two pistols in his hands, their long barrels almost touching the square's cobblestones. To Ella's mind, these pistols were like living animals — hounds of death that the sheriff held leashed at his heels. He could, in an instant, release them to vomit out fire and death upon the strikers.

The strikers themselves watched this as well. None stood so firm as the sheriff, but none seemed as if he would leave. Each striker fingered his weapon and crouched slightly, his weight shifting and his eyes darting this way and that as if debating between fighting or fleeing. Behind all of this stood the governor, tall and stark, his face ticking still, as if each twitch were the seconds left before the conflict. His hand wiped puss from his eye like the minute hand passing across the face of a clock.

Ella could hardly let herself breathe as she watched. Surely ten minutes had passed already. The onlookers now grew anxious themselves. Undoubtedly, this would end in a fight. Much of the crowd drew back further towards the square's edge, where they might find cover after the first shot.

Just then, a large man pushed past Ella. She looked over to see him carrying a rifle in one hand. He pushed close to the front of the crowd and stopped. Ella looked about her to see that many more men and women had arrived, each with a rifle and most bearing knives and tomahawks as well. These must be militia members coming to aid the sheriff in the inevitable fight.

Ella licked her lips. Still, the sheriff stood as immovable as death itself. Still, the strikers held the square. Still, the governor looked on, his face ticking out each second. Ella guessed that the strikers only had five more minutes left before the fight began. She tried to pull back towards the edge of the square, but Clerans took a step forward at that very moment, his hand on his tomahawk and his eyes fixed excitedly on the strikers.

Ella's heart sank. There would be a fight, and Clerans would probably abandon her to help in the glory of assisting the sheriff in his administration of justice. She, on the other hand, was likely to be the casualty of a stray bullet.

Ella could hardly make herself breathe now. She had read the term 'slaughter' in her books, and she had always read the word with a twinge of romanticism. Yet now, for the first time, she saw what it must be like, and nausea built up in her throat at the thought of seeing these strikers lying dead in the square.

She glanced at the crowd of onlookers and the militia members ranging themselves around the sheriff. How many of them had families and loved ones? What had they been doing that morning before they jumped into the action? How many of them would still be alive when this was over? When the fighting started, how many innocent people would die?

Then Ella looked at the factory workers, and her stomach twisted itself into a knot of anxiety. Mrs. Blaeith was there, and so many other women stood behind the fence — many younger than her. How would they fare once the shooting started? They were all pressed up against that fence, and they had nowhere to go. Mrs. Blaeith could easily die if things turned violent.

Ella stared at the strikers again, looking into their eyes for the first time now. Her heart sank inside her. At last, she could see their wounded human hearts behind their guarded eyes. They were doing what they thought was best. And so was the sheriff, and so was the governor. Why did she have to watch this? There was no good way for this to end.

Sheriff Laei raised his pistols to point skyward. "You tain one minute left."

The strikers cocked the flints in their guns back to full position as they checked their priming. The spokesman bowed cheekily to the sheriff.

"You jist shoot one o' us dead when ye are ready, then."

"Save yer lives. Return to Nychweni Square," the sheriff said.

"We tain no more life left to save." The spokesman replied. "The Company made sure to ceive that from us. So here we are."

"Anoint you all," the sheriff cursed. "I wish you would leave. This is your own fault now."

The spokesman stared at the sheriff. "Do ye think ye cen intimidate us? We are desperate men, sheriff." He looked around him, and the strikers nodded bitterly, "Do ye no see the brink o' ruin our country is on? Do ye think that we stand here simply as a spoiled child seekin' our own desires? The Company, who ha' been my life an' my bread fer my whole life, ha' stabbed me in the back an' left me to starve or seek other employment. I could trive up more work, but that would be self-seekin'. I ha' to trive a solution fer the other men who the Company will betray. Is that no a just cause? Would ye oppose us and threaten us in yer mock justice? Fie, and shame upon ye."

The sheriff stood, unmoved. "Yer means, sir, are the antithesis o' justice. That is the crux o' the matter. Be yer intentions ever so noble, I will oppose yer foul means. There is law, and there is order; abide by it, or, in seekin' yer noble aspirations, ye will make a hell o' yer paradise."

The spokesman's eyes flashed with hate. "Foul means? Ay, ye ha' no seen foul means, sir. No yet, no yet."

"You will see mine, at least." So saying, the sheriff aimed his pistols into the crowd of strikers.

"Archi Laei!"

The sheriff looked up in alarm, and at that moment, the crowd parted, and Miss Nansi pushed her way into the square. She panted, her headscarf falling off, but her eyes glowed with determination as she marched towards the sheriff, standing between him and the strikers. A handful of others followed Miss Nansi, placing themselves as a shield before the strikers. The women wore headscarves instead of hats — like Miss Nansi. Were these Rectificationists, then?

"Archi Laei!" Miss Nansi said again, pure indignation in her voice. "What fer the love o' yer sacred kirk ha' gotten into ye?"

The sheriff clenched his jaw. "This does no concern ye, Nansi, nor any o' the rest o' yer Rectificationist do-gooders."

"Does it no?" Nansi replied, folding her arms. "I expect once ye shoot me, it will concern me."

"I am no goin' to shoot ye," the sheriff replied through clenched teeth.

"Ay?" Miss Nansi fired back. "Then wos that threat to shoot every striker in the square bald flummery?"

The sheriff frowned. "Do no be a fool, woman. What side are ye on?"

"I am on the side o' justice."

The sheriff tilted his head to one side. "Then get over here an' out o' my way."

Nansi held up her finger, and her eyes narrowed. "Justice does no always stand on the side o' the law, sheriff."

The sheriff rolled his eyes. "These men are tryin' to starve the factory workers to death. Do ye think that is just?"

Miss Nansi waggled her finger at the sheriff. "An' ye mean to gun them down an' start a bloody street fight. Is that any better?"

The sheriff sighed and lowered his pistols.

"What is this?" the governor growled. "Anoint ye, Nansi. What are ye tryin' to do?"

Nansi turned on the governor, her hands on her hips. "I am jist tryin' to keep yer city from dissolving into anarchy."

The governor wiped puss from his eye. "I thought ye Rectificationists wanted an anarchy."

Nansi ignored the comment but turned to the strikers instead. "Gentlemen, I want to see you succeed in this. You are hard workin' men, an' you do no deserve this treatment from the Company, the sheriff, or the governor."

The strikers murmured in ascent.

"But why are you sieging the factory?" Nansi asked.

The spokesman shook his head. "Ye missed my entire speech. I explained it merri well already. We must put pressure on the factories so that the government will take over the Company."

Nansi shook her head. "If ye want the Company to change, then put pressure on the Company. Bringin' the factories into this jist makes everyone hate ye more than they already do."

The spokesman folded his arms over his chest. "Ye think I'll will take a woman's advice?"

Nansi laughed. "Ye are clearly no from around here, dearie. Now come on, there's a big commons by my house — room enough for all o' you."

Nansi motioned for them to follow, and she turned out of the square, the crowd parting to let her through.

"After me, gentlemen. I may no tain enough tea fer all o' ye, but we cen all sit down an' tain a productive conversation about how to proceed."

Without a moment's hesitation, the crowd of strikers piled after Miss Nansi, until only the spokesman stood in the square. For a moment, he looked after his retreating comrades and back to the factory, and then he turned once more to the sheriff with a cheeky bow.

"Another time, perhaps."

And with that, he rushed after the other strikers, resentment echoing in every footstep.

24

WAYWARD

For a moment, Haeli felt nothing but the rush of wind all around her. She could see only the open sky above her and the ragged cliff edge as it rose steadily before her. Below her, she could hear the ocean's terrific booming against the cliff.

Then her body hit against something. A dozen tangled branches seemed to envelop her, all slapping against her and raking across her body. She stretched out her hands, and her fingers grabbed hold of something solid. She lurched to a stop.

Haeli's heart pounded in her throat, and she gasped for air. Slowly, she looked around. The top of the cliff was some twenty feet above her now. She had landed in a very tangled hawthorn tree that clung to the cliffside, hanging out almost horizontally from the cliff face, twisted and gnarled like the forgotten web of an orb weaver.

With great effort, Haeli looked down. Below her, the sea raged against the cliff, but it must be some forty feet below her. As another wave thundered against the cliff face, the surf splashed upwards, and a shower of ocean mist splattered her, the smell of the briny waters wafting all around her.

Her hands burned from the thorns' cuts, and Haeli knew she could not hold on to the hawthorn tree's branches forever. She could see the tree's trunk a little to her left. Kicking out with her legs, she swung one over the slender trunk. Then she let go of the branch she was holding onto with one hand, and, stretching out as far as she could, she got that arm around the trunk too. Now she swung the rest of her body onto the trunk and clung to it with her knees and arms as if she were clinging to the back of a wild elk that was trying to shake her free.

The ocean again slammed against the cliff. Haeli closed her eyes and tried to calm herself, swallowing hard.

Breathe, breathe, breathe.

She had to get control of herself. Losing control was how she had gotten herself into this mess. What in the world had happened? Who was that strange blind man? What was it he wanted? Was Martyn all right? Why had the griffin come back?

Breathe.

Haeli took in another deep breath and exhaled it slowly. There wasn't much point overwhelming herself with a dozen questions when she couldn't even answer the single question of how she was going to get out of this hawthorn tree.

Haeli surveyed her surroundings again. One or two other hawthorn trees jutted out from the cliff, but they were all much smaller and hardly looked like they would hold her weight. Otherwise, the cliff was uneven, with a good deal of rocks protruding from it. Haeli guessed these rocks would make excellent hand-holds. Still, she had never done much cliff-climbing before and wasn't sure how well she could climb with her torn hands — especially if she had to make it twenty feet straight up or fall to her death.

She remembered how Tomas had taught her to climb trees, staying patiently behind her and putting his hands on her waist to give her extra support when she needed it.

The Cliff

"Do not worry, Haeli; you are doing great. Remember, height can not kill you. It is only falling that is dangerous."

Looking below her, she could see the ocean again throwing itself against the cliff face. There did not appear to be any rocks below her, so she might be able to dive straight down into the ocean with no harm to herself. Then again, if she were to dive into the ocean, the ocean would probably oblige her by smashing her into a million pieces against the cliff face.

She could hear her father's voice in her head now, a memory from the first time she had gone to the ocean.

"That ocean is an uncanny beast. I find it better to stay away from it altogether."

"But cannot you swim in it?" she had asked.

Da shook his head. "Your Ma can teach you to swim. But I still stand by what I said. The ocean is an uncanny beast."

Haeli let out her breath slowly.

Up, then, was her best option.

Haeli slid backward on the tree trunk until she had scooted up to the cliffside, then she sat up. Pain coursed through her hand, and she winced. She clung to the hawthorn trunk even harder with her knees and looked at her hands. Her left hand was fine — only a few scratches on it — but her right hand bore several deep cuts where she had grabbed the thorn bush. There appeared to be some thorns still stuck in that hand.

Gritting her teeth against the pain, she picked at the thorns in her hand. She pulled most of the thorns out with effort, but at least one reasonably sized thorn was embedded too deeply for her to remove with her fingers. Haeli sighed in frustration and felt a lump forming in the back of her throat. How was she supposed to climb this cliff with thorns stuck in her hands?

Haeli swallowed again. Tears started to spill down her cheeks. She dashed them away hurriedly. Ma would tell her to ride her emotions like a horse and let them out, but she failed to see the use right now. That wouldn't help anything. She just had to focus and get up that cliff. Besides, the reason she had fallen off this cliff was because she was riding her emotions and not holding back. She couldn't do that again.

Haeli let out her breath slowly. She could do this. She had to do this.

Grabbing onto another branch, she pulled herself onto her feet. For a moment, she balanced precariously on the slim trunk. Reaching out with her hands, she grabbed onto a rock that jutted out from the cliff face and pulled herself up.

Almost at once, the rock broke off from the cliff and slid free. Haeli tumbled backward, still holding the rock in her hands. Her back hit the hawthorn trunk, and she wrapped herself around it like a leech. The rock continued to plummet downward and downward until the ocean surged up against the cliff and swallowed the rock into its foaming maw.

The pain of landing on the trunk coursed through Haeli's body, and her hands throbbed in pain. She felt bile rising in her stomach, and she retched. Her entire world seemed to narrow into a black tunnel. For what seemed like only a moment, her vision went black.

Haeli opened her eyes. She felt weak. Had she thrown up more than once? She was still clinging to the hawthorn trunk for all her life, but her muscles felt sore and stiff, as if she had been holding on for a very long time. She looked up at the sky. The sun was past its zenith. Was it midday already? Where had the time gone? And to the south, Haeli could see clouds gathering as if threatening a storm soon. But those clouds had not been there a moment ago. Had she fainted?

Slowly and shakily, she sat up and pulled herself back to her feet. She had to climb that cliff. She had to get out of there. She did not want to be exposed on this cliff face when the storm hit. It would be hard enough to climb back to the top of the cliff while the rocks were dry. The sea thundered below her again, taunting her. Haeli looked up to the top of the cliff and set her jaw firmly. She had to climb quickly if she were to get to the top before the storm began. Once more, then.

God, help me climb!

She could hear Tomas in her mind. "You are doing great, Haeli. Just relax. You can do this."

She grabbed hold of the cliff and tested it first to make sure that it would hold her weight, then pulled herself up. Her feet found a good hold, so she reached up with one hand, selecting the next rocky projection to hold her weight. Now she pulled herself up a little farther.

Pain coursed through her right hand as the thorns protested, but Haeli refused to listen to them. Her life depended on getting to the top. She had to keep going. She had to push through the pain.

Now a memory of Yohni came to mind; from that time, he tore the palm of his hand open while breaking in a filly. Haeli had wrapped his hands up afterward while Da cleaned the blood from the reins. But Yohni never flinched.

"How did you do it?" Haeli had asked. "That had to hurt a merri good deal."

Yohni had only looked at her with his large nymphine eyes. "You cannot fight the pain by tensing up and pulling away from it. Pain is part of your life. Lean in. Relax into it."

Haeli let out her breath, reaching for another handhold. "Lean into the pain," she said to herself.

It was slow going. She selected each new handhold with care and caution, testing them all before she trusted her weight to them. She could take her time. It was better to go slow than to fall again — especially because this time, she couldn't be sure that the hawthorn tree would catch her.

She looked down. The hawthorn tree was a good way below her now, and she marveled at how insignificant it looked with the sea crashing against the cliff underneath it. How had it ever held her weight?

"Do not look down," her memory of what Tomas said in her head. "That will only make you dizzy. Stay focused."

Right. Stay focused. She was getting closer now. She simply had to push through.

After several more minutes of grunting and sweating, Haeli reached the top of the cliff. She felt weak from the exertion, but she had conquered. She set her face towards the western mountains as the clouds obscured the peaks, and now the rain fell in a gentle drizzle. Hurriedly, Haeli ran across the meadow up to the high road, wrapping her arms tightly about her to stave off the chilly rain. She leaped the ditch and hurried up to the little hollow where they had camped the night before.

Haeli wasn't sure what she had expected, but she certainly didn't expect what she found, which was nothing — nothing and no one. There was ample enough evidence of the camp: the fire ring, even some of their blankets still lying on the ground. There was also ample evidence of the blind stranger, as the smoldering remains of his meat still lay in the fire ring, and his strange canvas wrapper lay carelessly nearby. Too, there was plenty of evidence of the fight. Some blood was on the ground, coals from the fire all over the hollow, and the burned cedar tree.

All of this was still there. However, not a soul remained. The Eagle Griffin, the blind beggar, and Martyn had all vanished.

"Martyn!" Haeli yelled. "Martyn! Can you hear me?"

Her voice echoed back from the mountains like jeering taunts, answered only by the low rumble of thunder.

Haeli slumped on the ground, her exhaustion finally catching up with her. She felt almost sick, and a lump formed in her throat. For a moment, rational thought fled her brain, and she buried her face in her knees, sobbing. The rain soon soaked through her headscarf and ran in miserable streams down her neck and back.

Haeli's mind slowly processed her emotion. Ma was gone, Dafid was gone, Yohni was gone, and Da — oh Da! Da was gone forever. Now where was Martyn? She had felt alone when climbing the cliff, but now she was well and truly alone.

Haeli must have sat there weeping for several minutes, but there came a point when she could no longer cry. She imagined her Da wrapping her up in a warm hug. His strong arms had always comforted her. That helped. Leaning her head back against a tree, she brushed her hair out of her face. It was in her eyes and sticking to her moist cheeks. Haeli growled in frustration. Everything was wrong!

A deep resentment built inside her, replacing her grief. Why had all of this happened to her? How could God have let it happen? Wasn't He good?

Haeli swallowed hard. Yes, she knew God was good; she didn't doubt that — or at least if she did, she would never admit that she doubted it. She *wanted* God to be good. Yet, how could her father's death be good? God had control of that, right? Was she just supposed to accept that with a smile and a shrug and say, 'God will bring something good out of that'?

"Our emotions are like these horses," Ma's voice said in her mind. "Hope, Joy, Vengeance, Regret, Lamentation... God gave them to us as tools to help us do what we need to do."

Haeli pursed her lips. "Right now, the only emotion I feel is hatred. Hatred toward God. Surely you don't want me to ride that?"

"Some people will tell you," Ma went on, "that you shouldn't listen to your emotions, that you should only listen to your reason. But that doesn't work."

Haeli let out a muffled sob. "But it hurts. It hurts so much."

"Like a horse," Ma kept going, "you must break in your

emotions, but then — once there is trust between the two of you — you can ride them to accomplish great things."

Haeli wiped her tears from her eyes. "Great things? Like falling off a cliff because I lost control? Is that the great things you are talking about?"

There was a moment of silence, as nothing moved but the wind in the trees, the rain, and far away, the ocean booming against the cliff, matched now and again by the distant roll of thunder.

Suddenly, Haeli remembered her father's words to her before she had left him, the same words that Martyn had inexplicably repeated.

"Be strong, tain courage, and wait on the Lord."

Haeli pursed her lips and sighed heavily, wiping the tears from her cheeks one last time with the back of her hand. She *had* been strong. She *had* been courageous. But how was she supposed to keep waiting? Was God ever going to intervene and help her?

This was pointless. Crying would not get her anywhere, nor would it help anything. She was done. She had to deliver that letter to the Company for her Ma, and when that was done — when that was done, she could go south and find Ma and the Twengoli camp.

Haeli stood to her feet. She could almost physically feel herself grabbing hold of her emotions, wadding them up tightly, and shoving them deep down inside her where they would never come out again. She checked her pocket to ensure that she still had the packet for the Company, and then — with some trepidation — she checked that she still had the keys. There, she was ready to move on. Her legs felt like lead weights, and her shoulders pitched forward with exhaustion. But no, she couldn't give way right now. Now was not the time to be tired. She had to be strong.

Martyn probably hadn't deserted her. She could not understand why he hadn't gone looking for her or why he had left the blankets in the hollow, but that was beside the point. More than likely, he had simply gone on ahead to Entwerp. Probably he had assumed that's where she had run off to.

There was nothing else for her to do but follow him and make her way to Entwerp, too.

25

INVALID

At long last, Ella and Clerans reached Doctor Heyl's house. It was the same large, two-story, brick house, set all about with many-colored flowers — some were planted around the house, some along the road peeped out between the immaculate white picket fence, while other flowers spilled out of the window boxes which hung beneath every window.

As Ella and Clerans approached the house, Mrs. Heyl knelt in one of the flower beds. The little round woman worked contentedly, humming absentmindedly to herself, dirt covering her hands up to the elbows.

Clerans stepped up to the gate, pushing it open as he called to Mrs. Heyl, "God bless ye, Mrs. Heyl!"

Mrs. Heyl looked up and smiled warmly. "By the saint's beard! Well, how do ye do, Mr. Clerans? I hope ye are well?"

She stood hurriedly, trying to wipe off the dirt and mud that coated her skirt from the knees down. All she did was smear the dirt from her hands all down the front of her skirts. She extended her hand warmly to Clerans, dirty as it was. Clerans took it heartily and kissed Mrs. Heyl in greeting.

"It is merri good to see ye," Mrs. Heyl continued. "Why it

wos only last night when I wos speakin' to Charles, an' I says to him, 'Ye know Charles, I do no believe we ha' spoken with that little Blaeith boy recently. He is always merri o' an polite an' so well-mannered' — all o' yer brothers are jist merri o' an polite, an' you are all merri well-mannered — but I says to Charles, 'I wonder he does no pay us a visit on some fine evening.' Well, an' here ye are, an' it is sich a fine evenin' as anyone may say."

Clerans nodded, "Ay, that it is."

Then Mrs. Heyl turned to Ella, still smiling. "An' is this yer tryst?"

Clerans blushed, "Ay, no ma'am, this is–"

"Wait, a smudgeon," Mrs. Heyl interrupted, "Do no say, do no say." She looked at Ella quizzically. "Now then, dearie, I am certain that I'll ha' met ye a'fore, but I cen no fer the spiration o' me think what I'll cognize ye from. We ha' met, ay?"

Ella smiled. She couldn't help but love this bubbly, portly little lady.

"Yes," Ella replied. "You have seen me befo'e, but I'm not su'e you would say that we met."

Mrs. Heyl pursed her lips and then laughed lightly, pursing her lips again and looking closely at Ella. "By the saint's beard! I ha' seen yer face a'fore, I would swear to it, but I cen no think up yer name. Ye'll will forgive me, I am sure?"

Ella laughed. "Yes, I'm Ella Donne."

"O' course!" Mrs. Heyl said. "Ay, now I cognize ye! Ye are that new housemaid that the Pickering's hired fer to help poor Olyfia. Ay, an' it is good to meet ye officially, then."

And with that, Mrs. Heyl seized Ella by the hand and kissed her in greeting. "Well, now, I am merri glad you two vened to visit me. I do tain some water on to boil; you two will join me fer a cup o' tea? I do no doubt, but it will rain soon, an' then you will want to be indoors, anyway." As she spoke, she bustled over to the door. Ella couldn't help but think that the brightly painted door matched the whole cheery nature of that house with its overabundance of flowers and its cheery mistress.

Clerans smiled roguishly. "I would be happy to oblige ye there, Mrs. Heyl. Miss Ella, however, wos on her way here–"

"Oh, ay, o' course!" Mrs. Heyl interrupted. "It is after Sir Saemwel, she would be." She opened the door and called inside, "Charles, my love! Charles, we tain some visitors who ha' vened to see ye!"

A slow voice answered from a recess of that large house, "Ay love, I will be with ye directly."

Mrs. Heyl led them to a bright kitchen with large windows in almost every wall of the room, lightening up the space with beams from the afternoon sun. A scent of lavender settled upon Ella as she entered. It was a very inviting smell, and she couldn't help but sigh to herself as she surveyed the large kitchen. What a far cry this was from the crowded kitchen at the Pickering's manor house. Compared to this homey kitchen, the Pickering's kitchen looked like a dismal place.

The entire room looked much more modern than any Ella had seen before — especially in Llaedhwyth. The stove, in particular, caught Ella's eye. She had only heard of closed ranges before — they were so modern — yet here one was, standing right before her eyes. Supposedly, these closed ranges cooked more evenly as they recycled the smoke to extract more heat before it escaped through the chimney. The stove had a large oven to one side of the firebox and a massive boiler on the other. Nestled into the corner next to this marvel of modernity was a washbasin, which appeared to have a water pump next to it — a water pump in the kitchen itself! Various herbs and spices hung from the ceiling rafters, and, by the looks of them, Ella guessed that Mrs. Heyl had picked the herbs fairly recently — perhaps even that morning.

Ella couldn't help but smile to herself as she thought that any woman would become as cheery as Mrs. Heyl if she were surrounded by so many flowers and given such a remarkable kitchen to work in.

Mrs. Heyl bustled over to the boiler and filled three mugs with steaming water from the tap, talking the whole time.

"Well now, Miss Ella, ye are welcome in my house, sich as it is, an' excuse the mess. I am happy to make ye as comfortable as I'll may. Charles takes good care o' me, as ye see. Ay, that man knows how to spoil me rottener than a two-year-old cabbage leaf. Ay, an' here is the man himself!"

As Mrs. Heyl spoke, Dr. Heyl entered the room. He was the same slim man Ella remembered, though now large, dark circles hung from his dark eyes, and he walked in slowly, almost dragging his feet. His clothes hung about him in disarray, and his hair stood up on his left part in a ridiculous cowlick. He had rolled his sleeves up past his elbows, and his hands were wet as if he had just washed them. As Ella met his gaze, the doctor smiled wearily.

"God bless ye, Miss Ella." The doctor shook Ella's hand and kissed her on the cheek.

"Charles, love," Mrs. Heyl said, "I wos jist fixin' the younkers some tea. Ye'll will take some maté will no ye?"

Dr. Heyl nodded. "Thank ye, love. I would appreciate that."

"If ye'll tain matè," Clerans interjected politely, "I'll will ceive some as well if ye'll do no mind."

"If that is what ye would like," Mrs. Heyl replied courteously, pouring a mug for the doctor and handing it to him. "Here, Charles, sit and rest a smudgeon."

Dr. Heyl smiled weakly. "I'll would love to, but I'll do tain more patients..."

"An' Clerans, darling," Mrs. Heyl went on, "The maté will keep ye awake, an' being that it is already the evening, perhaps I could interest ye in some chamomile-ginseng-an'-lavender tea. It calms ye right well after a long day o' work. That is the tea I wos plannin' to make fer myself."

Clerans nodded. "That sounds like jist the tea fer this evening."

Dr. Heyl smiled at Ella again, that same tired smile. "Ye would be after Sir Saemwel? I'll will duce ye to him."

Ella followed Dr. Heyl from the kitchen, Mrs. Heyl's voice still audible behind them as the doctor led Ella down a long hallway. "Ye are a merri sensible younker, Mr. Clerans, an' I am merri happy ye stopped in fer tea. My poor Charles ha' been running crumunchlings fer the past four days now, what with Sir Saemwel, an' the riots an' all. He ha' about worked himself beyond his ability to keep his eyes open. Ay, but what cen I do as his wife, eh? Only keep smiling and givin' him little bits o' sunshine. He'll will vene through all the better fer it. Ay now, darling, an' what do ye think o' the tea?"

Dr. Heyl stepped around a pile of medical books that half-blocked the hallway. "Ye must apologize, er, I mean... forgive me fer the mess, Miss Ella."

Ella only smiled. "Of cou'se."

"The strikers," the doctor went on, "attacked a few people the other night, an' it ha' been a merri o' an ordeal... stitching an'... some long hours o' tendin' to them..." The doctor trailed off, looking back at Ella and trying to smile, but Ella could see lines of care and compassion crossing the tall man's face. "Well, three o' them will make it." He set his hand to the handle of one of the doors which lined the hallway, and he paused. "Ay, three o' them at least." He sighed.

"How many..." Ella asked, almost afraid to hear the answer. "How many we'e attacked?"

"Seven," the doctor replied. He looked at Ella again and tried to smile, but pain and empathy clouded his entire face. Ella remembered the brooding hatred in all those strikers' eyes and how they had threatened Governor Braedhwyc and Sheriff Laei. But they had dissolved so easily to Miss Nansi's rational pleas. Had they attacked and injured seven people, now?

Dr. Heyl opened the door and entered slowly. Ella followed. She found herself in a sort of antechamber, with a door on the opposite side which was cracked open. The entire room was rather dim and smelled of lavender. There was little in the room: only a washbasin with a cabinet above it, a large mirror, and a low couch in the corner. On this couch, Ella could see a tall figure — perhaps a young man of twenty — stretched out, fast asleep. At first glance, Ella knew that this young man was a faerie from his bulbous forehead and prominent cheekbones. She remembered from her books that these distinctive facial features would direct a faerie's sonar for echolocation. That had always intrigued her. What must it be like to see your surroundings through echolocation?

Dr. Heyl motioned to the sleeping young man and whispered, "Olafr, my assistant. The poor younker ha' no slept fer nearin' two days now. I insisted he ceive some rest."

"And when was the last time you slept, Docto'h?" Ella asked.

The doctor smiled wearily as he reached for the door on the other side of the antechamber. "Perhaps once Olafr is rested."

With that, the doctor entered the adjoining room quietly. Ella followed. As she entered, she looked around the room. It, too, was small, with only a couple of chairs, a large bed, and a small desk in the room's corner, which held several medical-looking books and tools. The curtains were drawn over the only window in the room, giving this room the same dim look as the antechamber.

Dr. Heyl crossed noiselessly over the soft carpet to the curtains and pulled them back just enough to let a beam of light through. By this light, Ella could see a form stretched out on the bed. Was this what Sir Saemwel was reduced to? As the light entered the room, Sir Saemwel groaned and shifted his position.

"We are free," he muttered to himself. "Let us get away from this accursed place."

Ella looked at Dr. Heyl in some perplexity. The Dr.

shrugged, saying in a low whisper, "He ha' been like that fer days; he is completely delirious."

Ella nodded, coming up to the bed. Poor Sir Saemwel lay before her, as if asleep, wrapped tightly in the doctor's bed quilts. Febrile sweat lay on his face and hands. His once noble face was sunken and hollow as if he hadn't eaten for days. Ella noticed a bowl of half-eaten porridge lying on the bed beside him. She looked back at the tired doctor and, for an instant, could imagine the doctor leaning over Sir Saemwel and patiently spoon-feeding the porridge to him.

Sir Saemwel groaned again and turned over. "It is here, Edwin."

Ella looked back at the doctor. "What is he saying?"

The doctor shrugged again. "I thought it wos jist sleep talkin', but I am pretty sure now that he is rememberin' conversations he tained in the past."

Ella looked back at Sir Saemwel and touched his hand, which peeked out from beneath his quilts.

"Si'h Saemwel?"

Sir Saemwel flinched; his eyes did not open, but Ella could see them moving wildly about beneath his closed eyelids.

"Si'h Saemwel," she repeated. "It's me, Ella Donne, you'h new housekeepe'h."

Sir Saemwel shook all over as if chilled. "No, it *must* be. I *must* go."

Ella settled down on the bed's edge, looking at Sir Saemwel closely. She had to say what she had come to say. He appeared to be in no state to answer her questions properly, but she had to ask him anyway. Perhaps she could find some clue as to the door — or her father in his strange answers.

She spoke now in quiet tones, "You told us about a doo'h, si'h, just befo'e you left us..."

Sir Saemwel seized her hand tightly and gasped, thrashing

about wildly in the bed. "Leave them there lest he follow them! Leave those accursed things behind the door!"

Dr. Heyl rushed over to the other side of the bed and hushed Sir Saemwel. "My dear sir, it is only a delusion. Ye need no trouble yerself so merri much."

Sir Saemwel settled back down, panting.

The doctor looked at Ella with a weary entreaty. "Please try no to excite him."

Ella nodded. "Yes, I apologize." She took a deep breath and turned back to Sir Saemwel. "Is the'e anothe'h way to open the... eh... do you have anothe'h key?"

Sir Saemwel groaned heavily. "No, Stifyn, take the keys. It is better that way. I do not want to see them again."

Ella felt a twinge of excitement at this response and tried to press forward. "Yes, Stifyn Blysffi had the key. Is the'e anothe'h? Can we open the doo'h anothe'h way?"

Sir Saemwel sighed as one who was in deep trouble. "'Those who make me do not need me, those who buy me do not want me, those who use me do not know me.'"

Ella shivered all over at this reply. Perhaps it wasn't worth pressing this point. She licked her lips as she thought of how to proceed.

"Did you know Silas Picke'ing?"

Sir Saemwel groaned again but made no response.

Ella felt discouraged; this wasn't going how she wanted it to go. She wanted answers, but she had none. She licked her lips.

"Did you know Silas Picke'ing?"

Sir Saemwel looked around this time, the name clearly resonating with him. "No, Edwin, that is completely unnecessary. I can do just fine on my own."

Ella could feel a lump in her throat. Here she had come, so near to one of her father's close friends. How many years had she been looking for her father so that she could have some idea of who he was and what he was like? Now she was here, next to perhaps the only man on earth who knew who her father was, but he was delirious and could no more answer her than some random beggar off the street.

"He was my fathe'h," Ella finally said. "I wanted to know something about him. I don't wemembe'h anything about him." Ella stared at Sir Saemwel with an unquenchable longing, knowing, even as she spoke, the futility of what she asked. "Can you tell me about him? Anything about him? I want to know who he was."

Sir Saemwel sighed. "I could never go back, Silas. That life is dead to me... Is it a sin for Saemwel Edwin Pickering?... I live what you would have lived."

Ella could feel tears coming to her eyes, and she sobbed. She buried her head in the bed-quilts and wept. What else had she expected? Her father was gone, and that was all there was to it. It was completely futile for her to search him out. She would never know what he was like, and she would never know who he truly was. He was gone. That was all.

Ella must have wept for several minutes before she felt Dr. Heyl's gentle hand on her shoulder. She looked up, wiping the tears from her eyes. "I'm so'y," Ella said. "I didn't mean to..."

The doctor smiled. "O' course no. Here, let me take ye to the kitchen. I am sure there is still some tea waitin' fer ye there."

Ella stood and followed the doctor out of the dim and disappointing room. The doctor sighed to himself as he closed the door behind him.

"I do no know what to do fer him," he said.

"Is the infection that bad, then?" Ella asked. "The'e is no chance of him getting well again?"

The doctor shook his head. "That is jist it. The infection is no bad. It outta-should ha' dissipated a week ago."

Ella looked at Dr. Heyl closely. "What a'e you saying?"

The doctor regarded her closely. "The old wound does no threaten his life. Sir Saemwel ha' *decided* to die. He ha' given up."

Ella furrowed her brow, not completely certain what to make of this.

Dr. Heyl sighed wearily. "He ha' lost his will to live. There is nothing I cen do fer him medicinally. I cen no cure a dead spirit."

26

DRAMA

"An' so the Sheriff stood there, with his pistols cocked an' his body poised like a wildcat that ha' been stalked by a bear." Clerans poised himself as well, imitating the sheriff's stance.

Elsi sat before him in wide-eyed wonderment while Miss Ella watched with an amused smile on her face. Pastor Daerl, Miss Nansi, and Mr. Hydmenton eyed Clerans critically.

After a moment's pause, Clerans continued his story, trying to imitate the sheriff's voice, "'You will, everyone o' ye, leave this square in ten minutes,' the sheriff said, 'or I will hold you as lawbreakers, an' kill you.'

"Well, the strikers did no take merri well to that, an' they mustered themselves up as if they'll would rush forward and kill Sheriff Laei right there where he stood. He glared at them sternly, like a hunter does at his hounds when they'll are misbehavin', an' they all stood still. No a one o' those varlets would come near to the sheriff."

Miss Nansi raised an eyebrow. "I do no believe that so many powerful men would jist fall back from Sheriff Laei gardin' at them."

Clerans shrugged and waved his hand dismissively. "Well, then, if you'll want to be wrong, ye can believe what ye want."

"I am jist sayin'," Miss Nansi replied, "that is no what I remember when I got there."

"Shush!" Clerans replied. "Ye do no want to spoil yer entrance! That wos s'posed to be a surprise." And Clerans waved his hands for attention. "I would ha' ceded to the sheriff and aided him, but then I thought to myself, 'Clerans, lad, ye ha' been commissioned to keep Miss Ella safe. Ye cen no desert yer post, man!' So I stood my ground and waited fer the fight, which garded like it wos about to ensue."

Miss Ella smiled. "I was ve'y glad you didn't leave me, Cle'ans."

Clerans bowed in affirmation. "Thank ye, thank ye. Surely ye know I would no desert a fair maiden in a predicament."

Miss Nansi leaped to her feet and pointed her finger at him in mock accusation. "Ah, but ye did, only jist this afternoon!"

Clerans did his best to act grievously offended. "An' jist *what* might ye be referrin' to?"

"This afternoon," Miss Nansi replied, "Ye abandoned *me* on yer stroll out into the town an' left me with a merri o' an pile o' dishes. Now, if that is no leaving a fair maiden in a predicament, I'll do no know what is."

Pastor Daerl laughed at this while Mr. Hydmenton grinned broadly.

"Ay," Mr. Hydmenton said. "She tains ye there, Clerans."

Clerans thought for a moment, formulating a response. The only thing he could think of saying didn't seem entirely appropriate, so he set aside his dramatic air for a moment and answered sincerely, "Miss Nansi, ye do no leave me merri o' room to reply without makin' fun at ye no bein' a *fair* maiden."

Miss Nansi smiled in victory. "The old hag still awaits a better response."

Clerans waved this aside. "In complete honesty, ma'am, I could no call ye an old hag."

"A *wicked* old hag, then?" Miss Nansi replied, smiling even broader.

Mr. Hydmenton snickered.

"Llifsa, no!" Clerans cried. "In complete honesty, as I wos sayin', I do no know why ye are still Miss Nansi after all, an' no a *Mrs.* Nansi Felonica."

Pastor Daerl chuckled, and Mr. Hydmenton cheered.

"Ay! There is one fer the boy, now."

Clerans looked at Miss Ella and Elsi for confirmation, and they both stared at him approvingly.

Miss Nansi only continued to grin. "Are ye makin' an offer, sir?"

At this, Miss Ella, Elsi, Mr. Hydmenton, and Pastor Daerl lost all composure as they roared with laughter.

Clerans could feel his cheeks grow hot. "I do no know that *Clerans Felonica* tains the right ring to it."

"Oh?" Miss Nansi replied with a chuckle. "Then ye ha' put some thought into this? What last name *would* ring right with *Clerans?*"

Perhaps it was best to change the subject. "As I wos 'splainin'," Clerans said, clearing his throat.

"He is admittin' defeat, ma'am," Mr. Hydmenton said to Miss Nansi.

Clerans cleared his throat again. "As I wos *'splainin'*, the villains would no cede near to the sheriff."

Miss Nansi smiled and folded her hands in front of herself, allowing Clerans to continue uninterrupted.

"So they stood, thus," Clerans continued dramatically, "with the good old sheriff on this side, and posed against him the whole merri crowd o' strikers, jist lickin' their teeth fer trouble. Then the governor speaks up. He says, 'You heard the sheriff. Now each one o' ye ha' better leave a'fore we open fire on you.'

"But those villains did no give a word o' response. Then, one o' those strikers stands up, as cocky as a bullfinch, an' says, 'yer threatenings do no sway us. Would ye oppose us in yer mock justice?'

"An' the sheriff garded at him like ye would gard at a piece o' rock that ha' trived its way into yer wheat grains. An' the sheriff says, 'Yer means, sir, are the antithesis o' justice, an' I will oppose yer foul means be yer aspirations ever so noble.'

"An' that cocky striker growls and opens his mouth as if he'll make a reply, but the sheriff held up his finger and says, 'There is law, an' there is justice. Abide by them, or ye'll will make a hell o' your paradise.'"

Clerans paused, allowing the scene he created to sink into the minds of his listeners. Pastor Daerl leaned over to Miss Nansi confidentially, though he spoke in a tone that everyone could hear.

"Ye know, Sheriff Laei could ha' saved himself a merri o' trouble. He should ha' jist set Clerans up in front o' those strikers an' had him talk them all to death."

Everyone laughed at this.

Clerans raised one finger in the air for attention — the way a senator might do at the Grand Synod when making a very important observation.

"An' so they waited — all o' us waited."

Clerans surveyed his audience again; they still snickered at Pastor Daerl's joke, but he had their attention.

"The strikers would no leave, an' Sheriff Laei would no back down. So they simply stood there. The sheriff, the governor, the strikers, an' all the rest o' us. An' the minutes slowly ticked by..."

Miss Nansi nodded. "Ay, they sure are! Are no ye supposed to cede back to yer mother's house fer the evening? If ye'll do no hurry yer story, I am sure she'll will be keepin' up supper fer ye."

"Ah, patience, patience, fair damsel," Clerans replied, congratulating himself on using the opportunity to contradict

Miss Nansi's self-imposed title of 'old hag.' "We *all* ha' to tain patience while we were waitin' fer the ten minutes to clude."

"I could feel the sweat rollin' down my face as we waited, an' the air wos as tense as a cloud in a thunderstorm. Now Sheriff Laei starts cockin' his pistols, an' it gards like the strikers are stickin' with their goal by vice or vail.

"Then, who should burst upon the scene, but—"

"Miss Nansi?" Elsi blurted out.

Clerans shook his head, a little deflated. "Now, how should ye know?"

Miss Nansi shrugged. "I did rather give that away, did no I?"

"Well, ay," Clerans went on. "Miss Nansi pushed her way through the crowd, standin' a'tween the sheriff an' the strikers."

"An' at my sheer beauty," Miss Nansi broke in, "they all apologized to each other, kissed the sheriff on the cheek, an' went home."

Clerans shrugged. "Sure. We'll cen go with that version o' the story."

Mr. Hydmenton laughed, shaking his head. "I must needs say that I never cen cern the truth from the fiction in yer stories, Clerans."

Clerans affected a shocked look. "Ah, Mr. Hydmenton. There is no fiction to cern out o' it. I tell ye the facts."

Miss Nansi raised an eyebrow. "But ye called me a 'fair damsel,' which is a fiction to cern from the fact."

Elsi and Miss Ella laughed lightly.

Clerans raised his hands in protest. "Well, now, you are all in luck, as I tain a witness to these *extraordinary* events aforesaid."

"Aunt Nansi?" Elsi asked.

Clerans shook his head. "She jist alleged that she was no a fair damsel, so we cen clearly no trust her testimony." So saying, he dramatically turned to Miss Ella. "I now vert to aforementioned witness. Miss Ella, what is the truth o' the matter?"

Miss Ella blushed slightly, and Clerans felt a little guilty for calling her out of the crowd, but he was enjoying this too much to give up now.

Ella licked her lips. "It's mostly accu'ate–" She stopped herself and started over. "He does have the facts right."

Clerans glowed triumphantly. "Ah! Ye hear that now?"

"It's just," Ella continued, "some of the events a'e out of o'de'h, and the details have been a little exagge'ated."

"Exaggerated?" Clerans asked, a little deflated.

Ella shrugged. "Maybe I should say dramatized?"

Clerans nodded. He liked that word better. He would settle with that.

27

____

OVER-TAKING

*E*rnest ducked under the boughs of a pine tree and peered out from under its edges. He could see a good deal of the road, and as he looked, a figure turned the corner, hurrying down the road with an alert look on his face.

Ernest could tell from his appearance that this man was a beacon-tender with knee-high boots, trousers, greatcoat, and tricorn hat. He held a long rifle over his shoulder and had a tomahawk and several knives tucked into his belt next to a long horse pistol.

Ernest lay still, hardly daring to breathe as this man walked past. He was young — probably a few years older than Ernest — well-built and healthy-looking. The man also bore several scrapes and bruises, as if he had recently escaped from a fight. Could this be the man who had routed the Archeomancer? He looked well-built and carried himself with the confidence and poise of an experienced fighter. If this man had indeed routed the Archeomancer, he was no man but the God of War himself!

As Ernest watched, the man came to the path which led to the campsite in the hollow. He turned down it, walking into the camping area briskly. Ernest couldn't see the man from where he crouched, but he could hear him rummaging through the camp's chaos.

"Haeli!" the man yelled loudly, his clear voice ringing off the mountains. "Haeli Blysffi! Do you hear me?"

For a moment there was silence, and then the man came back down the footpath and stopped on the High Road. He stood on the highway momentarily, examining the road as if searching for footprints. After a moment, the man straightened up and set off at a quick pace due north down the highway towards Entwerp.

Ernest watched with some admiration at the speed with which the man walked as he disappeared around the next turn in the road.

Ernest, Bill, Tell, and the Albino now rose from their hiding places. They looked down the road where the man had disappeared and then over at the Albino, who scowled darkly after the man. Ernest licked his lips nervously. Should he ask?

"Eh," Ernest began hesitantly, "was he, I mean, the... that man, he..."

The Albino let out his breath slowly and nodded. "Yes, he was the one pursuing me. I had the girl. She was mine. I caught her on the road. She ran from me that way," the Albino pointed off the road down the mountainside in the sea's direction. "It was futile. She could not run from me. I would have easily caught her — but that man attacked me." The Albino's voice dropped to barely more than a mutter. "He seemed protected from my power. I was nothing more than a normal man to him... and he was a Panhaplite..."

"A what?" Tell asked dumbly.

The Albino scowled. "A Panhaplite: the all-weaponed warriors. Did you have any schooling?"

"Oh," Tell nodded sagaciously. "I see."

The Albino now turned to the three pirates abruptly and looked them over. "That man will be searching for the girl now. He is a tracker, and he will find her. We must follow him. He will lead us to her."

With that, the Albino turned and marched after the man, matching his same hurried pace.

Ernest, Bill, and Tell looked at each other dumbly.

"Come now!" the Albino ordered without even turning his head. So the three pirates followed as best they could, having to jog now and then to keep up.

They continued for some time, stopping at every turn in the road and looking ahead to make sure the young man did not see them. Now and then Ernest could see the man, still walking briskly. It was the best that the pirates could do to keep pace with this man — the God of War, as Ernest had dubbed him.

They had not followed the man long before a thin drizzle of rain fell from the sky. However, as the man did not pause but simply hurried on, the Albino pressed them onwards, not letting them slack for a moment lest they lose the man again.

They had only walked a few miles before they mounted a ridge where they could see Entwerp Bay spreading out before them with the two rock sentinels standing at the bay's narrow entrance. The crystal-clear water lapped gently against these great pillars, the waves continuing on to mingle in the mangrove swamps in the mountains' valleys — or to slap against the dike wall before the little village of Entwerp Coastal itself.

Ernest could look down from this vantage point and see the entire highway as it wound its way down the mountain ridge, across the mangrove swamp, and into the little village. Not very far down the mountain, Ernest could see the young man still marching on briskly.

The Albino stopped suddenly.

The other pirates followed suit.

"What is it?" Ernest asked.

The Albino nodded slowly. "You three continue on. Follow that man and see where he leads you. Unless I miss my guess, he will show you where the girl is."

"You willn't come with us?" Bill asked.

The Albino continued to nod. "I should not show my face in there too rashly — not in the daylight, anyway. You three are sailors and not out of place on the road or in the city. There is no reason he will suspect you of anything. You three continue on your mission. Find that girl and bring her back to Holgard."

Without waiting for a response, the Albino turned from the road and disappeared into the forest up the mountainside. Bill, Tell, and Ernest exchanged glances quizzically. They stood there on the road for a few minutes, saying nothing.

Finally, Ernest broke the silence as he cleared his throat, looking down the road at the man they had been following. He didn't mind that the Albino had left them.

"If'n we don't hurry, we will lose him," Ernest said.

Bill nodded. "Right."

And he plunged down the hill. Tell and Ernest followed right behind.

The descent was easy. The road was well-maintained and wound steadily downhill. Still, the pirates had to push themselves to keep up with the man ahead of them. The man paused for about a minute right before he reached the bridges that spanned the bog at the bottom of the mountain, examining the road, most likely looking for tracks. This gave the pirates enough time to reach the turn directly behind him before he entered the city. Here, several other people trickled into the city from other smaller roads which joined the High Road before the series of bridges.

Bill turned back to Tell and Ernest. "We should split up. We shouldn't be seen together. I will follow the man as closely as I dare. Then Tell, you follow me at a distance. And Ernest, you follow Tell."

This agreed upon, Bill stepped out confidently onto the bridge while Tell and Ernest stayed behind, concealing themselves as best they could down one of the smaller paths that led into the mangrove swamps.

When Bill was about halfway down the bridge, Ernest nudged Tell and told him to follow. Tell obeyed mutely. Ernest sat in his place, peering after Tell. The God of War had completely disappeared from his sight — he was probably in the town by now — and Bill was indiscernible, one of four or five people on the bridges. When Tell had crossed the bridge about half way, Ernest stepped back onto the main road, walking along briskly now and trying not to look suspicious. He passed a few locals, who nodded to him and tipped their hats. Ernest knew that the sight of a sailor was not at all unusual, and they wouldn't suspect him of being a pirate, but he couldn't help but wonder if his nervousness showed as he returned each man's greeting and tipped his hat in return.

Ernest swallowed hard. He had a right to be nervous. Under Llaedhwythi law, a pirate could be shot — or worse, beheaded — on sight by any officer of the law. Ernest shivered. What a mission this had turned out to be.

Still, following Tell proved rather easy. Tell stood out of any crowd, head and shoulders taller than anyone else. Ernest followed him neatly at every turn. It was almost an enjoyable little walk — probably the first part of the trek that Ernest enjoyed. The rain stopped as suddenly as it came, and, in its place, clear evening sunshine poured down from cracks in the clouds, making all the puddles of rain in the cobblestone streets sparkle like jewels.

Before long, Tell ducked into a small alley a little way down a less-traveled street. Coming to the alley, Ernest ducked down it himself. There, he found Bill and Tell crouching, waiting for him. It was a very narrow and well-shaded alley, casting Bill and Tell in deep shadow.

"Where's the man?" Ernest asked. "What about the girl?"

Bill pointed down the little street they had stepped off of. "He went into the fifth house down. I haven't seen the girl yet."

Ernest pressed himself against the walls of the alley as he came close to the entrance. He looked around the corner just enough to get a view of the house that Bill had mentioned. He counted down to the fifth house and studied it. It was a low structure with no second story — indeed, only a few houses here had a second story. The house was made of stone, and there was a barn next to it with some chickens. It looked cozy enough, Ernest thought.

Just then, he heard the noise of someone coming down the little street. He ducked back down the alleyway, but not before he glanced down the street the other way to see who was coming.

It was the girl—Lady Death herself.

Ernest's heart lurched in him at the memory of her. The moonlight in her hair, the raptor bird fluttering up behind her, and the cold gun barrel pointing down at his head.

Lady Death.

Ernest glanced back at his companions. "She's coming; she's on the street!" He whispered.

Bill flashed a greedy smile and slunk to the alleyway's entrance, poised like a spider against the wall.

Ernest's heart pounded in his chest. Why was he so nervous? It was only a young girl. They were three strong men. There wasn't much she could do against them. Besides, while he didn't get a very good look at her, he was pretty sure she wasn't armed.

She crossed right in front of the alleyway, and Bill sprung. One of his long arms caught her around the mouth, and the other snatched her by the waist. It was the act of an instant. Bill dragged her into the alley, and Tell caught her, clamping his massive hand over her mouth as well.

Bill stepped back, grinning from ear to ear. "Nicely done, eh?"

The girl stood there, a look of sheer terror across her face. She didn't even try to escape. Ernest looked at her closely. This was Lady Death? Yes, it was the same girl, but all the fire seemed to have gone out of her. She looked like she was in the last stages of exhaustion. Her whole countenance exuded brokenness, like a half-drowned field mouse or a fawn that was still living after being run over by a cart. Her eyes met Ernest's with an expression somewhere between betrayal and accusation.

Ernest felt a knot in his gut. Yes, this was Lady Death, but he pitied her — he pitied her deeply. She was so weak, so helpless. How could he take advantage of her now? Besides, she had spared his life; he owed her something in return.

"Do we bring her back to Holgard now?" Tell asked.

Bill chuckled. "Who says we can't have some fun with her first?" And he winked knowingly.

A smile spread over Tell's face.

"Hold on," Ernest said, feeling sick. "Holgard said to bring her back to him, nothing about..."

Bill licked his lips, his eyes glowing with a wicked leer. "He do'edn't say we couldn't peel her first."

Tell giggled. "Why not?"

Ernest looked back at the girl. What was he supposed to do? He couldn't stand up to Bill and Tell; there wasn't any point in trying. The girl looked at him intently — pleadingly — with Tell's big hand clamped tightly over her mouth. Ernest clenched his jaw. He had to try.

Bill stepped towards the girl, his long fingers reaching for the hem of her dress.

"Wait," Ernest interjected. "Stop, we don't... I mean... eh... we shouldn't..." He felt sick in his gut, and he trembled all over.

Bill turned on him, looking him over curiously. "Why so reserved, Ernest? What's your problem?"

"I..." No words seemed to come to him. What was he doing? This was stupid. He looked like a baptized idiot. He should stop. Whatever happened to the girl now, it wasn't his fault.

Bill's face widened in a hideous smile as he jabbed Ernest with his boney elbow. "You do'edn't shy away from that rabbit-lipped leprechaun."

That hit Ernest like a kick in the groin. Shame and guilt washed over him, and he almost stumbled backward at the blow. He didn't dare look back at Lady Death. He could almost see her standing behind him with judgment on her brow.

"You are an evil man, Ernest. You are a cowering worm and a disgrace. You are bad entirely, and an utter failure."

Ernest swallowed, but he did look back at the girl, and she was still staring at him — as if *he* could help her! Ernest wanted to walk away. He wanted to forget this had happened. He wanted to forget any of this anointed mission had happened. His stomach lurched in him, and he gagged. For a moment, he felt certain that if he vomited, it would make everything feel better, but he held it down.

The girl still stared at him. What did she want from him? What could he do? He was a weak and evil man. He couldn't help her if he wanted to. But still she looked at him, her eyes pleading. Ernest ground his jaw together.

Tell forced her to the ground, and Bill leaned over her.

"Stop!" Ernest growled, and his hands curled into fists.

Bill looked back at him in confusion. "What?"

"Stop!" Ernest said again as he pushed Bill away. "Don't! I willn't let you!"

Bill doubled back, but then he came forward, punching

Ernest full in the face. Ernest lost his footing and fell to his knees, covering his face in case Bill should hit him again.

Bill stood over him in exasperation. "What's gotten into you?"

At that moment, Ernest heard the sounds of vociferous whistling coming from the little street off the alley's other end. All three pirates froze and turned toward the sound.

2 8

INTERVENE

His entertaining done for the day, Clerans stepped out of the Pickering manor and faced the eastern horizon. He let in a long breath of the crisp alpine air and exhaled. This was the life for him. How could it get any better?

With that, he trotted briskly down the stairs in front of the manor, holding his rifle (which was slung over his shoulder) as he bounced down each step. He paused briefly at the bottom to wave his hat back at Miss Ella and Miss Nansi, who still stood in the doorway.

"I'll will return, ladies. I do no know when, but I am sure I'll will."

Miss Nansi smiled. "What about tonight?"

"Tar and needles," Clerans replied. "Ye need me to return tonight?"

Miss Nansi laughed, though it sounded hollow. "I'm sure I will manage." And she waved her hand out over the commons to the south.

Clerans followed her gesture to see small groups of strikers setting up tents along the common's southern end, not too far from Miss Nansi's house. He shifted his hold on his rifle.

Miss Nansi shrugged. "I would no mind if ye'll would pop by, or send one o' yer brothers, or Lexi, to pop by tonight. Jist to see that my meetin' with them goes well."

Clerans nodded. "I will discuss it with Ma, but I am sure I'll cen do that."

Mrs. Nansi sighed. "Thank ye, Clerans. This old hag is merri grateful." And she turned, walking back inside.

"Farewell, fair damsel!" Clerans replied, and he turned to head down the road toward Entwerp Coastal. He heard the manor door close behind him, but he stopped abruptly as someone said his name.

"Cle'ans?"

Clerans turned to see Miss Ella walking down the front stairs.

"Ay, Miss Ella, what is it?"

Ella looked nervous. "It's just." She sighed. "Please do not tell anyone about the note I showed you."

Clerans nodded and smiled. "I will leave that to you, ma'am."

Ella smiled in return but still looked nervous. "And... and if you think of an answe'h to the widdle..."

Clerans shivered at the memory.

"Please let me know," Ella concluded.

Clerans forced a smile. "O' course I will. I'll will be runnin' errands fer the company around town all week, so with any luck at all, I'll will run into ye an' let ye know if I'll come up with anything."

Ella smiled. "Thanks, Cle'ans. I'm glad I let you in on this."

Clerans nodded, puzzled at Ella's desire for secrecy. "If ye'll do no mind my quirin'," Clerans finally said, "who knows?"

"About the lette'h?"

Clerans nodded.

Ella shook her head. "Just you and I. I wouldn't mind if Haeli or Lexi knew, though."

Clerans nodded. "Lexi should be here by tomorrow, so ye cen tell her then."

Ella nodded. "That would be wonde'ful."

With that, Clerans kissed her goodbye and pivoted on his heels for home.

It would be a few miles walk, but what was that for him? He loved the fresh air and open space, and, more than anything, he loved the solitude of it. He took a less-used path to the north — avoiding the commons the strikers were requisitioning and Entwerp Proper all together — circling around the dale's edge before catching up with the main road to the coast at the pass through the mountains.

Clerans breathed deeply and smiled to himself. The entire valley was beautiful, still green, but with a definite hint of autumn coming on. Some leaves were turning, and the grain fields to the south were turning amber. The mountains on all sides hemmed in the city, forming a picturesque wall to the north, east, and west. To the south, the dale ran to the horizon in a hundred shades of green. Especially after the rain that afternoon, all the colors stood out in vibrant detail everywhere Clerans turned his eye.

Clerans continued his walk at a brisk pace. Yes, this road would be longer than the main road, and it would be considerably less maintained, but that was the whole beauty of it. He was all alone, by himself, on God's good earth, with God's good creation all around him, almost as if God were leaning over to give him a hug.

Clerans smiled at that thought. That sounded like the makings of a poem. "A hug from God." No, that wasn't grandiose enough. Maybe a title like *An Autumn's Eve, Like God's Embrace* would be better. Besides, that title had a better meter: it was iambic tetrameter.

Clerans whistled idly to himself, hearing the words to the meter of his song.

> *"An autumn's eve, like God's embrace,*
> *Across this valley, face to face,*
> *A testimony to His grace..."*

Clerans stopped whistling for a moment. What should his fourth line be? "And of His boundless favor" seemed to spring up in his mind, but he didn't think that would quite work. He had three lines already that rhymed, but he thought the fourth shouldn't. No, the fourth line should rhyme with the fourth line of his next stanza. Then again, it wouldn't be easy to come up with a rhyme for 'favor,' so maybe he should come up with a different line.

How about "Unto a wayward sinner?" That sounded better. He liked the alliteration in "wayward," and besides, the concept of a sinner would complement the concept of grace that he had brought up one line previous. Then again, it wouldn't really be any easier to come up with a rhyme for 'sinner' than for 'favor.' Be that as it may, 'sinner' it was.

Clerans kept whistling as he went along, but the second stanza didn't come to him immediately. Just then, he heard a twig snap in the underbrush behind and to his left. Clerans stopped whistling and pivoted around, scanning the woods and mountains nearby in the way Sheriff Laei had taught him. His right hand strayed towards the tomahawk at his side, and his left hand moved towards his skinning knife. He didn't think that anything was stalking him, but Sheriff Laei insisted that he always train himself to reach for his weapons.

"When it venes to a fight, ye must trust yer instinct," he could hear the sheriff saying, "which means ye must train yerself to tain an instinct which is worthy o' yer trust."

Nothing seemed out of the ordinary. The trees bent slightly in the wind, and a few sparrows played hide and seek between the boughs. Down on the ground, only a few wildflowers poked their heads out between the rocks, and a ground squirrel eyeing Clerans from a distance.

Clerans shrugged and was about to turn back to the road and continue his jaunt when a thought occurred to him. Hadn't he seen a wild apple tree a little way ahead on the road? Clerans didn't look to confirm. He simply grabbed the strap of his rifle, standing poised and ready. He breathed steadily and consciously relaxed himself. In order to shoot accurately, he had to be relaxed.

Now he pivoted on his heel and unslung the rifle from his shoulder. It rolled out beautifully. He felt the butt of the stock slide up against his shoulder as his eye scanned for the apple tree. There! He fixed his gaze on a sickly specimen of an apple near the tree's top, not much larger than a cherry. He halted his spin, his feet still about shoulder-width apart, and then he raised the gun to his eye, cocking the flint back with his thumb as he did so. The front and back sights touched, and Clerans pulled the trigger smoothly and firmly. The entire operation was one swift and fluid movement.

The rifle fired, sending a loud report echoing all along the mountainside. Clerans still had his eye fixed on his mark, and he smiled with satisfaction as the apple vanished — obliterated into a thousand pieces.

Clerans whistled to himself some more as he set the butt of his rifle on the ground and reloaded his gun. That was a nice shot; Sheriff Laei would be proud of it. He slung the rifle over his shoulder again and continued on his way with a little more spring in his step, whistling stridently.

He kept up his brisk pace and soon rejoined the main road before plunging into the canyon which led to Entwerp Coastal. He passed several men on foot and stood to the side for a couple of carriages — tipping his hat to each one — but there weren't that many people out this evening. All the while, Clerans kept up his vociferous whistling. He was still trying to come up with a second stanza of his new poem.

"An autumn's eve, like God's embrace,
Across the valley, face to face,
A testimony to His grace,
Unto a wayward sinner."

Clerans reached the bridge across the Entwerp River, dropping a stone down, down, into the raging water as he crossed over. Still he whistled, and still he thought. What could be his rhyme for 'sinner?' 'Winner?' No, that was too cliché. Ah, but now the next few lines came to him:

"This dim reflection, deftly made,
This sampling glory, here displayed,
To wholesome, wicked, man, or maid..."

But what came next? It had to rhyme with 'sinner.' What if he simply reused the word? Perhaps his last line would be something like "To saint, or sordid sinner." He did like the alliteration in that line.

Clerans now passed the kirk and turned down another less-used path that cut along the town's circumference. It would bring him home the back way, through the little alleyway. Sure, it would take him a little more time, but he was in no hurry.

His mind returned to his poem, and he recited the second stanza in his head.

"This dim reflection, deftly made,
This sampling glory here displayed,
To wholesome, wicked, man, or maid,
To saint, or sordid sinner."

Yes, that worked. He'd let it pass for now. He wasn't certain it was his best poem, but it was from the heart, and that's what counted.

He continued to whistle merrily as he walked along. Now, the question came, would every successive stanza end with the same theme — ending with the word 'sinner' — or would every two stanzas simply end with the same word?

Clerans walked in silence, pondering this question, turning from his little path to follow another that plunged down into the town. He glanced up and could make out his own home amidst the rows of low houses stretching down to the dike wall. He whistled again. Perhaps he should wait on the poem until he reached home. He could write it all out, which should give him the inspiration he needed to finish it. Besides, when he saw it all written out, he could correct any awkward wordings in the first two stanzas.

Clerans now passed into a street on the outskirts of Entwerp Coastal, ducked between a few houses, crossed a square with a well in the center, and turned down another street. He was almost home. He was sure he could smell his Ma's supper in the air. Ma's supper smelled different from the neighbors'. Everyone else's supper smelled like food; Ma's smelled like heaven. Perhaps that could be the subject of his next poem.

Clerans pivoted around the corner into the alleyway that would lead him to his street, and he froze. There, standing before him, were three figures, all dressed like sailors. Two were gnomes, one long-armed and hairy, the other slim and puny. The third was a human, huge, hulking, and brutish. These three figures stooped over a fourth form, a young girl who was clearly near complete exhaustion. Was it Haeli Blysffi? She looked similar to Haeli, whoever she was. The puny gnome was picking himself off of the cobblestones and holding his head as Clerans turned the corner.

Was this a robbery he had interrupted? Maybe an assault of a darker nature? Murder, perhaps?

Clerans immediately felt his pulse quicken. Sheriff Laei's words sounded in his head. "Relax, breathe deeply. Ye can no afford tunnel-vision." Clerans let in a deep breath, filling his abdomen with air and breathing it out slowly through his mouth. Relax.

This was it. This was the real thing. He had trained for this moment for so long, and he knew he was ready. It wasn't that different from when Sheriff Laei would surprise him in an alley or ambush him on the road. He would use all the same strategies. But it was different. This time, it was real.

Clerans actively relaxed his body, yet held every muscle ready to snap into action at the slightest provocation. He had to stay poised yet calm, monitoring the broad picture.

Clerans opened his mouth, but the long-armed gnome preempted him. Striding forward in one swift motion, the long-armed gnome grabbed Clerans by the shoulder and looked him in the eye menacingly.

"What's this, now? Do you think you can just walk in here?"

The brutish man chuckled.

Clerans kept himself relaxed, resisting the urge to move his hands to his weapons.

"What is happenin' here? What do ye ruffians ween ye are doin'?" Clerans asked.

The long-armed gnome sneered at him. "Oh, and you think *you* can be the one asking the questions now? You willn't find out, and you willn't tell anyone what you seed."

Clerans and Bill

And with that, the long-armed gnome drew out a dirk and poised it over Clerans' neck. A wide, hideous smile spread over the gnome's face. "You will die first."

Clerans still forced himself to stay calm. The sight of a dirk wasn't that alarming to him. He was familiar with many weapons and was intimidated by none. Besides, the gnome wasn't holding the dirk right; Clerans could disarm him effortlessly. Still, the entrance of a lethal weapon into this situation seemed to give Clerans reason to assume that he could respond in kind.

"An' what o' that girl?" he asked the gnome.

The gnome's smile broadened. "A good boy like you shouldn't hear such things." And the gnome raised his dirk ever so slightly.

That was all Clerans waited for. He sprung, hardly feeling a conscious choice of what he did. His hands moved by instinct. His left hand caught the gnome's dirk hand by the wrist and twisted it back, as his right hand, in the same instant, snatched his tomahawk from his belt. Swinging his right arm back, he swept the gnome's hand from his shoulder. Then he brought the tomahawk forward. He could feel the blow starting in his toes, coursing up his leg, gaining power in his hips, arching through his back, down his arm, and into the tip of his fingers. With the force of his whole body, he thrust his weapon between his opponent's eyes.

The gnome dropped to the ground like a rock, tearing the tomahawk from Clerans' hand. Clerans, however, had no time to look down. The brutish human bellowed like a wild bull, charging at Clerans and drawing a cutlass from his belt.

Clerans breathed deeply again, remaining calm as he unslung his rifle from his shoulder. The weapon rolled into the crook of his shoulder as it had a hundred times before. With practiced poise, Clerans raised the rifle and fired. The shot's force at such close range swept the brute from his feet, throwing him in a heap to the cobblestones.

Clerans did not wait for the second gnome to attack. He drew out his bayonet and affixed it to the end of his rifle in two smooth motions. Then he advanced on the second gnome, the last of his assailants. The puny gnome, however, gave no resistance. He threw himself on the ground in terror, holding up his hands in desperation.

"Please, don't hurt me!" the gnome sobbed. "I do'edn't do it — I willn't do it. Just please don't hurt me!"

Clerans stood over him, gripping the rifle and bayonet. In an instant, he could have thrust his weapon downward and snuffed out the puny gnome's life. But the pleas for pity stayed his hand, partly because the gnome was no longer a threat and partly because his conscious brain was catching up with his actions.

He had just killed two people.

The gnome continued to grovel on the ground in front of Clerans.

"Please! I told them not to. I told them not to."

Clerans swallowed. He had to continue to stay calm. He let his eyes glance across the alleyway, seeing the mangled heap of the brutish man and the long-armed gnome laying dead a few feet away with the tomahawk still embedded in him. Clerans felt bile rising in his stomach. He forced himself to breathe. He had done no wrong. Anyone could see that. He had been defending himself and the girl.

Wait, the girl! Clerans glanced over at her to see Haeli standing shakily to her feet. So it had been Haeli Blysffi. What was she doing here?

Haeli regarded Clerans with an air of shock. Her eyes exuded relief and gratitude, but she looked too shaken and exhausted to speak.

Clerans suddenly realized that the puny gnome was no longer pleading. He turned back to him. The gnome was still prostrate on the ground but looked up at Clerans with a look of desperate hope for life.

"What do ye tain to say fer yerself?" Clerans asked levelly, still holding his bayonet poised over the gnome's head.

"I told them not to," the gnome repeated. "I do'edn't do anything."

Clerans shook his head. "What are ye blatherin' fer? Who are ye?"

The gnome swallowed, either unsure which question to answer or unwilling to answer.

"Are ye a pirate?" Clerans nearly spat out the word.

The gnome hung his head in shame. "I do'edn't do it at all, at all!" he pleaded.

Haeli now spoke, her voice shaky and barely above a whisper, "Clerans, he tried to stop the others."

The gnome looked up excitedly. "Ay, I do'ed! I told you I do'ed!"

"Be quiet." Clerans snapped.

The gnome hung his head again.

"Ye are a pirate," Clerans continued. "By Llaedhwythi law, ye cen be executed by an officer o' the law on sight."

"Clerans," Haeli spoke again, "do not hurt him. He stood up for me."

Clerans looked at Haeli briefly and then back at the puny gnome. What was he supposed to do, anyway? He couldn't kill this man. He was not an officer of justice and had no jurisdiction except in self-defense or protecting life. What was he supposed to do with this man? He wasn't threatening anyone — at least not anymore.

"Swear to me," Clerans finally said, turning back to the pirate, "that ye will no seek to harm me, Haeli, here (or any lawful citizen o' Entwerp, fer that matter) ever again."

"I swear it," the gnome whined. "I'd swear anything, just don't hurt me, please!"

Clerans still looked on sternly. "Swear it in the name o' the Almighty God." He wasn't sure why he felt he needed the gnome to do this. Maybe he was letting his power over this gnome go to his head.

The gnome swallowed. "I swear it in the name on the Almighty God."

Clerans nodded and turned to Haeli. "Haeli, cen ye walk?"

Haeli nodded slowly.

"Get Da or Ma, or Lexi, or Robert, or Roland, or whoever ye cen trive. I'll need help ceivin' this man into custody."

Haeli nodded and limped off as best she could.

29

HAVEN

aeli stumbled to the end of the alley and turned down the street towards the Blaeiths' house. Her head hurt, and her legs trembled. She felt weak, as if she would collapse at any moment. Her stomach felt like a hollow pit in the middle of her body, like something had seized her bowels in its fist, twisting them into a tight ball.

Yet even in her state of exhaustion, her heart pumped blood frantically through her veins. Hardly was she out of the alleyway when she began to run, tripping blindly over the cobblestones that formed the street. She had to get to the Blaeiths' house before anyone else tried to abduct her. She had to get out of the open.

She reached the door in no time and collapsed against the door frame. She gasped for air, her mind still reeling after her narrow escape from the pirates. Haeli raised her shaking fist to pound on the door, but before she could deliver the first knock, the door opened slowly of its own accord.

Haeli found herself staring into Martyn's face. Martyn jumped in surprise as soon as he saw her.

"Haeli! I wos jist gardin' fer ye–"

Haeli collapsed against Martyn. "Martyn! Oh, Martyn!"

She sobbed, shaking all over. A wave of relief washed over her, and she fell to her knees, unable to keep herself upright for another moment. She was finally safe!

Martyn drew her inside. "Haeli? Are ye all right? What ha' happened to ye? Who ha' done this to ye?"

Haeli trembled all over, suddenly remembering what Clerans had asked her to do. But the words stuck to her tongue. Her head was still spinning, and she couldn't think in coherent sentences. "Clerans!"

"Clerans did this to ye?"

Haeli clung to Martyn more tightly. "No, Clerans stopped them... the pirates... in the alleyway... help! He needs help!"

Martyn sat bolt upright. "Clerans needs help?"

Haeli nodded.

Martyn hurriedly placed Haeli in a nearby chair. "Da! Lexi! Clerans is in trouble with pirates in the alley!"

Martyn snatched up his rifle from beside the doorway and flew outside, followed closely by Lexi and Mr. Blaeith.

As they slammed the door shut behind them, Haeli laid her head against the chair's back, hugging her legs tightly to her chest. For the first time, she looked out across the cheery room to see Robert and Roland sitting across from her, staring at her with wide eyes. She trembled all over.

Mrs. Blaeith moved up to her slowly and knelt in front of her. "Dear Haeli, what ha' they done to ye?"

Haeli leaned forward, throwing her arms around Mrs. Blaeith and continuing to sob.

"There, there," Mrs. Blaeith said soothingly, "ye are all right now."

Mrs. Blaeith picked Haeli up from the chair as if she were only a newborn infant, carrying her down the back hall.

"Robert," Mrs. Blaeith said in a calm and even voice, "get me a bowl o' the stew, an' a piece o' bread, please, an' bring them back to me."

Haeli still trembled all over. She let Mrs. Blaeith carry her without objection. She didn't know if she could walk another step. Pushing open the door to Lexi's room, Mrs. Blaeith entered and set Haeli down gingerly on the bed.

Haeli clung tightly to Mrs. Blaeith, so the kindly woman sat down on the bed with Haeli, stroking her hair. Haeli buried her head in Mrs. Blaeith's lap, still sobbing inconsolably. She had no conscious thought. She didn't even care that she was crying. It was a release. She didn't have to think anymore; she could just feel. Finally, she was back on a horse, galloping at full pace, though she did not know which emotional horse she was riding now. She was safe at last. That was the important thing.

Haeli didn't know how long she lay there weeping, but a furtive knock at the door interrupted her.

"Vene in," Mrs. Blaeith said softly.

Robert shuffled awkwardly through the door, holding a steaming bowl of soup in one hand and a chunk of rye bread in the other. Without saying a word, Robert placed the food on the dresser, looking at Haeli wide-eyed before hurrying from the room.

Mrs. Blaeith tenderly lifted Haeli to a sitting position. "Are ye hungry? Cen ye eat?"

Haeli trembled all over. She was starving. She had been starving all day long. But could she eat after what had happened to her?

Mrs. Blaeith dipped a large spoon into the soup and held the thick broth to Haeli's lips. Haeli accepted it gratefully. The savory stew tasted rich and wonderful in Haeli's mouth, but as she swallowed, her stomach lurched in rejection. With an effort, Haeli forced the bile back and swallowed the spoonful of stew.

"I want to eat," Haeli finally said, "but I do not think I can right now."

Mrs. Blaeith looked at her with empathy. As her eyes met Haeli's, Haeli felt that Mrs. Blaeith knew exactly what she had been through. What a relief it was to be safe at last! Haeli wanted to cry all over again, but her mind had better control of her now. She couldn't start crying again. How was that supposed to do any good? This lack of control wasn't getting her anywhere. She had to pull up on the reins and slow this horse down.

Mrs. Blaeith squeezed Haeli's hands in hers. "Ye look as if ye'll could use a warm bath. Would ye like me to draw one fer ye?"

Haeli nodded, sighing heavily. After two long days on the road, exposed to rain and frost... yes, a hot bath sounded like heaven.

Mrs. Blaeith squeezed Haeli's hands once more before stepping out of the room. "Robert! Cen ye and Roland bring me the bath? An' set some water on to boil if ye will!"

Then Mrs. Blaeith stepped back inside and sat next to Haeli again, taking her hands in her motherly hands. Haeli felt another lump in her throat. Yes, only her mother could care for her better than Mrs. Blaeith. As it was, Mrs. Blaeith was just the woman she needed at that moment. This thought brought a question to Haeli's mind. Where was her mother, anyway? Had she made it safely to the Twengoli village? Was she even now implementing her plan to cede all the Company's land in Indigie Law back to the tribes? Or had the pirates attacked her, too?

Mrs. Blaeith continued to look at Haeli sympathetically. "Do ye want to talk about it?"

Haeli took in a deep breath and let it out slowly. "Not particularly."

Mrs. Blaeith smiled sadly. "I understand. Poor dear."

After a moment's pause, Mrs. Blaeith continued. "Talkin' about it will do ye good, Haeli, jist like cryin' over it helps."

Haeli tried to swallow back the lump in her throat, and she

trembled as she took another breath. She was on the verge of tears again. Had crying about it actually helped, though?

Mrs. Blaeith squeezed her hands again. "Ye cen talk when ye'll are ready. I will be listenin'."

Haeli licked her lips, concentrating on breathing steadily and often. Mrs. Blaeith was probably right. She had better tell someone what she had been through, and Mrs. Blaeith was probably the best person to tell. However, her mind refused to go back over the events of the last few days. All she could see was an obscure bundle that was her father and the gnome's leering look as he forced her to the ground. Haeli shuddered all over and closed her eyes. She was safe now. She was safe.

Haeli licked her lips again, forcing herself to speak. "They attacked the fort. They... they... pirates. It was pirates. They attacked the fort and killed..." Again the lump caught in Haeli's throat, but she forced her words through it. "They killed Da."

Tears streamed down Haeli's cheeks again, and she buried her head in Mrs. Blaeith's lap. Her whole body wracked with sobs.

"I just want it to go back to the way it was before everything went wrong!"

Mrs. Blaeith stroked Haeli's hair tenderly. "Hush. Hush."

"Martyn," Haeli spoke again, her voice sounding muffled in the folds of Mrs. Blaeith's dress. "Martyn, and Laendon, and Meriwedhr came. I rode to them... they were bringing us..."

"Martyn told us," Mrs. Blaeith said softly. "He told us about the pirate raid."

Haeli looked up at Mrs. Blaeith desperately.

Mrs. Blaeith's eyes exuded sympathy. "The pirates followed ye here, did no they?"

Haeli nodded.

Mrs. Blaeith sighed tenderly. "Are ye willin' to tell me more?"

Haeli took a deep breath. "I fell off of a cliff." She paused, unsure if she could continue. She *needed* to continue.

Mrs. Blaeith nodded encouragingly. "Ay, that explains why Martyn could no trive ye."

Haeli swallowed. She needed to tell Mrs. Blaeith what had happened. It would help. "I scended back to the road. I walked all the way here. That is when they found me." Haeli's words stuck in her mouth. Her tongue would not move.

Mrs. Blaeith squeezed her hands. "Ay?"

Haeli winced. Her right hand was still tender from grabbing the thorn bush. Yet somehow, the pain seemed to give her the energy she needed to keep going.

Haeli took another breath. "They had me. They would have... they would have... But they did not. Clerans stopped them. I am all right. They did not assault me." She looked at Mrs. Blaeith closely. Was that enough? She didn't need to go into any more details, did she? She wasn't sure that she *could* go into any more details.

Mrs. Blaeith squeezed Haeli's hands again. "I understand."

Haeli sighed. She felt like crying again.

Mrs. Blaeith pursed her lips, and Haeli realized with surprise that Mrs. Blaeith was about to cry. "Oh, dearie, I am glad to hear it. God protected ye from the worst o' it."

Haeli nodded. She had no words to say.

Then there was another furtive knock at the door. Both Haeli and Mrs. Blaeith hurriedly wiped their eyes.

"Vene in."

Robert pushed the door open slowly, dragging in a tall metal trough. Roland followed close behind with two large buckets of water. As Roland filled the tub slowly, Robert left the room, returning a moment later with two urns of boiling water. He poured one into the tub, and the water immediately erupted in a burst of inviting steam. He left the second urn by the tub's side, mumbling something about, "in case ye'll will need it warmer," then he and Roland hurried from the room.

Mrs. Blaeith squeezed Haeli's hands one last time and stood

up. "I will be jist outside if ye'll need anything, an' I will be back with some clean clothes fer ye. Please try to eat some food while I am gone."

Haeli nodded. "I will."

Mrs. Blaeith paused at the doorway, then turned back and knelt in front of Haeli, stroking her hair soothingly.

"Haeli, ye know that this is no yer fault? None o' this is yer fault."

Haeli nodded. "I know."

Mrs. Blaeith looked satisfied. "Do no ever let yerself believe that this was yer fault."

And with that, Mrs. Blaeith exited the room, shutting the door gently behind her.

Haeli wasted no time in undressing and slipping into the inviting bath. A sigh of satisfaction escaped her as the warm water enveloped her. She hadn't even noticed how achy she was until now. Oh! How good that water felt!

Tears formed in her eyes again. Haeli submerged all of herself but her head, closing her eyes and letting the tears stream down unchecked. She was safe now. She was safe at last.

As the hot water soaked the soreness from her muscles, it also seemed to soak through the sharpness of her emotions. She didn't need to fear her memory anymore. After all, she was safe. She could let her mind remember.

With this permission, images flooded back over her, images of the past few days: The pirates' attack, her father's desperate conversation with her in the back room, her mad-dash flight from the pirates, her father's burial, the long hike, the griffin's two attacks, the arduous climb up the cliff, the near assault in the alley... She was all right. She was safe now. God had protected her. It was not her fault. None of it was her fault.

Haeli sighed again, opening her eyes again. Yes, it was true. None of it was her fault — but she could have done more. What had she done through it all, anyway? She had been so passive, *letting* the events happen to her. She should have fought those pirates in the alley herself — and she would have if she hadn't been at the end of her strength — and she could have killed them just as effectively as Clerans, too!

Still, it was not her fault. There was nothing she could do about it now. But from now on, she would shape events and not let them shape her.

Sitting up, Haeli scrubbed at the cuts in her hand until she was sure they were clean. At last, she pulled the last thorn out. That felt so much better. Haeli reached over to the dresser and took the piece of rye bread, eating it slowly. Yes, that was what she needed: a hot bath and food. She would be as good as new in the morning. She would have her strength back. Then let any pirate try to get in her way.

Haeli had finished the bread and was nearly done with the bowl of stew as well when there was a gentle knock on the door.

"Haeli, dear, it is me," Mrs. Blaeith said from the other side of the door.

"Vene in," Haeli said, surprised at how confident her voice sounded. She *was* feeling better. She would be her usual self again soon.

Mrs. Blaeith slipped into the room with an armful of laundry. "Here are some towels fer ye an' some clean clothes. They are Lexi's, but I believe they'll will fit ye all right until I cen get yer other clothes washed. Would ye like me to ceive them an' wash them now?"

Haeli suddenly remembered the two keys and the letter to the Company, still hidden in the mass of clothing she had taken off. Yet she did not let her face lose its composure. See! She was doing much better already. She had control of her emotions again.

"Let me get dressed first if you do not mind."

Mrs. Blaeith laid out a clean outfit on the bed. "There ye are,

Haeli. Now, once ye are dressed, I am afraid that the others would like to talk to ye in the front room."

Haeli inhaled sharply. "They do not... I do not have to... I mean... I could tell Martyn, if I must, but I do not think I could..."

"Oh no," Mrs. Blaeith said reassuringly. "Ye do no need to tell them what ye told me. But they do tain that last pirate in the front room with them. They are no sure what to do with him. So, if ye'll tain anything to say (for or against him), then I think it would be most welcome."

Haeli let out her breath slowly. That last pirate was still alive — that coward.

Mrs. Blaeith smiled sympathetically. "Ceive all the time ye'll need, Haeli. Ceive all the time ye'll need."

And with that, she slipped from the room.

Haeli climbed from the bath and dried herself slowly. What was she to do about that cowardly pirate? Frankly, she wanted nothing to do with him. She should probably let Mr. Blaeith and Martyn deal with him and stay out of it.

Yet Haeli felt a prick of her conscience at this thought. No, she could not do that. That would be the passive thing to do. She had just now resolved to be more active. Well, here was her first opportunity.

But what was she to do with this pirate then? He was such a coward. He was the one whom she had shown mercy to after he had chased her along the Ocean Road. Now he had abused that mercy by trying to capture her again.

Then again, he had stopped the other two pirates — or at least tried to stop the other two pirates — from their attempts to violate her. She would be coldhearted indeed if she did not show him some leniency for that. There must be some mercy, then. Perhaps Mr. Blaeith would be a judge of what kind of mercy to give. Still, she had better speak up for the pirate.

With this finally determined, Haeli finished dressing herself in Lexi's clothes. Hurriedly, she snatched the two keys from her old clothes, again hiding one in her headscarf and the other in her bodice. Finally, she stuffed her Da's letter to the Company into her skirt pocket. She was ready now. She would be passive no longer!

And Haeli marched from the room, her jaw set firmly as she moved towards the front room.

30

DESERVING DEATH

*E*rnest lay in terror before this dreadful boy in the alleyway. If the girl was Lady Death, then this boy was Lord Vengeance. Ernest was still reeling with disbelief at how quickly and efficiently the boy had killed Bill and Tell. He could hardly believe that it had happened at all. How could Bill and Tell be dead? Could that really be their bodies lying in two heaps on the cobblestones?

Ernest watched out of the corner of his eye as Lady Death disappeared around the corner. He was terrified of this boy, but not with the same primal state of fear he had felt after his initial run-in with Lady Death. He had a strong hope that he might survive this whole ordeal. After all, *he* hadn't been doing anything wrong. Bill and Tell might have, but *he* hadn't. Too, Lady Death had stood up for him. That was surely a good sign, wasn't it?

Ernest eyed Lord Vengeance, trying to read the boy. Was he inclined to spare Ernest's life? What did he mean about taking him into custody? Was he going to turn him over to the officials? Hopefully not, as that would mean certain death for a pirate, even if Lady Death stood up for him. Ernest shivered, and his stomach tightened in a knot.

He had sworn the oath Lord Vengeance asked of him. Surely that would help him in his plea for life. Wouldn't it?

Like the sun's slow dawning, Ernest realized that he still had his pepper-box pistol in his breast pocket. Might he be able to get at it without being suspected by this Lord Vengeance? Ernest continued to eye Lord Vengeance carefully. He was only a boy, but he bore the confidence and mastery of a seasoned warrior.

Ernest's palms grew sweaty at this thought, and his heart raced. Could he risk it? His eyes fell on Bill's corpse with the tomahawk still protruding from him. Ernest's stomach churned. Perhaps a better question would be, was it worth the risk?

After watching the speed and skill with which this Lord Vengeance had taken out Bill and Tell, Ernest didn't relish the thought of having that same speed and skill used against him. No, he would have to wait, hoping that his good deed in standing up for Lady Death would erase from these Llaed-hwythis' minds the fact that he was a pirate.

He had come to this conclusion when three people rushed into the alleyway from the street. All three were armed and vicious looking. The first was the man Ernest had been tracking — the man who had been hunting down the Albino. On a closer look, this man was the spitting image of Lord Vengeance, only taller, more terrible, and probably much more lethal. Ernest decided he was right to think of him as the God of War.

The second newcomer was another gnome — a woman gnome — short and beautiful, yet carrying a rifle with the earnest confidence of a soldier. Behind her, was a man whose age and similarity to Lord Vengeance and the God of War led Ernest to conclude was the father of these two demigods.

The God of War reached Ernest, his rifle pointed directly at

Ernest's back. "What is happenin', Clerans?" he asked. "What is this all about?"

"Ay," the she-gnome said as she, too, joined the circle of rifles trained on Ernest. "Did this man hurt Haeli?"

"On me honor!" Ernest replied, thinking it best not to use vulgar language in front of his betters. "I do'edn't so much as touch her at all, at all."

"I do no tain a clear idea o' *what* happened myself," replied Lord Vengeance — or Clerans, as his name appeared to be.

The she-gnome glared at Ernest, glancing disdainfully at Bill and Tell's corpses. "What villainy would harm a sweet girl like Haeli?" She turned again to Ernest, raising her rifle menacingly. "I would be merri obliged to ceive that villain's hide."

Ernest cowered back. Maybe this would not turn out well for him after all. "It wasn't me!" he pleaded. "I do'edn't do anything!" Where was Lady Death now to stand up for him when he needed her?

The father now strode up. "Do no jump to any conclusions, Lexi," He said. "I, too, would like to reach the bottom o' this ordeal."

Ernest chanced a glance towards the father and another towards the she-gnome. So her name was Lexi?

"Stand to yer feet, pirate," the father ordered.

Ernest leaped to his feet, standing like a soldier at a drill.

The father looked him up and down. Finally he said, "Ye will vene with us an' answer our questions, or I will vert ye over to Sheriff Laei and tain ye shot. Do ye understand?"

Ernest nodded vigorously. "Ay, sir."

The father nodded and turned on his heels. The God of War, Lord Vengeance, and the she-gnome called Lexi motioned Ernest forward with their rifles, and then they followed directly behind him. Leading them out into the street, the father marched into the low house where Ernest, Bill, and Tell had traced the God of War only a few minutes earlier.

Only a few minutes ago? How could so much have changed in so little time?

Once inside, the father and the rest of Ernest's captors set up a hasty court. The father sat himself down in a large wooden chair, and the God of War placed Ernest in a chair directly facing him. Lord Vengeance — or Clerans — positioned himself between Ernest and the father, while the God of War (wasn't his name Martyn?) and Lexi stood behind Ernest, exchanging their rifles for pistols trained on Ernest's head. Off in the corner, Ernest could see the mother and two more boys sitting, observing the proceedings with interest.

The father raised his hand as if he were a judge beginning a trial. "I would like to know why I tain a pirate in my livin' room, why, Clerans, there are two dead pirates in the alleyway, an' finally, what to do with this pirate now that I tain him in my custody."

"Don't turn me over to the sheriff, please, sir," Ernest said.

The father held up his hand sternly. "Will we allow the accused to speak?"

"What am I accused on?" Ernest asked.

"Certainly no," Lexi replied, prodding Ernest with her pistol.

Ernest winced. Where was Lady Death? She was supposed to speak up for him. Was he defenseless in this court?

"Now, wait a moment!" Clerans interrupted. "I tain questions o' my own, sich as, what is Haeli doin' here, anyway? An' ye, Martyn, why are ye back from the mountain so early?"

The God of War — Martyn — sighed heavily. "It is a long story. I only jist finished telling everyone here, but ye see, the pirates raided the Blysffis' fort–"

Lexi gasped, prodding Ernest with her pistol again. "The *villains!*"

"What're you prodding *me* for?" Ernest asked, a little upset.

"Ah," the father cleared his throat. "An' were ye there, Mr. Pirate, at our friend's fort?"

"He might ha' been there," Martyn replied, "though I do no recognize him."

The father held up his hand. "Ay, but let the pirate speak fer himself."

Martyn nodded. "I will, only I do no imagine that we cen trust what he'll says."

Ernest licked his lips. For some reason, he didn't feel he could lie to this regal old man. Maybe Martyn's clear mistrust made Ernest want to be trustworthy.

"Yes," Ernest admitted.

Lexi jabbed him with her pistol again, and he added hastily in his defense, "But I wasn't *in* the fort. I was in the barn! I wasn't involved in the raidin' or the killin'–"

Lexi prodded Ernest with her pistol again. "Ay, but he was still *involved*."

"The killin'?" Clerans gasped in alarm.

Martyn clenched his jaw. "Ay, they killed Stifyn Blysffi."

Clerans' jaw dropped open, and his hands went for his knife. "Ye killed Mr. Blysffi?"

"It wasn't me!" Ernest protested.

Clerans began to draw his knife from its sheath, but Martyn leaped forward and grabbed his brother by the wrist before he could.

"There now, Clerans, calm yerself!"

Ernest trembled all over. "I already sayed I wasn't in the fort. I do'edn't have anything to do with the killing. I do'edn't kill anyone!"

Clerans' eyes flashed with fire. "I should have stuck ye in the alley. I should no ha' spared ye!"

"Peace, now!" the father thundered. "Clerans, control yerself."

Clerans let go of his knife handle and clenched his fists tightly. Martyn let go of him, resuming his position behind

Ernest with his pistol. Ernest squirmed in his seat and eyed Clerans nervously. His honesty wasn't getting him anywhere.

Clerans breathed deeply a few times, trying to calm himself. "Mrs. Bysffi and Dafid? What o' them?"

Martyn waved his hand dismissively. "Safe, as far as I know."

Clerans stared long and hard at Ernest, biting the inside of his cheek. "If I'll ha' known that..."

Martyn shook his head. "Come now, Clerans. Let us continue this trial now. I will tell ye the whole story when we'll are done."

"Ay," the father said. "Clerans, I would be merri interested in hearin' what happened to ye in the alleyway."

Clerans shuddered all over like a man remembering a nightmare. "I wos venin' home from the Pickerings." Clerans stared at Ernest, and he shook his head. "They were in the alleyway, an' they tained Haeli. I killed the two o' them that resisted. Fer better or fer worse, I let this one live."

"For better," Ernest said, nodding. "Definitely for better."

"Silence, *villain*." Lexi hissed, whacking him on the head with the barrel of her pistol.

Ernest winced. "Do you have to do that?"

Lexi brandished her pistol menacingly. "Ay, an' I will do it again if ye'll say sich as a mumble!"

The father sighed. "I would merri much like to know what Haeli ha' to say about all of this."

The mother now spoke for the first time. "I do no think she is fit to speak o' it, Henri."

The father nodded and rubbed his head. "I understand that. Still, without her testimony, I do no know what to do with this... this..."

"*Villain?*" Lexi offered.

"Really?" Ernest cut in.

Lexi whacked him with the pistol barrel, viciously this time. "I *told* ye no to say a word!"

"Wait a moment," the father said, a peculiar light in his eye as if he were a man a step away from solving a great mystery. "Here is my question to you, Mr. Pirate."

"Ernest, if you don't mind," Ernest said, feeling he may as well give them a name besides '*villain*' to call him by.

The father nodded. "All right, Ernest, my question to ye is this: why did ye and yer comrades attack the Blysffi fort?"

Ernest's heart sank in an instant. How was he to answer that without linking himself to the atrocities done at the manor house in Entwerp Proper? Ernest's mind worked at a mile a minute. "Ah, sir, that's a hard question to answer. See, well," Ernest licked his lips. There wasn't anything he could say but the truth. "We were looking for a key."

At this, the father, Clerans, and Martyn all perked up as if lightning had struck right next to them. Lexi, however, didn't seem to find this a noteworthy piece of intelligence.

The father leaned forward. "A key?"

Ernest swallowed. Maybe he had said too much already.

"A key fer what?" The father eyed him suspiciously.

Ernest could feel his heart pounding in his chest. "Well, sir, you know as well as I that most keys open *doors*."

Would that be vague enough?

The father leaned forward further, his interest making Ernest feel sick to his stomach. "A door?"

Ernest shrugged, struggling to look clueless. "I presume."

"An' I am sure ye know *what* door?"

Ernest swallowed again. "By my honor, how should I know *what* door, sir?"

Martyn now prodded him with his pistol. "We could vert ye over to the sheriff..."

"Ah, please sir!" Ernest whined. "I'm only a lowly cook's-mate. Why should I be privy to the captain's council?"

"You are no as clueless as ye would tain us believe," the father said flatly.

Ernest sunk down in his chair. "Blind prelates! All I know is something about some treasure, or ancient country, or something."

Lexi let out part of a laugh. "Did ye jist say, 'blind prelates'?"

"The Gwambi Treasure?" The father pressed.

Ernest nodded. "That would be it, sir."

The father's eyes narrowed thoughtfully, and the pit in Ernest's stomach grew heavier. "Why did ye search the Blysffi's fort fer the key?"

Ernest squirmed nervously. Anything he answered to that could very well be used as proof that he was present at the rabbit-lipped housekeeper's torture and final confessions. The very memory of that night sent shivers down his spine. It wasn't his fault he had been there. He wasn't guilty of anything — at least nothing *too* bad. It was Holgard's order to be there. He didn't have a choice in the matter. These people wouldn't understand that.

Ernest swallowed and took a deep breath. "I'm just the cook's-mate..."

The father cut him off. "That will no pass, Mr. Ernest. Ye tried that once, and I know ye are lyin'. Now answer the question truthfully."

Ernest felt sick. Was there any way he could get out of answering the question?

Martyn prodded Ernest in the back of the neck meaningfully with his pistol barrel. Ernest shivered. For a moment, the image of the tortured housekeeper flashed in his mind: her countless screams for mercy and the terror of the Archeomancer's supernatural torments. His stomach leaped to his throat, and he swallowed back his own bile so as not to heave on the floor in front of him.

He looked up to see the father still staring down at him, with Clerans, Lexi, and Martyn, too, waiting for him to answer.

"Why were ye searchin' in the Blysffi fort fer the key?" Martyn prodded.

Ernest wanted to disappear. Why wasn't Lady Death here to clear his name?

"Answer his question, *villain!*" Lexi smacked him on the head again with her pistol. "Where did ye think ye were about to trive that key, eh?"

Ernest winced, more at the question than from the blow.

"The gardener."

The father leaped to his feet at this comment. "The gardener?"

Ernest swallowed. "We were looking for a gardener, and they thinked what he lived at that fort."

"Who thought?" The father pressed.

"The Captain and the boatswain," Ernest replied, his heart pounding at a mile a minute.

"They thought the key belonged to a gardener?" the father asked.

"Yes," Ernest replied. He had started talking now. There wasn't anything else he could do. "They have a wizard — an Archeomancer they call him — and he telled them that the gardener haved the key."

"Who told him?" the God of War asked.

Ernest swallowed. In his mind, he could hear the rabbit-lipped housemaid's withered shriek. "Stifyn Blysffi!" Ernest shivered and held his stomach.

"Whose gardener were they gardin' fer?" the father asked.

"They raided a manor house," Ernest finally blurted out. "The housemaid told the wizard that the gardener haved the key, and somehow they traced him to that fort."

There, he had said it, and he had said nothing about him doing anything to the housemaid. He desperately hoped that the line of questioning would end there.

The father stepped back and sat down again. Ernest dared to breathe again. Was the interrogation over?

"The housemaid?" Lexi cried. "Olyfia! They killed her."

Lexi drew back her hand as if she would smack Ernest on the head again, but he covered his head with his hands.

"No, me! It wasn't me! It was that wizard, the Archeomancer. He tortured her, and she screamed." Ernest shook all over with terror. "She screamed! Oh, that wasn't me what do'ed that."

The father drummed his fingers on his knee thoughtfully. "Well, I would accept Ella's testimony about this pirate. If only Haeli felt up to givin' us some information about him. Even jist something as simple as 'guilty' or 'innocent'." And the father looked over at the mother.

The mother sighed and stood to her feet. "I do no want to press her, but I will ask."

As the mother disappeared down the back hall, Ernest licked his lips, looking around cautiously. The father had mentioned Ella. Then these people must know her. Surely, his help for her must mean something to them. Would that be enough to convince them to let him live?

Ernest cleared his throat. "Ye mentioned Ella..."

Lexi smacked him on the head with her pistol barrel. "You *villains* captured her, too!"

"That wasn't me either!" Ernest cried. "I helped Miss Ella. My messmate an' I, we helped her. We gived her a dagger. Do'edn't she ever show ye the dagger what we gived her?"

Lexi caught her breath. "A dagger?"

A spark of hope rushed through Ernest. "That's what I said. We gived her that dagger. It was for her protection, you see. We wanted to help her. It wasn't my fault she was captured, but I didn't want any harm to come to her, just like I do'edn't want any harm to come to Lady Dea... I mean Haeli. Isn't that her name? You said, Haeli?"

As if on cue, the mother walked back into the room,

followed a moment later by Lady Death. Haeli looked like a new woman from the cowering, exhausted creature in the alley an hour ago. She had undergone a complete transformation. She wore a clean woolen dress. Her hair was still wet from a bath, but her features were hard as flint, and she looked at Ernest with eyes like steel.

Ernest caught his breath. Was she going to exonerate him, after all? Perhaps she would condemn him in the end — and after he had gone through so much trouble to stand up for her, too.

"Haeli," the father said gently. "If ye'll cen do us the favor, would ye mind tellin' us if this man ha' done ye any wrong? At yer word, I will vert him over to the authorities to be shot."

Ernest stiffened, holding his breath.

Haeli took a deep breath. "He tried to stop the others. I would show him mercy."

Ernest breathed again, nodding several times to Haeli. "Thank you, ma'am. I'm greatly indebted to you standing up for me."

Haeli looked him squarely in the eye. "You already were indebted to me."

Lexi now seemed confused. "Is he no a villain, then?"

After a long pause, the father finally spoke again. "Well then, either by luck or by conviction — an' I am inclined to think by luck — ye ha' kept yerself clean o' hurtin' anyone o' us."

"And he helped me once," Haeli added.

"There we go," Ernest said. "Listen to the lady."

Neither Martyn nor the father seemed perfectly satisfied, but they said nothing.

Finally, Martyn broke the silence. "What do we do with him, then?"

Clerans shrugged. "Give him to the sheriff."

Ernest started in alarm. "Don't do *that*, sir!"

"Sheriff Laei would shoot him," the father said flatly. "He is a pirate, an' that is the law."

Martyn nodded. "Ay, he *is* a pirate, no matter what he'll may claim he'll never did."

Ernest panicked. He could feel his heart racing again. Was that whole stressful confession for nothing? He should have kept his mouth shut if they were going to kill him anyway.

Haeli spoke again. "He tried to save me."

Martyn shrugged. "He does tain that in his favor."

Clerans shook his head. "Though who knows what other women he ha' taken advantage o' (pardon me fer sayin'), but the only testimony we tain fer his innocence, apart from one incident, is his word, an' I fer one never trust a pirate."

Lexi perked up now. "I ha' seen the dagger he gave to Ella. He does tain that in his favor."

Haeli fixed Ernest with an icy stare. "He is a pirate, and he is also a despicable coward." Here she glanced at Ernest meaningfully. "But all the same, he helped me in the alleyway just now, and as a result, I do not think we should simply vert him over to be shot."

Ernest nodded. "Ah, listen to her. She's an awful wise lady."

The father cracked a slight smile at this.

"He probably deserves to be shot," Clerans replied bluntly.

The father nodded at this comment. "That is merri true, son. He deserves to be shot. But on the flip side, do no we all? Are we no all sinners deservin' death?"

There was silence in the room as each person present bowed their heads.

"An' how would ye escape death?" the father asked, looking Ernest in the face.

Ernest shifted his position in his chair nervously, unsure of this sudden change in the continuance of his inquisitors. "Eh?"

"What is yer plea, Mr. Ernest?"

Ernest swallowed. "As the young lady has said time and time again, I *do'ed* save her from Bill and Tell."

A look of deep empathy filled the father's face, and in that look, Ernest saw what might have been the archetypal face of all fathers lovingly teaching an erring child. *His* father had never looked at him like that.

"Mr. Ernest," the father finally said, "do ye think that yer one noble deed will erase the many evil deeds ye ha' done?"

Ernest swallowed and bowed his head. There was a point in that.

The father continued. "How many innocent men ha' ye killed in yer acts o' piracy? How many widows an' orphans tain reason to curse yer name when ye killed their husbands and fathers and lived off o' the plunder? No, Mr. Ernest, ye deserve to be shot. Ye could never do enough good things to erase that simple fact."

Ernest felt a weight come over his whole soul. He knew that every word the father spoke was true. He was a pirate. He was evil. He *did* deserve to be shot. He couldn't respond to that statement. It was true.

The father continued looking at Ernest with loving pity. "Ye only tain one hope o' livin', Mr. Ernest, an' that is by receivin' grace from yer judge."

Ernest looked up at this, daring to hope again that he might live. Clerans shifted positions but said nothing.

"It is the decision o' this court," the father said, straightening up dramatically, "It is the decision o' this court that the accused, Mr. Ernest, be sentenced to a thorough family devotions time, be fully catechized, an' then be locked in the barn fer the night where he will reside at all times when he is no bein' devotioned or catechized. He shall remain thus until further notice."

The father banged his fist on the table for a gavel, and the court adjourned.

31

AFTER THOUGHT

Once the dinner was cleaned up, Clerans and his brothers settled on stools before the fireplace, preparing for devotions. Da had them sing the longest and densest hymns in the hymnal and then brought out the scripture, lecturing for an hour on sin, damnation, grace, salvation, repentance, and sanctification. It was a wonderful sermon, Clerans thought.

Then, Da pulled out the catechism (the larger one, of course). This made even Robert and Roland squirm. Da only brought out the catechism on especially verbose occasions. This was certainly a special occasion; it wasn't every day that you got to sermonize a real live pirate! Clerans shook his head and allowed himself a small smile. He was over his initial desire for revenge. Maybe this pirate hadn't been involved in Olyfia or Mr. Blysffi's murder. If so, a thorough devotioning was appropriate.

Clerans decided he was going to enjoy this. He wondered what Pastor Daerl would say when he heard Da had catechized a pirate. There Da was, leaning forward like he always did when he was intent on teaching.

"'What are you?'"

The pirate looked at Da blankly.

"Now," Da said, looking up from over the top of the catechism. "Ye repeat after me: 'I am a sinner, justly deserving the wrath and damnation of God.'"

The pirate got that easily enough, so Da moved on to the second question.

"What hope do you have?"

And slowly, Da taught the pirate the answer with just as much patience and conviction as he had taught Clerans, Robert, and Roland.

"'My only hope for salvation is in the Christ, the Son of God, who died in my place as my sacrificial propitiation of sin, that I could inherit the glories of God.'"

And when the pirate had that answer down, Da moved to the third question.

"'How can you claim this hope?'"

Clerans knew these questions backward and forwards (and that was no figure of speech; he, Robert, and Roland would quote them backward to each other for the fun of it), but he hadn't reviewed them since Da had taught Roland the catechism. However, the nostalgia of the questions and answers was far eclipsed by the fun of watching this poor pirate struggle through them. That pirate was probably the most perfect heathen and hadn't the nearest idea to what religion was — he probably hadn't even heard the term 'gospel.'

The pirate twitched nervously and screwed up his face — just like Clerans himself had done when Da had catechized him. But here the pirate was, at least ten years Clerans' senior.

"'I must repent from my sins and look to the Almighty God alone for grace and forgiveness, for only He can save. I must make Him the Lord of my life and submit to His rules.'"

Then Da moved on to the fourth question.

"'And how are you saved?'"

And slowly, he taught the pirate the answer:

"'By the grace of God alone, through faith in Him, which is gifted of His Holy Ghost, and not by any deed of myself.'"

Robert and Roland grinned at each other, both probably finding this entire scene as humorous as Clerans found it. Even Ma seemed to enjoy this, though she was still nervous around this pirate. Lexi still stared at the pirate skeptically with her arms crossed and a wide scowl across her face, though even she had the beginnings of a smile playing at the corners of her lips.

When Da had finished the fourth question, he went through all four again until he was convinced that the pirate knew them all by heart. Then Da put away the catechism and sighed contentedly.

"Well, now, Mr. Ernest. I hope ye ha' ceiven good care o' those questions. Ye are no likely to hear anything truer. But I think the first four are enough fer ye this evening. Tomorrow, perhaps, I shall teach you the next four."

The pirate seemed to wilt at the news that there were four more questions.

"Eh, sir," the pirate finally said, "if'n you don't mind my asking, how many questions are there?"

Da smiled broadly. "Three hundred and fifty."

The pirate's eyes bugged out, and Robert and Roland snickered, no longer able to hold in their mirth.

"What was that again?" the pirate gasped.

"Three hundred and fifty," Da replied.

The pirate swallowed. "Ah, now, that's a bit."

Da kept smiling. "No too merri fer a grown man like yerself. All o' my boys know the catechism by heart."

"Ay, that we do," Roland cut in, and Robert nodded emphatically.

The pirate swallowed again.

Clerans smiled and said, "Perhaps, Mr. Pirate, ye'll will wish that we ha' shot ye a'fore this whole catechism is cluded."

The pirate shook his head vehemently. "Oh, no. I'd go through a hundred catemchizements before I'd wish to be shot."

Da stood up. "That bein' settled, we will now lock ye in the barn, Mr. Ernest. Vene with us."

And with that, Da and Martyn took the pirate out the back door.

Ma now whisked Robert and Roland off to their bedrooms while Lexi washed the supper dishes. Haeli had disappeared. She must be in the back somewhere. Clerans was about to join Lexi when Da poked his head back inside.

"Clerans, Martyn, an' I are cedin' to the alleyway to clean away those two pirates and bury them. Would ye like to join us?"

Clerans' stomach felt like it was tying itself into a knot. He had blissfully forgotten about those two dead pirates in the alleyway — the two that he had killed himself. He felt sick just thinking about them. He remembered how effortlessly his tomahawk embedded in the long-armed gnome, and how the hulking man had dropped like a rock with one shot from his rifle. Clerans felt dizzy, and he put out his hand to steady himself.

Still, he should help to bury those pirates; he had killed them, and that would be the responsible thing to do. He supposed he didn't owe them anything — he had killed them out of self-defense — but he did sort of feel that he owed them a burial as it *was* he who had struck them dead.

"I..." Clerans stopped. He could feel bile rising in his throat. Those were *dead* bodies in the alleyway. "I..." he started again.

Da smiled at him sympathetically. "Martyn and I will take care o' it, then." He turned as if to go but then looked Clerans in the face. "No one outta-should enjoy doin' that, an' I am glad to see that ye do no. I am merri proud o' ye, son. Ye did the right thing, and ye tain the right attitude about it." Then Da turned and shut the door, but he immediately threw it open again. "Ah, right! Lexi, would ye mind bringin' that pirate some blankets? Thank ye!"

And then he shut the door for good.

Lexi grumbled. "Llifsa! That nasty *villain* outta-should tain to sleep a few chilly nights. It would do him a merri o' good." But she walked off towards the linen closet.

Clerans still felt sick, so while the others were occupied, he slipped out the front door and sat on the doorstep. Immediately, he felt like vomiting. Somehow he kept his supper down, though. He leaned forward and wrapped his arms around his knees. It was chilly out that evening. Why hadn't he grabbed his coat?

A damp breeze blew in from the bay, carrying with it the scent of far-off rain, but otherwise, everything was still in that little village. Here and there a dog barked, and behind the house, the chickens clucked as they settled up in their roosts for the night. The sun hung behind the mountains, painting the entire sky with red streaks — a deep red, almost like the color of blood.

Clerans groaned and buried his face into his knees. He had killed two people today. He had *killed* two *people* today. Taking a deep breath, he swallowed down the urge to vomit. Stop; there wasn't any reason to beat himself up about this. He had done the right thing. He had saved Haeli from who-knows-what sort of torture by acting quickly and decisively, just like Sheriff Laei had taught him. There was nothing to be ashamed of.

Though he could come to this decision rationally, his gut feelings didn't seem to be inclined to listen to his head on the matter. His stomach continued to tie itself up in vindictive knots. Clerans ground his teeth together. He had done what was right. He had done what he was supposed to do. Why did he feel so horrible about it?

Just then, the door opened behind him, and he straightened up, trying to act like he wasn't having an argument with his stomach. Looking behind him, he saw Haeli slipping out of the door. She noticed Clerans and took a step back.

"Oh, Clerans... I did not know you were out here."

Clerans shrugged, trying to look casual. "It is all right."

Haeli closed the door and sat down on the ground next to him. Clerans shifted his position nervously. Haeli simply made him nervous; that was all there was to it. Maybe this stemmed from the fact that Martyn could get along so well with Haeli, yet Clerans couldn't. To be honest, Clerans didn't even try to get along with her. She was simply a family friend, and that's how Clerans left it.

Then again, Clerans would admit to himself (and only to himself) that he did like Haeli. She was very sweet, hardworking, strong, and very pretty for a girl of her age. All of this added together to make Clerans naturally attracted to her. Because of this, he felt duty-bound to dislike her — or if not dislike, at least treat her with indifferent civility in public.

Come to think of it, this was probably the closest that Haeli had ever been to him before — sitting where she was directly next to him, almost touching him. Clerans felt uncomfortable with this, but (at the same time) he felt a twinge of a romantic thrill in it — and come to think of it, these two emotions perfectly summed up his relationship with Haeli.

Finally, Haeli broke the silence. "I did not know you were out here, but since you are, I just wanted to thank you for what you did for me."

Clerans blushed, feeling very uncomfortable now. "Ah, ye do no need to mention it..."

Haeli looked him directly in the eye. "That was merri brave and chivalrous of you — and of course, I would not expect you to do anything less — but still, I am merri thankful. You saved my..." She stopped and started over. "You probably saved my life."

Clerans shrugged and squirmed awkwardly, not willing to

meet Haeli's gaze. "Now, ye need no keep sayin' that. I did what I did, an' honestly, ye are makin' me feel merri embarrassed by keepin' talkin' about it."

Haeli laughed lightly at this — it was such a pretty musical laugh. Clerans had always liked the way she laughed. "I suppose you are right. I will shut up then." After a pause, she added, "I thought that what your father said was so sweet that I wanted to say something to you that would be equally meaningful."

At this, she grew somber and looked away. Clerans turned towards her now and examined her. In that moment, he saw Haeli differently than he had ever seen her before. She wasn't simply an annoyingly attractive girl, or even a family friend; she was another human being with a soul, with deep emotions and longings. Beyond that, Clerans could see a deep wound in her eyes. He hadn't allowed himself to admit that Mr. Blysffi — Haeli's father — was dead, killed by the pirates. It didn't *feel* real, and it unsettled him to think about it. Still, as he watched Haeli sitting on the ground next to him, he allowed himself to absorb the reality of what Haeli had been through.

Her father was dead. She had spent a weary day on the road, and was now separated from her mother and brothers, too. He tried to put himself in Haeli's place. It must feel awful, very lonely, and very bleak.

Clerans could sense somehow by her position and by her down-cast face that she was even then mourning her father. That would be so painful. It would change your entire view of life. Would she feel betrayed by Him? Perhaps a better question would be, what would *he* feel in that situation? Clerans wasn't sure how he would feel, but he knew he wanted never to question God, but to come to God with desperate cries for help in his grief. That felt more spiritual, anyway.

Haeli clenched her jaw, and for a moment, Clerans thought she was going to cry. Clerans had a strong desire to reach out and hug her or offer her what comfort he could. She was visibly hurting, and he couldn't help but feel for her. His stomach ached just looking at Haeli. If only there were something he could do to make her pain go away. Still, he kept his distance. He couldn't put his arm around her; he had already allowed himself to get too close to her.

"Are ye thinkin' about yer father?" he finally said in a low tone.

Haeli nodded, but she didn't look at him, and she didn't open her mouth.

"I am sorry." He couldn't think of anything else to say. "I..." He trailed off. Anything else he could say would probably sound ridiculous. "I am sorry," he finally said again.

Suddenly, Haeli straightened up. Clerans watched with a twinge of horror as Haeli seemed to swallow down her emotions forcibly, leaving only a stone-cold expression on her face.

"Haeli," he breathed, "are ye all right?"

"I am fine," she replied.

Clerans furrowed his brow. Haeli was obviously *not* fine. "Haeli…" he said, but she broke in.

"I tain a favor to ask of you."

Clerans nodded. "All right. I will do it."

Haeli looked at Clerans closely. "That is it? You do not want to hear what it is first?"

Clerans shrugged. "Look here, Haeli; I want to help ye in any way I cen. It is hard enough fer me to sit here, no knowin' what to do, but if ye tain a favor that needs doin' then ye cen count on me to do it."

Haeli regarded him for nearly a minute (as Clerans shifted his weight awkwardly) before she finally pulled a weathered packet of papers from her pocket. "I need you to deliver this to the Company offices for me."

Clerans took the letter and nodded. "That is easy enough.

The executive office, the service office, the warehouse office, or the coastal office?"

Haeli pursed her lips. "Whichever one would process a legal prosecution?"

Clerans raised an eyebrow at this. "Are ye prosecutin' the Company?"

"Ma is," Haeli replied. "Or rather, Da is." And she went silent again.

After a moment's pause, she finally said, "It is a long story. You can read the letter if you like. And I do not expect you to carry through on this if you are not comfortable."

"Llifsa!" Clerans exclaimed. "I will deliver this letter to the executive office. I ha' already agreed to that. And if it tains something to do with yer Da, then I'll will be all the more certain to see it done right."

Haeli looked him in the eye, but her face looked dead and emotionless.

Clerans licked his lips. "Haeli, are ye all right?"

"Ay," Haeli replied stiffly. "I am fine." And she stood up. "I just wanted to thank you; that was it."

Clerans looked at her for a moment before he spoke. He was trying to be diplomatic. He didn't want any hard feelings. "Haeli, ye cen sit down. Ye do no ha' to be upset. Come now, sit back down, and we'll cen talk some more."

Haeli looked away.

Clerans clenched his jaw, speaking softly. "Haeli, ye are no fine. I cen tell ye are hurtin'..."

But that was as far as he got. Haeli turned on him, glaring. "And what if I am, you...!" But she apparently couldn't come up with the right word to describe him, for she spun on her heels and walked off around the corner of the house.

Clerans sat there for a moment, stunned. He felt like she had stabbed him between the ribs. After he had let himself connect with Haeli, probably more so than anyone else outside of his family, in an instant, she had shoved him away and left him there alone. He had only been trying to help her. Hadn't she thanked him earlier for helping her?

Clerans was upset, but he tried to calm himself down. There wasn't any *real* reason to take offense at Haeli's outburst. She was still grieving the loss of her father. Perhaps if *he* were grieving the death of *his* father, he would have done the same thing. No, he didn't blame Haeli — but he still felt like she had stabbed him.

Clerans simply sat there for a few minutes all by himself in that little street. He heard a tapping sound a little way up the street and looked to see a blind beggar coming slowly down the cobblestone street. Clerans stood. He didn't want company just then, even if the company was a total stranger who was likely to ignore him. Clerans took one last look around the corner where Haeli had disappeared and sighed.

Lord, he prayed, *help poor Haeli. She is hurting, and I cen no help her (actually, I do no think she wants me to help her — an' fer that matter, I am no sure I want to be the one who helps her). You cen though, so please help her.*

With that, he opened the door but paused right before entering his house. Miss Nansi! She had asked him to check in on her with her meeting with the strikers. Had that started already?

FREE FROM SAFETY

*E*rnest stood all by himself in the 'barn,' as the father had termed it. He could hear the father locking the door and walking off. So that was that. He supposed he could be in a much worse situation right now. The catechizing had been tedious, for sure, but it was certainly better than anything else he could have hoped to endure at the hands of Llaedhwythi justice.

Ernest allowed himself to look around. It was a small barn, not much more than a shed. There was a single stall where a large draft horse stood slowly eating his straw and a pen full of fat and lazy chickens all huddled together on their roosts next to the horse's stall. Apart from that, a wagon filled the rest of the space in that little barn. Various tools hung from the walls; a pitching fork, a few shovels, and a hoe or two. As Ernest sighed, the sweet scent of clean straw filled his nostrils.

The father had left Ernest with an oil lantern, so he now set this on the wagon. There was plenty of hay about. He could easily scoop some into the wagon and make a very comfortable bed for himself to spend the night in. This wasn't all that bad; he had a warm place to stay and a full belly. He might have been dead already. Thank goodness that nice little family hadn't turned him in to the sheriff. Still, he could have used a blanket or two.

Just then, he heard a key in the lock, and the door opened slowly. He looked up to see Lexi standing in the doorway. She had her pistol in one hand, pointing it at the ground with the calm confidence of a skilled marksman. But what was that in her other hand? Two blankets? Ernest simply stared at her for a moment, and in the light from his oil lamp, she looked like an angel. The straw in front of her feet glowed ever so slightly, and the lantern light gleamed off of her white cheeks; Ernest couldn't think that he had ever seen a gnome who was so beautiful.

He stepped towards her, and she fixed her eyes on him coldly, her hand tightening on her pistol ever so slightly. "Ye do no move another muscle, sir."

Ernest remained perfectly still.

Lexi took a single step inside and dropped the blankets over the wagon hitch. "There."

"Thank ye kindly, ma'am," Ernest said, trying to be polite, although the words came out in an awkward rush.

She took one step backward and looked him over once more. "I would ha' let ye freeze tonight, but Mr. Blaeith asked me to bring ye the blanket, so do no thank me, thank him."

Ernest nodded. "Yes, ma'am, I see."

Lexi eyed him closely. "Did ye really give Ella that dagger?"

Ernest nodded eagerly. "I do'ed, and isn't that the truth."

Lexi continued to eye him suspiciously. "That is the only thing that you ha' said that makes me think I cen believe you. Ye could no ha' known about that dagger if ye'll were lying."

Ernest took a deep breath, hardly knowing what he was about to say. "Ay, but you're the prettiest gnome I've ever laid eyes on."

Lexi fixed him with a reproving glare before she slammed the door shut, locking it forcefully.

Ernest sighed contentedly as he walked over to the blankets and began making himself a bed. First, he grabbed a pitching fork and bailed several fork-fulls into the wagon's bottom, then he laid one blanket over the top, laying the other over himself as he settled down on top of his makeshift bed.

He had nothing to complain about. He would likely spend the night better than he ever would have on the pirate ship. If he hadn't been captured, he would probably be making his way back to the ship now, slogging away throughout the night, only for Killjelly and Holgard to interrogate him when he got back. He might have a few hours to sleep before he would have to wake up and begin the day's work with the other crew members.

He could get used to sleeping in this barn with nothing but a few chickens and a horse to keep him company. It looked as if he was likely to eat well, and if all he had to endure was a catechizing once a day, he wouldn't have much to worry about. Hadn't the father said there were three hundred and fifty questions? At four a day, he would be here for... well, maybe a month. That wasn't so bad. He could spend a month here pretending to be a good little gnome, learning his religion from the father, and catching a glance of that enchanting Lexi any chance he got. He could get used to all of this.

The God of War would probably have him work for his keep, and that was all the same to him. Hadn't he been thinking that morning that he wanted to get a piece of land and settle down, leaving his life of piracy behind him? Well, maybe this was his chance. He could learn a trade from the God of War, or Lord Vengeance, or the father, or whoever would teach him, and then he would settle down like a respectable gnome. Maybe if he showed them all that he had reformed, he could marry Lexi.

Yes, that would be very nice. He could stand being married to that beautiful gnome. She was as enchanting as a summer's evening under a full moon. True, she was slimmer than he had imagined his wife would be, but that was all right. She would fatten up with time.

He would miss Lewis, for certain. There wasn't any way he could send a message to him, was there? He wouldn't mind if Lewis could settle down with him. Still, there wasn't much of a way that could happen. Lewis was back on the pirates' ship, and he was stuck there in the barn, held captive by... well, by a nice little Llaedhwythi family.

Still, if this were all to work out, he would have to convince this nice family that he was reformed, and probably the best way to prove that would be to prove that he had got religion. That wouldn't be too hard; after all, he had gone to school at the monastery, plus he knew how to do righteous cussing, thanks to Lewis. He just had to keep a sharp mind during the catechizing, and he'd have them convinced in no time at all.

He nestled down into his straw bed some more and sighed contentedly, reciting his lessons from the evening before falling asleep.

"What are ye?"

"I am a sinner, justly deserving the wrath and damnation of God."

"What hope do ye tain?"

"My only hope for salvation is in the Christ, the son of God, who died in my place, as my sacrificial propitiation for sin, that I could inherit the glories of God."

"How can you claim this hope?"

"I must repent from my sins and look to the Almighty God alone for grace and forgiveness, for only He can save. I must make Him the Lord of my life and submit to His rules."

"How are you saved?"

"By the grace of God alone, through faith in Him, which is gifted of His Holy Ghost, and not by any deed of myself."

They were nice questions and answers. Ernest didn't know what half of it meant, but they were nice questions and answers for all that. He was rather glad they were short and not long and impossible, like the monks' litanies and loricae. That made it a lot easier to remember.

Just then, he heard a sound as if someone was messing with the lock on the door. Earnest opened his eyes and sat up slowly. Could it be Lexi again? Probably not. She seemed rather sensible and wouldn't have come out to the barn twice. She would have remembered everything the first time. Most likely, it was Lord Vengeance or the God of War looking to see that he was still there.

The door creaked open slowly and cautiously. Glancing at his visitor, Ernest recoiled in terror. It was the Albino. He looked haggard, but a sinister light shone from his pink eyes. In his arms, he held a large bundle, which looked to be little more than a pile of rags in the dim light.

"Come, scribe," the Albino said in a harsh whisper.

Ernest dared not show any sign of resistance, but his heart sank to his toes. So much for his plans of leaving his life of piracy. He could not refuse the Albino. He had to go. If Longfinch had come to fetch him personally, Ernest might have found it inside himself to refuse and stay with this nice family, but there was something about the Albino — some power that seemed to emanate from him — which Ernest could not contradict.

Slowly, he climbed out of the wagon and walked to the door.

"Quietly, now," the Albino said. "You have made this hard enough on me already. We must be back at the galleon before midnight."

Ernest tried not to groan. He had been looking forward to a long, peaceful sleep in the barn. He didn't want to trade it for another sleepless night. It would take them *hours* to get back to the bay where Holgard's galleon lay in anchor. Even if they made good time, they could hardly make it back to the ship by midnight.

The Albino looked Ernest over critically. "Fed, rested, and ready for the journey, I see."

Ernest ground his teeth together. "Not much rested, really. I haven't getted a wink on sleep."

The Albino smiled grimly. "Expect little of that for the next few days." So saying, the Albino handed Ernest the wadded bundle. "You are in a better state to carry her."

Ernest took it, realizing with horror that it was a person, limp and swaddled in a ragged blanket. He looked closely at his new burden. Yes, it was indeed Lady Death. The Albino had done it. Their mission was successful. Ernest groaned involuntarily.

The Albino only smiled ruthlessly. "Come now, the night is wasting away. We must be going."

33

SEDITION

Clerans marched briskly through the commons, his eye fixed on Miss Nansi's cottage. He had come as soon as he finished his evening chores, but that had taken longer than he had wanted. Was he too late now? The last carmine glow of the sunset lingered over the western mountains, but in half an hour, the dale would be black as pitch, as neither the moon nor the daystar had risen yet. Already, the strikers had pitched their tents around the commons, having moved their things out of Nychweni Square. Clerans shifted the strap on his rifle. The strikers seemed gruff and shifty to him, not to be trusted. They looked even more desperate after their retreat from the factories. It was a good thing he was here to protect Miss Nansi. What did she think she could do with these wild men? They would not listen to reason.

Finally, Clerans reached Miss Nansi's door. The furniture from her front room sat outside, leaning against the wall of her cottage. That was odd. The door itself was wide open, and various strikers filed in. Pursing his lips, Clerans joined them. Entering, he found the whole of Miss Nansi's front room converted into a conference room, the furniture out of the way, and long boards laid across barrels and hay bales to form makeshift benches. Most of the strikers were still standing, talking together in muffled tones, while Miss Nansi pushed her way through the crowd with a kettle of maté. She must have run out of mugs, for she was pouring the maté into whatever containers or drinking vessels the strikers had on hand.

Clerans folded his arms over his chest and put his back to a wall. He felt distinctly out of place in this group. Though he felt a little cheeky thinking about it, he was the only *clean* person in the room. But as he scanned the room again, he realized that this was not entirely true. There were a handful of respectable-looking people crammed into this ersatz conference room, and when Clerans looked at them closely, he recognized them. That was Mr. and Mrs. Gingrich (the farriers from Entwerp Coastal) sitting at the front, and there was the young couple who were beacon-tenders together; what were their names? His name was Chaerls, but Clerans only knew her by her last name: Miss Flalowen. Still, seeing these couples here wasn't that shocking. They were both Rectificationists like Miss Nansi. Of course, they would support these strikers.

While waiting for the meeting to start, Clerans sat in the corner of the room, leaning against the wall and looking around intently. After a moment of waiting, he pulled Haeli's letter out of his pocket. Haeli had said he could read it to make sure that he was comfortable delivering it. So, now was as good a time as any to figure out what this was all about.

Unfolding the paper, he perused its contents. It was a legal document (filled with all the confusing and archaic language of lawyers), but this didn't bother Clerans much. He had to take dictations now and then for the Company, so he was used to this kind of dense vocabulary. It didn't take him long to figure out the letter's main gist. It was a notice of a lawsuit that Mrs. Blysffi was taking up for the indigies's sake: the indigies were suing the Company to reclaim lands that the Company had taken without payment. That was pretty easy to figure out, but what land exactly were they talking about, and which tribe was Mrs. Blysffi representing?

Clerans scanned the letter again, and finally, the full implications of this letter dawned on him. Mrs. Blysffi was suing for *all* the land which the Company occupied within the boundaries of Indigie Law because the Company had not paid for any of it. Clerans bit his lip. That would be almost every beacon station the Company owned and probably half the forts. If Mrs. Blysffi won this court case, then the Company would all but cease to exist on the coast; the only presence left being the offices and warehouses in the towns and villages.

Clerans shook his head. This was insane. This was a complete revolution. There was no way that any Llaedhwythi court would let this pass. Why was Mrs. Blysffi doing this anyway? Then Clerans reached the last line, and he furrowed his brow. Mrs. Blysffi mentioned something about prosecuting the Company under Indigie Law. What did that mean? Clerans thought back to other legal documents he had taken dictation for. Wasn't it customary to include which court you were suing in at the end of the letter? So whatever Mrs. Blysffi was saying about Indigie Law, it was instead of saying which court she was suing in.

Clerans paused. No, Indigie Law was the court Mrs. Blysffi was suing in. That was what this was saying. Mrs. Blysffi was suing the Company for the tribes' rights, but doing so in the tribal courts. This was brilliant. Sure, the implications were terrifying (this would shut down the Company, bring the economy to a screeching halt, and flood the city with unemployed wild men like the strikers), but it was still brilliant.

Just then, a burly man sat down next to Clerans, interrupting his train of thought. Clerans glanced at the man and recoiled in disgust. The man's face was badly mutilated (like a severe burn that had never healed right), and he was missing his right arm.

Clerans buried his nose in the letter, hoping the man would not talk to him, but no sooner had the man sat down next to Clerans, than he nudged him with his shoulder.

"And what is yer story, Yonker?"

"Me?" Clerans looked up in alarm. He tried not to gag at the stench which emanated from the man's disfigured face.

"Ay," the man replied. "What made ye join the cause?"

Clerans shrugged. "Oh, no, sir, ye misunderstand. I am no part o' this. I am jist here to watch."

The man eyed him suspiciously. "So ye are a spy, then?"

Clerans shifted away from the man as best he could. "If I'll wos a spy, do ye think I would merri well tell ye outright like that?"

"Who sent ye?" the man pressed.

"As it happens," Clerans nodded to Miss Nansi, "I am a friend with the owner o' this cottage, Miss Nansi Felonica, an' she asked me to come by."

The man still eyed him warily, so Clerans cleared his throat and changed the subject. "Merri well, my good man. Why do no ye tell me what made ye 'join the cause,' as ye put it?"

The man looked him up and down for a moment and finally nodded. "I wos a beacon-tender near Naeswyth Bay, served there for twenty-three years. Burned my face badly one night when I fell asleep while tendin' a beacon, an' I never complained about it. Then one day while I wos harvesting wood fer the beacon with my comrade, the tree fell on my arm an' crushed it. After the gangrene set in, they got me drunk on whiskey an' sawed it off."

The man wagged the stump of his right arm to emphasize the point. Clerans shuddered.

"Well then," the man went on, "I could no tend beacons anymore, so I turned up to the Company office fer my back pay. An' they fired me on the spot."

Clerans pursed his lips. "I do no mean to seem unsympathetic."

The man shook his head. "That probably means that ye are."

Clerans sighed. "Gard here, I cen see this both ways. Sure ye were hard done by the Company, but surely ye understand the business sense o' the Company. They'll cen no lose money by payin' someone who cen bring no value to them."

The man shook his head. "If I'll wos a horse, or a cow, or any kind o' livestock, then that way o' thinkin' may hold some truth. But I am a person, made in God's image. That should count fer something, ay?"

Clerans drummed his fingers on Haeli's letter absentmindedly. "Sure, I s'pose. So what are ye tryin' to accomplish?"

"Here is the way I see it," the man replied. "The Company refused to give us a saw-mill or any equipment that would keep us safe while we worked. They put us in an unsafe situation — an' that is the reason I lost my arm. So, if they'll refuse to pay the money necessary to keep their workers safe, then they'll outta-should pay fer the damage done to their workers."

Clerans tilted his head to one side. "I s'pose there is some sense in that."

"Ay," the man replied, "an' it is scriptural. Does it no say in the Laws to repay a man fer the loss o' his arm?"

Clerans nodded slowly. "Ay, ye are right. That is in the Laws."

The man held up his good hand dramatically. "Well, there ye tain it."

The man motioned to a middle-aged nymph on the bench before them. "That man there, he's been a beacon-tender fer forty years."

"Forty years!" Clerans gasped. "Why didn't he ever get promoted to a fort-tender or a warehouse manager? Did he jist like tendin' beacons that much?"

The man shook his head. "He tried fer promotions. But he is an indigie. Beacon-tending is all the Company will let him do."

Clerans furrowed his brow. "Well, that is no fair."

The man nodded. "Ay, no. It is no." The man paused fer a moment. "Are ye part o' our cause now?"

Clerans looked the man in the face and pursed his lips. He had never talked to a striker before (though he had judged them severely every time he saw them in Nychweni Square). But somehow, this seemed a lot more reasonable. He had always assumed that these men were lazy and irresponsible (which is why the Company fired them) or else that they were radical Rectificationists (like the Blysffis). But now he saw they were rational people with good reason to feel the way they felt and do the things they did.

The one-armed man seemed to read Clerans' thoughts, for he sighed heavily. "It is easy enough to judge us harshly because o' the way we look. We seem rough an' wild, do no we? Ay, and the irony is that we are rough an' wild because that is what the Company made us. We ha' to be rough an' wild to live. Yet now, the Company will use the same qualities they fostered in us to discredit us."

Clerans licked his lips. "I ha' never heard this strike explained like this a'fore."

The man looked at him critically. "Did ye ever ask?"

Clerans pursed his lips. "This is no what yer spokesman said at the factory."

The man shook his head. "Ay. We are all in this fer different reasons, an' most o' us tain different ideas o' how to run this strike. But whatever we decide, we must stick together."

Just then, Miss Nansi stood up at the front of the room and clapped her hands. The strikers fell silent and looked at her.

"All righty, dears," Miss Nansi said. "Now, I wanted to call ye together to discuss our methods."

A man suddenly stood up in the back — it was the

spokesman from the confrontation at the factory. "There is no anythin' wrong with our methods. We must put pressure on the sheriff, on the town, on the entire country! That's the only way that anyone is goin' to listen to us!"

"Ay, ay!" several strikers assented.

Miss Nansi shook her head. "I do no condone violence in this strike."

"Bah!" the spokesman replied. "Then ye do no tain stomach enough to see justice done."

"Ay, ay!" several more strikers agreed.

The spokesman went on. "They ha' been doin' violence against us fer years. Ye saw the sheriff, how easily he would stoop to violence against us. Sometimes violence is the only way what there is to get yer voice heard."

Miss Nansi sighed. "I do no object to violence per se — I am no a pacifist."

"Prove it!" someone yelled.

Miss Nansi folded her arms over her chest. "Look here, ye varlets. I supported independence. I even served with Caedmon Wilkins in the wars. Where were ye when we were fightin' the Empires?"

The strikers sat silently. Only the middle-aged nymph stood.

"I was a patriot, too. The Hrufangi murdered my tribe. I fought back." And he pulled back his sleeve to show a long scar all the way down his arm. "I took a bayonet defending Mininoich."

The nymph sat down, and everyone sat in respectful silence for some time.

Finally, Miss Nansi spoke. "I do no call into question your bravery or your ideals. But I ha' fought a war a'fore, an' I know what it is like. I think I'll know a thing or three about violence then."

The spokesman folded his arms over his chest. "Merri well. Enlighten us. Why was it all right fer ye to push out the

Hrufangi violently, but we must never raise a finger against the Company?"

Miss Nansi held up a hand in objection. "First off, ye were no raisin' a finger against the Company. Ye were raisin' a finger against the innocent factory workers."

The spokesman shrugged. "Ay. So? How else are we s'posed to get our point across?"

Miss Nansi shook her head. "Ye are impossible."

The spokesman held up his hands in exasperation. "Go on then!"

Miss Nansi sighed. "I do no tain a perfect solution."

"There!" the spokesman called out defiantly, and several other strikers murmured.

Nansi clapped her hands for attention. "That's the whole reason I called this meeting. We tain strength and power because we come to decisions together, maugre blindly followin' one leader." Here she stared pointedly at the spokesman.

The spokesman folded his arms over his chest and sneered. "It is no my fault that I ha' come up with the best way forward."

Miss Nansi shook her head. "Gard here: if we'll want to see the Company pay us fer the harm they'll ha' done us, then we must tain support. Committing violent acts on the populace will only alienate people from our cause."

"But the sheriff will use violence," someone said.

Miss Nansi held up a finger. "There is the point. I know Sheriff Laei. He is a friend o' mine, an' here is what he knows that ye do no."

Miss Nansi gazed at her audience. "The moment he pulls the trigger o' his gun or fights back against us, the entire population o' Entwerp will support him — no matter how unreasonable or unjustified he may be. He is the sheriff, an' so the people will let him be violent. He does no need to be careful — but we do."

Here Mr. Gingrich broke in. "Is no that the entire problem?

After the revolution, we thought we gained equality, but we are still under the yoke o' government an' companies. Tear them all down, I say!"

"Ay!" Mrs. Gingrich cried. "Let us establish the Anarchy!"

Nansi shook her head. "One problem at a time, please."

"Look," the spokesman said. "We already tain an answer to our problems. We jist need to nationalize the beacon system. That is it. That is what I told the sheriff at the factories."

"Ay," someone else joined in. "If the beacons do no need to earn a profit fer the owners, then they will be able to support more o' us workin'."

"Nationalize the beacons?" Mr. Gingrich snorted. "An' give the government more power over our lives? Better to tain no beacons at all than submit to sich slavery."

The spokesman's eyes went wide in alarm. "But the economy!"

Mr. Gingrich shook his head. "We cen no sacrifice doin' the right thing because o' some fool idea about the economy. I would rather be right than rich."

"Well, I would rather be rich!" a striker cried out.

Miss Nansi clapped her hands for attention. "One problem at a time. Fer now, we must think how best to put pressure on the Company."

"Barricade the factories," the spokesman said.

"Never!" Nansi and several strikers called out in unison.

The spokesmen shrugged. "Barricade the bank, then."

"Are ye moon-drunk?" Nansi replied.

"Ye may be, fer all I know," the spokesman shot back. "It is a good plan. There would be minimal loss o' life 'cause no so many people work at the bank, but it would be sure to get us noticed. We would get national attention."

"National infamy, ye mean!" Mr. Gingrich snorted.

"Same thing," the spokesman said with a shrug. "Any attention they give us is good fer the cause."

Miss Nansi shook her head. "But what good does that do us to barricade the bank? Everyone will hear o' us, fer sure. But how does that put pressure on the Company? Their finances are independent o' the National Bank. We would jist harm our country, an' the Company could carry on as before."

"Ay," several strikers agreed.

"We must put pressure on the Company," the man with one arm suddenly said. "I am no opposed to violence, but we must leave the factories and the bank, an' the sheriff alone. We outta-should direct our efforts on the Company, an' only the Company."

The spokesman folded his arms over his chest and sneered. "But what kind o' pressure could we put on the Company that would only affect the Company?"

Clerans suddenly stood, and he held up the letter from Haeli. "I think I tain an idea o' how you could do that."

A KEY MATTER

The night was well advanced, and the sky let down a drizzly rain when Ernest and the Albino finally reached the bay where Holgard and Longfinch's ships lay in anchor. Ernest could make out the two ships' outlines. The carpenters and sailors must have been busy all that day, as there wasn't a rigging line out of place. The two ships looked as good as new, ready to hunt again on the high seas.

The Albino pulled a little skiff from underneath a low-hanging branch on the water's edge, and in this, the Albino, Ernest, and Haeli skimmed quietly over the water toward the galleon. Haeli lay perfectly limp this whole time, and Ernest suspected the Albino had put her under some sort of spell; no one slept that soundly while being carried for miles along a rocky mountain road.

Ernest groaned and slumped down in his seat in the skiff. All his muscles hurt from his long march, carrying Lady Death — Haeli, that is — the whole time. To add to this, he was soaked through with the rain, and his head throbbed from lack of sleep. When would this end? Why couldn't he have stayed inside that nice little barn and lived with that nice little family for the rest of his life? Why did he have to go back to this misery?

They reached the galleon's side, and the watchman on duty hailed them. "Who's there? What do you want, and where do you come from?" He was gruff and not in the best of moods. Ernest recognized him as a carpenter, a leprechaun named Frank — or Walter — one or the other.

Ernest waved up at him. "It's me, Ernest, the cook's-mate."

The watchman peered down at them. "Ernest? What the sacrament are you doing down there?"

The Albino now spoke, his voice low and authoritative. "Tell Holgard and Killjelly that we have returned."

The watchman wilted, then scurried off across the deck to the captain's cabin.

"Get us a rope, at least!" Ernest cried, but the watchman must not have heard him since he didn't turn back.

"Haloo!" Ernest called out, trying to be quiet enough that the pirates on Longfinch's ship wouldn't hear him. "Haloo there! Get us a rope!"

After a few minutes, Ernest heard some more footsteps on the ship, and another watchman peered over the gunwales at them. This was a human — Roe, right? Ernest was pretty sure he was Frank's messmate, which would explain why they were on the watchman's duty together.

"Ernest?" Roe said softly. "Why are you down there? Weren't you here all day?"

"No," Ernest replied, getting frustrated. "No, I wasn't. I've been running a baptized chase throughout the mountains on a sacrament on an errand from Holgard. Now throw me an anointed rope so that I can get aboard and get out on this anointed rain."

Roe ducked his head back behind the gunwales, and in a moment, he threw a rope down to the little skiff. Ernest climbed aboard, and then the Albino tied Haeli to the end of the rope. After Ernest had hauled her up to the deck, he threw the rope back over the side, and the Albino climbed up.

Just as the Archeomancer's foot touched the deck, Holgard marched out of his cabin, flanked by Killjelly, Ynwyr, and Frank. He marched up to the Albino and looked him over, snorting in irritation.

"Do'edn't I give you three on my men?"

The Albino only smiled, pointing to the bundle on the deck, which was Haeli. "I brought you someone else in their stead."

With that, the Albino spoke a mumbled word or two, and Haeli stirred. Ernest had noticed the Albino looking gaunt and tired for most of the hike back, but as he watched, even more energy sapped from the Albino's frame. The Archeomancer leaned back against the gunwales, but he smiled with a kind of crooked satisfaction.

Haeli sat bolt upright with a wild look in her eyes. "Where am I?"

"Hold her still, sure," Killjelly ordered.

Frank and Roe sprang forward as she struggled to her feet, and they caught hold of her. Her eyes darted back and forth like a caged animal until they fell on Ernest. Ernest could feel his heart sink with guilt as she stared at him accusingly. "What have you done? This is how you pay us back for keeping you alive?"

"I do'edn't have a choice," Ernest whined.

"You coward!" Haeli spat. "And after I stood up for you, too!"

Holgard snorted and turned to the Albino in irritation. "I don't want a girl. That isn't what I sended you for."

"Ay," Ynwyr nodded. "What do'ed you think we'd want a girl for?"

The Albino smiled. "You said that you wanted the key. Here she is."

Holgard growled as he stared the Albino in the face. "I meaned a *key* — like a physical, metal key — for unlocking doors!"

"She knows," the Albino replied. "You look for answers. You should look for people."

Holgard straightened up and put his hand on his pistol butt, pacing back and forth in frustration. "Time is running out. Longfinch is getting ready to make his move. Pennywraith will be here before much longer. And now you want me to waste more time on interrogations? Look what we getted done with Jock by all our interrogating: Longfinch haves him now, and there's no telling what Jock's told him that we don't know about! What do you think it will take before Longfinch steals this girl, too, and interrogates her? I don't need another person. I need the key to the Gwambi door!"

The Albino smiled. "You think you can find this treasure by following the clues, do you not? You think Jock looked over each clue academically and solved this great mental problem to find the treasure. That is not at all what happened, though. Jock never found the treasure. The treasure found him. To find it yourself, you must know the people he knew. It is not a mental search; it is — and always was — an emotional and relational search."

Holgard growled but said no more.

Killjelly turned to Haeli, looking at her closely. "I know you, sure. You were there at the fort — you were the bar-maid. Your father gave you a key before he died, sure?"

Ernest looked from Killjelly to Haeli. Wait a moment, hadn't Killjelly told them to get the girl? Why was he acting surprised that the Albino would come back with the girl? Come to think of it, why didn't Holgard know about the girl? Were they both putting up a show? Ernest studied Holgard closely. No, he wasn't acting. But what about Killjelly? Something wasn't adding up.

Haeli shut her mouth tightly and looked at the leprechaun boatswain defiantly — even angrily.

"Where is that key?" Killjelly asked.

"You killed him, did not you?" Haeli said, speaking in a low and even tone. "You shot him."

Killjelly shrugged apathetically. "You've got to clean up after yourself."

Haeli clenched her jaw, pure hatred burning in her eyes.

Killjelly shrugged.

Holgard continued to storm across the deck, glaring first at Haeli and then at the Albino. He began stroking his fingers through his long beard in frustration. "We need that key before we can make our move. Everything else is ready, but *you* were supposed to bring me the key!"

"I brought you something better," the Albino replied coolly, though he looked annoyed.

"I don't have time for this," Holgard growled, turning on his heels, marching toward his cabin.

Killjelly motioned to Ernest, Frank, and Roe. "Do what you want with her, boys. We'll make her talk, sure."

Frank and Roe hooted in amusement as they threw Haeli to the deck. This time, she was not as passive as she had been in the alleyway. Frank had hardly got her to the deck before she lashed out at his knee with a kick like a stallion. Frank jumped back with a cry of surprise. Haeli scrambled back to her feet and landed a solid punch to Frank's gut, but Roe caught her by the hair and yanked her to the deck.

Ernest could feel his stomach tying itself in a knot. It was the same thing all over again — only this time, there was no Lord Vengeance to bring it to a stop. And too, there was the Albino and Killjelly standing by. Ernest may have been able to stand up to Bill and Tell, but he couldn't stand against Killjelly's direct command with the Albino looking on. Ernest simply stood there, rooted to the deck like a tree. He couldn't — no, he wouldn't — join Frank and Roe, but neither could he bring himself to stop them.

As Roe yanked viciously at Haeli's hair again, her headscarf slipped free and fell from her. Yet as it hit the deck, Ernest heard a metallic thud. Peering closely, Ernest thought he could see the slightest glint of metal in the wadded scarf.

"The key!" Ernest cried as he rushed forward, knocking Frank and Roe aside and snatching up the scarf. Yes, that was a key hiding in the scarf.

"The key!" Ernest cried again, holding it up for all to see.

Holgard turned around and rushed back, a smile spreading across his face. "Weel, where was it?"

"She had it," the Albino replied. "Did I not say as much?"

Holgard shrugged, "You might have, but you speak in riddles." And with that, he snatched the key from Ernest's grasp.

Frank and Roe now crowded around, wanting to get a good look at this key that had disturbed their quiet watch. The key was, in fact, drawing the attention of everyone present — except for Ernest. Ernest knew this was his only chance. Stepping forward, he snatched up Haeli from the deck.

"What are you–!" Haeli cried.

"Get away from here now, little lady," he whispered. "I don't want to have to stand up for you again."

And with that, he pushed her over the side of the ship. A moment later, he heard her splash into the bay's gently rolling waters.

Frank and Roe cried in alarm, and all eyes turned on Ernest. Ernest could feel his heart beginning to race. He hadn't exactly disobeyed orders, but it felt like he had, and there stood Holgard and Killjelly as witnesses. He wiped the rain from his eyes and tried to look confident.

"What's the meaning on this?" Killjelly hissed.

"She saved my life," Ernest replied. "They killed Bill and Tell, and they would've killed me too, but she speaked up for me. I owed her that."

Holgard chuckled, turning the key over in his hands. "Weel,

now, we will let it pass this time, Ernest. Good job with the key. Pour yourself a pint on grog and get some sleep."

Ernest looked at Holgard closely. He wasn't sure he had ever seen the dwarf captain in such good humor, even when he was drunk.

Holgard turned back to his cabin and clapped Killjelly heartily on the back. "Weel, tomorrow's the day then? Off with our chains! This calls for a drink or two."

Ernest shuffled towards the stairway that would lead him below deck. Frank and Roe muttered briefly together, but otherwise went back to their posts. The Albino, however, stayed leaning against the gunwale, and Ernest could feel the Archeomancer's eyes glaring at him as he climbed below deck. He was exhausted, but his stomach was still coiled up like a viper ready to strike, and his heart still raced as if it were trying to outrun a horse. He hoped he could get some sleep tonight. Maybe a pint of grog would help.

NIGHT VISITORS

Ella woke with a start. Sweat covered her whole body. Her nightgown clung to her like a leech. Her head swam with confusion. What was happening? Why had she woken up? Her blankets were soaked. She felt them hurriedly, shaking all over. Was that blood on her sheets?

She reached out for her candle, and after a few tries with her shaking hand, she finally got a match to strike. The pitiful flame leaped and spluttered at the stick's end, and she hastily lit the candle with it. However, the dim light didn't seem to clear her head at all. Her mind swirled in a maelstrom of bewilderment. Her heart beat rapidly, her pulse throbbing in her head. Why had she woken so suddenly? What was flustering her so much?

She felt the sheets again. Yes, they were soaked, but in the light, she could tell that they weren't bloody. She had soaked her sheets with her own sweat. How had she managed that? Still, the idea of her sheets being bloody was absurd. Why had she even thought of that? Why was that the first thing that had occurred to her? What had she been dreaming about?

Ella slid out of her bed and stood up, shaking so much that she could hardly keep her balance. She tried to wipe the sweat from her face, but her hands were equally sweaty. She wiped her hands on her nightgown, but it was completely soaked through.

She flopped onto the bed in frustration. What had happened to her? Why had she been sweating so much? She wanted to cry. Calm down, Ella. Calm down. Nothing happened. Did it?

In the dim light, she noticed a couple of pieces of paper on the desk beside her cot. There! She could fan herself and dry off the sweat. That should calm her down. After that, when her mind was clear again, she could try to figure out what was going on. She snatched up one of the pieces of paper and fanned herself. Yes, that was better. She sank back into her bed and sighed.

Just then, she noticed a scrawled message on the paper. She gasped involuntarily. With a flicker, the candle went out. Dropping the piece of paper, she grabbed at the matches again.

She trembled all over again, and she could hardly even pick up a match. There, she had one between her fingers. Now if she could only strike it. Once, twice. Still no luck. All right, Ella, just breathe. Calm down. Didn't you write something down before you went to bed?

Ah! The match burst into light, and she set it carefully to the candle wick. Pausing for a moment, she took in a couple of deep breaths. She didn't remember writing anything down, but she must have. Who else would have written on the paper on *her* desk?

She shivered. She didn't want to think about the answer to that question.

But where was the paper, anyway? She looked around and saw it lying face down on the floor. Picking it up carefully, she flipped it over and held it close to the candle.

There she found four names written in a scrawled and blurred handwriting:

Saeilas Pycerivg
Joc Blwhwrdr
Saemwel Pycerivg
Syd Cortwraeit

Ella read the names slowly, sounding them out carefully from the odd Pistosian script. "Silas Pickering, Jock Blowhoarder, Saemwel Pickering, Syd Cartwright."

At the first name, Ella caught her breath, but as she read the other names, she grew more confused. What did her father have to do with these other three men? Sure, Sir Saemwel had known her father. Had the other two? Was Jock Blowhoarder the same as Jock, the beggar from Blisa who was captured with her? Had *he* known her father?

The memory of sitting in the back of the wagon with Jock that first night when the pirates fled her village flashed in Ella's mind. Hadn't he said something about the less she knew about him, the better? What did he know that had to be kept secret?

Then who was Syd Cartwright? Wasn't that the same name she had seen carved into the shed wall? She had assumed it was an alias, but was he actually a friend of her father? Or perhaps this list had nothing to do with a friendship between the four men. It looked more like a hit list. This thought sent chills down her spine. Silas Pickering — killed at sea. Jock Blowhoarder — in the custody of pirates, being tortured to death. Sir Saemwel — on his deathbed, suffering from an old grenade wound. Syd Cartwright — who knows? Maybe he was dead already.

But who wrote this list? Ella now looked up, and for the first time, she realized the door to her room was open. Her heart raced, and she could feel the sweat on her forehead again. She was certain she had closed the door before climbing into bed. She shook all over. Who had come into her room while she slept? Was that why she was sweating? Had she somehow sensed his presence?

Ella snatched up the candle and stood to her feet. She hardly thought about what she did as she stepped softly out of the room. She had to find whoever it was who had entered her room. He couldn't have gotten far.

She peered both ways down the hall, but the dim light from her candle didn't reach more than a few yards in either direction. Both ends of the hall lay shrouded in darkness and could have concealed any dread phantom. A loud creak sounded from the stairway down the hall to the right. Ella started and almost dropped the candle. She caught herself in time and padded towards the stairway with bated breath.

Pastor Daerl slept in the room at the bottom of those stairs. She should probably wake him. If there was someone in the house, he should know; that way, Ella wouldn't have to face whoever it was alone.

Ella took a deep breath and stepped down the first step. She tried to step as lightly as she could, but to her ears, in the night's stillness, each stair seemed to creak like a cackling crone. What if the person who entered her room was still on the stairs? What if he turned and attacked her before she even reached Pastor Daerl's door?

She held her breath and kept walking, each stair creaking and groaning under her. Finally, she reached the bottom and hurriedly turned towards Pastor Daerl's door. She could hear a sound like drums in the other direction. No, that wasn't drums; that was her heart pounding in her ears. Ella shook her head as if that would clear it. What was wrong with her? What had gotten her so spooked? Who had come into her room?

She tapped lightly on Pastor Daerl's door but got no answer. A wave of fear seemed to wash over her, and she threw off all of her attempts at being quiet.

"Pasto'h Dae'l!" She wasn't yelling, but it sounded like she was in the deathly quiet of that house. "Pasto'h Dae'l!"

The door flew open, and the huge satyr stood in the entryway. He still rubbed sleep from his eyes, but he was wide awake and alert. "What is it? What is the matter?"

Ella sobbed. "The'e's someone in the house. He came into my w'oom..."

Just then, there was a crash from the kitchen. Ella started and backed away. Pastor Daerl strode forward with determination, grabbing a pistol from inside his room.

"Haloo! Who is there?"

There was no answer from the darkness.

Ella crept forward, staying behind Pastor Daerl at all times. She was still terrified, but having the pastor's imposing figure near her helped.

"Who is there?" Pastor Daerl asked again, his big voice booming through the kitchen as he entered. "I tain a pistol, an' I will no hesitate to shoot. Show yerself now, or it will go poorly fer ye."

Ella came to the entrance to the kitchen and held out her candle. All was as it should be. There was no sign that anyone had been in there, not even a clue as to what might have caused the crash. All the dishes were neatly stacked on the counter, with the sour bread set to rise. The smaller table and chairs sat alone in the corner, and the rug covered the trapdoor in the other corner. Everything was in place.

Pastor Daerl scanned the room, holding his pistol ready.

"Where are ye?"

As if in answer, the rug in the corner flew aside with sudden violence as the trap door burst open. Pastor Daerl turned at this sound and discharged his pistol. The sound of the shot rang through the entire house, and gunpowder smoke filled the room. Still, Ella could see no one. No one had touched the trapdoor. How had it opened? Ella shivered all over. She could feel the pounding in her ears louder than ever. Was that her heart?

Pastor Daerl's eyes went wide, but not with terror; the look on his face seemed more like a look of revelation than anything else.

The pastor pointed at the open trapdoor with authority. "Ye tain no power in this house. Ye are a defeated foe. I rebuke ye in the name o' God Almighty! 'If He is fer us, who cen stand against us?' Be gone!"

There was a feeling of tension in the air, like an intense heat, and then it vanished. Ella's heart was still racing, but the pounding in her head was gone. She could breathe again and no longer felt like someone was walking behind her, watching her every move.

Just then, there was a loud noise down the hallway as if a door was flung wide open, and Mr. Hydmenton came dashing into the kitchen, carrying his rifle, three pistols, a skinning knife, and a cutlass.

"What wos that? Are we bein' invaded?" He looked around wildly, glancing first at the pastor and then at Ella.

Ella felt a little ridiculous, standing there in the kitchen in bare feet, with her nightgown clinging to her, still soaked in sweat. Pastor Daerl's enormous frame, however, seemed to command the room — even if he was in his nightgown, too.

"Are we bein' invaded?" Mr. Hydmenton asked again.

Pastor Daerl shook his head. "It is over now."

"What wos it?" Mr. Hydmenton hopped about excitedly, like a schoolboy aching to get outside. "I heard a gunshot. Who ha' been hurt?"

Pastor Daerl took a deep breath, his face setting into a hard, determined edge. "A pistol will do no good against the *power* that ha' invaded this house. We tain other weapons to use in sich warfare."

This seemed to stop Mr. Hydmenton dead in his tracks. He stood stock still and looked at Pastor Daerl acutely. "What do ye mean?"

Night Visitor

The pastor shook his head. "The pirates ha' awakened some-thing — something that outta-should no ha' been awakened."

Mr. Hydmenton wrinkled up his brow. "Did they do it on purpose?"

"I do no know," Pastor Daerl replied.

"I'm still confused," Ella admitted. "What just happened?"

A lightness came over Ella, and suddenly the floor seemed to rise to meet her. The candle fell from her grasp, but Pastor Daerl caught her before she collapsed.

"Miss Ella, are ye all right?"

Breathlessly, Ella stood again. That was strange. She had never lost her balance like that before. It was like fainting; only she was wide awake the whole time.

"Miss Ella?"

Ella put her hands to her head. "I'm all wight — at least I think I am. I just need some ai'h."

So saying, she turned from the kitchen, but again that same lightness came over her, and her knees buckled. Pastor Daerl held her by the shoulders, keeping her upright.

"Come along then."

Pastor Daerl and Mr. Hydmenton helped Ella to the front door and walked her out onto the porch. The cool air on Ella's face helped. Yet no sooner had they stepped outside than Mr. Hydmenton inhaled sharply.

"Llifsa! Will they ever rest?"

It was black as pitch outside, with only the stars out to light the world. Before them, they could see the twinkle of lights that was Entwerp Proper — a few street lamps still burning, and here and there, a candle flickering behind a windowpane. The dark mountains were barely discernible against the slightly less black sky. Ella squinted, trying to see what Mr. Hydmenton had seen in the darkness.

Yes, she could make out shapes in the darkness moving along in the common area between the Pickerings' Manor and the outskirts of Entwerp Proper. Now and then, she saw a brief twinkle of light as of someone carrying a lantern. Were those nebulous shapes the strikers? Why were they moving out into the commons? Ella bit her lip. That's right, Miss Nansi had said something to the strikers about the commons by her house. They must have all moved.

"What are they doin'?" Mr. Hydmenton asked.

"I do no know," Pastor Daerl replied.

"Are they mobilizin' fer something?" Mr. Hydmenton asked. "Like they are about to start a siege? Did no they threaten to siege the bank?"

Pastor Daerl shook his head. "The bank would be on the other side o' town. Maybe they are movin' to a place with more room? They could ha' jist been too crowded in Nychweni Square."

Just then, Ella saw a rather larger light appear, as if someone had lit a torch. For a moment, she could see figures of dark and brooding men by the light. They were certainly the strikers. Then the light burst into a regular blaze. The light momentarily blinded Ella. She heard a loud cheer from the strikers and several gunshots.

As her eyes adjusted, she could see the horde of strikers ranged about in knotted groups along the commons. A large crowd was gathered around a small cottage, which was now being consumed by a wall of flame. As she watched, the strikers threw something against the cottage walls — jars of oil, perhaps? — and the flames burst out anew, devouring the little cottage.

"That is Miss Nansi's cottage!" Mr. Hydmenton texclaimed, raising his rifle as if he meant to fire upon the strikers.

Pastor Daerl pushed the rifle back down. "Do no fire, man. They will kill us, fer sure."

Mr. Hydmenton nodded and lowered his rifle. "What are we goin' to do?"

Ella stared at the mass of strikers eerily illuminated by the burning cottage. What kind of savage country was she living in? Was Miss Nansi in the cottage?

Pastor Daerl let out his breath slowly. "Fer now, we stay inside an' lock the door."

DREAMS

To his great surprise, Ernest entered the kitchen and found that a lantern still shone brightly over the galley. There, by the counter, sat Lewis with his little black book open in front of him. He looked up as Ernest entered and smiled wearily. There were deep rings under his eyes.

"Another adventure, eh, boyo?"

Ernest nodded, pouring himself some grog before he sat down beside his messmate. "You look terrible, Lewis. Are you all right?"

Lewis smiled weakly. "Having some trouble sleeping, that's all. So I figured I'd read my scriptures."

Ernest took a long sip of the grog. "Couldn't sleep?"

Lewis sighed. "I've been thinking about what you sayed last time we talked."

Ernest looked at him blankly. "What do you mean?"

"About God being powerful."

Ernest tried to think. This wasn't a good time to talk about deep subjects. He wasn't in a mental state to think right now, nor could he readily remember what Lewis referred to. "I'm afraid I don't follow you," Ernest finally said.

Lewis sighed, closing his book and wiping his eyes. "You asked if'n God was powerful, then why do'ed he let evil exist?"

Ernest shrugged. "I might've." He wasn't a captive of that nice little Llaedhwythi family anymore. Did he have to bother with religion now? Still, this seemed very important to Lewis, and the least he could do for his messmate was to listen.

"Well, I can't figure it out," Lewis continued. "What I finded is that God *is* indeed powerful. His seers fought with demons and spirits and Hellings in his name, and even ghosts couldn't stand when God's name was spoken."

"Ghosts?" Ernest asked. This sounded a little more interesting.

"Ay," Lewis replied. "Surely you know about the ghosts?"

Ernest sipped at his grog again. The alcohol was having its effects; already, he could feel his heart-rate slowing and exhaustion catching up with him. "I thinked that you believed in a heaven and hell like an orthodox believer, nothing about people's souls becoming ghosts."

Lewis chuckled at this. "Well, boyo, I'm not Orthodox, Helen Maria, no! But I believe in a heaven and hell. That isn't what a ghost is, though. The monks never telled you about ghosts in all their learning on you?"

Ernest shook his head. "The most they ever sayed was that they were 'humbugs.'"

Lewis chuckled. "On course they'd say that. No, ghosts are as real as you or I, but they aren't dead people's souls; they're living demons. They were the demons present at the great orgy in Sarnach when the devil Evlis summoned all the kings on the earth to himself, and they took Aydon, the prophet on God, and sacrificed him on their altars. That was the time when God judged the people and destroyed that pagan city on Sarnach with salt and fire from heaven. And he cursed the demons in that city so that they would have bodies, needs, and pains like any mortal, yet they would still be immortal. That's who the ghosts are."

Ernest nodded. "It's a good story."

"The monks do'edn't even tell you about the destruction on Sarnach?" Lewis asked incredulously.

Ernest shook his head.

Lewis banged his fist on the table forcefully. "Blind prelates! Those Orthodox are worse than I thinked."

Lewis sat there in silence for a long time and frowned. "Well, it comes to my mind," he finally said, "that if'n God created all on those spirits and cursed some on them to make them ghosts, then he must be awfully powerful, and he could do away with all evil forever whenever he wished."

Ernest nodded, drinking the last of his grog and setting his tankard on the counter. "Sounds reasonable."

"But why doesn't he?" Lewis asked.

Ernest looked over at Lewis quizzically. Did he expect Ernest to answer, or was that a rhetorical question?

"I suppose," Lewis replied with a dejected shrug, "it's a good thing he doesn't, since we'd just as likely be destroyed with all the other evil people."

There was a long and very melancholy silence following this remark. Ernest looked at Lewis closely. He didn't think he had ever seen his messmate look so depressed in all of their time together. Lewis was always so sanguine. He couldn't have come to this point researching Ernest's question — Ernest didn't care that much about the question, anyway.

Ernest wrinkled his brow in thought. He should just go to bed. Then again, could this struggle Lewis was going through have anything to do with those late-night conversations with Killjelly? Perhaps he was up late tonight only because he had conversed with Killjelly again. This thought sent a shiver down Ernest's spine. What were those two up to, anyway?

Lewis groaned. "I don't want to do this anymore, Ernest. I'm done."

Ernest raised an eyebrow. "Done with what?"

Lewis waved his hand ambiguously at the kitchen. "This."

"You're done with cooking?"

Lewis cracked a smile at that. "No, boyo, I hope I'm never done with cooking. It's..." he swallowed and leaned forward, looking intently in Ernest's eyes. "Don't you ever wish we could stop being pirates? Don't you ever wish we could settle down and be done with it all — all the killing and plundering?"

Ernest nodded, speaking in a low tone. "I know what you mean. I might have done it myself only just this evening."

Lewis perked up at this. "Ay?"

Ernest nodded. "That adventure I was on, well, it do'edn't go very well. We ended up getting attacked, and this boy killed Bill and Tell, and he would've killed me too if'n I hadn't begged on my knees for mercy."

Lewis winced. "Helen Maria."

"Well," Ernest continued, not wanting to get long-winded. "I haggled with them, and finally, they sentenced me to a catechizing and locked me in the barn."

Lewis' eyebrows shot up. "A catechizing? Ernest, you happened upon some regular Weldronists — or else Elderians — God bless them!"

Ernest shrugged. "Well, I don't know about that, but what I know is that they haved the most beautiful gnome lady with them, and I haved half a mind to forget about you and Holgard and everyone else, learn their religion, and marry that gnome."

Lewis sighed. "What was her name?"

"Lexi," Ernest replied, certain that he was blushing. "And she was as fiery and feisty as you could have wished for."

Lewis nodded. "You should've done it, Ernest; you should've leaved us behind."

Ernest only smiled. "I do'edn't want to leave you out on it."

He knew he couldn't mention the Albino, so he had to give another excuse for why he came back.

Lewis shrugged. "I'd just as soon leave this life myself. Maybe I'd open a restaurant in a big city."

Ernest smiled. "You'd do well at that. I reckon noblemen would come from miles around to eat at your restaurant."

Lewis waved his hand modestly. "Ah, now, you needn't say that much. Though the governor might fund my restaurant once he sees the sewer-rat population decrease around my shop."

Ernest sat back contentedly, choosing to ignore Lewis' comment. "I'd prefer to get a piece on land and start a little farm. I'd get me some pigs and maybe a cow or two for to make cheeses."

Lewis nodded. "That's not a bad plan, boyo. Helen Maria! You could grow the food, and I'd cook it for the restaurant."

Ernest smiled at this idea. "What about the sewer rats?"

Lewis grinned from ear to ear. "Oh, no, I'd save them for special occasions, like for weddings, or coronations, or earthquakes."

Ernest shook his head. "There's no way, Lewis. You know as well as I that Holgard would probably hunt us down and have us tortured or keelhauled if'n we tried to leave. That's what they do'ed with the Blowhoarder — Jock — when he double-crossed Holgard."

Lewis leaned forward intently and stared Ernest hard in the face, dropping his voice very low. "Ernest, there's about to be..." Lewis stopped and licked his lips as if trying to decide if he should keep going.

Ernest looked at him closely. A good deal of the color had drained from Lewis's face, and he looked haggard and tired, like a man who has come back from an arduous journey to find there was no house waiting for him at the end — the sight of Lewis like this unsettled Ernest.

Lewis swallowed and started over. "There's about to be some changes — some big changes."

Ernest leaned back and crossed his arms. "This has nothing to do with Pennywraith, does it? I keep hearing that he is coming."

Lewis grimaced. "That is hardly a change compared to what is about to happen."

Ernest nodded. "All right, what kind on changes?"

Lewis licked his lips again, looking very uncomfortable. "I'm not allowed to say."

Ernest leaned back and studied Lewis closely. "You look like you've seen a ghost yourself, Lewis."

Lewis didn't laugh; he simply looked away, staring hard at the wood stove's glow.

"Ernest," Lewis finally said, "you have to promise to do as I say. I will get you through this."

Ernest nodded slowly. "All right. I trust you, Lewis. I will do what you tell me to do."

Lewis suddenly stood up and walked over to the other side of the kitchen, and began rummaging through some of his bags of spices. Ernest looked closely after him but couldn't make out what Lewis looked for in the dim light. He heard a rapid clicking noise and knew Lewis was using his sonar to find whatever it was he searched for. With a sudden flourish, Lewis pulled a few slips of paper from hiding and returned to the bar. He handed the papers to Ernest solemnly.

"These are for you... in case."

Ernest squinted at the pages, trying to make sense of the scrawled handwriting. "Fish and potheen, no potatee... ah, fish and potato... harsh? No, hash. I see now: Fish and potato hash: lard to coat the pan–" Ernest stopped and looked up at Lewis in surprise. "Lewis, is this...?"

Lewis nodded solemnly. "Those are my recipes."

Ernest simply stared at Lewis in shock. Was this actually

happening? Was Lewis sharing his recipes? What could have driven him to this extreme action?

"In case," Lewis said again, then he sighed. "We will start our restaurant yet, boyo, you will see. We'll make it through."

Ernest continued to look at Lewis closely. "Lewis, you're scaring me. What is this about?"

Lewis forced a wide smile and laughed nervously. "Don't worry about it, boyo, it's nothing much. Just hold onto those for me until... until we start our restaurant."

INFERNO

The spokesman turned on Clerans sharply. "An' who are ye? Ye are no beacon-tender."

"Let the boy speak," the one-armed man said.

Clerans swallowed hard, suddenly aware of everyone staring at him. Why was he so nervous? It wasn't usually that difficult to talk to a group of people. He was used to being the center of attention. But this was probably the first time he was trying to say something serious and intelligent to such a large crowd.

"This letter," Clerans said slowly, "is from Stifyn an' Minni Blysffi, an' it is startin' a lawsuit 'gainst the Company. I am certain some o' you know Stifyn an' Minni Blysffi?"

The Rectificationists nodded.

"An' what's that got to do with us?" the spokesman asked.

"Let the boy speak!" several other strikers broke in.

"Ay!" Miss Nansi said, looking at Clerans with some interest. "What is this about?"

Clerans cleared his throat nervously. "The short o' it is that Minni (I am sorry, it feels uncanny to call her that. I always know her as Mrs. Blysffi. Let me start over). Mrs. Blysffi is suin' the Company on behalf o' the indigies."

"An' what've the indigies got to do with us?" The spokesman broke in again.

"Let the boy speak!" nearly the entire room yelled out in response.

Clerans cleared his throat again. "Most o' the Company's infrastructure (the forts an' the beacons, specifically) are on indigie land. They never paid fer it, they jist started usin' it. Mrs. Blysffi is suin' them fer it. Demandin' that the Company gives the land back."

The spokesman shook his head. "That would shut down the entire Company."

Clerans held out his hands. "You wanted to put pressure on the Company an' only the Company. Well, here is the way to do it. What better pressure cen ye think o', but to threaten the very existence o' the Company?"

Mr. Gingrich shook his head. "I like the idea, an' it is a merri just move on the Blysffis' part, but ye'll know as well as I that no court in Llaedhwyth would uphold sich a bold breach o' precedent. Our legal system is too corrupt an' in the pocket o' the Company."

Clerans held up his hand, warming to his topic. This felt like the drama he enjoyed performing. "Now that is where the brilliance o' this suit venes into play."

"An' that is?" the spokesman asked with irritation.

Clerans paused for a moment, letting the effect build. "Mrs. Blysffi is no goin' to sue the Company in any court o' Llaedhwyth." Clerans paused again, looking over his audience. "She is suin' them under Indigie Law."

The spokesman snorted. "What does that even mean? Are ye jist makin' up words at this point?"

"Ye do no know what Indigie Law is?" Miss Nansi asked in alarm. "Where wos yer beacon? I cen no think o' any beacon that is outside o' Indigie Law."

The spokesman shrugged. "Maybe, I jist never heard o' it."

Miss Nansi looked at him critically. "Where wos yer beacon? I do no think ye ha' ever mentioned it."

"How could ye ha' never heard o' the Indigie Law?" Mr. Gingrich broke in. "Ye were a beacon-tender, an' ye never heard o' Indigie Law?"

The spokesman frowned. "Look, there jist weren't many indigies near my beacon."

"Where wos yer beacon?" Miss Nansi pressed. "Are ye even a beacon-tender?"

The spokesman straightened up in anger. "How dare ye accuse me like that! Look at everything I ha' done fer the cause, an' now ye mean to accuse me like a common criminal?"

Suddenly, the middle-aged nymph stood on his bench and clapped to get attention. "We are all missing the point that this boy has brought up. All the crimes the Company committed against us — whatever they were — were done to us while we were at our beacons or our forts. In other words, the Company committed these crimes against us within indigie territory: within Indigie Law. As such, they must be held accountable to Tribal Law."

Miss Nansi laughed triumphantly at this. "Clerans, ye are right! This is outside the jurisdiction o' the Llaedhwythi government or courts. All we must do is appeal to tribal justice!"

The spokesman shook his head. "An' how would that help? What could the tribes do for us that the Llaedhwythi government couldn't?"

Mr. Gingrich nodded slowly. "Ay, the tribal judges are outside the Company's corruption. It jist might work."

The middle-aged nymph smiled broadly. "They could put the owners to Moa-Fire."

"What?"

The nymph looked at the spokesman critically. "The Trial by Moa? Have you never heard of it?"

The spokesman shrugged. "Never. An' what good would it do us?"

Miss Nansi now stared suspiciously at the spokesman. "Now gard here, younker. You still ha' no answered my question. What beacon did ye tend?"

The spokesman looked between Nansi, the nymph, and Clerans. Finally, he sighed. "Ay, I've haved about enough on this."

He nodded at the dozen strikers closest to him. "Come along, lads, let's clean this up."

Suddenly, the group of strikers stood to their feet and leveled guns at the crowd. Clerans' mouth went dry. The spokesman pointed a pistol directly at his head. He didn't even have time to sit down before the spokesman and his squad opened fire. There was a terrific thunder from the guns firing in the enclosed space, and immediately the air filled with gunpowder smoke. Clerans braced himself for the feeling of boiling-hot lead tearing through his flesh, but instead, the one-armed man's fleshy body slammed into him, bowling him to the ground. Something hot and sticky washed over Clerans' face and neck. He scrambled to his feet, trying to escape from under the one-armed man. The man convulsed like a reptile, and Clerans suddenly realized that he had a gruesome bullet hole in his back. Had he jumped in the way of the spokesman's pistol to save Clerans' life?

The man wheezed and coughed, blood in his mouth. "Get that letter out o' here, younker."

And he convulsed again.

Clerans wriggled out from under the dying man and turned towards the door. There was another blast of gunfire, and the air around him hummed as if a bullet had passed close by him. The smoke was so thick he couldn't see anything. Everyone was screaming. Sheiks of pain and cries of indignation filled the air. How was he supposed to get out of here?

Then Clerans remembered Miss Nansi. Turning towards the front of the room, he rushed forward furiously. Bodies (living and dead) blocked his way, but Clerans bowled through them, pushing through the mass of people and smoke. A third time, the guns fired, and more shrieks of pain split the air. The floor was already slick with gore, and Clerans breathed a silent prayer of thanks that he could not see the carnage around him for the smoke.

Clerans tripped as he pushed through the last wall of bodies, falling down at the front of the room. As he hit the ground, Miss Nansi formed in the smoke before him. She was on her hands and knees, wheezing.

"Miss Nansi!" Clerans called, grabbing her shoulder and helping her to her feet.

"Run, Clerans!" Miss Nansi cried. "Get out o' here."

"No without ye!"

Clerans turned. There was no way he could make it back to the door. It was a miracle he had made it through the throng once. He would never make it back through with Miss Nansi in tow. Besides, the spokesman and his goons were closer to the door. They undoubtedly had the entrance sealed and would gun down anyone trying to escape that way.

His pulse pounded in his head. He took a deep breath, trying not to gag on the gunpowder fumes and ignoring the cacophony around him. He couldn't see right now, but he knew what this room looked like. There was a window in the bedroom at the end of the hall.

"Vene along then!"

Clerans seized Miss Nansi's hand and rushed to where he knew the hallway to be. Stumbling over a corpse on the ground, and trying not to slip on the blood, Clerans rushed down the hall. The air was a little clearer here, and he could see the door to the bedroom. Clerans slammed his shoulder into it, and the door gave way. The smoke had not yet entered the bedroom, but to his alarm, several boards lay across the window, nailed to the frame from the outside.

"Varlets!" Miss Nansi cried in alarm.

Hastily, Clerans unslung his rifle and rushed at the window with the butt of his gun. He slammed all of his weight into the blow. The glass shattered, and Clerans drove the butt forward with enough force to knock a board loose.

"Holy Sacrament!" someone cried from the other side of the window, and the face of a striker loomed into the hole Clerans had created.

Effortlessly, Clerans spun his rifled around and fired at point-blank range. The man disappeared, and Clerans set to work with his rifle butt again, knocking out all the boards from the window.

"Here, here!" A voice yelled. "Someone's trying to get out!"

Clerans jumped through the window, and he collided with someone.

"Baptize it!" The man cried.

Clerans lashed out with his fists, finding the man's face and pummeling him as hard as he could. His blood was up, and he reacted with the instincts of a wild animal. Another striker loomed into his view, carrying a rifle with a bayonet on the end.

"Demon younker!" the striker called out.

Clerans disentangled himself from the man he was punching and bulled into the second man's knees. He heard something snap, and the man collapsed to the ground with a stifled scream. Clerans caught his rifle before it fell and discharged it into the first man (who was regaining his feet). As the second man struggled to stand with his broken knee, Clerans thrust the bayonet into him. His pulse still pounded in his head, and Clerans could hardly think. He was just doing. He never stopped to see if his opponent still moved, thrusting the bayonet into him several times for good measure.

There was a noise behind him, and Clerans wheeled about, the bloody rifle in his hands. Miss Nansi had crawled through the window and gaped at him in alarm.

"Clerans!" she gasped.

Clerans took a deep breath and dropped the rifle.

"We ha' to get out o' here."

With some satisfaction, he noticed several more people climbing out of the window he had opened. Mr. and Mrs. Gingrich were first, followed by Chaerls and Miss. Flalowen. So most of the Rectificationists would survive. But what of the committed strikers? The middle-aged nymph? The one-armed man?

"They're escaping!" someone called out.

"Run!" Miss Nansi screamed.

Just then, a wall of flames erupted from the cottage, lighting up the entire scene in eery, crimson light. Clerans could see the spokesman sauntering away from the cottage with a smirk. He walked like a sailor, Clerans realized.

"Shoot them!" a striker yelled as he pointed at the escapees. "Don't let them get away!"

The spokesman shrugged. "They're harmless now. Leave them alone."

While Miss Nansi and the others scattered into the night, Clerans stood still, his throat tightening as he watched the fire's chaos. The strikers hurled jars of oil on the cottage, igniting every inch of the little house. There were still people inside. Clerans' eyes burned from the smoke, and he clenched his fists.

The spokesman turned and looked at him, a light in his eyes. "Shall I shoot you down, too, younker?"

"Ye will pay fer this!" Clerans screamed.

The spokesman shrugged. "Me? The strikers did it. What've I got to do with this?"

"Ye are no a striker, are ye!" Clerans yelled.

The spokesman waved at those around him. There was a twinkle in his eye, and his accent betrayed him. He was a seaman: a common pirate. "Come on, lads! We've maked our decision. To the bank. We siege the bank tonight. Everyone will hear on our cause!"

3 8

HALCYON

*I*t was Tomas who had taught Haeli how to swim. Da had taken her to several lakes and let her splash around in the shallows. He had taught her how to float and tread water because it was "important." But it was Tomas who had taught her to swim.

"That ocean is an uncanny beast," Da had said. "I find it better to stay away from it altogether."

So, of course, Tomas had taken her to the ocean to swim.

"You have never swum before — never felt it for real — until you have swum in the ocean," He had said.

And that's when he had taught her to swim. Keeping her head above the water, navigating the waves, staying away from the rocks, avoiding the currents, tasting the salty brine — Tomas had been thorough. And thank God he had been! Tomas might be dead, but her memories of him and his lessons could save her life.

Getting out of the bay was the simple part. The waves weren't that bad in the bay. It was once Haeli got out into the open ocean that things got interesting. All she meant to do was to swim to a beach close by, get to land, and run away. But

345

either she wasn't as good a swimmer as she remembered, or Tomas hadn't prepared her well enough. Maybe she caught a rip tide. Whatever it was, she missed the beach, and the tide took her out to sea.

Haeli remembered nothing of the night but a constant heaving of the ocean. Hour after hour, the waves washed over her, and the salt stung her eyes. Now and then, the salt water would flood her mouth, and she would come up spluttering, gagging, and coughing, only to have another wave wash over her. The sickening taste of brine clung to the back of her throat. As the hours wore on, she succumbed more and more to exhaustion. She couldn't even see the coastline anymore. She wasn't swimming, only keeping her head above the water.

"That ocean is an uncanny beast. I find it better to stay away from it altogether."

Sorry, Tomas, I am going to have to agree with Da on this one.

And while the waves buffeted her, her mind reeled with the implications of what had just happened. Those pirates had taken one of her keys. How had she let that happen? Why couldn't she have stopped them? Could they accomplish their goals now, or would they need the other key? Her whole mind was in turmoil. She didn't want to admit that it had happened. How could she have lost one key already? What would Da say?

She didn't know how long she struggled like this, but, at some point, she felt something hard — a rock perhaps — strike her leg. Then there was a touch of something hard underneath her feet. Another wave washed over her, and her head hit something solid.

She must have lost consciousness, for she suddenly became aware of two muscular arms seizing her waist. The waves were not nearly so high, and she floated on her back. She guessed it was morning, for though she couldn't feel the sun on her face, there was more light in the air — enough light to make out the large shapes of mountains on the horizon — and the confused and large shape of her rescuer. The water rushed over her face, and she closed her eyes again.

"Come on, Halfdan! Why won't you do anything? Help me get her out!"

The voice that spoke was desperate and high-pitched in excitement, but the speaker sounded as if he were a man of some size and strength. Haeli could feel the arms around her tighten, and her back brushed against something hard. Was she on land?

"What would be the use?" This second voice was even and spoke with no tone.

"Devil have you!" the first voice replied.

"It is a sin to swear," the second voice stated with the same lack of emotion.

"She could be dead by now, you layabout!" the first voice cried.

"If she is dead," the second voice said, "then her soul is most likely in heaven, experiencing more joy than we could ever hope to give her on this barren island."

Haeli could feel herself being dragged across something very hard — probably solid rock. Whoever was dragging her laid her down gently after a few steps.

"Don't you have any tender feelings?" the first voice asked, irritated.

There was a brief pause, and then the second voice responded, "I am not sure what you are asking."

"Devil have you!" the first voice said again.

"I told you already," the second voice replied, still unaffected, "it is a *sin* to swear."

The first voice growled. "I never swore until I met you, you feathered-head!"

Haeli tried to open her eyes, and they came open slowly — almost as if she were dragging gravel across her eyes. The day was overcast — which was probably a good thing — so she didn't have to adjust to much light. As she peered about her, she could make out a blurry shape of a man leaning over her and the cloudy sky above, but that was as much as she could make out before her stomach retched.

She turned suddenly onto her front — kneeling on her hands and knees and disgorged the little she had in her stomach. She knelt on a rock face. All around her was solid rock. She could feel a hand pressed lightly on her shoulder, and the first voice spoke again. The strain and excitement had left it, and the voice was now slow and soothing.

"There, there, now, darling, you will be, eh, you will be all right. See Halfdan; she's still alive, and no thanks to you and your sermonizing."

"As I said before," the second voice said in the same emotionless monotone, "nothing I could have done would have helped her."

Haeli took a couple of deep breaths, fighting the urge to throw up again. She could feel her whole body trembling, a gnawing hunger in her gut, and a dry feeling in her mouth. This mixed with the taste of brine and bile in her mouth, and she shuddered. She desperately wanted to lie down on that rock and die. God didn't seem to want her to die, though. He only seemed to want to make her miserable — in every way possible.

She was still alive, thanks in part to these two strangers who had pulled her from the water. Haeli considered standing up for a moment but knew that would be futile. She hardly felt like she had the strength to continue kneeling. She rolled to her side and tried to sit up as best she could.

Looking up, she could see more clearly the man who had pulled her onto this rock. He was rather tall and very broad around the shoulders. He looked to be about the age of her own father, with a sun-tanned complexion and a brow line forever wrinkled into a pensive expression.

She looked at the man suspiciously for a moment before turning her head toward the second voice. Looking to see who her other savior might be, she saw only a large bird perched on a nearby rock that jutted out from the rest of the rock she sat on. Haeli blinked and looked closer. Yes, it was a harrier — a male harrier. Aarushi was the only harrier she had ever seen before, so she wasn't as familiar with the male harrier's feather pattern.

The harrier cocked his head and stared at her closely, then he spoke in the same emotionless tone. "I believe you look hungry."

Haeli could feel a lump forming in her throat. She wrapped her arms around her knees and shivered. "I am," she said, her voice croaking like that of an old hag. She swallowed and tried to get the bile out of her mouth before speaking again. Really, she didn't want to speak: she wanted to cry. No, not now, Haeli, hold yourself together. Not in front of a stranger.

Haeli swallowed again, pushing back her emotions. "I am hungry. Thank you for asking."

The harrier nodded. "I have nothing to give you to eat, but it is good to know that you are hungry."

"What kind of help is this?" the man cut in, storming over to the harrier and waving his finger in front of its beak. "Are you just going to sit there?"

The harrier stared at the man blankly. "I sense unprovoked and unholy rage, both of which are sins."

The man continued shaking his finger at the bird. "I'm surprised you didn't become a preacher, buzzard."

The harrier blinked. "No, I would never have been a good preacher. People hire preachers to tell them what they *want* to hear, not..."

"I suppose you're right," the man cut in. "You'd make a terrible preacher. Look at what you've done to me, for instance:

I was a good and honest man, and you've turned me into a swearing destitute!"

The harrier shook his head. "That is an unfair accusation. I did not induce you to start swearing. It was your choice and your responsibility before God..."

"And it will be your responsibility before God," the man interjected, "if you don't get this girl something to eat before she starves to death."

"Her death would not be my responsibility," the harrier replied evenly. "Why should I bear the blame for the frailties of your mortal conditions?"

"And what about good works, eh?" the man replied. "Aren't you supposed to do good works?"

The bird tilted his head to one side. "All of our good works are as menstrual rags to God."

"And what the devil is wrong with menstruation, you unnatural creep?" the man fired back. "Except that I assume you do not do it."

"Firstly," the harrier replied coolly, "I am male and therefore do not have a fertility cycle. Secondly, we birds do not have to suffer through menstruation."

"Well," the man replied hotly, "for us frail mortals, it's a normal and healthy part of our lives."

The harrier blinked. "Why are we arguing about menstruation?"

"You brought it up," the man said. "You said that good works are like menstrual rags. In which case they are good and healthy things to do."

The bird stretched out a wing and nodded slowly. "Your exegesis is fascinating. I have never heard the scriptures handled in such a novel way. I can not say, unfortunately, that you are wrong, though. You have a point."

"Well," the man cried. "Are you just going to keep talking, or are you going to do some good and find this girl something to eat?"

The harrier looked like he was about to say something, but thinking better of it, he flew off.

The big man now turned back to Haeli, squatting in front of her.

"Don't eh, don't mind Halfdan," he said. "He's a bit of a nuisance, but, eh, he means well."

Haeli nodded.

The man looked her in the eye for a moment; then he extended his hand. "My name's Titus Donne, by the way."

Haeli shook his hand and tried to smile. "Haeli Blysffi." She said. So his name was Donne? Hadn't she heard that name recently? He seemed nice enough, but she knew better than to trust a stranger.

Titus nodded. "I'd, um, I'd welcome you to my island, but, eh, I'm afraid there's not much to offer you here. You're, eh, you're welcome to whatever part of this rock you want." He smiled briefly but then let his face become pensive again.

Haeli took a moment to look around. There wasn't much to this island. That was true. All she could see of it was a pile of granite rocks rising out of the heaving sea, though some of the taller rocks cut her line of sight short. Where was she? Could this be part of the Faeroteisi Islands? That sounded likely. She looked up at the sky and could see the sun's pale orb through the clouds low down by the horizon. So that direction must be east. She looked in the opposite direction, hoping to see the mainland, but a large boulder blocked her view.

Titus watched her and asked. "Are you, eh, are you looking for something?"

Haeli nodded. "Land."

The man nodded. "It's over there. Maybe, eh, maybe a hundred yards off."

Haeli looked at him closely. "How long have you been here?"

"Two nights now," Titus replied.

"And you haven't tried swimming to shore yet?"

The man shrugged and looked at his hands. "I, eh, well... eh, I can't swim, see."

Haeli nodded. Talking to this man seemed to take her mind off her misery, so she continued. Perhaps she might find out a little more about him, enough to know if she should be concerned that she was stranded on an island with him. "How'd you end up here, then?"

The man sighed. "My, eh, my ship was attacked by pirates. I jumped overboard and got washed up here."

"You don't look like a sailor," Haeli commented.

Titus nodded. "That's true. I'm not much of a sailor. I'm a logger from Slyzwir."

Haeli furrowed her brow. He was a Donne from Slyzwir? Could he possibly be related to... "Pardon me for asking," she said, "but you have a daughter?"

Titus looked up at her in surprise. "I do, eh, well, that is, I have a step-daughter."

"Ella Donne?"

The man jumped to his feet, his voice rising to the same excited pitch it was in when he had been pulling Haeli from the sea. "How do you know? Have you met her? Is she all right?"

Just then, the harrier — hadn't Titus called him Halfdan? — came flying back. He had a pear in each talon, and he fluttered down to Haeli, setting them beside her before he settled back on his rock.

"Courtesy of the mainland," the harrier said in his dull monotone. "I hope that may help stave off the hunger."

"Thank you," Haeli said as she took a pear and bit into it. The sweet taste and gritty texture seemed to explode in her mouth, washing over the lingering taste of salt water and bile. Never had she enjoyed a pear so much. She wolfed down the first — juice running down her chin, neck, arms, and elbows — and then she started into the second, before remembering that she should probably be better mannered. She slowed down, nodding to Halfdan again in thanks.

Titus still stared at her intently, and as soon as she finished with her second pear, he resumed his questioning. "Have you met my daughter?"

Haeli nodded. "I did. She is fine, as far as I know. I last left her in the care of a gentleman of Entwerp whom I know."

Titus squatted down again and sighed. "Then Ella's all right. How about that? That's the only good news I've heard in a while."

Haeli looked at Titus closely. "So, you are Ella's father?"

Titus nodded. "I, eh, yes, I had to come and find her. Do you know what happened to her? It's not very clear to me, eh, myself."

"Perhaps," Haeli said, throwing the two pear cores away from her, "you had better tell me what your story is, and then I can fill in the gaps as best I can."

ASSEMBLY

*A*s Pastor Daerl and Mr. Hydmenton rushed Ella inside, more gunshots sounded from the other side of the commons.

"What is going on?" Ella gasped.

"Quickly now," Pastor Daerl said, ignoring Ella's comments. "We ha' best barricade the door."

"They are venin' this way!" Mr. Hydmenton replied, slamming the door shut and locking it. "We will ha' to fight them off. Hold down the house at all costs. No doubt one o' us will die tonight."

"Jist barricade the door," Pastor Daerl replied.

Mr. Hydmenton rushed down the hall and returned, dragging a dresser behind him with one hand and a suit of armor with his other hand. Hurriedly, he threw these against the door before rushing down the hall to find more furniture.

"What is going on?" Ella asked again. As the pastor did not answer, Ella pressed again. "That *was* Miss Nansi's house, wasn't it? I wasn't just imagining it."

Pastor Daerl nodded grimly. "Ay, ye were no imaginin'. That was Miss Nansi's house."

"Was she inside?" Ella gasped.

Pastor Daerl was silent as Mr. Hydmenton rushed in, throwing another dresser and an armful of books against the door. Finally, he answered Ella.

"I pray to God she was not."

Mr. Hydmenton looked at them. "Did no Clerans say that Nansi had called the strikers to a meeting at her house?"

Ella's heart sank. "Yes. She did. That's how she got them to leave the facto'y."

Mr. Hydmenton shrugged. "There you tain it. That's what comes o' dealin' with strikers. They ha' killed her now."

"We do no know that," Pastor Daerl broke in.

Mr. Hydmenton shrugged. "Ay, but it wos her house they burned down. They probably roasted her to a crisp."

Just then, someone pounded frantically against the door.

"Llifsa!" Mr. Hydmenton exclaimed, jumping into the air with fright and grabbing at his pistols.

"Who is there?" the pastor called out.

"It is me," the voice of Miss Nansi called out from the other side of the door.

A wave of relief washed over Ella. "Oh, thank God!"

"Is it?" Mr. Hydmenton called out suspiciously. "Or are ye jist another spirit?"

"What fer a thousand cubits are ye carryin' on about?" Miss Nansi replied.

"Jist open the door," Pastor Daerl said.

Hurriedly, Mr. Hydmenton cleared the brick-a-brack he had thrown against the door, and Miss Nansi tumbled inside. She was panting and pale. Her eyes were wide and wild looking. Ella threw her arms around the older lady, sobbing. "Oh, Miss Nansi! You a'e all wight! You a'e all wight!"

Miss Nansi suddenly composed herself, looking at Ella with some alarm. "Dearie, are you all right? Were you so worried about me? You've completely sweated through your nightgown!"

Just then, Elsi stumbled down the hall from her room. She, too, was still in her nightgown, and she blinked groggily. "What is goin' on?"

Mr. Hydmenton piped up helpfully.

"The strikers tried to kill Miss Nansi, an' Miss Ella ha' seen a ghost! It wos hauntin' her last night."

"A ghost?" Elsi asked in alarm.

Miss Nansi scowled. "Do we tain enough troubles here already, with the strikers burning down my house, an' I vene here fer refuge, an' trive out that you ha' gone mad?"

Ella took a deep breath. She fingered the piece of paper she had found on her nightstand — the paper with the four names on it. She didn't want to show anyone that piece of paper. Maybe she would show it to Clerans or Haeli when they next met, and they could help her make sense of it.

"It is t'ue," she said, releasing Miss Nansi. "I woke up, and I was sweating all ove'h, and I thought that the'e was someone in my w'oom."

Miss Nansi raised her eyebrow. "What made ye think that there wos someone in yer room, now, dear?"

Ella shrugged and licked her lips. How was she supposed to answer that? She had just felt it, as if some dark and nebulous phantom stared out at her from the night's blackness. "It was..." she paused and tried to start over. "I just felt..." She took a deep breath. "The doo'h was open. I had closed — and I think locked — it when I went to bed."

Mr. Hydmenton nodded. "That is how the Hegrydis knew there wos a ghost in their house last year."

Miss Nansi shook her finger vigorously at Mr. Hydmenton. "That is enough o' that! I do no want to hear *one* more mention o' an ghost."

Pastor Daerl cleared his throat and spoke calmly. "Nansi, we all know that ye and the other Rectificationists object to the idea o' spirits, but ye cen no jist ban us from speakin' o' them. There appeared to be somthin' o' the supernatural about the house tonight, an' thus we must gard into this occurrence from every angle. If we'll want to discover the truth, we cen no simply preclude ghosts from the discussion."

Miss Nansi shook her head. "This is what I ha' to deal with then? The strikers burn down my house, and you are all concerned about ghosts?"

Mr. Hydmenton turned back to Ella. "So the door wos open?"

Pastor Daerl shook his head. "We cen let this rest. Miss Nansi is right. We tain more important matters to attend to."

"I thought that I hea'd someone walking down the stai'hs." Ella blurted out.

"More important matters?" Mr. Hydmenton said. "More important matters than a ghost who is hauntin' this house?"

Pastor Daerl shrugged. "The strikers jist burned down Miss Nansi's house. I am certain they killed some people, too."

"But there is a *ghost* in this house!" Mr. Hydmenton replied.

Miss Nansi held up her hands. "At least we should sit in the dining room."

"Should I get some tea?" Ella asked weakly.

Miss Nansi shook her head. "We ha' all had enough to do, by the sound o' it." And she guided Ella into the dining room and sat her down. "I think we all should take a few breaths together."

Ella squirmed in her chair, turning the piece of paper over in her hands underneath the table. "Should we be conce'ned if the'e is a ghost? I mean, I think it is haunting me specifically."

"Cen I get ye some tea, Aunt Nansi?" Elsi asked meekly.

Nansi laid her head on the table. "Do no worry about it, dearie."

"I told ye there wos a ghost," Mr. Hydmenton said excitedly, sitting down across from Miss Nansi.

"Ye know what?" Miss Nansi replied. "I ha' tained about enough rubbish fer one night."

Ella licked her lips. That paper was solid evidence that someone — or something — had been in her room last night. But she couldn't show that paper to everyone, could she? Was there any harm in it? She was certain that it had something to do with the Gwambi Treasure, and she didn't want to include too many people in her search for that treasure.

"I *felt* like someone was the'e," Ella finally said. It was a pretty lame argument, but that's all she could think to say.

Miss Nansi took a deep breath and raised her head from the table. "I do no mean to make light o' yer fear, Ella dearie. I just do no understand why ye and Mr. Hydmenton seem to think there wos a ghost in this house."

"I saw the trapdoor open by itself," Pastor Daerl said.

Miss Nansi shrugged. "That might ha' only been a stray gust o' wind."

Pastor Daerl shook his head. "From underneath the house? No, I do no ween that merri likely."

Ella swallowed. She had to show them. This conversation would get nowhere productive if she wouldn't give everyone the key piece of evidence. Pulling the paper out of hiding, she set it on the table in front of her. Mr. Hydmenton strained to see what was written on it.

"I found this," Ella said, "sitting by my bed when I woke up. I didn't w'ite it, and I didn't put it the'e."

Mr. Hydmenton read the names on the paper. "Silas Pickering, Jock Blowhoarder, Saemwel Pickering, an' Syd Cartwright. What do they tain to do with each other?"

Miss Nansi flinched visibly. "What were those four names?"

Ella read them now, enunciating clearly. "Silas Pickering, Jock Blowhoarder, Saemwel Pickering, and Syd Cartwright."

Miss Nansi shook her head. "It could no be."

"What is it, now?" Pastor Daerl asked.

"I mean," Mr. Hydmenton said, "We know Silas an' Sir Saemwel, an' everyone knows who Jock Blowhoarder is. But ha' any o' you heard o' this Syd Cartwright?"

Miss Nansi only shook her head, but before she could speak, a forceful knock sounded at the door.

"I will get it," Elsi said softly as she slipped from her chair and headed to the door.

In a moment, she returned with Clerans in tow. Blood covered much of Clerans' face and matted his hair. His clothes were torn and disheveled, and he plodded into the dining room with a hollow expression on his face. Yet when his eyes fell on Miss Nansi, he gasped in relief.

"Miss Nansi! Ye are safe!"

"Clerans!" Nansi called out, jumping to her feet and throwing her arms around Clerans. "Clerans, dearie, ye are alive."

Clerans toppled into a chair and began sobbing. "They killed them, did no they? They killed all those people?"

Ella watched Clerans in horror. The gore all over Clerans was shocking enough, but for Clerans to show so much emotion was even more terrifying. What had shaken him out of his jovial state?

"Are ye injured?" Miss Nansi asked, looking Clerans over.

Clerans shook all over, and he continued to sob.

Just then, another knock sounded at the door. Elsi dashed off and soon returned with Sheriff Laei close behind. The Sheriff glanced around, but his eyes stopped when they fell on Miss Nansi.

"Thank God you made it here."

Miss Nansi stood and dusted herself off. "Ay, an' ye cen thank Clerans fer that. If he'll had no been there to bust open the window an' kill those varlets who were guardin' the house, then I am certain I would ha' been burnt alive."

Elsi stumbled back in shock. "You killed someone, Clerans?"

Clerans took a deep breath, obviously trying to choke back his emotions.

Mr. Hydmenton chuckled, and Sheriff Laei sighed with relief. "Well done, sir. I see I ha' trained ye well fer yer task."

Clerans blushed and took another long breath, finally bringing his sobbing to an end.

Yet just then, Elsi burst into tears. Miss Nansi leaped up and wrapped her in her arms.

"There, there, now, child. What is wrong?"

"It is jist everything," Elsi sobbed, "all o' it, an' the strikers burnin' down yer house, Aunt Nansi, an' Papa no here an' — oh!" and she burst into a new fit of tears.

Ella sighed and felt an urge to cry herself, though mostly out of sympathy for Elsi.

"Come now," Miss Nansi soothed. "Let us be off to yer room now. Ye do no need to sit through this. There is no need fer ye to be further upset."

As Miss Nansi ushered her niece from the room, Sheriff Laei turned to Clerans. "Ye heard what the strikers were up to then?"

Clerans didn't acknowledge that the sheriff had spoken to him, but only stared into the distance with a vacant look on his face. Was he all right?

"Clerans?" the sheriff said.

Clerans stirred, throwing a sloppy salute. "Ay, I am ready fer duty."

The sheriff pursed his lips. "What are the strikers up to?"

Just then, Miss Nansi reentered the room and sat beside Ella. She sighed heavily and leaned over to whisper in Ella's ear. "Cen I tain that list o' names, dearie? I tain a notion o' what they are."

Wordlessly, Ella handed Miss Nansi the mysterious slip of paper.

"They burned down Miss Nansi's house," Mr. Hydmenton said helpfully. "An' we tain a ghost hauntin' this house!"

The sheriff fixed Mr. Hydmenton with a steady gaze. "What are ye sayin', man?"

Miss Nansi cleared her throat. "Archi, ye served with Sir Saemwel in the wars, did no ye?"

The sheriff nodded. "We were in the same tent, the two o' us, an' Silas Pickering as well."

Ella jumped at that statement. Had Sheriff Laei served in the army with her father, too? How had she not known this before?

"Ye fought with Silas Picke'ing?" Ella asked.

The sheriff looked at her closely. "Ay, an' how would ye cognize Silas?"

Ella was about to answer when Miss Nansi interrupted.

"Perhaps, ye cen shed some light on a matter fer us, Sheriff Laei."

The sheriff shifted his position nervously. "I would be happy to."

Miss Nansi took the piece of paper and laid it on the table in front of her. "Some mysterious visitor left this by Miss Ella while she was sleepin'. It is jist four names. Ye would no happen to know what they'll all ha' to do with each other, do ye?"

The sheriff only looked at her cautiously.

Miss Nansi now read the paper, "Silas Pickering, Jock Blowhoarder, Saemwel Pickering, and Syd Cartwright."

The Sheriff continued to look at Nansi with a blank face, though Ella was pretty sure he forced the look.

Clerans suddenly stirred from his chair as if regaining consciousness. "The bank!" He gasped. "They said they were cedin' to the bank!"

The sheriff turned on Clerans. "The National Bank?"

Clerans nodded. "The strikers said they were goin' to siege it tonight."

The sheriff straightened up with determination. "It is time to call out the Regulars, then. Clerans, cen ye walk?"

"Give us a minute," Clerans replied, taking a deep breath and staggering to his feet. "Ay, I am ready."

The sheriff looked him up and down and finally shook his head. "Ye ha' done enough, Clerans. Get yer rest."

"But I cen help."

"After ye ha' rested," The sheriff replied. And he turned towards the door, his metal braces on his arm creaking with determination as he strode out of the dining room.

"Wait!" Ella rushed after him, and the sheriff paused at the door.

"Miss Ella," the sheriff sighed. "This is urgent. I must get the word out if I'll am to prevent the entire country from descending into lawlessness."

"You knew Silas Picke'ing?"

The sheriff sighed, opening the door. "I do no tain time fer this."

Ella took a deep breath. "I only ask because he was my fathe'h. He left us when I was ve'y young, and I neve'h got to know him befo'e he died."

At this, Sheriff Laei's face broke into an expression of horror.

Ella took a deep breath. "I've always wanted to know what he was like f'om someone who knew him."

The sheriff stiffened. "I am sorry, but I must get to the bank a'fore the strikers."

With that, the sheriff slammed the door without looking once behind him.

Ella was stunned at this sudden and graceless rebuttal to her request, which she thought was reasonable enough. The sheriff looked like he was hiding something — but what was he hiding? What did he know that he wasn't telling anyone else? Perhaps Ella had been right not to trust him when she first met him.

Ella stumbled back into the dining room and collapsed into a chair. She was so exhausted. Clerans lay slumped in his chair, pale as the moon, while Mr. Hydmenton leaned forward with his head in his hands. Pastor Daerl stood in the corner, stroking his chin thoughtfully, and Miss Nansi leaned over the paper and chuckled to herself. "'Sir Silas, Jock Blowhoarder, Sir Saemwel, *and* Syd Cartwright.' Well, well, well."

Clerans stood shakily to his feet. "I ha' best be off. The sheriff will need me."

And with that, he stumbled from the room. A moment later, the front door slammed shut, and Ella heard Clerans stumping slowly down the front steps. Should she go out and stop him? He didn't seem rested enough to help the sheriff.

Miss Nansi put a hand on her arm. "He jist needs some air, dearie. He ha' been through too much tonight as it is."

They all sat for a moment in silence until Mr. Hydmenton sighed. "So now we are jist alone with the ghost again?"

Suddenly, Pastor Daerl slammed his fist down on the table.

"There is only one thing fer it!" And he stood up abruptly.

"What?" Mr. Hydmenton asked.

"Somethin' ha' been tryin' to scare Miss Ella and the rest o' us too," Pastor Daerl replied. "I ween that same thing can give us a few more answers. So there is only one thing fer it."

With that, the massive satyr strode from the room into the kitchen. Ella craned her neck to see what he did and gasped in horror as she saw Pastor Daerl throw the trapdoor open.

"We confront it!" the pastor cried.

CHANGING TIDE

*T*here were drums — sounding, resounding, echoing, reverberating, on and on and on. Everything was black. Ernest could feel nothing. He could see nothing, and he could hear nothing but that omnipresent drumming of some heathen litany.

Then there was fire. It burned and danced. There were screams and the sounds of gunfire. Ernest took a step forward but tripped over something. He looked down and saw dead bodies around him. He could see Bill, and Tell, and quartermaster Harold, Killjelly, Ynwyr, Holgard — all of his crew, all of his friends. They were lying there against his feet. He looked back at the fire, but it was gone. He tried to shake himself free from the corpses that entangled his feet, but when he looked, they were not his shipmates after all; it was that nice Llaedhwythi family that lay dead all around him. His eyes searched each of their faces until his eyes found the lifeless body of Lexi, her eyes wide with horror, as the rabbit-lipped housemaid's eyes had been when she died.

Ernest couldn't close his eyes. He couldn't move. He couldn't scream. Though he opened his mouth, no sound came out. Perhaps if he could try harder...

Just then, a low and breathy voice spoke from somewhere beyond his vision in the wicked blackness.

"So they all will pass. What are you doing here, anyway? What did you think you could do?" The voice paused, chuckling sinisterly. "What are you, anyway?"

Something seemed to crystallize in Ernest's mind. He didn't even open his mouth, but he heard himself responding to the ghastly voice. "I am a sinner, justly deserving the wrath and damnation of God."

The wicked voice snickered. "And what hope do you have, then?"

Again, Ernest heard his own voice answer, "My only hope for salvation is in the Christ, the Son of God, who died in my place, as my sacrificial propitiation for sin, that I could inherit the glories of God."

The voice let out a low hiss, saying, "How can you claim this hope, eh?"

Was the darkness lifting? Ernest still couldn't see what putrid essence spoke to him from the shadows, but the darkness slowly dissolved. "I must repent from my sins and look to the Almighty God alone for grace and forgiveness, for only He can save. I must make Him the Lord of my life and submit to His rules."

"How are you saved?" The horrible voice spoke again, pain and anger simultaneously rising in the tone.

Ernest heard his own voice respond once more, ringing out as clear as a trumpet, "By the grace of God alone, through faith in Him, which is gifted of His Holy Ghost, and not by any deed of myself."

All was silent for a moment, and then the sinister and wheezing voice chuckled softly, "But you are not saved, Ernest. You are mine."

Then all was dark again. After a moment, the drums sounded again. Again the vision came to him, again the wheezing voice spoke, and again he answered. All was quiet and dark, and it began all over again.

Ernest must have dreamed this same dream four or five times before finally waking up. Ernest shivered. Looking around the crowded room, all about him, his fellow pirates hung in their hammocks, many knocking against each other as the ship swayed gently. A soft light — as of the morning's first warm rays — trickled through the open gunports and down the open hatch. As he watched, Frank and Roe tramped down the steps from the upper deck and headed for their own hammocks. The night shift was just over, then.

Several other pirates stirred, and a couple slid from their hammocks, stretching and yawning widely. Ernest yawned himself. Quartermaster Harold would wake them soon, and he would need to serve out breakfast to the crew. So long as he was awake anyway, there wasn't much point in waiting for the quartermaster's rude awakening. He may as well report to Lewis to see if he needed any help.

Ernest swung out of his hammock, but he had no sooner slipped into his over-clothes than the quartermaster's shrill whistle burst through the crowded cabin.

"Up and about now, lazies! We have new orders in this morning."

Ernest hurried over to the kitchen and slid behind the bar to take his stand by the ale barrels. As Ernest scuttled past, Lewis added the last few ingredients to his stew.

Lewis looked up and winked. "You rested well then, boyo?"

Ernest nodded. "Not too bad, some weird dreams, but not too bad."

Just then, the first crew member arrived at the bar. Lewis dished them out their portion of stew while Ernest served out a pint of beer for each man. He couldn't help but notice a dark and almost brooding look in everyone present. This perplexed Ernest a great deal. It had only been two evenings ago when he had last served out the food and drink to the crew, and they had been so merry and jovial — dancing, fiddling, and swearing. He supposed there had been a whole day intervening that time and this. So what could have happened yesterday to sour everyone's spirits? Perhaps that was why Holgard was in such foul humor last night before he found the key.

The stocky fiddler from two evenings ago shuffled past, and Ernest handed him his pint.

"Jimmy," Ernest said in a low voice, "what's happened to you all? You all look a hair upset."

The stocky fiddler looked at Ernest with a raised eyebrow. "You don't know?" He smiled bitterly. "Ah, that's right, you were off scouting. You weren't here yesterday."

Ernest nodded enthusiastically. "Yes, that's right. I was scouting, just like you say." That must be what Killjelly had told the crew.

The stocky fiddler looked sideways as if afraid someone might overhear what he was about to say. He lowered his voice confidentially, "You remember Nugent? How he was tramping up on the table a few evenings ago impersonating Vania Bloodrummer?"

Ernest nodded.

"Well," the stocky fiddler continued, "somehow, Longfinch heared about it, and he haved Nugent hanged from the yardarm while we all watched."

Ernest's eyes went wide. "Longfinch hanged Nugent? Nugent wouldn't hurt a fly!"

"That's true," the fiddler said, looking at him meaningfully. "What's the point in hanging a man for an innocent jest? That's what *we* all want to know." And he walked away moodily.

Ernest thought on this for a moment while he served out the

last of the beer. How could that have happened? Longfinch couldn't have hung Nugent.

Not that Ernest couldn't imagine Nugent being hung — he was impertinent and perhaps deserved a good hanging. What Ernest couldn't believe was that Longfinch had done the dirty deed. He had seen Longfinch, and the elfin captain had always seemed so decent. It was hard for Ernest even to imagine Longfinch in a sour mood. How could such a captain order a crewman's hanging simply over a joke gone too far? It didn't seem possible.

Ernest started drawing himself a pint of beer when he felt Lewis' hand on his shoulder.

"For the life on you," Lewis hissed, "don't take a *sip* on that beer."

Ernest turned towards his friend in surprise, but Lewis only smiled broadly and winked, turning away and whistling merrily to himself.

Ernest looked at the back of Lewis' head in perplexity and then at the half-full pint of beer in his hand. What was all of this now? Ernest's mind flashed back to the evening before and Lewis' cryptic warning. Did this have something to do with Killjelly's night visits to Lewis? What was wrong with the beer, anyway?

Just then, Killjelly himself came walking down the stairs into the galley. Ernest looked at the beer in his hand, and an idea came to him. He could test his hypothesis that Lewis' strange behavior was linked to his conversations with Killjelly. As Killjelly walked past the bar, Ernest offered him the pint of beer.

"Some beer, sir?"

Killjelly smiled politely. "Thank you, sure, but not at the moment."

Ernest looked back at Lewis, who still whistled merrily with his back turned. After another moment of thought, Ernest set down the pint of beer on the bar.

Killjelly now walked to the middle of the cabin, and the pirates grew quiet as all eyes turned to the officer. Killjelly looked over the crew closely, then he spoke in an even and matter-of-fact tone with a blank expression on his face. "Holgard orders every man on deck for a special announcement."

A few pirates murmured a "Yes, sir," and they all stood, following Killjelly as he returned to the deck.

Ernest followed too, falling in line near the back. As he emerged onto the deck, he could feel the warm morning sun falling on his back. Looking about, his eyes fell on Captain Holgard, who stood on the poop deck in his full uniform, with Ynwyr standing at the helm behind him. To Holgard's right stood the dark figure of the Archeomancer.

Ernest gasped in horror. What was he doing out in broad daylight?

Many of the crew whispered to each other, pointing with questioning glances at the Albino. As for himself, Ernest felt his stomach turning at the sight of the Archeomancer. What was he doing here? Why was Holgard revealing him now? Ernest shivered. True, it was cold out this morning, but he wasn't shivering from the cold. This was turning out to be an unpleasant morning.

But what was in that beer, anyway?

41

AVANT-GARDE

*T*itus Donne nodded. "Fair enough."

He sat down with his back against a rock. Haeli settled herself down at a safe distance, unsure how much she could trust this man. Since she knew Ella, she presumed that Ella's father would be a trustworthy man, but she could never be too careful.

Halfdan fluttered up onto a granite rock and looked at Haeli and Titus as they spoke, not making a sound or any other gesture that might betray what he thought.

"Well," Titus began, "eh, I, eh, I'm not sure where to start. Um, it, eh, was about a month ago — was it? Nearly a month at least — when my daughter, Ella, that is, went out one night with some bread. She said she was bringing it to a beggar or something. Well, eh, she was gone for several hours, and, eh, finally, eh, I went looking for her. We searched the entire village, and finally, I found the bread she had taken with her lying in some alleyway. In that bread, there was ah... well, I guess there was a note, eh, shoved into the crust, and it said something about Entwerp."

Titus licked his lips before continuing. "Well, eh, I started looking and asking and found out that some folks, er, just further down the mountain had seen a wagon of unsavory-looking people riding down, eh, down the mountain at a, eh, well, quickly on that same night Ella disappeared. Someone said they looked like sailors. Then, er, I found out that Entwerp was a town out in this area of the... ah.... globe. So, eh, I got a... eh, well, I had the idea that maybe Ella was kidnapped and taken to Entwerp, so, eh, I got a cabin on board a whaling ship to sail across the sea. Well, we no sooner got here than some, eh, some pirates attacked us. I jumped overboard in the fight, and now, eh... well, here I am."

Titus was silent for a moment. "I wasn't even, eh, I didn't know Ella was here until you said you had seen her. I was, er, well, I was chasing a hope." Titus stopped as if choking on a lump in his throat.

Haeli nodded. "I am pretty sure we are talking about the same Ella. I met her over a week ago in the spice markets of Entwerp Coastal, and we made friends. She apparently was captured by pirates in Slyzwir, but escaped from them off the coast of Entwerp. Ever since she got into town, she has been looked after by someone I know. So believe me, Mr. Titus, she is in good hands."

Titus nodded. "That's, eh, that's a good thing for a father to hear."

Haeli looked over at the harrier and back at Titus. "May I ask how you came upon this fine bird?"

"I can answer that," Halfdan replied, still speaking in a monotone. "I was a scout for the whalers since I could spot the whales from farther away. The captain was a good Weldronist, and he thought I improved the moral character of his crew. When the pirates killed them all, I helped this poor soul, although he swears worse than any of those whalers." Halfdan spoke with perfect evenness as if he were simply repeating a long string of facts and not passing any judgment on them.

Titus, Hafdan, and Haeli

"I don't know how those whalers put up with him," Titus muttered under his breath.

Haeli shook her head. "I would bet that those pirates who attacked you were the same ones who captured Ella."

Titus looked pale at this and swallowed. "Eh, do you think?"

Haeli nodded. "They have attacked me three — maybe four — times. I escaped from their ship last night."

"What do they want?" Titus asked. "Are they in the business of capturing young girls?" He turned even more pale and shuddered as he spoke.

Haeli shook her head. "I think it was just a coincidence." She wasn't sure if she should mention the Gwambi Treasure or not. Ella had seemed pretty secretive about the whole thing, and Da had been very insistent on the key's secrecy. She probably shouldn't flippantly discuss the treasure with an all-but-stranger.

Ah! The keys! Haeli felt her heart sink down into her gut at the thought. The pirates had one of them now; it wasn't a secret any longer. How could she have let that happen? How could she have let her father down? Haeli felt a sob coming on, but she forced it back down. No, she would not think about that right now. Crying wouldn't do herself any good now. Once she had some time to think, she would come up with a plan of action. That's what she needed.

Just then, Halfdan perked up his head. "There is someone on the far shore."

Titus leaped to his feet and scrambled around the boulder that blocked their view. Haeli also struggled to her feet, finding with some satisfaction that she now had the energy to stand. She walked shakily over to where Titus stood.

Sure enough, the shoreline stretched before her — only fifty yards off. She could see those same majestic mountains she knew so well, stretching out of the water for miles and miles along the coastline. By her memory of the mountain range, she guessed she wasn't much further down the coastline from Entwerp than her family's fort was — maybe a little closer.

"Are you sure you see someone?" Titus asked.

Haeli strained her eyes at the far shore. It was hard to make out much of anything in the woods and cliffs, though a small beach lay directly across from the island. Still, she could make out no figure on the far shore.

"I can see them clearly," Halfdan replied methodically. "There are two women and a young boy; all of them nymphs."

Haeli looked closer at the shore, catching sight of some movement. Yes, that looked like a person. Titus must have seen this too, as he waved his arms wildly and shouted, his voice again rising to a high pitch in his excitement.

"Halloo! We need help! Help us!"

Haeli could now see one figure distinctly, stepping out onto the beach and looking directly at them.

"With your luck, Titus," Halfdan said emotionlessly, "those will be native cannibals looking for lunch."

Titus immediately stopped shouting and turned to Halfdan abruptly. "Do you think?"

Just then, the figure dove into the water.

"He is coming towards us," Haeli said.

"She," Halfdan corrected.

"Well," Titus said, picking up a fist-sized stone and standing tall, "she will not have me for lunch, that's for certain."

"Do not kill her," Halfdan said with a slow blink. "That would be murder, which is *also* a sin."

"It's not murder if she's trying to eat me!" Titus protested.

Haeli shook her head. "The indigies are not cannibals."

A trail moved through the water as of something swimming right under the surface. In a moment, the waves broke, and a small woman stepped out onto the rocky island. She was an indigie nymph, with her amphibian-like skin and webbed feet and hands. Haeli guessed she wasn't much older than herself. She was about three feet tall and as lithe as a willow wand. She had long, jet-black hair, dark, oily skin, and narrow, black, squinting eyes. Her clothes looked to be made of supple animal skins, comprising a petticoat that reached to her knees and a light shirt that had no sleeves and left her stomach bare. By the look of her, Haeli guessed she was of the Twengoli tribe since she had those characteristic flat eyes. Few Skratsi had flat eyes.

The little woman smiled broadly at Haeli and spoke in Tylweni. "Good greeting do I give unto you."

"And may the Great Aeparon return your blessing unto you," Haeli responded.

Titus looked confused, staring back and forth between Haeli and the indigie. "Well, is she coming to eat us?"

"I can not understand them any better than you," Halfdan replied.

"Ye and your companion who is with you," the indigie girl continued in Tylweni, "do both appear as ones haplessly stranded upon this desolate island. Why for do ye not swim unto the shore? For it is not of a far distance and can easily be attained and achieved."

"I am weak," Haeli replied. "For I have only just now and presently been pulled from the waves of death which have striven with me for the purpose of taking my life all of the night long. Therefore, do I no longer have the strength for to swim. As for my companion, he does not understand the ways which are to swim."

The indigie laughed at this.

"Well?" Titus asked. "Is that a good thing if they laugh? Does that mean they're friendly? Or maybe they laugh right before they try to cook you."

"Your companion," the indigie said, "is a sad and lonely man who has not known the companionship of the sea, nor learned of the pleasurable deed that is to swim."

Haeli nodded. "He is a man from a far and distant land, even the eastern lands, who has come for miles and miles in great haste and distress over the cause of losing his daughter. He has come for the purpose of searching for her and finding her out."

The indigie grew sober at this, and as her smile lessened, her eyes showed dark and solemn. "Then he is a very sad and desperate man indeed. For not even the mother moa would search so far and so long for the purpose of finding out her young. I give unto him honor and obeisance." And she turned and bowed to Titus.

"What's this now?" Titus looked at the indigie in alarm.

"I give unto you the blessing of the Great Aeparon," the indigie said. "May you be given success and a mushroom unto you for your labors."

Titus turned to Haeli. "What is the little woman saying to me?"

"Well," Haeli replied, speaking in Helfenic again, "it would not make much sense to translate it literally, but basically, she is wishing you good luck in your search for Ella."

"Ah," Titus said, letting his guard down. "That's very nice of her. Thank her for me."

"My companion," Haeli resumed in Tylweni as she turned back to the little indigie, "gives unto you a most heartfelt feeling of gratitude."

The indigie smiled again, then turned back towards the shore. Haeli followed her gaze and could see two figures standing on the beach.

"They are desperate and poor people!" the indigie called across the water. "Wouldst thou bring unto them a boat?"

The two figures disappeared back into the underbrush, but in a moment, they returned, carrying a long canoe. They set this into the water and paddled over to the island.

As these two other indigies came closer, Haeli had some time to observe them. The one at the canoe's front looked to be a young boy — maybe no older than eight summers. He wore nothing more than a loin cloth, and his oily skin glistened even in the overcast light. In the back of the canoe sat a young woman. She was taller and appeared to be older than the indigie who had swum to the island first. Both newcomers had the same dark complexion as the first, with the same flat eyes.

As the canoe reached the island, the boy in the front leaped out of the boat and dragged it onto the rocky islet. The young woman stepped out with the air of aristocracy. She wore the same apparel as the first indigie, only over the top, she wore a long, loose-fitting dress dyed red around the hem and edges. It looked as if it was made of a muslin material. Haeli wondered if the first indigie possessed a similar outer dress but had removed it in order to swim to the island.

This newcomer padded across the rocks on her webbed feet until she had come up to Haeli. She bowed courteously.

"My name is Tiya-Aenji the Li, of the Twengoli tribe."

Haeli bowed her head. "Good greetings do I give unto you."

Tiya-Aenji nodded to this. "May the Great God return your blessing."

This response surprised Haeli. Typically, the indigies spoke of the Great Aeparon, not the Great God.

Tiya-Aenji now motioned to the other two indigies, pointing first to the indigie who had swum to the island. "These are those who are commissioned with the task of waiting on and tending to me. This is Sydni-Efylyn, and this is her brother, Nōlistrw-kagwyr."

"Good greetings do I give unto all of you," Haeli said in Tylweni, and then she turned to Titus, translating for him. "This lady here is Tiya-Aenji, and she is the Li of the Twengoli tribe. These other two are her servants, Sydni-Efylyn, and Nōlistrw-kagwyr."

Titus nodded to them all. "They're, eh, they are most welcome. But, ah, if you don't mind my asking, what is a Li?"

Haeli pursed her lips. She had heard the term before, but wasn't completely certain. She turned back to Tiya-Aenji and resumed speaking in Tylweni. "My companion, who is filled with gratitude and thankfulness which overflows his bowels, has just asked of you, if you could tell unto us what it is to be a Li?"

Tiya-Aenji smiled courteously. "Certainly, will I declare this matter unto you. That I am the Li is regarding the fact that I will succeed the Shaman, being that when he dies, will I, by necessity, enter the role of Shaman for myself. For to be the Li is to be the first orphan of a great warrior who was blessed with a mushroom."

Haeli nodded. What was it with the Twengoli and mushrooms? "In what meaning," she began slowly, choosing her words carefully and grasping at vocabulary words that she had only ever heard before and never used herself, "in what meaning is this that you speak of the mushroom? For this is to say and to ask, how is a warrior blessed with a mushroom?"

Tiya-Aenji continued to smile. "It is the teaching of the Shaman that when a man dies and is interred into the earth, out of his grave will spring up and grow a plant of some kind or nature, and it is according to this that his relatives might discover into what shape he has been reincarnated. For the man who is blessed with a fern has been born unto a deer, and the man who has been blessed with an oak sapling has been born as an eagle — but the man who has been blessed with a mushroom has been transfigured into the Great Aeparon and thus has passed beyond all things physical. Thus are the teachings of the Shamans from ancient times." Tiya-Aenji finished, and Haeli thought she could detect the smallest hint of a smirk on the corner of her lips.

"How is it then," Haeli began, trying to word her question

carefully to avoid any possible offense, "that you — a Li in line of the inheritance of Shamanship — gave unto us the greeting of the Great God?"

Tiya-Aenji's face now beamed with exuberance. "Are you a follower of the Great God, then? Of whom we have been told of by the people of the east?"

Haeli nodded. "I am a worshiper of the great God, the Almighty God of my forefathers."

Tiya-Aenji sighed. "It is on account of this that the Shaman detests me with a great detestation and would wish with his heart to have another Li who might enter into his place upon his death. Yet such is not the case, for I am the only Li in the tribe."

Titus cleared his throat. "What's the little woman saying now?"

Haeli took a deep breath and turned back to Titus. "Let me see, some of this is hard to translate literally. Basically, she, as the Li, is the heir to the Shaman of the tribe. But, it sounds like the Shaman does not like her because — if I understand this correctly — she is of our faith and does not believe in the religion taught by the Shaman."

"That is correct," Tiya-Aenji said in Helfenic, speaking with a confidence and precision that Haeli had never heard from an indigie before.

Titus stumbled back. "Ah, eh, why didn't you say so before?"

"You speak the common tongue merri well," Haeli said.

Tiya-Aenji nodded. "You speak the Twengoli tongue merri well."

Halfdan now spoke. "Tiya-Aenji, you are a remarkable woman and will be blessed for your labors on earth with the eternal bliss of heaven." He spoke with the same mechanical evenness, but Haeli thought she could sense the smallest hint of sympathy — though she may have imagined it.

"Thank you," Tiya-Aenji said, bowing slightly to the harrier.

Just then, Nōlistrw-kagwyr cleared his throat, muttering something under his breath. He spoke so rapidly that Haeli couldn't catch what he said; only she thought she heard something about an 'edict.'

"What is it your servant says?"

Tiya-Aenji sighed, still speaking in Helfenic. "He was reminding me of the chief's edict. Will you come with us into the boat? We will take you to shore."

"Absolutely!" Titus said enthusiastically.

"What edict?" Haeli asked.

Tiya-Aenji replied in Tylweni. "The Supreme Chief Iasaqi-Woni has issued an edict unto us which does declare and demand that all strangers who are not of the Twengoli tribe be brought unto him in the village, whether it is of their will or not."

Nōlistrw-kagwyr nodded enthusiastically at this and looked like he was about to speak, but Tiya-Aenji held up her hand, and he shut his mouth.

"For what purpose and unto what ends?" Haeli replied in Tylweni, suddenly apprehensive about stepping into the boat with Tiya-Aenji and her servants.

Tiya-Aenji shrugged. "He will question you closely with the purpose of discovering the truth and determining your guilt."

"Guilt?"

Nōlistrw-kagwyr nodded again, grinning from ear to ear. Haeli noticed now, for the first time, that he carried two *karambit* knives and a wicked-looking *kukri*. On looking at Tiya-Aenji, she noticed, with some surprise, that she was similarly armed, having, in addition, a long sling and a bag of obsidian sling-stones hanging from her shoulder. Only Sydni-Efylyn was unarmed. Should she resist getting into that boat? Titus was already climbing in. Besides, she didn't have enough strength to win a fight unless neither Nōlistrw-kagwyr nor Tiya-Aenji were trained fighters — which looked unlikely.

"Yes," Tiya-Aenji replied, still speaking in Tylweni and smiling as if nothing was wrong. "Guilt. For he wishes to ascertain who is guilty for the act of murdering his two sons."

42

OFF-BALANCE

Clerans trudged slowly down the road towards Entwerp Proper. His feet ached, and his eyes burned. His whole body felt like lead. What a pleasure it would be to lay down and let his body become one with the earth. But no, he did not have that luxury tonight. The strikers were moving on the bank. He had to be there to stop them. The cool night breeze wafted over his skin as he trudged through the darkness. That helped a little, though it made him more plainly feel the congealing blood on his face. A shiver ran through his whole body. Those strikers had murdered all those people in Miss Nansi's house. They would pay for it.

Then he remembered the letter in his pocket. Would he deliver it to the Company? It was likely to help the strikers, and at the moment, he did not feel very inclined to help them. They had just murdered so many people and were trying to shut down the National Bank. Then again, he had promised Haeli that he would deliver the letter. After all, this wouldn't help the strikers who were sieging the bank. This would only help Miss Nansi and whatever real strikers were left after the spokesman's purging.

Clerans tightened his jaw and walked with more determination. If he could get his hands on that spokesman…

He now passed through the commons, coughing as smoke blew in his face. That glow of embers beside the road was all that remained of Miss Nansi's house. The night was dark, and he couldn't make out much of his surroundings. Here and there, he could see shadowy figures moving. They must be strikers, stragglers who were still hanging out around their new camping site. He wouldn't waste any time on them. If they were still here, they weren't dangerous. It was those radical and homicidal strikers who followed the spokesman he was worried about.

Just then, the sharp crack of gunfire broke the still night.

Clerans quickened his pace, suddenly feeling much more awake. Those gunshots were not far away. That had to be the strikers. As he hurried on, he entered the city itself and the abundant whale-oil streetlights. At last, he could see more clearly, and ran forward now with more confidence. More gunshots echoed in the night, and he rushed towards them. Confused shouts and voices came from a square a little way down the street. The strikers must be there, and he would help stop them.

Turning a corner in the street, he came directly into a small square. A group of perhaps eight rough and wild-looking strikers (carrying rifles as they marched down the street) stood directly in front of him.

"Halt where you are!" Clerans cried out, grabbing at his own rifle.

Yet at that moment, a fusillade of shots rang out from the other side of the square. Most of the strikers before him collapsed to the ground with screams of agony and curses. There was a rush of wind in the air around Clerans and the buzz of musket balls skittering across the cobblestones only to lodge with sickening thuds into the striker's flesh or the stonework behind him.

Alarmed, Clerans tripped, falling into the pile of writhing strikers. Another fusillade of shots rang out, and those few strikers still standing collapsed, cut to the ground by the murderous fire. One man fell on top of Clerans, and he struggled to get back to his feet.

Looking toward the gunshots, he saw perhaps two dozen soldiers in gray uniforms emerging from the shadows, the whale-oil lamps' eerily light gleaming off their well-polished bayonets. Governor Braedhwyc himself led this group of Regulars, and he wiped puss from his leaking eye as he glared disdainfully at the dying strikers.

Clerans opened his mouth to call for help, but just then, the governor barked out an order.

"Cut them all down. If they'll are in the city, then they are up to no good. We cen ask them questions an' negotiate with them in the morning, but fer now, shoot them on sight."

Clerans shut his mouth, suddenly realizing that the Regulars had no way of knowing that he was not a striker himself. Perhaps it would be best not to move while the Regulars were here.

A couple strikers still writhed about on the ground, gasping and crying out in agony. A Regular stepped forward with his bayonet raised.

"Do no bother," the governor barked, his eye twitching. "They are no more danger to us now. We must get to the bank before the rest o' the lot. Vene along, then. We must needs hurry."

And the Regulars marched briskly out of the square.

Shakily, Clerans crawled out from under the striker who had died on top of him. On the bright side, the blood on his face was no longer congealed.

Yet as he stood up, a striker grabbed at his boot.

"Please!" the man sobbed. "Please!"

Clerans knelt beside the man. He couldn't be much older than Clerans was.

"Aye, ye tain my attention." But as Clerans looked the man over, his stomach turned. There was a gruesome bullet hole in his side the size of an apple.

"My mother," the man gasped. "My mother."

Clerans swallowed. "I do no know who yer mother is. I am sorry."

"My mother." The man gasped again. "Please. I need my mother."

Something seemed to snap inside Clerans' heart. He lifted the man up and threw his arms around him, heedless of the blood oozing from his wounded side. And then Clerans sobbed. This was wrong. This wasn't how war was supposed to be fought. There was supposed to be honor and bravery, and daring, and courage, but all he saw here was horrifying mortality. Why was this man bleeding out on the streets with no friend or family member to help him? Was he a follower of the spokesman, or was he another wronged man, like the one-armed man from Miss Nansi's cottage, a genuine believer in the strikers' ideals? Who was to say he was even on his way to the bank? Perhaps he was just an innocent person like Clerans, caught in the violence unawares.

Clerans held the dying man close, weeping uncontrollably. "I am sorry, I am so sorry. I do no know who yer mother is."

"Tell her." The man choked. "Tell her. I wos here."

"I am sorry," Clerans continued to sob. "I am sorry."

The man made a gurgling noise, and his body convulsed. Finally, he patted Clerans clumsily on the back. "There. It is all goin' to be all right. We will make it out…" Then his body went limp.

Clerans swallowed back the lump in his throat and let the striker slump to the ground. None of the other strikers moved anymore, either. So that was it. Slowly he got back to his feet, standing for a moment and looking at the group of corpses. Just that morning, he had been reveling in the chance to help the sheriff fight off the strikers from the factories. He had only ever dreamed about getting to fight hand-to-hand with an enemy. Well, now he had done it. He had killed several people already this evening. And now he knew he was pretty good at it (at least, he had kept himself alive somehow). Yet, for the first time, he wondered if this was something he wanted to be good at.

The sound of gunshots echoed from further to the south. Clerans sighed and readjusted the rifle on his back. He should get to the bank. Sheriff Laei would need his help. Yet as he turned to go, he heard a gun cocking into full position.

"Halt right there!"

Clerans jumped at the sound of the voice, pivoting towards it. "Lexi?"

"Clerans?" Lexi stepped out of the shadows and lowered her rifle. She had her hair tied back in a scarf and her skirt corners tucked into her belt in a sort of make-shift trousers. A tomahawk and two pistols hung from her hip, and the handle of a skinning knife protruded from her left boot. She only ever walked around like this when she was serving in the militia.

"What are ye doin' here?" Clerans asked.

"I could ask ye the same question," Lexi replied, putting a hand on her hip. Clerans suddenly realized that she had a red ribbon tied to her arm. What was that about?

Clerans shrugged. "I wos venin' to the bank to help the sheriff."

Lexi nodded. "Aye, they called out the militia."

"Which is why ye are here?"

Lexi tilted her head to one side. "That, an' I am gardin' fer that pirate."

Clerans felt his heart drop. "The one I captured?"

"Aye," Lexi replied. "He escaped. Slipped out jist after I brought him a blanket. Treacherous rogue."

More gunshots sounded in the night, mingled with muffled shouting. "We should get to the bank, should no we?" Clerans asked.

Lexi furrowed her brow. "Ye look exhausted, Clerans. It is no yer night fer militia duty, anyway. Ye ha' best get some rest."

Clerans shook his head, fingering the shoulder strap of his rifle. "I am here. I will help."

He cast a look at the striker who had died in his arms. He had to help the sheriff, even though he didn't want to. If only to prove that he could still do this.

Lexi slung her rifle over her shoulder and sighed. "Merri well. Let's get to the bank. Do ye tain anything red about ye?"

Clerans smiled darkly. "Aside from the blood all over me?"

"No," Lexi replied, nudging him on the shoulder. "I mean something red that ye cen wear." And she motioned to the red ribbon on her arm. "That's how the militia are markin' themselves out."

Clerans shook his head. "Clearly, no one took the time to tell me."

Lexi sighed. "Then ye'd best stay with me. The Regulars are on orders to shoot on sight."

Clerans let out his breath slowly, feeling a catch in his throat as he looked one last time at the dead strikers. "Aye, I figured that out already."

43

INDIGENOUS

It was only a short hike of a few miles before Haeli, Titus, and Halfdan, led by their three indigie guides, reached the Twengoli village. Haeli — though she had interacted with the indigies frequently — had never been to one of their villages before, and the sight of it took her breath away. It was settled around one of the area's many rivers on a decently steep slope, nestled among the great spruce trunks and broadleaf ferns.

They entered on an almost indiscernible path at the village's lowest edge. From here, they ascended, their path broken now and then by wooden landings which divided the village into terraces. The path followed the river's course closely, and the river itself was arrested in its mad, downhill career by various dams, causing it to pool at approximately the same levels as the wooden landings. All along the path were small huts built of vines, branches, fern leaves, and animal hides. Lower down, the dwellings were smaller and made entirely of plant matter, but the higher they climbed, the more the huts were made of animal skins dyed in ornate patterns.

From these dwellings issued hosts of indigies, all short and swarthy. Some were muscular, square warriors with knives tucked into every inch of clothing they possessed, six-foot spears in their hands, and slings and bags of obsidian sling-stones hanging from their shoulders. There were some older women, bent double with age, their wrinkled skin hanging from their bones, and richly colored scarves drooped over their heads. Naked, pot-bellied children peeped out of the entryways — or from behind their mothers' skirts. There were also many young men wearing only knee-length skins belted around their waists and young women in similar garb to Tiya-Aenji, looking on with deep, black eyes.

Haeli had never seen so many indigies in one place. She never would have guessed that their villages were so large. At the same time, she noticed, on the village's outskirts, several smaller huts — almost like tents — scattered here and there among the trees. Was this perhaps a gathering? Were many of these indigies visitors and not full-time residents of this village?

Here and there, Haeli could see a dead animal — a boar usually, or sometimes a bear — hanging from a tree, some completely skinned, others being skinned as Haeli watched. Many fires were also sprinkled throughout the village where all this meat was being cooked. Once, Haeli saw a small building with smoke oozing out of every crack as a young warrior hung thinly sliced meat inside. Was he preserving meat? Were these the preparations for some feast, perhaps?

But then Haeli noticed preparations of a more unsettling nature. She had seen warriors bearing many knives, but now, here and there, she could see more warriors — burly and calcu-lated — carefully and meticulously working out fine and brutal edges with whetstones on their *karambits, kukris,* and spears. Some other warriors knapped pieces of obsidian, turning them into razor-edged sling-stones — flat as a disc with a sharp edge all the way around. Haeli's mind connected the ends of each piece of thread she saw and weaved them together to make a single conclusion — the large group, the preserved meat, the care of weaponry — this was a military assembly. The indigies were going to war.

But against whom? The Twengoli would not attack another Twengoli village. This gathering looked too large to be a petty intra-tribal dispute. What about between tribes? The Twengoli and the Skratsi hadn't fought for seven years now. Governor Braedhwyc had mediated their last blood feud, and there had been no violence between the tribes since. The Uquibiwi couldn't be the focus of the Twengoli's martial activity, could they? They could be very warlike, according to all accounts, but she had never heard of the Uquibiwi picking a fight with the Twengoli ever since an Uquibiwi chief had taken a Twengoli chief's daughter for a wife and moved to the capital as an envoy for Caedmon Wilkins and the constitutional convention. Who, then, could the Twengoli be preparing to attack?

Something stirred inside Haeli. Had her mother reached the Iasaqi-Woni? If so, could she be the cause of all of this? Were the indigies going to war against the Company itself? This was not how she saw this lawsuit going down, and she doubted the Company would respond very well to an open attack by the indigies.

As Haeli pondered this question, they reached another landing which looked to be near the top of the Twengoli village. Here Tiya-Aenji stopped and motioned towards a large hut, speaking in Helfenic, "You should stop here, for now."

Then she turned to Nōlistrw-kagwyr, speaking in Tylweni, "Go unto the Supreme-Chief Iasaqi-Woni, and tell him with reference to his edict that we have brought more strangers unto the village for the purpose of his interrogation."

Nōlistrw-kagwyr flashed an impish smile and dashed off uphill.

Titus breathed a sigh. "This is, eh, well, incredible. I've never seen anything, eh, anything quite like it."

Halfdan only gave a low whistle, settling himself on a low-hanging tree branch but saying nothing.

Tiya-Aenji again motioned towards the large hut. "Go inside. You will find rest there."

Haeli turned towards the hut, noticing with no small anxiety the number of armed warriors loitering around it. A couple of other people also sat outside the hut, beacon-tenders by their looks. Haeli ground her teeth together. Why did she have no say in all of this? Why could she have no say in the events that happened to her? She wanted to *do* something, anything! But no, she was doing something. She was watching, and she was waiting. She might not know what part she would play in this drama with the Twengoli, but whatever it was, she would be ready to play it to the fullest.

Then Haeli froze. A familiar figure stood in the doorway, gazing at her. She almost doubted her eyes. Was she really seeing what she thought she saw?

The figure stared back at her with an expression that seemed to say the same thing.

"Yohni?"

The figure stepped forward, a wide smile spreading across his usually somber face.

Haeli ran for him, collapsing on her knees, hugging him tightly, and kissing him on both cheeks. "Yohni! You are here!"

Yohni accepted her greetings with civility, but he smiled broadly the whole time, finally saying, "Why are you here?"

Haeli looked him closely in the eye. "Wait, if you are here, then..."

At that moment, a shrill little boy's voice cried out from inside the hut. "Yali!"

Haeli didn't even have time to stand up as Dafid, closely followed by her very own mother, came dashing out of the hut.

"Dafid! Ma!" Haeli couldn't speak beyond that; any more

words caught in her throat. Dafid hugged her tightly around the waist, and Ma covered them all with her arms.

"Oh, Haeli!" Ma gasped, "Oh, my darling. You are here! How did you get here?"

Haeli could think of no words to say; she only wept. She grabbed Dafid and hugged him, then grabbed her mother and hugged her, and wept harder. Ma was weeping now too, but Dafid jumped up and down, shivering all over with excitement.

"Ma, do you see? Yali is here. Yali vened to be with us!"

Ma wiped tears from her eyes and hugged Haeli again. "Yes, Dafid, I see."

Dafid peered closely at Haeli and put his little hand on her cheek, feeling the tears that streamed down her face.

"Don't cry, Yali. Don't be sad."

Haeli smiled and hugged her brother tightly. "I am not sad, Dafid. I am just merri happy."

Dafid wiped more tears from Haeli's cheeks. "But then, why are you crying?"

Haeli smiled, still hugging her brother closely. "I am crying because I am so happy."

Dafid made a strange grunt at this, but he said no more. Haeli released her brother and embraced her mother one last time.

"Oh, Ma!" she breathed, but wasn't able to say anything else before she started crying again.

Her mother rocked her back and forth, kissing her on the cheek several times. Haeli sank into her mother's arms, relaxing in the embrace.

"Ride it, Haeli," her Ma murmured. "Ride it until it is all done."

For a moment, she forgot all about the trouble she had been through — the violence, the exhaustion, the terror. She forgot about her long night fighting the waves and the indigies' strange behavior. She even forgot that the pirates had stolen one of her father's keys. None of that mattered at the moment. For now, all that mattered was that she, Ma, Yohni, and Dafid were together again.

"O God," Ma whispered, "Thank you for bringing my child back to me."

Haeli held her mother tighter and sighed, thinking, *Yes, Lord, thank you*. With a feeling akin to pricking her finger on a needle, she realized she hadn't spoken to God since the afternoon by the roadside when she had yelled at Him, asking Him why. The emotions of that moment — the confusion, the anger, the hopelessness — threatened to interfere with this moment in her mother's arms, but she pushed them back. Not now, she would deal with them later.

After a moment, her mother released her and held her at arm's length. "Goodness, dear," she said, "You look like you have not eaten or slept since I last saw you!"

Haeli smiled and laughed nervously, wiping the tears from her cheeks and eyes. "That is almost true."

Just then, the whole ground shook with the sound of drums. There must have been a dozen or more drums beating in time, some so large that the entire mountain resonated with each strike, and others small and crisp, like the sound of bones rattling against each other. Haeli gasped in alarm.

"What is that?"

She had forgotten about Tiya-Aenji and Titus, but she now looked to where they stood a few feet away. Titus only looked back at her, barely concealing the terror washing over him. Tiya-Aenji, however, looked solemn.

"That is the summons. Iasaqi-Woni is calling you."

Ma gasped. "God help us."

Haeli now turned on her in alarm. "Is this because of the lawsuit? Did we start this?"

Ma shook her head. "I never got to talk to Iasaqi-Woni. He would not see me."

"Come with me," Tiya-Aenji urged. "You must follow."

Two warriors stepped forward, spears in hand.

Ma bit her lip. "Please be careful. The indigies are out for blood. I wouldn't bring up the lawsuit if I were you."

"Come," Tiya-Aenji urged again. "The Supreme Chief will speak with you himself."

"What does he want?" Titus asked, his voice rising in pitch.

Tiya-Aenji only shrugged. "He only wishes to ascertain your guilt for the death of his sons."

Haeli stood up, giving her mother a hug and kiss on the cheek. "I will be careful."

"God be with you," Ma whispered.

44

APOCALYPSE

s the last crew members settled themselves on deck, Holgard spoke.

"We've received orders from Captain Longfinch." He paused, looking at his crew, meeting their questioning gazes one by one.

Ernest could sense the confusion among the crew. What was all of this about? Why had Holgard summoned them? How were they supposed to react?

Holgard's eyes narrowed, and he pulled at his beard, grunting. "Longfinch orders us to move immediately to strike Entwerp Coastal this afternoon."

A pirate in the front cheered. A few more joined him and then quickly shut their mouths as they realized that no one else joined the cheer, and Holgard didn't encourage it.

Holgard regarded his crew in silence for a moment. He fixed his eyes on the pirate who had cheered. "Is that exciting to you? Do you wish to attack Entwerp again?"

The pirate looked at his fellows and then back to his captain, obviously not sure how to respond. Ernest noticed the Albino smirking at this.

Holgard smiled grimly. "How many on you want to go back

and do battle with that battery? Do you want to watch your good carpentry work splinter? How many on you want to guide our crippled ship *back* to this bay and then rebuild this ship what's taken us so long to rebuild already?" Holgard looked the crew over again. "Eh? Any on you?"

Ernest stole a glance over at Longfinch's man-o-war. Several crew members scurried about on deck, but none looked at the galleon. Were they able to hear Holgard? Surely the dwarf captain's voice carried well over the water, yet Longfinch's crew made no sign of overhearing what Holgard said.

Holgard smiled slowly. "That's what I thinked. The truth is that this plan on Longfinch's is baptized suicide, and it's a conversion on a stupid plan!"

Several crew members chuckled at this.

Holgard pointed at a sailor who had chuckled. "You there! Why are you laughing? Eh? Speak up now."

The pirate blushed, "Er, ah, sir, I just thinked it was funny."

Holgard snorted. "You were laughing at Longfinch, weren't you? Aren't you afraid to laugh at the captain? Yesterday, he hanged a man for making a jest on him. Aren't you afraid to snicker at him?"

A pirate in the back yelled, "Nugent didn't deserve a hanging! I amn't afraid to laugh so long as I have Captain Holgard with me!"

The crew all gave a cheer at this response.

Holgard smiled broadly. "Weel, now. You know the truth now. I think no more on Longfinch than you do. His crew doesn't work any harder than you."

"Far from it!" Killjelly interjected.

The crew cheered.

"He isn't any better on a captain than I, and none on his strategies work. I've telled him again and again that we have to wait. We can't go off and fight the battery again. We have to wait until Captain Pennywraith can reinforce us. But will he listen to me? No, on course not! Weel, this time he's come up with his worst plan yet, and we're going to bear the brunt on his bad idea."

The crew nodded in agreement.

"And why would we obey him, anyway?" Holgard asked.

Quartermaster Harold now spoke with some hesitation. "We *do'ed* swear fealty to him, so he *is* our captain."

Holgard scowled darkly at this. "*Who* is your captain?"

The crew replied in one voice, "You are!"

Holgard nodded in pleasure. "That's true; we only sweared fealty to him 'cause he threatened to kill us all two years ago when he captured our ship."

The pirates nodded, murmuring to each other.

"That isn't true fealty if'n we sweared it under duress," Holgard continued, "is it now?"

"Not at all, sure," Killjelly replied.

The crew cheered.

Holgard smiled and snorted. "Weel, it's time I let you in on a secret." Holgard regarded his crew intently, looking each one in the eye. "I've been working behind Longfinch's back."

The crew stood hushed, everyone hanging on to Holgard's words.

"When we started on this mission, I thought to myself, 'Why should we help Longfinch find the Gwambi Treasure, if'n he will take half on it when it's all said and done? And why would he take only half, eh? What's to say he willn't stab us in the back and take the whole treasure himself?'"

Holgard tapped his finger on the side of his head. "And so I planned to do my bit on working. That's about when I met this fine gentleman who stands beside me." Here Holgard motioned to the Albino.

The crew turned and looked at the foreboding figure of the Archeomancer. They had been eyeing him nervously the whole time already. Now they seemed to feel released to observe him more closely. The Albino simply stood where he was, making no acknowledgment of the crew's obvious interest in him.

Ernest shivered all over. What would the rest of the crew think if he were to tell them what he had seen the Albino do?

"This man," Holgard continued, "is an Archeomancer." Holgard ran his fingers through his thick beard. "That's just a fancy word to say he's a wizard what likes old civilizations, like the Gwambi's."

Ernest glanced around at the crew. They stood in rapture, looking the Albino up and down in wonder. Out of the corner of his eye, Ernest thought he saw Killjelly smiling a strange smile. Ernest turned to look, but Killjelly was simply standing there, looking on with equal admiration.

"Weel, now," Holgard said, putting his big hand on the Albino's shoulder, "while we were out slaving away for Longfinch, this man here haves been on the ground, looking for the Gwambi Treasure for us so that we could find it first and not have to share it with Longfinch and his crew."

The crew gasped, and one pirate in the back cheered. The rest of the crew took up the cheer.

Ynwyr smiled, a naïve confidence in his eyes. "Father, you are a brilliant man."

Holgard grinned widely. "Thank you, son, thank you. Weel, as I was saying, when we were fighting the battery, this man led a small party into Entwerp Proper, and he finded the entrance to one on the Gwambi tombs. There was only one problem: there was a door, and it was locked. So, while we've been fixing up our poor ship, this man has been tirelessly working to find the key so that we can open that door."

Tirelessly, Ernest thought, that wouldn't be the word he'd use. Maybe sleeplessly, not tirelessly. He was plenty tired.

"Weel, I amn't telling you this now just to get your hopes up," Holgard eyed his crew carefully and held up the key dramatically. "Last night, we finally finded the key!"

The crew now cheered louder than ever.

"Who needs Longfinch now?" Killjelly cried.

The crew cheered again.

Holgard smiled broadly. "That's true. We are our own masters."

Ernest looked back across the bay. Longfinch's man-o-war was a flurry of activity as the crew scampered about on deck, letting out the sails and hauling up anchor. He felt a sinking feeling in his gut. They must have heard Holgard's speech.

"Sir!" Ernest called out. "The man-o-war! Look!"

The crew turned to follow Ernest's gaze.

"They've heared us!" Quartermaster Harold cried in alarm.

"They're getting ready for battle!" another pirate said.

Holgard only grinned wider. "And why shouldn't they? We've bided our time long enough. Why should we put up with Longfinch's whims any longer? We don't need him."

"Down with Longfinch!" Killjelly yelled.

The crew repeated Killjelly's cry, "Down with Longfinch!"

"How are we going to defeat him?" Quartermaster Harold said in a panic. "No one haves ever defeated him."

Holgard smirked. "Weel, I've seen him defeated *once*. I was the boatswain aboard this ship when Jock Blowhoarder was captain. *He* defeated Longfinch, and I remember how he do'ed it."

The crew cheered.

"Quartermaster Harold!" Holgard commanded. "Bring out the arms! Draw up anchor! Out with the sails!"

The quartermaster reluctantly pulled out his whistle, trilling out orders as Holgard gave them.

The crew now dashed madly about the deck, many swarming below deck to work the cannons while others scampered up the shrouds like swarming bees to untie the gaskets and unfurl the sails.

Ynwyr set himself firmly at the stern, and as the ship inched forward, he pulled hard at the wheel. The ship turned lazily. Many crew members on deck hauled on the rigging, some releasing the buntlines and clewlines so that the sails unfurled, while others hauled the brace lines, turning the yards to catch the wind as the ship turned. Ernest ducked as a boom swung over his head. He scampered over to the gunwales, out of the way of the action on deck.

"Man the guns!" Holgard screamed. He still stood on the aft deck, his huge hands gripping the gunwales so tightly that his knuckles looked white. His eyes were wide with excitement, and his beard and hair blew madly in the wind.

Ernest felt a chill run down his spine as he looked at Holgard.

"Down with Longfinch!" Holgard screamed. "We fly to battle! We will throw off our chains on service! Down with Longfinch!"

"Down with Longfinch!" The crew echoed.

45

COURT OF JUSTICE

Haeli and Titus followed Tiya-Aenji, warriors flanking them on both sides as they marched further up the mountainside. The air outside had suddenly become hot and sticky. Even breathing was oppressive. There must be a storm coming on. Sweat trickled down Haeli's forehead as they climbed up to the next terrace, where a path showed them the way forward. Haeli trudged along compliantly through the humid air as the path now became a bridge over the river, leading to a platform that stood in the middle of the river in the basin formed below a moderately sized waterfall.

At the far side of this platform — on a tall throne with painted warriors ranged all around him on a dais, the waterfall trickling behind him in the height of honor — sat the Iasaqi-Woni, the supreme chief. He sat with a solemn scowl over his face, his webbed hands folded in his lap. His bare chest gleamed in the light, and his raven-black hair moved slightly in the wind. He had eagle feathers and faience beads braided into his long hair, and his hair looked burnt at the ends. Paint covered his entire face — red, blue, orange, white, and black — all radiating out from his face like spokes on a wheel. The bodyguard's face paint matched this same motif.

A long, wicked-looking *kukri* lay unsheathed on the Iasaqi-Woni's lap, and Haeli could see his extensive muscles twitching as if he longed to thrust the *kukri* into some poor soul. Haeli swallowed hard. He was huge — despite being a nymph. He was menacing and deadly and, by the look of him, blood-thirsty. Of course, the Twengoli had signed treaties with the government, so she hoped she was not in any real danger from the chieftain's wrath, but then again, she was in the Indigie Law; Llaedhwythi codes of justice no longer protected her.

Beside the Iasaqi-Woni stood an old wizened nymph who was as bony as the Iasaqi-Woni was square and muscular. He leaned heavily on a gnarled hawthorn staff decorated with eagles' feathers and faience beads. Haeli guessed that this man must be the shaman of whom Tiya-Aenji had spoken. A single streak of orange paint stretched from the center of his chest in a straight line until it disappeared underneath his skin kilt. Unlike the other warriors, who bore as many weapons as their meager clothing would allow, this shaman bore only a single *karambit* knife, though it was about twice the length of any other *karambit* Haeli had ever seen. This knife lay strapped to his left side in an ornately decorated sheath.

Behind the chief, seated above the waterfall, was a group of about two dozen drummers — wearing only loin-cloths — painted extravagantly from head to toe. Each drummer had his own drum, ranging from huge bass drums nearly double Haeli's height, to small brass *debruka* hand drums, to sets of six or eight-pitched drums. They pounded away in perfect rhythm, making the entire valley resonate with the sound. As Haeli and her party reached the platform, the drummers stopped abruptly. Haeli's ears rang at the sudden silence. The thick, humid air made Haeli feel all the more tense.

Tiya-Aenji now stopped before the Iasaqi-Woni's throne and

bowed. Haeli and Titus stopped on either side of her, and the warriors who had been following them this whole time formed a half circle around them, blocking any means of escape.

Haeli could feel her pulse rising. She had to stay calm. Whatever was going on here, she could get through it if she could only keep her wits about her.

The Iasaqi-Woni frowned, speaking in Tylweni. "Who, may it be inquired of, are these skinny people?"

Tiya-Aenji bowed again. "We have found them, O great and supreme chief, residing upon one of the islands of the coastal area. Upon discovering them, we have thought it prudent and wise to bring them before your all-powerful justice for the purpose of ascertaining if they might know of the guilt of the murder of your sons."

The Iasaqi-Woni grunted, but the shaman screwed up his face into a sneer, looking down at Tiya-Aenji with contempt.

"Far be it from you, O woman-of-the-useless-worship," the shaman croaked. "Far be it from you to see justice done in a proper way after the accordance and wishes of our ancestors."

A snicker went through the group of warriors around Haeli and Titus, but the painted bodyguards on the dais remained motionless.

Tiya-Aenji only bowed again, saying, "The young woman is wise in the ways of our language, and her mind is clear in the understanding of our speech."

The shaman banged the butt of his staff on the dais and glared at Haeli. "Thus is the language of pure beauty and wisdom, even the language of our ancestors, made common and profaned in the tongues of the east-folk."

The Iasaqi-Woni raised his hand, and the shaman stopped speaking, stepping backward with a hoarse growl. The chief now turned to Haeli.

"Are these words true which are spoken of thee by the Li?"

Haeli noticed that the Iasaqi-Woni addressed her in the

common person, as you would speak to a child. She had never heard this grammatical person used when addressing a stranger. More than likely, this was a privilege of the Iasaqi-Woni's rank alone. Haeli bowed as low as she could, trying to outdo Tiya-Aenji in civility. "The words of the Li are most true with regards to me, for I have been taught and understand the knowledge of the pure and beautiful language, even the language of your noble ancestors, O great and supreme chief."

The Iasaqi-Woni smiled. "Thou hast been well trained in the ways of civility, O dark-maiden-of the-curled-hair."

Haeli looked up and smiled. This was a good sign. Perhaps she didn't need to be afraid of this chief. Maybe he had no ill intentions, as she had feared.

The Iasaqi-Woni studied her for a moment. "We have belonging to us, and handed down to us, a saying of words from the ancient times. Even this saying I will relate unto thee: 'When you speak to a great chief with the speaking of words, proceed with careful words as though a knife were pointed against your gut.' Even so hast thou, O maiden, addressed me, the supreme chief of the Twengoli tribe. Thus is shown the supremacy of thy tact, for thou too hast a knife pointed against thy gut."

That did not sound promising. Was he speaking metaphorically of a knife, or was she in danger of physical harm? Haeli wasn't sure how to reply, but luckily, the Iasaqi-Woni spoke again.

"Thou and thy companion hast been summoned unto me for the intent of determining guilt. Dost thou bear among thy words a response unto this?"

Every warrior fixed their eyes on her as if in breathless anticipation of what she would say. Haeli glanced at Tiya-Aenji, but she would not meet her gaze. Haeli wasn't sure what the chief was asking her, but from the general atmosphere, she guessed she had just been asked an impossible question — though the question's cultural subtleties were lost on her.

"What's going on?" Titus asked. "What did he say?"

Haeli licked her lips, replying to the Iasaqi-Woni first, "The Iasaqi-Woni is most wise. If he does not know all things, then let it be said that he knows more than any other man who is drawing breath on the earth. In his great knowledge, therefore, has he asked of me this question. For how am I, a poor and ignorant girl of the east-folk who can hardly speak unto you in your own language, how can I know of what guilt the Iasaqi-Woni speaks?"

The warriors all nodded, and the Iasaqi-Woni smiled. Only the shaman remained frowning. Haeli let herself sigh; she must have answered well.

"Thou hast words," the Iasaqi-Woni said. "We begin to wonder if thou hidest a mushroom underneath thy tongue."

At this, the warriors laughed heartily, elbowing each other and nodding with approval. Haeli allowed herself a smile. This was shaping up well.

"What did he say?" Titus asked again. "Please, I, eh, I do not know what they are saying."

Haeli spoke to him now, "Well, the chief there, the Iasaqi-Woni as they call him, he asked if you preferred to be boiled in water or fried with garlic, and I said 'fried with garlic, naturally.'"

At this, Titus turned pale. "Oh, dear God, help us."

The Iasaqi-Woni suddenly frowned. "What is it thou hast said unto thy companion who is with thee?"

Haeli turned back to the chief, bowing and resuming her Tylweni, fairly confident now that she could please him with a response. "My companion whom ye behold with me has come from a faraway and distant country from far and away across the great and heaving ocean — even from the lands of the east. In the east-lands, the people frighten each other with terrible stories of the tribes in these lands, with stories as one might frighten a child. And it is of his belief that you bear the intention of eating the two of us at your feast."

At this, the Iasaqi-Woni leaned his head back and laughed. His bodyguard laughed with him in the same manner while the other warriors nudged each other and snickered. When the chief had finished laughing, he turned back to Haeli. "In this is shown the ignorance of those tribes across the great and heaving ocean. Tell thou unto thy companion who is with thee that he need bear within himself no fear of our eating him, for we are not Uquibiwi."

Haeli turned back to Titus. "The chief says he was joking, and he will not eat us."

Titus sighed. "Good, I, eh, I thought that... well, I'm glad."

The Iasaqi-Woni looked closely at Titus. "What does he say now unto us?"

Haeli smiled, looking at Titus, too. "Is there anything you would like to tell the chief? I can translate for you."

Titus nodded, swallowing hard. "I suppose, tell him, uh, tell him from me that he, eh, he looks like a nice old fellow, and the beads in his hair don't look half bad on him — even if I would never wear them — and tell him I, eh, I'm glad to have met with him and heard him laugh."

Haeli nodded and turned back to the Iasaqi-Woni. "My companion whom ye behold with me addresses himself unto you now, O supreme chief. He addresses you with the most respectful tone that our weak language bears, saying unto you that you are indeed a mighty chief, as is beheld in your royal attire and mighty entourage. He wishes you respect and blessing from the great Aeparon and wishes that you may always be in a state of pleasure to make you laugh."

The Iasaqi-Woni nodded. "Even so? Then thy companion is even as well-taught in his civility despite his foolish ignorance of my people. Declare thou unto him that I bear him good hospitality in my court."

Haeli turned now to Titus. "He says that you are a very polite person."

Titus blushed. "Ah, well, I never...eh, that's very nice of him."

The shaman now snarled and banged his staff on the dais. There was a sudden flash of lightning, arching down from the sky at catching the shaman's staff. The sound of the thunder echoed through the valley so loudly that Haeli felt it in her chest. For a moment, she stared in shock at the shaman, her heart racing. What had just happened? Had she really seen what she thought she had seen?

"Good heavens!" Titus cursed, shielding his eyes.

Yet the indigies remained where they were as if nothing out of the ordinary had occurred.

"But what of the matter of guilt?" the shaman hissed.

The Iasaqi-Woni frowned again. "Thou speakest true. Now, O civil-tongued maiden, declare unto me if thou canst, for my two sons are dead. We have found their bodies dead in the fort of the east-folk. I did send them forth from my tribe with wares and hides, and they left with jubilation and great joy for the purpose of doing trades and businesses with thy people. And such is the way that our trade and wares are repaid, even with the murder of my two sons!"

The Iasaqi-Woni's eyes now filled with wild anger, and he fixed Haeli with their gaze. "Dost thou know of such things?"

Haeli licked her lips. She tried to ignore the lightning for a moment. There was probably a natural explanation for that. Right now, she had to think about what the Iasaqi-Woni had said. Two indigies killed while attempting to do trade? Could they possibly be the two indigies whom the pirates killed in her father's trading fort? They had introduced themselves to her. What were their names? She could remember their sober looks, their civil demeanor, and the way the larger one had sat at the counter with her and told her the story of the Kwawpi. What was his name?

Slowly, like a spark spreading into a flame, a thought occurred to her. The pirates had killed the chief's two sons, and the entire tribe was getting ready for war because of it. A thrill ran down Haeli's spine. What were the chances that she could convince the Twengoli to attack the pirates? That would be ample retribution for her father's death. She might even get the Gwambi key back.

She would do it. She had to be careful with how she proceeded, but she had little doubt that she could succeed. If only she could remember that huntsman's name.

Then the name came to her.

"Aerlyn-withlygwyr?"

46

MUTINY

"**M**an the guns!" Holgard ordered again.

Quartermaster Harold whistled out the order shrilly. The gunners rolled out the guns below deck while others swarmed onto the swivel guns on deck.

"Load starboard side!"

Again, Quartermaster Harold whistled out the orders.

Ernest stepped forward, about to head to Killjelly and ask where he was needed, when Lewis appeared out of nowhere and seized him by the arm.

Ernest glanced at Lewis's face and recoiled when he saw his messmate's grim features without a trace of his typical joviality.

"Stay down," Lewis hissed. "Don't do a thing."

Lewis pushed him back to the gunwales and forced him down. "Hide. Stay out on the way."

Ernest looked up, and just like that, Lewis was gone, hurrying back below deck himself. Looking forward, Ernest could see the man-o-war wheeling to meet the galleon as she flew forward, the wind filling her sails.

Holgard yelled back to Ynwyr at the stern.

"Steer to starboard. We will pass the man-o-war close on the port side."

Ynwyr looked confused. "But you just said to load the *starboard* cannons."

Holgard flashed a roguish grin. "Do as you're told, son."

Ynwyr shrugged and pulled at the wheel. The galleon sped forward, bearing down on the man-o-war. Ernest could see the gun ports on the man-o-war's port side opening up.

"Hold your course!" Holgard yelled.

Just then, Ernest heard an explosion of obscenities from a gun master behind him. He turned to see a swivel gun crew struggling to load their cannon. The barrel monkey lay stretched out on the deck. It looked as though he had passed out right in the middle of shoving the powder into the gun. The other members of the gunning crew stood about stupidly, a couple blinking like owls.

"Baptize the lot on you!" The gun master screamed. "I could have haved this anointed gun loaded and fired by myself, you baptized heathens!"

Just then, Ernest heard a sharp report. He looked up to see a puff of gunpowder from the man-o-war. A cannonball cut across the ship's port side. The gunwale splintered where it hit, but the ball hurled across the deck harmlessly before plunging into the bay on the other side of the galleon.

"Hold your ground!" Holgard cried. "Hold the course, Ynwyr, my boy!"

The galleon continued full speed forward, guided skillfully by Ynwyr as it headed to face the man-o-war with a port broadside.

Ernest bit his lip. What was the point of this? The cannons were loaded on the wrong side. If they pulled to port, they would be open to Longfinch's cannons, unable to return fire of their own.

The space between the two ships closed rapidly. The swivel

guns on the man-o-war let off a few more shots, but with little to no damage done to the galleon.

"Return fire," Holgard ordered the swivel guns on his own ship. "Return fire, you layabouts!"

One of the swivels let off a hasty shot, but the charge landed in the water nearly thirty yards away from the man-o-war.

"What kind on a baptized shot was that, you anointed mules?" Holgard ground his teeth together, still gripping the gunwales tightly. "Hold your course, son."

Ernest looked at the man-o-war anxiously. Only a few minutes now and they would pass broadside of the man-o-war's murderous fire. Ernest clenched his teeth. What was the captain doing?

"Hard to port!" Holgard suddenly cried. "Pull, son! Hard to port!"

Ynwyr pulled hard on the wheel, and the ship turned abruptly. The sailors scampered about, hauling on brace lines and turning the sails again to catch the wind as they turned. The ship wheeled sharply, crossing the front of the man-o-war so closely Ernest could have thrown a rock between the two ships as they whirled past. Now the galleon bore down directly across the man-o-war's starboard side. Ernest wanted to leap to his feet and cheer. What a maneuver! The man-o-war had no guns loaded on that side. Now they had all the firepower.

"Give them fire, boys!" Holgard screamed. "Anoint them with cannon shot!"

Ernest waited to hear the cannons pounding as they all fired one after another. He peered over the gunwales, expecting to see the man-o-war's hull shatter before the heavy cannon fire.

The first two cannons fired as usual. Then there was a long pause. One more cannon got off a shot before the two ships had passed each other. Only once the opportunity of hitting the man-o-war had passed did the other cannons finally fire, hurling their shots uselessly into the bay.

Holgard stood speechless on the aft deck, still gripping the gunwales, though now all the color had drained from his face. He only stood this way for a moment, though, before he found his voice.

"Turn the ship! Wheel back! What kind on cannon fire was that? I will flay everyone on you with a rusty knife if'n Longfinch doesn't kill you first!"

Ynwyr turned the ship hard, and again the galleon wheeled in the water, wearing the ship to face back towards the man-o-war. The sailors rushed about, trying to turn the sails to catch the wind again. Ernest noticed now that a few of them lay passed out on the deck, and the others staggered like drunk men. They tugged at rigging lines, but they were the wrong ones. Several sailors even hauled on clewlines, yelling at each other as the booms swung chaotically above their heads.

Ernest watched in wide-eyed amazement. They couldn't even perform this basic nautical maneuver. The mainsail swung laterally with the wind and fell limp, while the mizzen's topgallant caught the wind from the front instead of the back, driving the ship backward. The galleon's turn came to a halt, and she floundered in the water like a great skipping stone before it sinks beneath the water's surface.

Holgard now stormed down from the aft deck, his face red with anger and spittle foaming in his beard. He shoved the sailors aside as if they were twigs as he seized the rigging lines.

"You call yourselves sailors? How many years have you been on this ship? Don't you know how to operate a sail?"

Single-handedly, the huge dwarf captain hauled the mainsail into the wind. The ship evened out, moving forward again. Ernest turned from the confusion on deck to see the man-o-war completing a neat turn, wheeling on the galleon like a massive bird of prey.

Captain Holgard

"You!" Holgard screamed, pointing at a swivel cannon crew. "What are you doing standing there? Get that gun loaded! Fire! Kill those baptized pirates. What is this to you?" He grabbed an insensible sailor from the deck and shook him vigorously. "This isn't some baptized vacation; this is war! Convert you, get this ship in order!"

The massive dwarf captain stood in the middle of the ship, looking around at the unconscious and staggering crew. The veins in his forehead stood out, and his beard bristled in fury.

Just then, a loud scream rent the air, and Ernest looked over at the man-o-war in time to see Cweel rise like a flash of lightning from the deck. The dreadful Eagle Griffin streaked through the air like an arrow before he crashed into the galleon's shrouds and rigging lines. His claws, beak, and fangs slashed through the ropes as if they were little more than spiderwebs. Then, with a stroke of his wings, he tore through the mainsail.

"Shoot that devil!" Holgard bellowed, pointing at the hideous griffin as he continued to cavort through the air.

Several of the pirates leveled their muskets and fired, but none could keep their hands steady.

Cweel wheeled to his left, beating his wings in deep strokes to gain altitude. He circled above the galleon for a moment, and then, folding his wings back, he fell from the sky like a demon falling from heaven.

Cweel landed directly on Ynwyr with his claws extended. The young dwarf screamed in pain as he collapsed onto the deck. Holgard rushed towards Cweel with a roar like a mother tiger's, drawing out both of his pistols as he came.

Cweel sneered and launched back into the air, carrying Ynwyr with him. Holgard discharged both of his pistols at the Eagle Griffin, but neither seemed to have any effect. Cweel laughed a wild, almost-diabolical laugh as he circled around the main mast once more. With another scream, Cweel hurled

Ynwyr's limp body into the rigging, where it caught and dangled like a fly tangled in a spider's web.

"Ynwyr, my son!" Holgard cried, but the dangling, limp body made no reply. Holgard threw one of his pistols to the ground and shook his enormous fist at the wheeling Eagle Griffin, absolute rage rising in his eyes. "Come down and face me, convert you! I will have your wings for my supper and skin you with a dull butter knife!"

Cweel cackled with laughter. "Perhaps *you* should come up and meet *me* here, captain!"

At that moment, Ernest heard several loud reports from the man-o-war. He stayed where he was, hunkered down below the gunwales, but watched as grapeshot cut across the deck, mowing down almost every man who was still on his feet. Holgard still stood, defiant and boiling like a summer thunderstorm.

"Baptize you!" he screamed, pointing his finger at the man-o-war. "Baptize every one on you!" He looked around wildly, desperation now mingling with his fury. "Killjelly, get the men in order. Prepare for boarding! Killjelly, where are you?"

Ernest looked around the deck, suddenly realizing that he hadn't seen Killjelly for a while.

Holgard growled in anger, reloading the one pistol he still held in his hand. "Stand your ground, men! Prepare for boarding!"

The man-o-war was now quite close, and even as Ernest watched, the first grapnel clanged against the gunwale. The two ships drew together. Ernest could see the host of leering pirates preparing to leap aboard the galleon as soon as they could. Looking back, he saw only two pirates on their feet next to Holgard, struggling to get their muskets loaded.

Ernest crouched lower and trembled all over, for the first time realizing that this was not simply an event he was a spectator of. *His* ship was about to be boarded. *His* crewmates were about to be slaughtered.

Ernest saw two puffs of gunpowder smoke from the pirates aboard the man-o-war, and the two pirates by Holgard dropped dead to the deck. The ships now touched, and Longfinch's pirates swarmed aboard with whoops and cries. Holgard stood like an immovable mountain, firing his pistol into the rushing throng of pirates. Just then, Ernest heard a shout, and Longfinch's pirates came to a swift halt. Longfinch strode out of the midst of his pirates, a smug smile on his face as he tasted the air with his long elfin tongue.

"You never were one to see the bigger picture, were you, Holgard? You probably can't even see that I planned this mutiny before you did. There isn't much point in continuing to fight now."

Holgard growled like a wild bull. "I never surrender. I'd like to see how many on you it takes to kill me."

Longfinch snickered. "That's what I always liked about you, Holgard. You are indomitable and unrelenting. That's also the reason I never trusted you. Let's make this easy now, shall we? Just give me the key."

Holgard frowned darkly but reached into his trouser pocket and brought out the iron key, holding it out to Longfinch. Longfinch took a step forward, reaching out his hand, but Holgard suddenly tossed the key over the ship's side.

"Go fetch it now," Holgard jeered.

There was a loud cackle from over the gunwales as Cweel flew up and alighted on the deck, the key caught neatly in his mouth.

It was now Longfinch's turn to sneer. "Still, this wasn't that rewarding on a victory, Holgard. Do'ed you think I would fall for that switching-broadside trick again? You were *so* predictable, I hardly even had to try. We do'edn't even get to use any on my contingency plans. That almost took the fun out on it — almost."

Holgard suddenly yelled with wild abandon, drawing his cutlass and charging at Longfinch. Several of Longfinch's pirates swarmed forward, eager to shed blood themselves, but they were no match for this enraged dwarf. Holgard struck out with his sword like an injured honey badger, shattering one of his opponent's rapiers in a blow. He took on the entire group of pirates with unstoppable fury.

Before Longfinch had time to call a halt, six of his men lay dead and dismembered on the deck. Holgard stood over their dead bodies, his eyes wild with war-lust, spots of blood now peppering his clothes.

"Hold!" Longfinch cried. "The dwarf is mine. I alone will fight him."

"Come for me, then," Holgard said, his eyes thrown wide in an unbridled rage. "I will avenge my son on you and on a hundred on your men."

Longfinch smiled patronizingly, fingering one of his long dirks at his side. "Or perhaps I should string you up from the yardarm here? You'd look rather nice, dangling helplessly next to your idiot on a son."

Holgard bellowed furiously and threw himself at Longfinch. If anything, the dwarf attacked Longfinch with an even greater fury than he had attacked before, yet the elf captain held his ground skillfully, holding his long dirk in his left hand and his *kukri* in his right. Holgard rained down blow after blow with his massive cutlass, but Longfinch parried every one with such skill as Ernest had never seen before.

Still, with the sheer force of his attack, Holgard drove Longfinch back. The dwarf ground his teeth together, his eyes wide with anger, spittle running down into his beard as he pressed forward with brute strength. Longfinch stayed light and nimble, with an ever-present smile on his face, as if he were mocking the great dwarf captain.

Every man aboard the deck watched the fight in anxious anticipation. Ernest watched his captain, hardly daring to breathe. Holgard fought with such unrelenting power, but how long could he keep it up? Surely he would tire soon.

Minute by minute, the fight wore on, yet Holgard still showed no sign of slowing. Longfinch backed his way up the stairs, which led to the fore-deck. Yet even with the advantage of high ground, Holgard continued to push him back.

Longfinch wheeled nimbly as he reached the deck, and for several minutes they fought across the foredeck, making a circle around the deck several times as Holgard drove Longfinch steadily backward.

Ernest's heart raced, beating in his throat as he watched the fight wear on. Holgard had the stronger presence in the fight, yet Longfinch seemed to have a better mastery over the situation. Holgard exuded strength in all he did, while Longfinch's precise and nimble motions spoke of an almost unequaled skill.

Longfinch's skill seemed to hold Holgard's strength at bay, yet if Longfinch made a single mistake, Holgard would crush him in a moment. On the other side, while Holgard's raw power kept Longfinch's skill perpetually on the defense, Ernest was certain that once his captain tired in his attack, Longfinch would begin his offensive part in the fight, and Holgard would never stand against the elf captain's superior skill.

Still the fight wore on, and still Holgard showed no signs of tiring. The dwarf continued his mad forward onslaught, his whole shirt saturated in sweat. Still, he didn't slow for a moment. Beads of sweat began trickling down Longfinch's forehead, and his smile was not nearly so confident as it had been when the fight first began.

With a sudden spring, Longfinch parried Holgard's cutlass to the side and vaulted back down to the mid-deck. Turning to face his opponent, Longfinch drew out one of his throwing knives, hurling it at Holgard. The dwarf captain batted the knife aside with his cutlass easily before bulling down the steps towards Longfinch like an unstoppable force of nature.

Longfinch stood to the side of the mainmast with a strange smile on his face. As Holgard came close, raising his sword to strike, Longfinch moved a stray piece of rigging with his foot. Holgard's feet caught on the rope, and he tripped. Quickly recovering himself, Holgard still delivered his blow at Longfinch. The small trip, however, had thrown him off just enough that his blow missed, embedding his cutlass in the mast instead of Longfinch. Holgard struck with such force that the cutlass sank several inches into the wood.

Before Holgard had time to recover, Longfinch sprang forward, slicing him across the wrist with his dirk to make the dwarf release his sword.

Holgard stumbled back, growling in pain; then he came forward again with his bare hands now, dealing Longfinch a harsh blow in the head with his left hand. The blow took Longfinch unprepared, and he crumpled to the ground at the sheer impact of Holgard's first.

The elf jumped back to his feet in time to dodge Holgard's next blow, and counter it with a stroke of his *kukri*, catching Holgard in the shoulder. Holgard bellowed, wheeling once more on Longfinch, but Ernest could see that even now, the fight was over. Holgard stood weaponless, with one arm hanging limply from his body, while Longfinch was still fully armed. The dwarf captain would fall before Longfinch's unmatched skill.

Longfinch struck Holgard with both his weapons at once. Holgard blocked one of Longfinch's blows with his forearm, but Longfinch struck him in the thigh with his other. Holgard collapsed to his knees as if all of his exhaustion were overcoming him at once. His face drained of color, and he panted heavily, his shirt soaked in sweat and blood.

Ernest looked once more at his captain and felt a pain go through his heart. He had never thought that he was fond of Holgard, but now, as he saw the dwarf captain there, struggling for breath, defeated on his own deck, he couldn't help but pity the poor dwarf, especially after he had put up such a fight.

Longfinch stared at Holgard levelly, breathing heavily himself as he held his dirk to the dwarf's throat. Holgard only looked on, his eyes glazed over and his face ashen, almost as if he had lost all will to live.

Longfinch spat out blood onto the deck and lowered his dirk. "Holgard, you represent all that I loathe in a pirate," Longfinch finally said, "and all that I have struggled to overcome in myself; you are simple, brutish, predictable, money-seeking... You will never understand the pleasure it gives me to watch you suffer."

Longfinch spat again and held his cheek for a moment. Ernest wondered if perhaps Holgard had knocked out some of the elf's teeth.

Longfinch spoke again as he sheathed his dirk. "Still, I have to admire someone what can put up that much on a baptized fight. I've never met your like before, Holgard. So I can't find it in me to kill you like the pig I think you are. I will make it quick instead."

With that, Longfinch drew out his pistol. He put it to Holgard's head and fired. Ernest flinched from where he hid. Holgard slumped to the deck. That once indomitable and hulking dwarf was now only a mortal wad of flesh on the deck.

Longfinch reloaded his pistol methodically, giving orders to his crew as he did so. "Bring me the co-conspirators. Kill everyone else aboard."

47

RECREATION

Clerans and Lexi hurried down the streets of Entwerp Proper, moving ever closer to the sounds of gunfire. Clerans knew the streets well, and even in the whale oil street lamps' strange light, he wound his way easily through the broad avenues. For several blocks, they passed no one. The citizens must sensibly be staying inside their locked doors. Yet, as they neared the National Bank, several other militia members joined them. They, too, hurried toward the sounds of fighting. Each militia member bore a red ribbon or handkerchief on their arm, marking them out clearly, even in the eerie lighting.

Finally, Lexi paused, and the other militia members paused with her. By now, there were around a score of them, all armed with rifles, pistols, skinning knives, and tomahawks. Clerans knew they were only a couple of blocks from the bank now, very close to the park, which lay on the east side of the banking complex. The gunfire was quite close now, and Clerans heard shouting and screaming from close by. They were moments away from getting into the action. He should be excited, but his stomach just felt sick. Thankfully, he wasn't feeling tired anymore. The anticipation cured him of that, at least.

"Any other sergeants here?" Lexi asked.

The other militia members shook their heads.

"Looks like ye are senior officer," someone said.

Lexi nodded. "Merri well. Make sure you are all loaded, then. I expect we'll will be in the thick o' it soon."

Just then, there was the sound of rushing feet. A group of six or seven strikers turned the corner, barreling toward them.

With no command from Lexi, the militia turned and fired, cutting down the strikers where they stood. Clerans was late in slinging his rifle from his shoulder, so he never had time to fire. At this close range, the militia was deadly accurate, and not a single striker rose from the street.

Yet hardly had the echoing of their fusillade died away, then more rushing feet pounded in the street; more strikers coming this way.

"Reload!" Lexi barked.

But there was no time for that. Over a dozen more strikers turned the corner and halted abruptly, staring with alarm at their dead comrades, and then at the disorderly line of militia. Those militia members who had not yet fired let off a few lethal shots into the crowd of strikers. Clerans himself sighted down the barrel of his gun, but he couldn't bring himself to pull the trigger. The image of that dying striker stuck in his mind, and his words rang in his memory.

"My mother. Tell my mother."

As the militia frantically tried to reload their guns, the strikers, too, began reloading their weapons. Clerans bit his lip and lowered his rifle.

"Idiots. Get out o' here!"

The strikers looked up in alarm, and the militia all turned on Clerans.

"What?" Lexi said.

Clerans waved at the strikers. "Do you want to be shot?

Then get out o' here, get as far away from the bank as ye cen. The regulars will no hurt ye outside o' the city."

The strikers looked furtively at each other and then back at Clerans.

"Vene on then," Clerans said, motioning with his head down a side street. "Away from the bank now."

Several of the strikers dropped their weapons, and they all hurried off as Clerans directed.

"What was that about?" Lexi demanded.

Clerans raised an eyebrow as he looked at her. "Is it no better that way?"

Lexi sighed. "Ay, I s'pose it is." She motioned to the other militia members. "Vene along then!"

She led the way down the street towards the bank. After they had stepped over the bodies of the strikers they had shot, Clerans and the others marched easily down the street, turned the corner, and in a moment, they entered the park on the bank's eastern side. But this was not the welcoming, brightly lit place Clerans knew so well. Not a single street lamp flickered here. The strikers must have shot them out or otherwise extinguished them. The line of street lamps by the National Bank still shown, however, casting eerie shadows amongst the park's oak trees and manicured gardens.

The militia groped their way along, bathed in deep shadow. Several times, as Clerans crept along, he stumbled against something fleshy that lay stretched out in the street — it was too dark for him to see if the corpses were strikers, militia, Regulars, or innocent bystanders. Once, he stumbled into a park bench. The whole thing rattled loudly as it collapsed.

"Shush!" Lexi barked.

"Someone else must ha' already broken it," Clerans whispered weakly.

Now and then, there was a flash of a gunshot, the night's darkness with yells of anger and screams of pain. From the park, it was hard to tell where the fighting came from (the darkness and the tree trunks obscured so much). Dark shadows moved past them, some running, some marching.

"Shall we fire?" a militia man asked.

Lexi snorted. "An' who are they?"

The man was silent in response.

"Clerans wos right," Lexi said. "We are here to guard the bank, no jist shoot strikers. So let us get to the bank."

So saying, she plunged on in the darkness.

Finally, they found the path which led out of the park, and deposited them in the square before the National Bank. Yet no sooner had they emerged from the shadows of the park's trees than a line of gleaming bayonets greeted them.

"Militia!" Lexi called out, holding up her red ribboned arm.

The line of Regulars lowered their weapons.

"Lexi?" It was Sheriff Laei who stepped out from behind the gray-coated Regulars.

Lexi gave a salute. "Here to serve, sheriff."

Sheriff Laei frowned. "You are the first militia I ha' seen all night. What ha' taken so long?"

"It is a mite difficult gettin' here an' no bein' shot," Clerans replied.

The sheriff turned when he heard Clerans' voice and looked him over. "Ye are here too? Ye outta-should be restin', Clerans."

Clerans only sighed. "Duty calls, sir. Is that no what ye taught me?"

Just then, a militiaman in the rear of the group cried. "Strikers!"

They all turned in time to see a group of rough-looking strikers emerging from the shadows of the park trees behind them.

The Regulars immediately opened fire, and the militia joined in as quickly as they could. Clerans (for his part) checked to make sure he could not see any red ribbons on them before he, too, discharged his rifle in their general direction.

Several strikers fell to the ground, some dead, while others writhed in agony. The rest disappeared as swiftly as they had come.

Hurriedly, the militia and Regulars reloaded their guns.

"They are slowin' down," the sheriff noted. "They do no tain the organization fer a unified assault."

Clerans smiled bitterly. "Probably 'cause most o' their leaders are dead."

"What is that?" the sheriff asked.

Clerans sighed. "At Miss Nansi's cottage. The spokesman killed nearly all the other leaders o' the strikers. It's jist him now givin' the orders, I ween. Though he is demented enough to give us trouble on his own."

The sheriff bit his lip. "Well, he ha' lost this round. I do no doubt, but we are through the worst o' it already. Though, who knows what they'll be plannin' next."

"The bank is safe, then?" Lexi asked.

The sheriff surveyed the square before him, and Clerans did likewise. Over a dozen bodies lay in the street, their mortal wounds obscured in the dim lighting. Combined with the other strikers shot down in the rest of the city, there was a grievous blood-letting for the strikers. Yes, this attack on the bank had cost them dearly, with not much to show for it.

How different this was from how Clerans thought it would play out. He had assumed this clash with the strikers and the law was inevitable, but he had always imagined it as some dramatic set-piece battle, the Regulars on one side of the square and the strikers on the other. He had imagined a violent confrontation full of honor and daring. How very different from this chaotic rushing around streets and feeling your way in the dark. Once again, he wondered if this was truly something he wanted to continue to familiarize himself with.

"Well," the sheriff finally said, taking a deep breath. "I expect they ha' jist about run out o' will to keep fightin'. We may see a few more o' them before the night is over, but I expect we are done fer now. Still, we will stand guard fer the rest o' the night, jist in case."

Lexi saluted. "Where do ye need us, sir?"

The sheriff motioned back towards the park. "You could monitor this path fer me."

The militia saluted and formed up in a rough line a little way from the trees at the park's outer edge. Yet as Clerans stepped into his place at the end, a striker they had shot reached out his hand toward Clerans' boot.

"Please," he choked. "Help. Please."

Immediately, Clerans knelt beside him and helped him to sit up. The man coughed heavily, choking and gurgling as he did so.

"There," Clerans said in a soothing voice. "Ye will be jist fine. I will see to ye."

"Please," the man choked again.

"Clerans," Lexi hissed. "What are ye doin'?"

Clerans ignored her as he looked the man over. It was impossible to see much in the trees' shadow here, but he could feel some kind of injury on the man's leg. There was the sticky wetness of blood, and it seemed bent at an unnatural angle.

Clerans let out his breath slowly. "Vene along then."

With an effort, he hoisted the injured man over his shoulder. The man cried out in pain as Clerans stood to his feet.

"Clerans," Lexi hissed.

"What are ye doin'?" the sheriff broke in suddenly.

Clerans looked the sheriff in the eye steadily. "I am bringin' this man to Doctor Heyl."

The sheriff looked confused. "But he is a striker."

Clerans' cheeks flushed at this statement. He could still feel the one-armed man's body against him as he took the bullet, which should have killed him. He could still see the middle-aged nymph's resignation right before they burned the house down around him. He could still hear the young man's sobbing before he died in Clerans' arms. Those had all been strikers, too. Was he the only one who saw their dignity?

"What happened to lovin' yer enemies?" Clerans finally said. "An' fer that matter, I am no certain they *are* our enemies."

The sheriff shook his head. "They are strikers, Clerans."

"Does that mean they are no longer people?"

The sheriff lowered his head and sighed. "Ay, ye are right. They are people, too. Merri well, get him to the doctor, then."

Clerans nodded and pointed himself toward the suburbs. He plodded forward slowly, his exhaustion suddenly coming over him again. The weight of this injured man on his shoulder wasn't helping.

"I did no teach you that," the sheriff finally said in a soft voice.

Clerans did not even bother to look behind him at the sheriff. "No. I ha' to learn that the hard way."

48

MOA-FIRE

Every warrior standing before the Iasaqi-Woni froze, fixing their gaze intently on Haeli. The shaman frowned and let out a low growl. The Iasaqi-Woni looked at Haeli closely and critically. "Even so. Just as thou hast spoken, so is called the name of my oldest son: Aerlyn-withlygwyr. Even he and his younger brother Felhedh-llasaryni traveled with wares unto thy people. Even the two of them did we find dead, killed, and murdered."

Haeli trembled all over with excitement. She had been right. Those two indigies whom she had traded with were the Iasaqi-Woni's own sons. This explained the Twengoli's actions in kidnapping all of those beacon-tenders. She had to be careful now. She would use the Twengoli's outrage for her own purposes. And why shouldn't she? Both she and the Iasaqi-Woni had good reason to join forces in extracting retribution on the pirates, and that hooked leprechaun in particular.

The Iasaqi-Woni still looked at Haeli closely. "What doest thou know? For I see in thy eyes even now the recognition of remembrances."

Haeli opened her mouth to speak, intending to tell the

Iasaqi-Woni what she had seen and how his sons had died, but the memory hit her like a foaming sea wave during a storm. Haeli closed her mouth and swallowed. Her heart raced, and the horse of her emotions threatened to take off at a gallop. Those were dangerous memories to invoke. She took a deep breath and swallowed again. Control yourself, Haeli. Calm down. She imagined herself reigning in her horse and bringing it to a stop. Haeli licked her lips and then swallowed again.

"You speak in truth, and even in wisdom does your tongue move, for I do bear within me, even within my own heart, the memory of your two sons. I, even I, was in that trading fort when your two sons, O supreme chief, came for the purpose of doing trades and businesses with us. For my father was the proprietor of that fort, being granted it by the Mighty Tribe of our people, and I am his daughter and was there to do trades and businesses with your sons."

At this, the shaman slammed down the butt of his staff forcefully on the dais. Once more, lightning crackled from the end of his staff. "Even so! Thus has the small one spoken! Thus does she proclaim against herself her own guilt!"

As if on cue, the drummers started up again, thundering away on their huge drums, while those on the pitched drums hammered out what was probably a war chant. Haeli could see the warriors around her bristle as the drums started, the blood flowing to their faces as they fingered their knives and the cords of their slings. Beads of sweat trickled down Haeli's face. She wiped them away with her hand hurriedly. The humidity was not helping her state of mind.

The Iasaqi-Woni waved his hand, and the drumming stopped. Haeli's heart pounded in the reigning silence; she could feel it pulsing in her throat. The Iasaqi-Woni eyed Haeli closely. "We will not judge so rashly, O great shaman. But on the contrary, we will all sit and listen until the maiden has spoken all of her remembrances. Though let her tread with care how she raises our royal fury of war."

Titus leaned over to Haeli, rather pale himself. "Eh, he didn't change his mind, did he? He's not going to eat us after all?"

Haeli swallowed. "Listen well, O great and supreme chief, and I will speak unto you. Understand, for I will teach. I declare with a bold proclamation: not by my hand, or the hand of my people, or by the hand of any agent of the Mighty Tribe were your sons killed. But they were set upon, I and my family with them, by–" Haeli searched for the right term. There wasn't a Tylweni word for 'pirate,' nor could she think of any concept by which to describe piracy in that language.

"Among my people," Haeli started over, "there are those who are wicked and lawless men, who answer with words to no man and will not abide by the laws of any people, and they heed not the speaking of our chiefs and despise the wisdom of our shamans. They belong to no tribe and abide by the customs of no people. These men do we call in our tongue *pirate*, for they kill maliciously those with whom they have no blood feud, and they sail about on the great and heaving ocean in great ships, and they work deeds of desperate wickedness on all coasts. Such are *pirate*.

"Even these men of whom I speak, these *pirate*, they did come upon the fort of my father while we did business with your sons. For my father had traded with Aerlyn-withlygwyr, and given unto him a new *karambit* knife for his uses. And even in the midst of our trades did these *pirate* descend upon us, even as a pack of wild dogs descends upon the suckling pig."

Haeli could again feel the memory of that night rushing over her in an intense wave of emotion. Her voice trembled as she went on. "Your sons, O great and supreme chief, showed forth the nobility of their blood in bravery and valor. For they fought with greatest courage against the savage *pirate* men and slew many of them. But those *pirate* fired upon your sons and slew them in blood and cut them down where they stood. Even my father–" Haeli choked here, but swallowed, forcing herself to continue. "Even my father died himself, in bravery and honor, defending me from the wickedness of those *pirate*."

The Iasaqi-Woni leaned forward, holding his head in his hands for a moment before looking back at Haeli. "Even so, hast thou seen? Even so, have the brave fallen in death?"

At this, a drummer beat his huge drum — one deep and resounding thunder that echoed across the whole valley. The other drummers raised a wail, an almost unearthly keening that curled the hair on Haeli's head. The Iasaqi-Woni raised his head again, and all was silent. "Yet speak unto me with a thoroughness of detail concerning these *pirate*, for you say they sail about the great and heaving sea in great ships? And of what is their description?"

Titus fidgeted nervously. "What is going on?"

"It is a lot to explain," Haeli said in a low voice. "I can explain it later. For now, you can know that we are in no great harm."

Then Haeli turned back to the Iasaqi-Woni. "They are sea sailers, O great and supreme chief, and go about in the garb as of a sea sailer. And they have on their ships great guns with which they do shoot and fire upon our ships to kill all those aboard..."

The Iasaqi-Woni raised his hand, and Haeli stopped. He looked at her closely. "But those *pirate* who were those men who killed my sons, even my two dear sons. How might they be recognized?"

Haeli could again feel every warrior's eyes looking at her. She considered this for a moment. "They were of many races, O great and supreme chief, of all the races of men, for among them were leprechauns, and nymphs, and humans, and dwarfs, and gnomes. Yet of their chief, of the leader of them whom it was who slew your sons and fired his gun upon my father — of this man, he was a leprechaun, yet in the place of and instead of his left-hand does he possess two hooks."

At this statement, the entire group exploded in excitement, all the warriors talking to each other in tones of increasing fervor.

The Iasaqi-Woni raised his hand, and the warriors settled down except for one who waved at the Iasaqi-Woni.

"It is even so, O great and supreme chief, for such is the man whom we have seen in the bay. For even in that bay, now sit two ships, and the men of those ships work in the woods and do bring back trees for themselves to repair their boats. Even in their labors have we seen this man of the two hooks."

"It is true!" another warrior cried. "Yet even now, the ships do fight and contend with each other, and they sail north towards the city of the east-folk, even the city of Entwerp!"

Haeli caught her breath. Was this true? Were the pirates coming back to Entwerp? She would certainly need the help of these indigie warriors.

The Iasaqi-Woni raised his *kukri* over his head. "Are not the warriors ready for battle?"

The warriors responded with a deafening cheer, and the drummers pounded on their drums. But this was all interrupted once again as the shaman banged on the dais with his staff. Lightning arched down from the sky, silencing the warriors. How was he doing this?

"Yet what of this man?" the shaman said in his strained and croaking voice. "What of the man-of-no-words from the ignorant and foolish tribes across the great and heaving sea?"

The Iasaqi-Woni nodded. "Even so. What of thy companion who is with thee, O tactful maiden? Why has he come here in ignorance from his land across the great and heaving sea?"

Haeli turned to Titus now. "The Iasaqi-Woni is now speaking to you. He wants to know why you are here?"

"Oh!" Titus said, "Eh, that's simple. I, eh, I came for my daughter, to bring her home."

Haeli turned to the Iasaqi-Woni. Every warrior present was bent on war with the pirates. She had succeeded. The Twengoli would make valuable allies if the pirates were indeed sailing on Entwerp. Perhaps Titus' story would be a good way of impressing on them the unity of their cause against the pirates. She had done so well thus far. Why not press a little farther? After all, the closer the Twengoli bound themselves to her and Titus, the less likely the chances were of them turning against her in the future.

"This man," Haeli said, "has come all this way on a paternal mission. For these that are *pirate*, even the same men who killed your sons, O supreme chief, these *pirate* did steal this man's daughter from him. Even for the purpose of retrieving his daughter unto himself, has this man crossed the great and heaving ocean and come unto your lands."

A hush fell over all the warriors, and the Iasaqi-Woni nodded gravely. "There is a saying which was spoken by our ancestors and is repeated and passed down to us. Even this saying do I speak unto thee, 'Even is the love of the mother moa for her hatchling.' For in this, does thy companion who is with thee show that he bears in his heart the passion of a father. For he has traveled at such a distance for the intent of recapturing his daughter. In this, we have misjudged him, for surely he is not so foolish as he first appeared."

Haeli turned to Titus and translated, "The Iasaqi-Woni says that you are braver than a mother moa, and he is impressed that you would go to such lengths to find your daughter."

Titus looked confused. "What is a moa?"

"It is a large, flightless bird," Haeli replied. "More relevantly, though, I think the chief would help us recover Ella if we asked."

Titus's eyes went wide. "Do you think? Eh, do we, eh... that would be a lot of help. We'd be sure to find Ella then, wouldn't we?"

Haeli nodded. "Shall I ask?"

Titus nodded. "It's worth, eh, it's worth asking, I suppose."

Haeli turned back to the chief. "My companion who is with me thanks you, O great and supreme chief, for your compliments to him. He understands that both you and him do bear a feud against these *pirate*. He therefore humbly implores of you that you would give unto him aid as he recovers his daughter unto himself."

All the warriors turned on the chief, looking at him with expectation in their eyes. The shaman smiled slyly.

The Iasaqi-Woni nodded slowly. "Even as he says, it is true. For these *pirate* bear on them the guilt of killing my two sons, even my dear sons. In addition, they bear the guilt of stealing this man's daughter. We are the same in this regard — thy companion and I — for we are both fathers, and our children were taken from us by these men who are *pirate*. Even so, does this man — thy companion who is with thee — seek to reclaim his child. Yet, would the Twengoli follow the mother moa into battle? Even the moa that has lost its child? Even so, was I tested with moa-fire, and even so must this man be tested that we may see if he seeks his daughter with the fervor which is more fervent than the fervor of the mother moa. Only then will we follow him in battle, to join in battle as an ally with him."

The shaman struck the dais with his staff again, bringing down lightning once more, and then he raised his arms above his head as if he were pronouncing a curse. "Let moa-fire begin!"

The drummers played again now, and Haeli could feel her skin crawling at the noise. Sweat trickled down her neck. The heat was unbearably obsessive; surely the storm was near.

With wild shouts and cries, the warriors circled around Titus and herded him away from the dais. Even the bodyguard surged forward, forming a ring around Titus. Tiya-Aenji grabbed Haeli by the shoulder, drawing her out of the throng and pulling her up onto the edge of the dais. Out of nowhere, the bodyguards ignited torches, holding them in their circle around Titus.

Titus looked around frantically, his voice rising in pitch in his uncertainty. "What's going on? What did he say?"

Haeli yelled across at Titus, "I do not know. He said they would put you through moa-fire."

"What the devil is that?!" Titus yelled back.

"I do not know," Haeli replied, her heart pounding in her chest. "The word 'fire' in their language can also mean 'test.' or 'ordeal.'"

Titus shook his head, looking about him wildly. "That doesn't sound good."

"Just stay calm." Haeli urged. "I think they are only trying to make sure that you will do whatever it takes to get Ella back."

"That much is true." Titus glanced around for any way out of the circle of torches, though he was clearly less frantic now. Sweat covered his face and arms, gleaming in the torch light.

"The chief said if you passed this trial, they will help you get Ella back."

"If only I knew what it was," Titus replied.

"Just remember, you are doing this for Ella!" Haeli said.

Titus stood firm now, his vast frame looking even more stalwart amidst the chaos of the swaying circle of torches. "I'll do anything to get my Ella back."

No sooner had Titus spoken these words than an injured scream echoed across the valley; it sounded something between a wounded panther's scream and a hunting eagle's war cry. Haeli could feel the blood draining from her face. She knew what animal made that scream: it was a moa's cry. Would this moa trial involve a *real* moa?

Just then, Nōlistrw-kagwyr came bounding across the bridge with something tucked under his arm, running as fast as his stubby legs could carry him. Haeli looked closely and saw, to her horror, that the little indigie carried a young moa, only a few weeks old. It was a pitiful sight, the bird already a foot tall with no wings on its downy body, kicking and struggling to get free from Nōlistrw-kagwyr. Haeli guessed that the spurs on the young moa's feet had probably not developed yet, and therefore the little indigie could carry the young moa without fear of harm.

Another scream rent the air, and across the bridge, a huge mother moa charged like a raging war horse. The warriors turned and intercepted her before she could reach Nōlistrw-kagwyr. Forming a circle around her, they waved their torches at her and shouted wildly. She hissed and screamed but halted her mad career, rising to her full height of twelve feet and stamping her feet in indignation. The whole time, the drums beat loudly and frantically.

Haeli looked at Titus and then at the female moa, and her mouth went dry. The moa towered over the large man and completely dwarfed all the nymphs who danced about her with their blazing torches. The moa bore three huge hooked claws on each foot and a wicked spur on the back of her heel. Her beak was relatively small for her enormous body, but it was hooked like a hawk's. Haeli knew very well that these giant, wingless birds were nothing more than fruit-eaters, yet they were very dangerous when irritated, and this mother moa looked far beyond irritated.

Nōlistrw-kagwyr now ducked into the circle surrounding Titus, glowing with exhilaration. He held up the poor, struggling young moa for all to see. It squawked and squirmed in his grasp. The mother moa heard the squawking and surged forward towards her fledgling. With shouts and war whoops, the indigie warriors drove her back again, waving their torches at her when she threatened to kick them with her wicked hooked feet.

The Iasaqi-Woni now stood, holding his *kukri* over his head. With an elegant toss, he threw the large knife to the ground before Nōlistrw-kagwyr. The little nymph snatched the *kukri* up and stood poised, the struggling moa in one hand and the *kukri* with his other hand.

Then, Nōlistrw-kagwyr flung the young moa to the ground and struck off its head with a single blow of the *kukri*. The warriors cheered, and the drummers beat faster. Nōlistrw-kagwyr held the blade in the young moa's blood for a moment and then bounded over to Titus with the *kukri*. Titus recoiled, his face filled with horror as he looked at the little indigie boy, and he blanched in terror as he looked past Nōlistrw-kagwyr at the towering, raging mother moa.

Nōlistrw-kagwyr laughed roguishly and pressed the chief's *kukri* into Titus' hand. Then, with another smile, the little indigie darted off as fast as he could, ducking outside the circle of torches. No sooner was Nōlistrw-kagwyr outside the circle than one of the bodyguards uttered a harsh cry. At this, the warriors holding the mother moa back parted and joined their comrades in a giant circle all around the platform before the Iasaqi-Woni's dais, leaving Titus in the middle of the circle with the mother moa. As if on cue, the drums suddenly stopped, and every warrior stood still, holding out their torches and looking on intently. Haeli hardly dared to breathe.

The mother moa, now unimpeded, charged forward with a savage hiss, coming to a halt before the body of her dead fledgling. The moa nudged at the body a few times as if in disbelief. Then, with the tip of her beak, she smelled the blood on the platform around her fledgling. Titus had stood stock still, all the color drained from his face, holding the Iasaqi-Woni's *kukri* awkwardly in his hand. The moa now moved forward with her nose until she had almost touched the bloody *kukri*, then her eyes fell upon Titus.

"Titus!" Haeli cried.

The mother moa screamed another ear-piercing cry and lunged at Titus with her head. He dodged at the last moment, but then the moa bulled into him with the rest of her body, throwing him across the platform with the blow. The *kukri* flew from Titus' hands as he rolled across the platform. The moa chased after him, hissing hideously, her claws tearing into the wooden platform. Titus stopped tumbling right against the circle of torches, lying on his back. He raised his head, but that was as far as he got. He simply lay on the ground, frozen in terror. The moa descended on him, prancing about madly.

Haeli could hardly bring herself to look on. She knew that, in an instant, the moa would leap on top of Titus and tear him to pieces with her massive, clawed feet. But at that moment, the Iasaqi-Woni shouted a single word, and the warriors leaped forward, driving the mother moa away from Titus with their torches.

The Iasaqi-Woni shook his head. "Verily, this one will never survive such a simple trial. Perhaps he is little more than the fool we believed him to be, after all."

Haeli ground her teeth together and looked back at Titus, who struggled shakily to his feet. The warriors whooped again and backed away, leaving Titus in the ring with the moa again.

"It is for Ella!" Haeli cried. "You have to survive for Ella's sake!"

"I can't kill this monster!" Titus screamed back.

The moa hissed at him and charged again.

"You have to!" Haeli insisted. "Fight it! You have to kill her if you want to find Ella!"

Titus jumped to the side, narrowly avoiding the moa's beak as she struck at him. He must have seen the *kukri* on the ground, for he dove at it. The moa screamed and wheeled at him, striking out at him with one on her feet. Haeli winced. How had that missed him?

Titus was back on his feet now and had the *kukri* in his hands. The warriors gave a shout when they saw this, and many started chanting. The moa charged again, striking at Titus with its hooked beak. This time, Titus did not back down. He pushed forward, swinging with broad, heavy strokes with his newly attained *kukri,* as if trying to fell a tree. One blow clipped the moa's neck, and she recoiled in pain, letting out a savage hiss.

"That's for Ella, then!" Titus shrieked.

Titus leaped forward again and swung the *kukri* at the massive bird. The blow caught the moa in the shoulder, and again she screamed in pain, stumbling backward.

The warriors yelled with excitement, waving their torches wildly. Haeli looked at Titus with an anxious gaze. The poor man hadn't the foggiest idea how to fight. She could tell that he was letting his adrenaline get to him. He swung that *kukri* about for all he was worth, as if *that* would somehow bring him victory. He probably thought he was winning the fight at that moment, but Haeli knew he was far more vulnerable than he realized.

The moa took one more step backward, and then she sprung, her head and long neck darting forward like a cobra. Her hooked beak caught Titus in the side and threw him to the ground. Titus yelled in pain, trying to struggle to his feet. The moa charged him again, prancing about wildly and threatening to kick him. Haeli saw the giant bird raise one foot and plunge it toward Titus's belly. She gasped, fearing that this was the end for Ella's stepfather. But what was this? Titus was still alive. He must have rolled away just before the moa's clawed foot raked into him.

Titus was on his feet again. His side was bleeding profusely, and he had a long, savage-looking cut across his thigh, but he was still standing. He clenched his jaw in determination, a look of wild desperation in his eyes that seemed something between undaunted bravery and barbarian savagery.

The enormous bird wheeled about, striking at Titus once again with her beak. This time, however, Titus was ready for her.

"*Ella!*" Titus bellowed. He swung the *kukri* up in a back-handed slash, catching the moa directly in the neck. The beast gave a startled yelp as it collapsed to the ground, convulsing violently in its death throes.

The warriors shouted, and the drummers beat their drums again, now at a slow and throbbing rhythm. Titus collapsed to his knees, flinging the *kukri* from him and holding his head in his hands. Haeli flew from the dais to Titus' side. She completely forgot about the fact that she had only just met the man; she was happy to see him still alive.

"You did it!" she cried. "You did it. Ella would be proud of you!"

Titus didn't even look up at her; he just moaned.

The Iasaqi-Woni stood, grinning from ear to ear. "Even so, is the trial determined. And thus have we witnessed that this man is not a fighter, yet he will fight the moa. Even so, he is worthy to reclaim his daughter and be our ally."

The warriors cheered.

"Tomorrow," the Iasaqi-Woni resumed, his deep voice booming out for all to hear, "we will hunt for the *pirate* men who killed my sons!"

49

EXORCIST

"We confront it!" Pastor Daerl repeated, looking back into the dining room. Ella sat stock-still. Was he suggesting what she thought he was? She remembered how he had stood there when the ghost had first awakened her; his finger pointed authoritatively at the trapdoor. Yes, he had confronted this thing already; he probably was going to do so again.

Miss Nansi stood to her feet, shaking her head in exasperation. "I will no be a part o' this. This is nothin' but spooks an' wooses. Ye'll will be makin' a fool o' yerself, Daerl, that is all."

Pastor Daerl shook his head. "We will trive out fer certain then." And with that, he descended the flight of stairs down into the basement beneath the trapdoor.

Ella could feel her throat going dry. She had nothing but bad memories of that basement. How could Pastor Daerl walk into it now? She looked over the table at Mr. Hydmenton.

He met her gaze and then shrugged. "Well, I will no miss it."

Following Mr. Hydmenton into the kitchen, Ella's heart sank to her toes as she viewed that hideous trapdoor, now open and bare. She could feel the blood pounding in her ears. That was where Olyfia died, down in that dusty basement.

Still, she couldn't miss this. Pastor Daerl was going to do something very significant down there. She had to witness it. With any luck, they might open the door and find the Gwambi Treasure. Wouldn't that be something?

Ella swallowed, and, with an act of willpower, she descended the stairs to the basement. As she reached the bottom, she looked around, the smell of must and mold settling on her nostrils. It was the same small basement she remembered with its bookshelves and that strange iron-supported door — without a handle — on the far side.

The very thought of that door sent chills down her spine. When she first found it, she was so elated; she thought she had found the Gwambi Treasure! Yet now — after all that had happened with Olyfia, the dreams, and the night visitor — that door seemed more like a festering monster than a solution to this great mystery.

Pastor Daerl stood directly before the door, looking it over carefully.

"There are no hinges," he commented.

"They are probably on the other side," said Mr. Hydmenton.

Pastor Daerl nodded. "Ay, and what o' a key? That is a lock, I see."

All of Ella's inhibitions about telling more people about the Gwambi Treasure seemed to roll off of her at once. Perhaps it was the terror of that door, or perhaps she finally realized how preposterous it was not to trust Pastor Daerl.

"Si'h Saemwel had the key, but he hid it, and then Miste'h Blysffi found it, and he took it with him to his fo't."

Pastor Daerl nodded slowly, feeling over the door's iron bands carefully. "But what is behind this door?"

Mr. Hydmenton shrugged. "Who knows?"

"Si'h Saemwel knew," Ella replied, "And so did my fathe'h, Silas Pickering."

"Well then," Pastor Daerl surmised as he looked around the room. "If we'll are to get to the bottom o' this first, then we'll ha' to open this door."

"But how?" Ella asked.

Pastor Daerl walked to the other side of the room from the door and winked at Ella. "Leave that to a satyr."

With that, he hurled himself across the room, flinging himself into the air and striking the door with his pointed hoofs. The door shuddered as if hit by a tremendous battering ram, but that was all. The pastor picked himself up off the ground, dusted himself off, and charged the door again, striking the door with all of his might. Ella was certain the door would splinter with the blow's power, but it still stood whole and undamaged.

The blood pounded in Ella's ears again, and her hands sweated. This was a dark and evil place. Why had she come down here? This wasn't worth the effort. She should just leave. She looked around the room at the bookshelves, the dust, and the pastor as he flung himself again and again at the door. Then she studied the door for a long moment. No, she had to stay. Something was going to happen here, and she would have to be there to see it happen.

Pastor Daerl flung himself at the door for about the fifth time and stood back to his feet, wiping sweat from his brow and panting. "Ye do no s'pose the Pickerings tain an axe about this place?"

Mr. Hydmenton shrugged. "Surely they'll do. Give me a moment."

He bounded up the stairs and was gone. After a few moments, he returned with an axe in one hand and a sledge-hammer in the other.

"How will these do, then?"

Pastor Daerl smiled. "Ay, that'll will do the trick, I s'pect!"

Mr. Hydmenton took the axe and motioned for Pastor Daerl to take the sledge.

"'Two are better than one,'" he said with a grin.

"Ay," Pastor Daerl nodded. "We may as well tain more scripture quoted here. It will no hurt anything."

Pastor Daerl and Mr. Hydmenton both advanced on the door. Ella was almost certain she could hear that pounding sound again, like tribal drums. Sweat dripped from her nose, soaking into her clothing.

The pastor and Mr. Hydmenton regarded the door, standing before it in the gloom of the basement like two soldiers about to make a desperate last stand before a great foe. Pastor Daerl gripped the sledgehammer in one of his massive hands, letting it dangle ominously beside him, while Mr. Hydmenton held his axe over his shoulder, gripping it tightly with both hands. Their two silhouettes stood out starkly in the dim light; the massive frame of the pastor — over seven-feet tall, with curled horns on his head and bristling hair all over his body — standing next to the smaller, yet still stocky, frame of Mr. Hydmenton.

"Why did no we try this earlier? We should ha' thought to break down the door," Mr. Hydmenton said.

Pastor Daerl raised the sledge, and Mr. Hydmenton raised the axe.

Pastor Daerl started the count. "One... two... three..." Was he purposefully counting in time with that throbbing pulse, or was that just coincidence?

They swung their tools at the door with as much force as they could muster. Ella heard a loud crack, and Mr. Hydmenton cried in surprise. The axe and sledge heads flew back and clattered against the far wall, leaving only the handles in the hands of Pastor Daerl and Mr. Hydmenton.

As Ella, Pastor Daerl, and Mr. Hydmenton looked at each other, a low and sinister laugh seemed to rise out of the ground like a vapor. Mr. Hydmenton jumped back in surprise, dropping the axe handle, his face as white as a sheet. "Tar and needles!"

Ella's throat was now totally dry. "It's him," she said, the words spilling out of her mouth of their own accord.

Pastor Daerl took one step back but continued to face the door, rising to his full height and planting his hooves firmly on the stone floor.

Mr. Hydmenton shook his hands as if they were in pain and looked at them. "What wos that? What happened?"

Pastor Daerl stood authoritatively before the strange door, his eyes narrowed, and his jaw set firmly. The hair on his head, the back of his neck, and his arms stood up on end as if feeling the air around them. The pastor pointed his finger directly at the door as if delivering a military command. His giant voice boomed in the little room, "I rebuke ye in the name o' the Almighty God."

The sinister laugh turned to a snarl, like that of a cornered animal.

"Who an' what are ye?" Pastor Daerl thundered. "Why ha' ye vened?"

All was silent for a moment. Sweat poured down Ella's back, and she had trouble breathing.

"So rash?"

The voice that spoke was at the same moment deep and threatening, yet gravelly, like the voice of a man who has not spoken in a long time.

Pastor Daerl spoke again, "Why are ye here?"

The voice chuckled again. "I will never leave you, nor will I forsake you."

"In the name o' the Almighty God, I bind ye!" Pastor Daerl replied. "Ye tain no power here, 'fer no power on earth or in hell may cern us from the love o' God.'"

The voice snarled again. This time, Ella was certain she could hear the voice coming from directly behind the door. Her stomach churned, tying itself into a knot. Whatever *he* was, he stood only a few feet away from the giant pastor, with only that strange door between them.

"They invited me here. You will not send me out."

"Who?" Pastor Daerl replied, still as indomitable as a stone wall, "Who invited ye?"

The voice laughed mockingly.

Pastor Daerl stomped his hoof on the ground like an impatient war-horse. "In the name o' the Almighty God, I command ye to speak: who invited ye?"

The voice snarled again. "I have already told you."

Suddenly, the entire room was filled with the sound of tribal drums. There was another laugh. "You will never be rid of me," the voice continued. "I know how to torture the human soul."

The pastor's eyes went wide with anger. "In the name o' God, I rebuke ye!"

The laughter turned to an unearthly wail, and then all went silent.

Ella and Mr. Hydmenton stood huddled against the stairway on the far wall, each looking on with terror and apprehension. Ella was certain that her dress was now soaked with sweat, and she could feel the sweat running down her neck and legs. Was it pooling on the ground? She swayed slightly. Why was she so dizzy?

Mr. Hydmenton trembled all over. "This entire house is haunted!" he whispered.

Pastor Daerl turned and faced Ella. His face was set hard like flint, serious and brooding. He looked like a man who had just seen his archenemy for the first time.

"Well then," he said gravely, "This *is* more than a physical war."

Ella pitched forward and vomited. She shivered as if suffering from an intense fever. For the first time, she doubted whether she should continue to search for this treasure. Perhaps this wasn't worth it. Perhaps she should simply let the pirates find it. It couldn't be worth all of this.

She could feel Mr. Hydmenton holding her. Was he supporting her? Had she fallen?

"Miss Ella," Mr. Hydmenton was saying. "Are ye all right? Miss Ella?"

Ella vomited again. This was too much. She was done. She would never look behind that door. It wasn't worth it. She would forget about all of this stupidity, the Gwambi Treasure, and everything. She was done. Her treasure hunt was over.

Pastor Daerl shook his head. "This changes our course of action."

Ella looked up at the huge satyr inquiringly but could not speak. Her head still throbbed from the encounter.

"What do ye mean?" Mr. Hydmenton asked.

The pastor shook his head. "This is no a safe place to stay."

Ella felt light-headed; she leaned against Mr. Hydmenton, unable to keep herself standing on her own.

"We cen no jist abandon the house!" Mr. Hydmenton replied. "What if the pirates vene back? What if they'll open that door?"

Pastor nodded. "We should stay here, though mayhaps we should send Miss Nansi, Elsi, and Ella elsewhere."

"But where?" Mr. Hydmenton replied. "With the strikers out, there *is* no safe place in this town."

Ella felt dizzy. The room couldn't be spinning, could it? No, she must just be light-headed. It seemed to get darker, somehow. Her vision blurred for a moment, almost as if she were looking down a very long, very dim tunnel. Then, for a moment, she saw the image of that portrait of her father which hung in Sir Saemwel's room — or was it her own portrait she looked at?

Had her father really found this treasure? Had he indeed encountered this nebulous being who lived behind the door? Perhaps he had, but he had given up, too — that's what his letter seemed to indicate — he had given up the Gwambi Treasure. Could Ella expect to succeed where her father had failed?

Suddenly, she came back to herself. She wasn't in the basement anymore, though; she was slumped in a dining room chair. Had she passed out? Elsi and Miss Nansi leaned over her, dabbing her forehead with damp rags. Ella opened her eyes blearily, looking slowly over the room. Pastor Daerl and Mr. Hydmenton stood a little way away, watching her anxiously.

"Miss Ella, most of all, seems in danger," Pastor Daerl was saying. "At the merri least, we should move her elsewhere, mayhaps to Dr. Heyl's place?"

"What?" Mr. Hydmenton said. "An' put the good doctor in harm's way himself?"

Miss Nansi clicked her tongue reprovingly. "Listen to you two; you sound like a bunch o' frightened schoolchildren!"

"This house *is* haunted," Mr. Hydmenton insisted.

Miss Nansi shook her head. "I will no believe it."

"Then explain it," Pastor Daerl urged, a hint of annoyance in his tone. "There is no other explanation but that we are dealing with a demonic spirit — a ghost, unless I miss my guess."

"Ha!" Miss Nansi said. "What kind of flummery an' flim-flam is this?"

"How cen ye call this a flim-flam?" Mr. Hydmenton asked. "Ghosts are a *scriptural* concept."

"Do ye no see Miss Ella?" Pastor Daerl interjected. "Do ye no see the danger she is in? We *must* move her from here before it gets merri more dangerous fer her."

Suddenly, words came unbidden to Ella's lips. "The'e's no use. He will neve'h leave me. It doesn't matte'h whe'e you take me, he will follow me."

Miss Nansi shook her head. "She is more in danger o' yer fantastical tales than this trumpery," Miss Nansi cut in emphatically. "We cen no move her. The strikers are too unpredictable.

With them jist outside the house, we cen no tell whether they will set on us if we'll try to leave."

Elsi hurried over to the bay window and pointed out. "Ay, Miss Nansi is right. Gard fer yourselves."

Ella peered out the window from her seat and could see the dark shapes of the strikers ranged all about the commons before the house. A large knot of strikers stood in the road itself. There were so many strikers, and even more joined them, trudging out of the city and taking their stand on the commons.

Mr. Hydmenton let out his breath slowly, and Pastor Daerl sighed.

Miss Nansi nodded. "See there?"

Mr. Hydmenton blew out his lips in frustration. "The issue o' the ghost is a moot point, then. Fer better or fer worse, we are closed in here."

Pastor Daerl nodded. "Ay. Then we tain no choice but to ceive the evil as it'll venes upon us."

HAVOC

Longfinch's crew let out several wild yells as they rushed forward to perform Longfinch's command. As they swarmed the deck, Ernest cowered in horror, watching as they carelessly shot or bayoneted every member of Holgard's crew they came across — even though most of the crew were unconscious on the deck. Ernest had never imagined a scene of such reckless slaughter. Suddenly, one of Longfinch's pirates spotted Ernest.

"Here's one what's still alive!" the pirate shouted. "We can have fun with him."

Ernest tried to back away and sink into the gunwales as fear gripped every inch of his body. He could hardly bring his mind to think about the torture he was about to endure.

Just at that moment, Lewis appeared out of nowhere, standing between Ernest and Longfinch's pirates. "No, you don't touch us, boyos. We were co-conspirators with you. Now take us to Longfinch, like he sayed."

The pirate looked visibly disappointed as he stepped forward, grabbing Lewis and Ernest roughly by the shoulders.

Ernest was still trembling all over, and as the pirate jerked him to his feet, Ernest pitched forward, hurling on the deck. The pirate laughed bawdily.

"Don't have the stomach for your own work, do you?"

And with that, the pirate dragged them off towards Longfinch. Ernest tried to steady his legs. He looked over at Lewis, and Lewis winked reassuringly.

As Ernest turned his eyes back towards Longfinch, he saw Killjelly, the Albino, and Quartermaster Harold being dragged to the elfin pirate as well. Ernest swallowed. Was Killjelly behind this, then? What part had Lewis played? Ernest looked back over the deck, which was now covered in corpses. Who was responsible for this?

As Ernest surveyed the deck, he noticed Vania Bloodrummer crossing over onto the galleon. Behind him, members of Longfinch's crew hauled four very large crates from the man-o-war over to the galleon.

Killjelly nodded his head in a bow as he reached Longfinch. "All as you commanded, sir."

Longfinch smiled. "You served me well." Then he addressed the men holding Killjelly. "Release him. He's one on ours."

Then Longfinch turned to the Albino. "And you, sir, it is an honor to meet you at last." Longfinch reached into his shirt, pulling out an amulet that hung from his neck. It was in the shape of a circle within an upside-down triangle. "I've never had the privilege of meeting someone so high in our order. I'm afraid Killjelly is the highest-ranking officer what I have ever met."

Longfinch bowed before the Albino, almost kneeling to the ground. The Albino only looked on. At that moment, Ernest saw the amulet that the Albino wore around his neck and realized that it was the same as the one Longfinch had. But hadn't he seen that same amulet some-where else? Ernest turned to look at Killjelly. Yes, he, too, wore the same amulet around his neck. A numbing horror crept over Ernest. Were they all three part of some secret fraternity?

"The Order of the Ghost," the Archeomancer said, almost as if he could hear Ernest's thoughts.

The pirates who held the Albino looked in uncertainty from the Albino to their captain, who knelt before him. As if coming to the same conclusion, the men released the Albino and stepped backward.

Vania Bloodrummer now strode up, leaving the men behind him as they carried their crates down the hatch. Bloodrummer saluted Killjelly.

"Which is neatly done, whatever."

Killjelly returned the salute.

"It will be a pleasure," Bloodrummer continued, "to have you more overtly fighting for us."

Killjelly smiled. "It haves comed to that, sure."

"You!" The Albino suddenly said, pointing at Bloodrummer.

Vania Bloodrummer took a step back in surprise as the Archeomancer looked him over critically.

"You are not of our order," the Archeomancer finally said, "yet you bear the marks of wizardry upon you. Speak and declare your craft."

Bloodrummer seemed to relax at this, and he smiled. "Pyromancy, sir."

And with that, he held up his hand dramatically and snapped his fingers. Ernest thought he saw a spark dart out from between Bloodrummer's fingers, but he wasn't sure. Almost in that same instant, one of the pirates' muskets miss-fired. The pirate cursed loudly, looking his musket over incredulously.

"What the baptism go'ed wrong? It wasn't even cocked."

The Albino nodded, though the beginnings of a frown spread over his face. "Pyromagia, you mean. It is not true pyromancy because you are projecting with fire, not conjuring from it. Yet it is of the Craft, even if it tastes more of the stage."

"And yet," Longfinch replied, standing back to his feet, "it still pays homage to the Source. Vania's pyromagia carries many uses beyond simply the prestige on a cheap showman's trick. For he can handle that fire which is hot enough to re-knit flesh."

The Albino seemed to accept this, for he said no more.

Killjelly, however, cut in. "And these crates, Captain," he motioned to the last crate as Longfinch's crew carried it below deck. "May I make so bold, sure, as to ask on them?"

Longfinch smiled. "Dynamite."

Killjelly nodded. "That was my assumption. I have never seed it used before, sure."

Longfinch laughed good-naturedly at this statement. "You will; believe me. But now tell me about these others." Longfinch motioned to Lewis, Ernest, and Quartermaster Harold. "Was the conspiracy so large?"

Killjelly shrugged, pointing to Lewis. "The cook. He drugged the crew for us."

Longfinch nodded. "And the other two? They do'ed nothing for us?"

Killjelly nodded.

Quartermaster Harold spoke now, his voice desperate and strained. "I speaked for you. I sayed, 'Longfinch is our captain.' I do'edn't join in this mutiny. I was *true* to you, captain."

Longfinch smiled kindly and rested his hand on Quartermaster Harold's shoulder in a friendly way. "Good for you. Thank you for standing up for me."

Suddenly, Longfinch raised his pistol to Harold's heart and fired. Quartermaster Harold fell dead to the deck, and Longfinch's pirates cheered wildly.

Killjelly shook his head, a rueful smile playing at the corners of his mouth. "You've got to clean up after yourself, sure."

Longfinch started reloading his pistol and turned to Ernest now, still smiling that same friendly smile. "And what on you? What do you have to say?"

Ernest's mouth went dry. Was this the end? Lewis stepped up boldly, standing between the elfin pirate and Ernest.

"He is my messmate. He haved no part in the mutiny."

Longfinch smirked at this. "Yes, but he played no part in *my* plan, either, did he?"

Lewis stared at Longfinch defiantly. "You mayn't owe me much, captain. I'm sure you could've defeated Holgard if'n I hadn't drugged the crew. Still, I do'ed, and it helped your plan run as smoothly as it do'ed. Now, the least you can do for me is give me my mate's life."

Longfinch finished loading his pistol and stared at Lewis. "Life is never a small thing to give. I don't grant it carelessly. You served me, and for that, you get your *own* life." Longfinch fixed Lewis with a steady gaze, and his voice cut like a knife. "You don't make demands of me."

Lewis didn't budge.

Ernest now found his tongue. "But I do'ed help you, sir. After all, it was me what served out the drugged beer to the crew."

Longfinch regarded him contemptuously, his strange smile creeping back into his lips. "Gnome, if'n I decide to give you your life, it will only be because it isn't worth me spending a bullet to take it."

The crew snickered.

Ernest knew he had to talk; his life depended on it; his eyes looked between the lifeless forms of Captain Holgard and Quartermaster Harold, and then he looked at the Albino.

"But I do'ed help you, sir — at least, if'n the Archeomancer is on your side on the fence, as it would appear."

Longfinch looked back at the Albino inquisitively. The Albino nodded. "He was the scribe."

"*And*," Ernest said, "I served on *both* crews what went looking for the key. Come to think on it, I was the one what finded the key for you."

Longfinch seemed to take a few minutes as he absorbed this

bit of information. He stood there on the deck, tasting the air with his long tongue and fingering his pistol. He spat on the deck. Ernest noticed that there was blood in his spittle.

Killjelly cleared his throat. "Speaking on pyromagia and dynamite..." he motioned to Ernest.

Vania Bloodrummer chuckled. "He would be perfect for it, whatever."

Ernest got the distinct impression that Killjelly referred to something distasteful.

Longfinch chuckled. "I haved not thinked on that. You are right, Killjelly." He clapped Killjelly heartily on the shoulder. "I'm already glad you're on the crew."

Longfinch now strode forward jovially, fixing Ernest with his keen gaze. "I will grant you your life."

Lewis stepped aside, and Ernest let himself breathe again, though he was uncertain what would come next.

"For now, at least," Longfinch added with a smirk as he shoved his pistol back into his belt.

Ernest could feel his blood-chilling as Longfinch continued to look at him, still smiling that same unsettling smile. After regarding Ernest for several long moments, Longfinch spoke again.

"I will give you one very important task. If'n you succeed in that task, and if'n you survive it, I will give you your life. If'n you fail, you will die."

Ernest nodded. "I understand, sir. You willn't be disappointed."

Longfinch smiled and slapped Ernest heartily on the shoulder. "I hope not. You don't want to see me disappointed."

The crew laughed uproariously at this.

Longfinch continued to smile, still regarding Ernest with a keen eye. "Tell me, cook's-mate, do you know what a fire-ship is?"

WAR-MONGER

*H*aeli hugged Titus excitedly, hardly able to believe what she had just witnessed. "You did it!" she cried, "You won! Ella would be proud of you."

All around her, the indigies pranced about in a wild dance, waving their knives and *kukris* in the air above their heads. Several indigies pulled out their slings and now hurled sling-stones at the forest trees in chorus with the drums. Behind her, Haeli could hear the shaman cackling in laughter, then he shouted out in Tylweni,

"Let the blood of the *pirate* men be on their very own heads! May the Great Aeparon lay upon them disfavor and curses! May nothing sprout from their graves!"

Haeli heard Titus saying something. She held him at arm's length and looked him in the eye. "You did it!Wait until Ella hears what you did. We will find her in no time."

Titus looked at her blankly. "I... eh... I..."

Halfdan floated down from the sky and alighted on the platform next to Haeli. The harrier took one look at Titus and turned to Haeli, saying bluntly, "You fool, he is bleeding out."

Just then, Haeli realized Titus was holding his side, and

blood was seeping through his shirt and coat. There were even bloodstains on her dress where she had been hugging Titus.

"Llifsa!" Haeli cried. "Help! One of you indigies, help me! He is going to bleed to death!"

The indigies only continued to dance wildly around them. Haeli was desperate now; she yelled in Tylweni, "It is of imperative importance that we receive aid! I urgently request help and assistance!"

Still, no one replied. Haeli dashed the sweat from her forehead in frustration. Titus looked at her pitifully and tried to smile. "So, eh, this is it? Well, eh, tell Ella that she... eh... that I was looking for her."

Halfdan shook his head. "Your swearing will soon be held to account before the Almighty God. I told you it was a sin." The statement sounded to Haeli as if the harrier was trying to be sympathetic.

Haeli looked at Titus in desperation. "No! You can not just die. Hold on!" She looked around at the dancing indigies again. "Will one of you help us?"

At that moment, Tiya-Aenji pushed through the crowd. She grabbed Titus by the arm and raised him up as best as her slight stature would allow. "Nōlistrw-kagwyr!" she called.

The little imp appeared out of nowhere, grabbing Titus by the other arm. Between the two of them, the nymphs half-carried, half-dragged Titus out of the mob of dancing warriors. Ella followed behind.

"Will he be all right?" she asked.

Tiya-Aenji's jaw tightened as she replied, "Let me get him to my hut."

They moved on hurriedly, and Haeli noticed with some surprise that none of the indigies in the village seemed to pay any heed to them. They simply turned away and continued their work as Tiya-Aenji and Nōlistrw-kagwyr hauled Titus past.

The Iasaqi-Woni

Finally, they reached Tiya-Aenji's hut. Tiya-Aenji rushed Titus inside and laid him down on a cot. She tore his shirt open and ripped off the leg of his trouser with her teeth to get to the wounds in his side and thigh.

"Sydni-Efylyn!" Tiya-Aenji cried. "Bring unto me the bandages, and stitchings, and comfrey and goldenseal."

Haeli didn't watch the operation much longer, but turned to see her mother sitting with her back to the wall. Several other Pistosians were here as well — beacon-tenders by their looks — and they looked on darkly. These must be the other people the Iasaqi-Woni captured for questioning.

Haeli slumped down next to her mother. She felt miserable. The air in the hut was even more oppressive than the air outside. She was hot and covered in sweat from head to toe, and her hair was a frizzled mess. Little Dafid craned his neck to see the excitement around Titus.

"What happened to the man? Why is he bleeding?"

Ma held Dafid close, but she turned to Haeli.

Haeli sighed. "They released a moa on him."

Ma's eyes clouded with concern. "What for?"

Haeli sighed. "I made the mistake of saying that he was garding for his daughter. They said he had to prove his paternal instincts by killing a moa. I should have kept my mouth shut... I should not have said..."

Haeli's voice caught, and she could feel tears coming to her eyes. No, she couldn't cry. She didn't have any good reason to cry.

Ma wrapped her arms around Haeli. "It is all right, Haeli. It is not your fault."

Haeli knew she wasn't crying because Titus was injured. That was upsetting but not the real reason she was so upset. The thought of poor Ella losing her father made her think of her own father, and that thought was more than she could handle.

No, not now. She couldn't let herself think about that. Haeli swallowed hard, seizing those emotions, wadding them into a tight ball, and pushing them back down. She couldn't go there. She wouldn't go there.

She wiped her eyes and stared ahead vacantly, refusing to look at her Ma lest the feelings return. Her heart pounded in her chest, pounding, pounding, pounding... like a tribal drum. Haeli felt a chill run through her, and she could feel the key's slight weight in her bodice. She shivered. She still had a key — one of the two — at least. The doom of that one key still surrounded her like a palpable mist, just as strongly as when she had both keys.

Ma stroked her hair, whispering to her. "Haeli, it is not good to hold it in. Let it out."

Haeli did not respond. She refused to look her mother in the eye.

"You can not hold your emotions in," Ma said with a sigh. "They are like a horse. God gave them to us as tools, to help us do what we need to do."

Haeli took a deep breath. "That is not what I have experienced."

Ma tilted her head to one side. "You must break in your emotions, but then — once there is trust between the two of you — you can ride them to accomplish great things. You only have to let your emotions free."

Haeli clenched her jaw, turning on her mother. "Maybe for you, but it does not work that way for me."

Just then, Tiya-Aenji came up and squatted before Ma and Haeli. "He will be fine," she said in Helfenic. "I have stopped the bleeding, and the skin should close in time. There was no damage to the inside of his body. He lost a good deal of blood, but that was all. I will give him my medicines, and I expect him to be walking soon."

Ma sighed. "That is very good. I am glad to hear it."

"Why," Haeli asked, "would not anyone else help? Why did they ignore us?"

Tiya-Aenji smiled sadly. "My people believe that if they offer hospitality or help another person, they will give themselves bad merit and will bring down disfavor from the Great Aeparon. Only the Li of the village will give hospitality and aid and medicine so that the Li may take all the bad merit of the village upon themselves."

Haeli raised an eyebrow. She welcomed this interruption of her dark thoughts. "Why is that?"

"Because," Tiya-Aenji replied, "the Li will become the shaman in time and will therefore earn enough good merit in the eyes of the Great Aeparon to cancel out all the bad merit which the Li previously accumulated."

Haeli nodded. "So basically, you do all the village's dirty work?"

Tiya-Aenji smiled. "That is correct. I did so begrudgingly until the missionary explained to me that the Almighty God came to earth to be the Li for all men on all the earth." Haeli could now see a bright spark showing from Tiya-Aenji's eyes. "He would take the guilt and bad merit of every man upon himself and pay for it with his own good merit. Then, he did not become the great shaman, but the Great Lord and Son of the Almighty God." Tiya-Aenji sighed happily. "That was when I believed."

Tiya-Aenji looked over at Ma suddenly. "Would you like another *esoci*?"

Ma smiled. "I would not refuse."

Tiya-Aenji motioned to the far side of the hut where Sydni-Efylyn leaned over the fire, wrapping vegetables in flatbread. "If you speak to Sydni-Efylyn, she will make you more."

Ma nodded and stood to her feet. "Thank you, I will do just that."

As Ma walked over to Sydni-Efylyn, Tiya-Aenji turned to Haeli and looked at her closely.

"I know what troubles you."

Haeli couldn't help but smile incredulously at this claim. There was no way that this little nymph woman knew what Haeli was going through. "And what is that?" Haeli asked.

Tiya-Aenji looked at Haeli seriously. "I, too, have climbed the Gwambi Tower."

Haeli raised her eyebrows in surprise at this claim. Tiya-Aenji had climbed the Gwambi Tower? No one survived that. How could Tiya-Aenji have survived climbing the tower? Why did Tiya-Aenji think Haeli had climbed it, too?

Tiya-Aenji must have sensed Haeli's confusion. "You have seen the ghost?"

Haeli furrowed her brow. "I am not sure what you are talking about."

Tiya-Aenji simply regarded Haeli for a moment. "You bear that doom upon you, the doom of one who has seen the ghost. The doom of one who has dreamed the dreams that he gives."

Haeli remembered the strange dream the night her Da died; the griffin, the pteranodon, the rocky pinnacle, the knife, the strange chanting. Was that what Tiya-Aenji was referring to?

Tiya-Aenji looked over Haeli's face as if searching for something. "His power is terrible."

Haeli shook her head, trying to clear that strange dream from her mind. "What are you talking about? A ghost? What in the world do you mean?"

Tiya-Aenji only studied her more closely. "You have the Almighty God inside of you. By his power are all other spirits bound and defeated. You need not fear the ghost's doom."

Tiya-Aenji regarded her closely for another moment. "Be strong, have courage, and wait on the Lord.'"

Haeli flinched. "I have waited long enough."

Tiya-Aenji looked at Haeli for another moment and then

shook her head. With that, the little nymph stood to her feet and strode out of the hut, leaving Haeli alone. Haeli remained for several minutes on the floor with her back against the wall, her mind reeling.

Ma returned with two *esoci*. She handed one to Haeli and settled down beside her.

"If this whole matter is settled," Ma began, "hopefully, the Iasaqi-Woni will only see me. I can bring up the matter of the lawsuit with him."

Haeli nodded, her mind not on her conversation with her mother. What was Tiya-Aenji talking about?

"Tiya has clarified that we can stay here indefinitely," Ma said.

Haeli shrugged. "Sure."

Why did Tiya-Aenji think that Haeli had met a ghost? *Had* she met a ghost? There was no such thing as ghosts, though; that was only Elderian mumbo-jumbo. That age had ceased, hadn't it?

She put her hand to her bodice and felt the key there. A sense of impending doom came over her as if she were standing at the top of a giant cliff, about to be hurled down to whatever waited below.

Yes, she stood on the edge of a great nightmare and had but a moment — just enough time to take a deep breath — before that nightmare began. Then she would be falling, falling, falling, but there would be no hawthorn tree to catch her this time.

Suddenly, a loud shout sounded from outside the hut. Haeli had just enough time to look up before the supreme chief and his bodyguard entered the hut. As they passed through the hide which hung over the entrance, they brought with them a wafting of cool air, rich with the smell of rain. The storm was almost upon them.

The Iasaqi-Woni and his bodyguard filled what space was left in the hut. Haeli could not help but feel intimidated by this gathering of warriors — even though few of them stood above three feet from the ground. Their weird war paint looked even more intimidating in the hut's dim light, and their features looked cruel and terrible. Each warrior stood with a stone face, knives, *kukris*, and spears bristling from their bodies, with their webbed hands crossed in front of their chests, and their oily skin flickering back the firelight.

The Iasaqi-Woni strode directly up to Titus, with the wizened shaman a step behind the great chief.

The chief stopped only inches from the cot where Titus lay. Titus sat up in surprise, seeming to be in much better condition than Haeli had feared. Maybe he hadn't been that close to bleeding out after all. Haeli looked closely at Titus' face. No, he was still pale. He seemed to sit up only through force of will, or else a great fear of this mighty nymph chief.

The Iasaqi-Woni nodded to Titus, speaking in Tylweni, "Hail, O great warrior who doth fight even for the recovery of his dear daughter, for whom thou dost shed blood, even the blood of the mother moa."

Titus nodded back, licking his lips. "I...eh...I..."

The Iasaqi-Woni drew out his *kukri* in one smooth motion. The blood of the moa was still on the blade, beginning to dry. Titus recoiled in terror. Haeli couldn't help gasping. Now what was going on? What was the Iasaqi-Woni trying to do? He would not intimidate poor Titus anymore, was he?

A toothy smile now spread across the Iasaqi-Woni's face, showing his double rows of canine teeth, and Haeli guessed it was supposed to be a show of friendship. Then, turning the *kukri* around so that the handle faced Titus, the supreme chief offered the weapon to him. The big man looked hesitantly from the large knife to the web-handed nymph warlord standing before him. With some reluctance, he took the *kukri* from the Iasaqi-Woni.

The shaman cackled. "Even so! Thus is the accomplishment of it!"

"Even so!" the bodyguard echoed.

The chief, however, remained perfectly silent as he stood before Titus. He remained so for several minutes as, with an air of dignity, he leisurely picked his nose clean. Then the Iasaqi-Woni bent forward and took Titus by the foot.

Titus seemed to view the chief with a great deal of revulsion and apprehension, but remained perfectly still throughout the ceremony. Haeli couldn't help but smile a little at this sturdy man's confusion. True, it was confusing to her what exactly was going on, but she guessed she witnessed some kind of treaty ceremony.

"Even so," the Iasaqi-Woni now said. "Thus are we allied together with each other, and thus do we pledge ourselves against those *pirate,* and do declare ourselves in opposition to them for the purpose of seeking their doom and damnation. Thus are we allied together even as allies in this search. And so shall we recover thy daughter unto thee, and so shall we together work a great revenge and reckoning upon those men which are *pirate!*"

"Even so!" the bodyguard echoed again.

Haeli now smiled again, but not at the humor of the situation. Here were nearly twenty warriors pledging themselves — and their entire tribe — for the pirate's destruction. She looked over each of those dreadful warriors and shivered with excitement and apprehension. These would be dreadful foes for the pirates to contend with! Haeli had a part in bringing this about, and she felt a sense of vindication that she could help in bringing revenge on those pirates who murdered her father.

At that moment, a clap of thunder shook the little hut. As if in answer, the rain suddenly fell in sheets from the sky. Haeli could only imagine the force with which the rain fell, for it seemed to pass through the forest canopy unabated and drive against the hut's roof. The hide-and-thatch roof leaked in a dozen different places as the rumble of the rain filled the air inside like the roll of a drum. To Haeli's mind, it sounded as if nature itself gave the marshaling cry for war.

The hair on the back of Haeli's neck stood on end as another blast of thunder split the skies. Yes, the Twengoli would go to war, and she would go with them. The pirates would regret the day that they raided the Blysffi fort. Haeli would have her revenge. She had waited long enough.

PRONUNCIATION KEY

Most of the proper nouns in this book are transliterations from Llaedhwythi Tylwen, except for a couple from Helfenic. The following is a guide to the pronunciation of Llaedhwythi Tylwen:

Consonants – as in English with a few exceptions:

- **c** - always hard as in *c*lub, never as in *c*ertain.
- **ch** - as in Ba*ch* never as in *ch*urch. Strictly not used in pure Llaedhwythi Tylwen, but often in other forms of Tylweni and foreign words.
- **dh** - like the *th* sound in *the*n, never as in *th*istle.
- **f** - v as in of.
- **ff** - f as in off.
- **g** - always hard like *g*irl, never as in *g*entle.
- **ll** - sounds almost like *dl*, in technical terms, a voiceless alveolar lateral fricative.
- **r** - flapped, as in Spanish.
- **rr** - trilled, as in Spanish.
- **th** - as in *th*istle, never as in *the*n.

Vowels:

- **a** - short as in Ell*a*. This vowel can never take the accent.
- **e** - short as in f*e*d.
- **i** - long as in sk*i*.
- **o** - short as in p*o*t, or long as in h*o*me.
- **u** - short as in p*u*t.
- **y** - short as in h*i*t. When followed directly by a vowel becomes a consonant, as in *y*olk.
- **w** - long as in pl*u*me. When followed directly by a vowel becomes a consonant as in *w*alk.

Diphthongs:

- **ae** - short as in *a*pple.
- **ei** - long as in h*ay*.
- **aei** - long as in sk*y*.
- **aey** - similar to *aei* but ending farther back in the mouth.

Subjunctive: the subjunctive case represents uncertainty or doubt, and is signified by the ending *'ll*. Example "They'll will eat," means "They might (or might not) eat."

PISTOSIAN WORD GLOSSARY

'll – subjunctive suffix used to denote uncertainty

cede – to go, or to yield (as in con*cede*)

ceive – take, hold (as in re*ceive*)

celer – fast, quick (as in ac*celer*ate)

cern – separate (as in dis*cern*)

clude – close, shut, end (as in ex*clude*)

cognize – know in a relational sense (as in re*cognize*)

duce – to lead (as in de*duce*)

fiscate – buy

gard – look, watch (as in re*gard*)

kye – cattle

legate – send, especially as a messenger

lieve – lift, raise (as in re*lieve*)

llifsa – interjection of general surprise or consternation

merri – much, very, lot

maugre – instead of

petticoat – a crude, derogatory term for a woman

plete – fill (as in com*plete*)

pose – put (as in inter*pose*)

prehend – grasp (as in *prehen*sile)

prive – rob, steal (as in de*prive*)
priver – petty thief, pickpocket
quire – ask (as in in*quire*)
ruth – pity (as in *ruth*less)
scend – climb, rise (as in a*scend*)
spire – breathe (as in con*spire*)
sault – leap, jump (as in as*sault*)
tain – have (as in con*tain*, or ob*tain*)
trive – find (as in re*trieve*)
tryst – as a verb: to have a romantic meeting. As a noun: a beau
vail – power (as in pre*vail*)
vene – to come
vert – turn (as in a*vert*)
voke – call, yell, cry (as in *vo*cal)
ween – imagine
ye – second person singular pronoun
you – second person plural pronoun
younker – youth

ABOUT THE AUTHOR

Amos Christian Wilson is a history enthusiast, bagpipe player, fantasy cartographer, theology nerd, home-school graduate, and award-winning storyteller. His inspirations come from his love of nature and history, as well as his experience across a wide range of blue-collar trades, including carpentry and piano tuning. Amos currently lives with his wife and children in the scenic Flint Hills of Kansas.

Sign up for A. C. Wilson's newsletter to receive updates on upcoming books, and receive a free e-book prequel to *My Father's Land*!

www.ACWilson.net
and
acwilson.substack.com

ALSO IN THE GWAMBI TETRALOGY

This series draws as much from J. R. R. Tolkien and Indiana Jones as it does from Charles Dickens. With a focus on immersive world-building that features fully developed fantasy races, deeply religious colonists, and labor riots, "The Gwambi Tetralogy" is black-powder, epic low fantasy, bordering on magical realism, with a faith-based, and character-driven plot.

Book 1 - *My Father's Land*

☞ https://wisepathbooks.com/products/my-fathers-land

These pirates who just kidnapped Ella seem to think that she knows the location of the Gwambi's Lost City of Gold. Sure, her father died looking for the Gwambi city, but that doesn't mean she knows anything about it. Her mother wouldn't even let her read the one book they owned on the lost Gwambi city. Mind you, she read every other book in the house—every other book in the parish—so she knows a thing or two. The question is, can she do anything with all that head knowledge? I mean, does it matter if she can positively identify the difference between a gnome, a leprechaun, and a nymph, if she can't defend herself when they are trying to stab her in the gut? And let's not even start talking about the sorcerer...

With a focus on immersive world-building that features fully developed fantasy races, deeply religious colonists, and labor riots, *My Father's Land* draws as much from JRR Tolkien and Indiana Jones as it does from Charles Dickens.

Book 3 - *My Father's God* - coming soon

Clerans must protect his village. It's the easiest thing ever. All he has to do is fire the cannons, and no one ever gets past the Entwerp battery. But now he is being sent out to board a highly explosive fireship and steer it away from the battery. How hard could that be? I mean, the only time the battery is vulnerable is during the lowest tide of the year. Oh wait, it *is* the lowest tide of the year. And if Clerans can't stop the fireship, then Longfinch's pirates will murder everyone in the village. And why doesn't he call for reinforcements? Well, the reinforcements are tied up trying to prevent the strikers from burning down the national bank.

Book 4 - *My Father's Will* - coming soon

After finding God, things couldn't be better for Ernest. I mean, it would probably be better if he wasn't trapped in the ancient Gwambi catacombs, with no food or water to speak of. It would also be better if Clerans wasn't about to be skinned alive by the pirates, or if Martyn wasn't slowly bleeding to death from a traumatic head injury. But no fear, there *is* someone else trapped in the catacombs with them, someone who — if he doesn't kill them — has the medical knowledge necessary to save Martyn's life: Killjelly…